'£20 million.' He smiled, seemingly pleased with his wealth 'I want the money invested with a good return and I want to pay no tax. But as I say most importantly I want no one to be able to get to it. I want no one to know it exists.'

'Well, I will do my best. All transactions leave some sort of paper trail. It is not possible to make money completely disappear. However, I think with a little luck I will be able to create a structure that will please you.'

His eyes met mine and for the first time I realised how cold they were. His gaze was fixed and resolute. 'You are too modest Dr Stuart. I have heard it said that when you hide money God can't find it.'

First published in Great Britain in 2005 by Summara Books

Published by Summara Books

Summara Books is the trading name of Summara Limited

Printed and bound in Great Britain by
Mackays of Chatham

CIP catalogue record for this book is available from the British Library

ISBN 0-9550724-0-9

THE LAUNDRYMAN

TREVOR THOMAS

Gay

Best Wishes

Trevor

7 11/13

SUMMARA BOOKS

To Zofia, Myles and Nicholas

Prologue

Even those who wanted him caught still marvelled at his work. He was a magician, using sleight of hand in financial transactions that bewildered the authorities. He made money disappear and reappear at ease. But his vocation was beyond mere art. It had a purpose. He turned dirty money into clean money. He received the proceeds of crime and, for a generous fee, washed them, returning to his clients funds which were seemingly legitimate, their origins wholly untraceable.

The police knew of him; that is, they knew of his existence but they didn't know who he was or how he operated. Originally those officers assigned to the Special Crimes Unit believed that each drug organisation had its own money laundering system, or a multitude of such systems. But over time the intelligence obtained from infiltration, observation and surveillance gave rise to a pattern which indicated that principally the cartels were all using a single system operated by a single person. He was known only as 'The Laundryman.'

To the police he was a major target, viewed as a criminal mastermind. To identify and apprehend him became a priority. Instant promotion and peer group accolades awaited the team that caught him. But he proved as adept at evading detection as he was at financial illusion.

To the drug baron he was an expensive necessity. The Laundryman managed the final process that enabled the cartels to enjoy the fruits of their labours. Necessary, not to the reckless dealers - they took their chances and usually ended up in jail. When apprehended they were often damned not by their possession of drugs but by their inability to explain how they financed their lifestyle - Mercedes sports cars, several houses, Rolex watches and an executive box at the Arsenal - when they didn't even have a job. No, the Laundryman tended to the more organised dealers, those drug cartels that operated along business lines, those with disciplined operating and financial procedures. Those sophisticated enough to use the offshore financial structures the Laundryman would provide. Those with powerful contacts. Those in the know.

Mazzinni was not in the know, but he needed the Laundryman. The start of the new millennium had treated him well. He had money to hide. A lot of it. And quickly. Sitting alone on the balcony of his newly-rented large beachside villa in Andalucia, southern Spain, naked but for his sheer silk robe, he thought again of the valuable information he had just obtained from the woman now standing under the shower in his bathroom.

'And where should I go with my little problem?' he'd asked her earlier.

'To the financial capital of the world,' she whispered.

'New York?' he asked apprehensively.

'London,' was her cool reply.

Mazzinni smiled. London was the right place. He was getting closer. 'Do you have a name for me?'

'I have two,' she replied.

He pondered the names now as he gazed appreciatively at his panoramic view of the Mediterranean Sea. It had impressed his guest too. After some fifteen minutes, she emerged onto the balcony dressed for work in a single-breasted navy blue blazer with its three gold stripes on each sleeve, worn over a brilliant white blouse, her dark woollen skirt falling just to the knee. Her cap, with its gold symmetrical wings on its peak flowing back from the centre, rested under her arm.

'Of the two names,' Mazzinni asked, 'who is the best?'

'Dr Andrew Stuart,' she said without hesitation. 'A J Stuart & Co.'

'Thank you,' he said and bade her goodbye, suggesting they get together again the next time she had a stay-over in Malaga.

Happy and relaxed, Mazzinni was enjoying his new lifestyle. Finding the Laundryman could not have been easier. He rang and made an appointment. He would fly to into London's City Airport on Friday. He had a flat in Earl's Court, but he'd book into Langham's, enjoy a lazy weekend, a show, a dinner, maybe a little casino gambling. On Monday he'd attend to business. He had cash to collect. Then on Tuesday morning at 10.00am he'd meet the man. *The wrong man.*

Chapter 1

When I telephoned the salon I specifically requested Tania. It was 9.15 on Monday morning and I fixed the appointment for later that same day. Tania was BB's sister. Tall, black, elegant and strikingly attractive, she managed Shadowlands in Mayfair. That afternoon, as I walked the short distance to the salon from my offices in Wigmore Street, I felt increasingly tense. For though my hair needed attention, that was not the primary purpose of my visit.

'I knew I would see you again,' said Tania once I had settled myself into her chair, 'but I never thought it would be in here.'

Her words both pleased and puzzled me. It had seemed to me to be an excellent idea. I looked around the bright modern chrome and glass surroundings. 'Why not in here?'

'Because,' she teased, 'we're a hair and beauty salon, not a barbershop. Let's face it, you're fairly conservative, Dr Stuart.'

'Only on the surface,' I replied.

'OK then,' she asked playfully, 'what style would you like?'

'Same as I already have, only half an inch shorter.'

'See what I mean?' She laughed first; I followed. 'May I suggest something a little more daring?'

'Maybe,' I said slowly. 'I have a special occasion this weekend, but nothing too daring. I don't want my clients wondering if I have lost the balance of my mind.'

'I was thinking of cutting a lot more off. It will make you look much younger. Anyway, what's the special occasion?'

'A first date.'

'And how old is the lady?'

'Well, let's just say she's younger than me.'

'Definitely shorter.'

'OK, shorter but professional. Nothing spiky. Subject to that, I'm in your hands.'

With the styling agreed, I was led away to the basin area by a pretty young junior who washed my hair with unusual vigour, her ample breasts occasionally brushing against the side of my face. I made a mental note to give her a generous tip.

With a towel around my shoulders and my hair still damp, I was led back to Tania, who started combing and cutting. I watched her in the mirror. The movements of her hands were swift, almost cavalier. She knew what she was doing, she'd been doing it for years and it no longer required concentrated effort. The skill was second nature. 'Where are you taking the lucky lady?' she asked.

'Cayman,' I replied.

'A restaurant?'

'An island.'

She stopped and looked at me through the reflection in the mirror. 'You're taking a woman to the Cayman Islands on a first date?'

'Yes'

'Who the hell is this woman?'

'You,' I said.

Tania held my gaze through the mirror for some time. Then, without a word she continued styling, running her figures through my sandy-brown hair, lifting up the strands and snipping off the ends. She appeared to be enjoying herself. 'Ask me then,' she eventually said.

'Ms Tania Berkeley will you accompany me to the Cayman Islands this weekend on a date?'

'I'll need to think about it,' she replied.

'We'll have a suite. A bedroom for you, a bedroom for me and an adjoining living room. You'll have an ensuite bathroom and so will I. We'll breakfast together in the lounge. The weekend will be glorious and, I hope, romantic. Moreover, it will be a little longer than the weekend. We'll fly out on Wednesday morning and fly back on Sunday.'

'If you're taking me on a date Dr Stuart, we better move to first names, don't you think? And not Andrew. BB calls you Andrew. Does anyone call you Stu?'

'No one,' I said.

'Except me,' she replied.

'So you're coming?'

'I'll need to change my schedule.'

'Which means you're coming?'

'Yes,' she said.

Now my only problem was BB. He was coming to my house that evening for a chess game. Byron Berkeley, everyone called him BB, and everyone, I think, was a little afraid of him. A former amateur boxer, BB maintained a rigorous fitness regime. He had a presence, physical in nature: six foot one and very muscular. He also had a slight air of menace, which belied his often gentle manner. He ran a Boy's Club in South London, funded by the Council with the aim of keeping teenage boys occupied, off the streets and out of crime. BB worked hard, but he was swimming against the tide. He rarely talked about it, but I could often see the frustration in his face. He had the most expressive face and, when I saw his face that evening, I knew he'd heard. 'My little sister?'

'I can explain,' I said.

'I'm listening.' He started setting up the chessboard.

'She's beautiful BB. This is not a conquest. I want to love her.'

'It's not going to work, Andrew, trust me. Anyway, she's 26. How old are you?'

'Two years younger than you.' He glared at me. 'I'm 39,' I added quickly, 'but that's not the point. Look, she's agreed to go away with me so I don't think the age gap bothers her. We'll be away for five days. If it's not going to work we'll know soon enough.'

'Five days of sun, sand and sex, right?'

'No, five days of courtship. I have plenty of sex. I'm looking for love BB. We've discussed this before. I want to make love to Tania, sure. But the love has to come first. I'm not going to jump on her as soon as we land in Georgetown. I don't intend jumping on her at all. She'll have her own room, you know.'

'Yeah, she told me.' He'd set the white pieces up for himself, the black for me. It was his running joke. I had all the advantages of being white and he all the disadvantages of being black, except when we played chess. As he looked down at the board, I studied his dark face, the chiselled features, the smooth skin. He too was beautiful. He moved his king's pawn two spaces. 'Just treat her right, OK.'

'I will. Still friends?' I asked.

'Your move,' he said.

I first met BB at a chess club at London Bridge, which prided itself on the cosmopolitan make-up of its membership. I like to think I play an elegant game á la Dr Alexander Alekhine, the Russian Grandmaster of the 1930s and 1940s with an emphasis on combinatorial chess, though I played clearly nowhere near as well as Dr A! BB played a brutal and unforgiving game in the mode of a young Mike Tyson: all direct attack, every move made *with bad intention to a vital area*. He played with his whole body – taut, athletic, full of restrained energy. Once he'd made up his mind, and he made up his mind quickly, he moved the pieces with swift determination and then glared, not at the board but at his opponent. He was a good player, made the club's first division, and though when we played I usually won, each match was an exhausting experience.

Our friendship developed over time. I tend not to cultivate close associations with anyone. But a rule of the club was that our addresses were posted and made available to other members and, much to my initial annoyance, BB took to turning up at my house, often late, with his folded board and box of plastic pieces, saying that he'd come by to 'kick my ass.' Studiously ignoring the finely crafted mahogany set in my drawing room which rested on the highly polished glass table which served as the chess board, BB would walk to the kitchen, raid my fridge for a sandwich and a beer, before setting up the cheap set on the breakfast bar.

Once when I was working at home under a tight deadline on the transfer to an offshore company of the personality merchandising rights of a premier league footballer recently transferred from Juventus, BB had turned up late with his usual refrain, and I had rebuffed him at the door. I did not see him again for some three months except at the club where his response to me was icy, despite my attempts to explain my brusque behaviour that night. Strangely for me I began to miss his visits. Recourse to the club's address list led me to his flat on a council estate in South-east London. I deliberately left my visit till after midnight. When he answered the door I said, 'Do you fancy a game?'

He grinned, clearly happy to see me, but said, 'What's the problem, missing your regular ass kicking?'

I suppose BB is the only friend I have outside of my practice. Apart from my passion for chess, and my quest for sex with love, my work consumes virtually all of my energy. So it will come as little surprise that when the trouble began part of it at least started in my office, though at the time I saw nothing unusual in the day; nothing, that is, unusual for the international tax practice that bore my name. It was the day following my visit to Shadowlands and a new client was booked in for 10.00am. I take on no clients at an annual fee level under £50,000. My PA, Anita, had made this clear to the client, who had said that the money was not a problem provided that I was as good as people say. 'Oh, he's not as good as they say,' Anita told me she had replied. 'He's much better than that.'

The comment was typical of Anita's fierce loyalty. She had worked with me for eight years. We were the practice. I had a network of freelance professionals that I regularly called on but A J Stuart & Co was Anita and me, and we loved our work. Anita was fifty years old, looked it, and dressed accordingly. But her face could light up like a teenager's when engaged in the intrigue, secrecy and intricate planning that are an intrinsic part of the international tax minimisation structures I create. They appealed to the sense of adventure behind her staid exterior. They challenged her intellect beyond The Times crossword, which she finished every day. Moreover, Anita enjoyed working with the firm's varied clientele, and she was always as excited as I was with the prospect of a new assignment.

With the client in the boardroom, coffee and biscuits on the table, Anita buzzed for me to make my entrance. Always a grand entrance; I find high net worth individuals enjoy a little theatre. I was wearing a white Turnball and Asser sea island cotton shirt, double cuffed, the gold cufflinks sporting my AS logo. My grey pin-stripped suit was from James & James of Old Burlington Street. There were real buttonholes on each sleeve. This is one of the many features, which distinguishes the made-to-measure from the off-the-peg. I sometimes leave the last button open to emphasise the point to the sartorially discerning. I did so today. My shoes, also made to measure, were of course highly polished. The picture was completed with a red silk Nicole Manier tie. That was the outside. To be ready on the inside I choose one of a multitude of inspirational quotes and repeat it to myself over and over like a mantra. Today I chose Anthony Robbins: *It is in the moment of our decisions that our destiny is shaped.* That done, I walked to the boardroom humming *Hail to the Chief.* As I entered, Anita said to me, "Dr Stuart, this is Mr Mazzinni." And turning to the small, neat, dapper new client, "Mr Mazzinni, Dr Stuart."

We shook hands and I took my seat. 'How did you hear about us Mr Mazzinni?'

He smiled. 'I wish my affairs to be treated in the strictest of confidence Dr Stuart.' His accent was pronounced. 'Let's just say I have been recommended to talk to you by a private commercial pilot.'

Robin Brocklehurst. Aviator, entrepreneur and client. Most pilots, being salaried employees of their airlines, have little use of my services. But Robin is a freelance pilot who operates through a company, RB Aviación SL, a Societat Limitadad, registered in Andorra. The company, which I set up, enables Robin's business income to accrue in the Co-Principality which has no taxes on income or gains. And RB Aviación enjoys a good income, its principal clientele being the nouvelle riche of France and Spain.

'That's sufficient.' I said. 'How can I help you?'

'I think I need, how do you say?' His small hands fluttered in the air. 'A piggy bank.'

'A piggy bank,' I repeated with a degree of amusement.

'I have a large amount of money that I need to place somewhere secret. I don't want anyone to know about the money. No one at all. If anything happens to me I want certain people to be able to enjoy the money. But as of now I don't want those people even to know the money exists. After this meeting I will not be contactable for, say, two to three weeks. When I return I want everything already set up. Then I will transfer the money to you. Can you do that?'

'Yes,' I said, 'but first I need more information to determine the structure that will suit you best. For example, will you need access to the money?'

'Not in the immediate future.'

'How much money are we talking about?'

'£20 million.' He smiled, seemingly pleased with his wealth 'I want the money invested with a good return and I want to pay no tax. But as I say most importantly I want no one to be able to get to it. I want no one to know it exists.'

'You seem' I said 'to be asking me to set up an offshore asset protection trust.'

'Quite so, Dr Stuart,' he replied, clearly warming to the theme. 'I need you to protect my assets. That is why I am here. I need my assets protected from prying eyes.'

'Well, I will do my best. All transactions leave some sort of paper trail. It is not possible to make money completely disappear. However, I think with a little luck I will be able to create a structure that will please you.'

His eyes met mine and for the first time I realised how cold they were. His gaze was fixed and resolute. 'You are too modest Dr Stuart. I have heard it said that when you hide money God can't find it.'

I am not immune to compliments, though that was hardly a phrase I would use in a corporate brochure. I studied Mr Mazzinni's face. It was animated; as if he had found the man he was looking for and wanted to conclude his business swiftly. I was right on the money. 'I have your deposit with me,' he said and reached for his briefcase. '£50,000 in cash.' He pulled out ten bound wads of £50 notes.

Robin, Robin, I thought, this time you've gone too far. 'Mr Mazzinni,' I said, 'I cannot accept a cash payment. I'm sorry. I am not even sure I can accept this assignment.'

His expression immediately hardened. 'Why not?'

'The money laundering legislation is quite strict. I must assure myself that your funds are legitimate.'

There was suppressed anger in his voice. 'How are you going to do that?' he asked.

'With your help,' I replied quietly and opened the blue folder on the boardroom table. 'I have here a Know Your Client Schedule. I will ask you a range of questions about you, your businesses, your assets and liabilities. The purpose of the questions are to ensure that I have taken all reasonable steps to avoid any suspicions on my part that the structure you are asking me to develop is part of a money laundering operation. Are you ready?'

'Whose side are you on?'

'I'm on your side Mr Mazzinni. Trust me. Shall we get started?'

He looked at me with some apprehension. 'Go ahead.'

We went through the form slowly and carefully. I did most of the talking, raising the questions, re-phrasing some answers he gave, suggesting some answers he failed to give. After half an hour we were done. Gathering my papers together, I said, 'We can proceed.'

'Do you need the names of the people who will get the money?'

'The beneficiaries of the trust? Yes, their names, addresses and passport numbers, together with their countries of residence and domicile.'

'I will give you those details when I come back, if that's OK.'

'That's OK,' I said.

He reached back for his briefcase. 'So, I can give you the money now?'

I genuinely would have preferred a cheque. But as I now Knew My Client, I could see no harm. 'Sure,' I said.

That evening Julianna, my housekeeper, was packing my clothes as if the trip to the Cayman Islands were to be purely business. I told her again that I was taking Tania. She had not met Tania but, of course, she knew her brother BB. Both Julianna and BB had been born in Jamaica, and sometimes before or after (but never during) a chess game, they would converse in patois, which I found pleasing to the ear. Julianna's accent was the more earthy. She was 30 years old and had only been in England for two and a half years, the last two of which she had spent in my employment. She had a very easy manner and a relaxed attitude toward housework. This suited me. Indeed, we had a rather easy and relaxed relationship.

'Put in some shorts, T-shirts and two pairs of swimming trunks,' I said.

'You can't swim'

'I know, but I might want to paddle OK. Just pack them'

My tension reflected my excitement. Tomorrow Tania and I would be on our way, British Airways, first class, direct to Georgetown. My whole body felt light, as if just slightly intoxicated. And I sensed a familiar stirring in my loins. I would sleep with Julianna tonight, which was good. I did not want to step on the plane feeling craven. This trip was to be a quest for love. I would woo Tania. We would eat in some of the finest restaurants in the Caribbean, charter a yacht and circle the islands, walk along Seven Mile Beach, talk a lot and laugh a lot. Tania may wish to swim in the sea; I would content myself with paddling.

Of course I would have to take a day out to conduct my business. The already complicated financial affairs of a UK resident client wanted them rendered yet more complex by the establishment of a Caymanian trust under the Special Trusts (Alternative Regime) Law 1997, known for short as a STAR Trust. I needed to meet with a firm of attorneys, a firm of accountants and a bank. Normally that would mean three separate days work, each with a very long interlude for lunch. Anita had re-scheduled the appointments so that they all take place on the same day, though I would still bill the client for three. He would expect nothing less.

The Cayman Islands have received much negative press over the years. They are too often seen as an unregulated tax haven, and a centre for money laundering. In fact the Cayman Islands are both a highly regulated and highly successful offshore financial centre, indeed the fifth largest financial centre in the world. There are no taxes within the islands on income, profits, gains or inheritance. This arose, according to legend, from the Wreck of the Ten Sails. In 1788 the Cordelia, the lead ship of a convoy of merchant ships heading for England from Jamaica, ran aground on the Caymanian coral reef. The island natives displayed great heroism in rescuing the shipmates and no lives were lost. Unbeknownst to the islanders one of the lives saved was a member of the royal family and for this King George III granted the islanders freedom from conscription and freedom from taxation.

It is the absence of direct taxes that make the jurisdiction a valuable tool in international tax planning and asset protection. There is, to my mind, nothing shady about the Cayman Islands. Its professional infrastructure rivals that of most of the countries in the developed world. But mention in your local pub that you are flying to Cayman at the weekend and even those who should know better ask you which of your two suitcases contains the clothes and which contains the money.

Even Tania was not immune from this view of our destination, however romantically I portrayed it. 'Tell me about Cayman,' she said as we settled into our wide, fat, comfortable leather seats in the first class compartment of BA.

'Well technically there are three islands, Grand Cayman, Little Cayman and Cayman Brac. We'll be staying in Grand Cayman. It has a more level terrain than Jamaica, and the pace of life is quieter. The beaches are wonderful. We'll be staying on the Seven Mile Beach.'

She admonished me. 'You sound like a tourist guide, not an international tax consultant. Tell me about the money. How did it become a tax haven?'

'I prefer the phrase "offshore financial centre."'

'Whatever,' she said with some exasperation. 'Tell me how a country just jumps up and says give us all your money, we'll look after it, no questions asked and no taxes!'

'It's not like that Tania.' But it was no good. She wanted the popular guide to Cayman, The Tax Haven, and I gave it to her.

'You know that the Cayman Islands could have become part of Jamaica in 1962 when JA received its independence.'

'Sure.'

'Then you also know that they elected to remain part of Britain as a crown colony. Well, the British government was hardly going to bankroll them. The Queen's ministers would have preferred that the small islands had linked up with Jamaica, like Tobago did with Trinidad. So Cayman was left with having to find a source of income. They choose two: tourism and offshore financial services. And they choose very well. To attract the offshore business they enacted legislation that allowed for a range of different types of companies to be incorporated within their jurisdiction, each with minimal filing requirements.'

'What?'

'No Cayman company had to file accounts for public inspection, nor have those accounts subject to an independent audit.'

'So no one could find out what was going on?'

'No one – turnover, profits, assets, liabilities, all confidential. Moreover, the companies were not subject to taxation.'

'Paradise.'

'And it gets better. The companies could issue bearer shares.'

'You've lost me.'

'When you have a company, whoever owns the shares owns the company. Shares are usually registered in the names of their owners, the shareholders. Bearer shares are registered in the name "bearer"; that is, whoever bears, or holds, the shares owns the company. Bearer shares provide for the complete anonymity of company ownership.'

Her face registered the expression of someone who was losing the plot, but she was tenacious. 'Explain.'

'OK, I set up a Caymanian company, say, with bearer shares issued to me. I deposit £250,000 in the company account. To transfer the company to you I just give you the shares. No paperwork is involved. You now bear the shares and, technically, you can go and collect the £250,000. Or give the shares, or sell the shares, to someone else. No one knows who owns a company with bearer shares except the bearer.'

'That's legal?'

'Oh yes, and that's simple. You want to see some of the things we get up to in my offices.'

'I can only imagine.'

The pilot interrupted us with information we did not need and would not remember. Tania leaned back in her seat and closed her eyes. I chose to do the same. We would soon be taxiing to the runway. We had hours to talk. No need to rush. Things were going rather well.

We were airborne, and well pampered with champagne and smoked salmon, when she returned to the subject. Without preamble she asked: 'So if I set up a Cayman company and ran a business through it I would pay no tax right?'

'Possibly right, possibly wrong. You see, the term offshore company is applied to a company incorporated in an offshore jurisdiction, like Cayman or the Bahamas, but if the company is controlled from the UK it becomes resident in the UK and subject to UK taxation. You couldn't for example run the hair and beauty salon you manage through an offshore company.'

She seemed chastised. 'I know that,' she said.

'But with the right sort of trade if you appointed company directors resident offshore and those directors were responsible for the central management and control of the company then, in the right circumstances, yes, you could trade tax free, until the profits were repatriated.'

'Repatriated?'

'When you brought the profits back into the UK you would pay tax on them.'

'I see,' she said.

'How come you're so interested?'

She smiled with such warmth I just wanted to embrace her. 'I just like to keep myself well informed. How difficult is it to find these offshore directors?'

'Not difficult at all. The service is offered by offshore banks, offshore trust companies and international company secretarial agencies. There's decent money in it.'

So it's expensive?'

'Not necessarily. You could take advantage of the 'Sark lark'.'

What's the Sark lark, Stu?'

The 'Sark lark' is the term applied to appointing directors resident in the small island of Sark in the Channel Islands. These directors take no interest in the affairs of the company. They simply accept fees for serving as directors. They will sign anything, approve anything. They even pre-sign their letter of resignation so that you can dismiss them whenever you want. As they don't really do anything their fees are low.'

How much?'

Say, £200 per annum'

That's not much. How do they live?'

Remember, they don't work for the company. They just collect fees for signing documents. Half of them are farmers. Mind you, I happen to know of one Sark resident who is a director of over 5,000 companies. That's £1 million a year for signing paperwork he doesn't have to read.'

Do you use the Sark lark?'

'Not any more. It's fallen into disrepute. In my field you've got to remain on the cutting edge. Moreover, I no longer compete on fees. My fees are high and my structures, I like to think, are sound.'

'I'd love to do what you do.'

I made no reference to the years of study and the lonely nights spent analysing abstruse tax legislation from all over the world. Instead I said, 'Tell me about Shadowlands.'

'It's a hair and beauty salon.'

That's it?'

That's it.' The door was closed with such finality, I wondered if she thought I was patronising her. She turned away, leaned back to the headrest and closed her eyes. I looked at her lovingly, her high cheekbones, small nose, wide mouth, smooth dark skin. Beauty, however, is so much more than the sum of the parts. All I can say is that looking at her made me feel warm all over. Without moving or opening her eyes she said, 'You're staring at me Stu.'

No,' I said. 'Just admiring your beauty.'

'That's all right then,' she purred.

The first time I saw Tania she was leaning against the piano holding a crystal flute of champagne in Ronnie Scott's Club Room at the fortieth birthday party I threw for BB. She looked casually elegant in a long cream sleeveless dress. I may be mistaken, but I think her eyes lit up when she saw me. She walked across the room and held out her hand. "You must be Dr Andrew Stuart, I'm Tania Berkeley, BB's sister," she said and, because it seemed the most natural thing to do, I raised her hand and kissed it. She giggled and teased me about my formality. I complimented her on her appearance. We danced and drank and talked through the evening. She told me how protective BB was about her choice in men, and she made me laugh with her impersonation of Macy Gray. I told her about my first love affair and how I'd never quite gotten over it. She told me I needed to love again. As we parted, she said, "I feel I've known you for years." And I felt the same. That's the thing about love. You just know.

But it took me over a year to do anything about it. At first I was in denial. It was lust, I told myself and it would be wrong to lust after BB's sister. And if not wrong, it would be dangerous. If it was sex I wanted I had a large choice via the Agency. I did not want to damage my friendship with BB over a matter as simple as sex. But I just found myself thinking about Tania all the time. I replayed our evening's conversation over in my mind interminably. I often visualised her eyes, penetrating and knowing, heard her mellifluous laughter and felt her undulating body as we danced. I thought about her every day until it had become an obsession. And when I was certain that this was love, I planned the date and walked into her salon.

We talked only in brief snatches during the flight. We watched the movie together and I nudged her each time the food and drink came around. For the rest of the time Tania snoozed, her eyes closed and her breathing soft. I worked on my laptop sketching out the report I would later present to the bank, occasionally stealing glances at this woman of striking beauty whom I yearned to make my own.

I finished the report in the hotel. As it flowed, I typed with increasing pace. Everything fell into place. It would be ready within the half-hour. The hotel's business centre would print the report from disc and bind it for me in readiness for tomorrow's meetings. It was 3.00pm and I had the rest of the day for Tania.

There was a gentle tapping at the adjoining suite door. Not now, I thought, and immediately checked myself, anytime Tania. 'It's open on my side' I said.

Tania entered wearing a sarong. She seemed to glide into the room. It was as if her motion required no effort. The brightly coloured attire served only to highlight the smooth darkness of her skin, reminding me, not for the first time this trip, of how different we were. Moreover, she was so beautiful, so graceful, so at ease with herself that I felt I did not deserve her. I suppose she represented at some level the unattainable, but I preferred to see her as my perfect love.

She sat down on the bed and as she crossed her legs I drank in every moment. 'Tomorrow I want to swim with the stingrays,' she softly declared.

'Not tomorrow, Tania,' I said. 'This report will soon be done and then I'm all yours – but tomorrow I have meetings throughout the day. Sorry. I did say before, or I thought I had.' I felt like I was letting her down.

'OK,' she said simply.

But I felt the need to explain. 'First I have to meet with the bank, then–'

'Can I come?'

'What, to the bank, sure. We can go into Georgetown together in the morning. You can do some shopping and we should be able to meet up again for a little while before I have to see the attorneys. You can show me what you've bought.'

'No,' she said, shaking her head. 'Can I come to the meeting?'

'Why?'

'I would like to.'

24

'Tania, it's a business meeting. Of course you can't come. The affairs of my clients are totally confidential.'

'OK,' she said and paused. 'Can I meet with your bank manager after you?'

'Tania, don't be silly. This is a private offshore bank. It only deals with high net worth individuals. Please don't do this.' I tried to keep the irritation I felt out of my voice. 'I know we're here to have fun, but the bank meeting is not one of the fun parts. It is business, and business is business.'

'I'm not being silly, Stu. I want to open an account.'

'No, you're right, you're not being silly, just slightly unrealistic. Look, even if you could walk into the bank and open up an account, which you can't, it would do you no good – certainly not from a tax perspective. Any interest you earn on a Caymanian account must be disclosed on your UK tax return. It will be subject to UK tax in exactly the same way as if you had the account in the Barclays Bank in the high street. There are ways of doing these things Tania.'

'And you know the ways.'

'Yes, I know the ways.'

I had made my point. She got up and walked to the window. She looked out over the swimming pool to the beach and the sea. With her back to me I admired her figure, her legs, her curves, her perfect bottom. Without turning she said, 'So I can't just walk into the bank and open up an account.'

'That's right.'

'Why?'

'Because you need a letter of introduction.'

'Who from?'

It was time to close this down. 'From a professional person of unimpeachable integrity.'

She turned from the window, looked at me and smiled. 'Write me a letter of introduction Stu.'

'Tania, you're crazy. The minimum balance accepted by the bank on a private account is US$100,000.'

'Just write me a letter of introduction.' As far as she was concerned the discussion was over. 'Now, let's eat.'

'I have my report to finish, Tania, and you're playing with me. Don't. Don't do this.'

'I'm not playing Stu. Finish your report, then write my letter of introduction, then we'll have lunch.' She glanced at her watch. 'Or dinner.'

I could not judge this. She appeared serious enough. I decided to take her request at face value. Maybe it could be part of the wooing. 'I'll do it.' I said. 'One thing though, why do you need an offshore account? Maybe I can structure matters in a way that better meets your needs, through a company perhaps or a limited partnership.'

'I just need the account. Don't ask me anymore questions. My affairs are as confidential as those of your clients.' She walked back to the adjoining door. 'Now don't be long,' she said and returned to the lounge.

There are those who consider an offshore account to be a status symbol, a fashion statement on par with Gucci sunglasses and Valentino shoes. This type of thinking tends to lead to very muddled financial affairs. I didn't know Tania's income bracket, but it couldn't have been high enough to make an offshore account worthwhile. After all, she only managed a hairdressing salon, albeit an exclusive outlet in Mayfair. My mind drifted. Was there a wealthy boyfriend in the background? She'd never mentioned one, but then I'd been careful not to ask. She dated, of course, and she was stunning and, in Mayfair, she moved in the wealthiest of circles. A rich boyfriend (soon, I hoped, to be ex-boyfriend) was certainly a possibility. Or she was acting on behalf of another, her employers maybe. She asks for time off, tells them that she's going to the Cayman Islands, and they ask her to open an account so they can funnel away some of their profits. That would be tax inefficient on their part, but the idea was plausible. Or was there something else, something darker. I brought my mind back into focus. There were a thousand wholly legitimate reasons to want to open an offshore account. I would write the reference - but carefully.

Once the report was completed, I turned to Tania's letter and crafted something I thought suitable, which read:

Dear Mr Canolla
TANIA BERKELEY
I write a letter of introduction for Ms Berkeley. She is a long-standing family friend who is interested in opening an account with your bank. Ms Berkeley is a respectable and responsible individual who would not, in my opinion, enter into any obligation she was unable to fulfil.

Yours sincerely
Dr Andrew Stuart

I then telephoned Paul Canolla. 'Paul'

'Andrew, great to hear from you. Listen, I got a call from Anita, she said you can only spare an hour tomorrow. I'd ruled out the whole day. We can still do the day if your plans have changed.'

'Thanks Paul, but I do have to stick to the new agenda. In fact, if you have time available there's a small favour I would like you to do for me. After my meeting could you see a friend of mine? Her name is Tania Berkeley. She wants to open an account. I've prepared a letter of introduction.'

Paul was silent for what seemed to be a long time, but it was probably only a matter of seconds. He asked slowly, with a hint of apprehension in his voice, 'Why is that a favour Andrew? That's business.'

'Well, you see, I am not advising her as such. She is not a client, and I suspect she will not meet your minimum balance requirements. I am not asking you to waive those requirements, just to let her down gently with her dignity in tact. She's a friend Paul.'

'She'll bring your letter with her?'

'Sure.'

'Have you completed an account opening form?'

'No.'

'Please do so and I'll see what I can do for her. Tania Berkeley you say?'

'Yes'

'How well do you know her Andrew?'

'Very well.'

'Will you be sitting in on the meeting?'

'No'

'I'll see her after I see you. I'm making the diary entry as we speak. Now tell me, how is the wonderful Anita?'

Tania and I arrived in Georgetown half an hour early for our appointments so we strolled around the picturesque little Caribbean city for thirty minutes. The air was warm and carried that musky smell that rises from the tropical earth after a rainfall. It was not too long before I began to feel damp from perspiration. Though I had spent much time in the tropical offshore financial centres, I had never grown comfortable with the climate, certainly not in a shirt, tie and jacket. I suggested to Tania that we head for the bank and wait in reception until our 11 o'clock meeting. As soon as we entered the bank she knew why. The air-conditioning was chilling.

The Island Bank was located on the second floor of a discrete small block of offices set back from the main road. There were no tellers, most transactions being conducted by telegraphic transfers. The waiting area was Olde English in decor: wood-panelled walls and Chesterton furniture. The receptionist offered us coffee, which came in a china pot on a silver tray with those small china cups with ornate handles so small that even a young child could only get a single finger through the loop. The rest of humanity had to pinch the handle with thumb and forefinger. Thankfully after two or three sips the cup was emptied and the entire charade was over. I disliked the pretentiousness. Tania was enthralled. 'This is posh,' she whispered.

'Sure,' I said.

Even though we were early we weren't kept waiting long. Paul Canolla himself came out to greet us. His fair coloured hair ran to his shoulders and his physical definition reminded me of his favoured leisure activities: yachting, swimming and tennis. He was not muscular, just very fit, and it showed. Wearing his trademark red braces, white shortsleeve shirt and red tie, he strode toward us as if he owned the bank. 'Andrew,' he announced in a booming voice, rich in its texture and confidence. 'And this must be Tania Berkeley.'

'Tania,' I said, rising. 'This is Paul Canolla, the managing director.'

'Call me Paul,' he interjected.

'Tania,' she said, a mite demurely.

'Right,' said Paul. 'First Andrew, then you Tania. Can I get you anything while you wait?'

'I'm fine Paul,' she replied. 'The coffee is lovely.'

I walked with Paul to his office, a large affair bereft of any evidence of hard work. His desk, as always, was clear; the room smelt fresh and there was not a trace of paperwork anywhere. There were two creased leather sofas facing each other by the windows separated by a mahogany coffee table. I sat on one sofa; he sat on the other. On cue, his secretary came in with two large mugs of coffee. I wrapped my fist around the handle. It felt good.

'I believe you're setting up a STAR trust, Andrew. What role would you like us to play? As you are aware we have a subsidiary trust company that can serve as the corporate trustee.'

'At this stage, Paul, I am looking primarily to you for banking and investment services. The fiduciary role will be handled by attorneys and the financial administration by accountants. My client likes to invite as many people as possible to the party.'

Paul, I thought, would have been a little disappointed but he didn't show it. I gave him a copy of my plan, which he read in front of me. He then invited into the meeting one of his portfolio managers and the three of us spent an hour working out the details together. When we were finished and again alone, Paul asked me whether there was anything he should know about Tania before the meeting. I told him there was nothing I needed to add to our earlier telephone conversation. He buzzed the secretary and asked her to show Tania Berkeley in. As she entered, I rose to leave. 'How long will you be?' I asked Tania.

'About twenty minutes,' she suggested.

'At least an hour,' said Paul.

I took the opportunity to pay a brief visit to some of my favourite jew-
ellers in the Caribbean. I bought a pair of diamond studded elongated caymanite earrings for Tania, and two pairs of gold mounted caymanite cufflinks for myself. Caymanite is a semi-precious gemstone found only in the
Cayman Islands. I wanted us both to have a permanent reminder of the
place in which our romance commenced. When I got back to the bank, a
little after the hour, I was shown straight into Paul's office. He was sitting
behind his desk and Tania opposite him in one of the wicker guest chairs.
'All done?' I asked.

'Yes, I think so,' said Paul. 'Tania?'

'All done. Thank you.'

'Fine,' said Paul. 'Tania would you mind waiting outside. I want to
have a quick word with Andrew. Man to man stuff.' And he winked at
Tania.

After Tania had left I said, 'What was that about?'

'Just flirting,' said Paul. 'You can't blame a man for flirting. In fact that
leads me on to what I wanted to discuss. I'll be in London in a couple of
weeks and I was wondering if you could sort me out, you know, with a
date.'

'Do you want a date or do you want sex?'

'Sex,' he said.

'Well there's an agency I use. Expensive, but very discrete.' I gave him
the number. 'I must say though that I'm finding out love is better than sex.'

'I'll only be in London for a few days Andrew, I won't have time for
love.'

It felt like I had all the time in the world. The rest of the vacation went
as planned: eating, sailing, shopping, dancing, sightseeing, snorkelling,
swimming (and paddling). No sex. We held hands when we walked, we
embraced when we danced and we kissed goodnight, but we slept in our
separate rooms. It was how I had wanted it to be, though I'm not sure I
could have had it any other way. When it was time to leave, I felt we had
embarked on a love affair and I was exhilarated.

30

I whizzed through my work the following week. I called Tania everyday at the salon. I had intended to work on Saturday too, but Julianna persuaded me to stay in bed. There is an easy sexual relationship between Julianna and me, born of a complete absence of love. We have a ritual. We have sex with music. My preference is jazz, hers is reggae. We put together a cassette of our preferred tracks. It starts with some slow tracks from the Pat Metheny Band. This is a time for kissing, stroking and caressing. The tape eases into some vintage Gregory Issacs. There were no rules, but I usually found my head between her legs during *Night Nurse*. From lovers rock to ragga, pure penetration with as much rhythm as I can manage, missionary, doggy-style, her on top, the works. A little Barry White, then back to smooth jazz.

We finished our session around ten. We were spent, moist and sticky with no place to go, bodies intertwined, basking in the final part that could last for hours: the afterglow. The timing had been consummate. Grover Washington Jr was easing into the first track of Reed Seed, and, as if the gods wished to bestow their blessing, it had started to rain. A perfect Saturday morning.

My mellow mood, and Grover's, was interrupted by the telephone. Julianna's arm reached over me and I playfully slapped her hand. She would have picked up the receiver and put it back down again. She'd done it before. Few people had my home number. I was ex-directory and the only personal number I gave my clients was my mobile. It would be a friend and I would deal with it quickly and return to my sexual cocoon. I lazily put the phone to my ear.

'Stu?' Oh Christ! I swung my legs from the bed, stood up and turned to Julianna holding my index finger to my lips. Julianna pouted. Tania was insistent, 'Stu?'

'Yes, I'm here. This is a surprise. I was just, well, sleeping. Well, not sleeping, you can hear the music, I was just having a lie in, you know, as you would say, chillin'.'

She raised her voice, 'Stu!'

'Yes, sorry Tania, what is it?'

'I've been arrested.'

31

Chapter 2

Over twenty years ago I'd been arrested myself. I was sixteen years old and terrified. Tania's call unearthed the pain that had long remained buried within me. Particularly her words, "I've been arrested." I uttered the same with the one call I had been allowed, but my mother never came. No one came, except the duty solicitor and social welfare officer - those who were paid to come.

'Stu?'

'I'm still here.' I said. Everything stood still. My legs became jelly. I could no longer hear the music. I could no longer smell the sex. My reaction was purely emotional. I was sixteen and the bastards were hurting me again. I eased myself back onto the bed, and forced myself back into the present. 'I don't understand, Tania. What are you talking about? Where are you?'

'Last night the police came to the house and arrested me. There were about ten of them, with dogs and everything. I'm at South Norwood Police Station. They held me overnight.'

They had locked her up. Me too. I had cried then. The tears came quietly now, for her and for me. Someone had hurt my love; someone had damaged my world. My voice, I think, remained strong. 'Are you all right? Did they harm you?'

Tania wasn't listening. 'Stu,' she said, her voice shaking, 'I'm scared. Please help me.'

'I'll do everything I can.' I would have rattled the gates of Hell itself. 'Do you have a solicitor?'

'No'

'I'll arrange it. You say you're at South Norwood Police Station, right?'

'Yes'

'What were you arrested for?'

'Money laundering. Laundering the proceeds of trafficking in cocaine. I'm innocent, Stu.'

'I know,' I said. But I didn't, not really. My mind flew back to the Cayman Islands and her request for an offshore account. Was it the wealthy ex-boyfriend? The tax evading employers? Or the something darker?

I went into the bathroom and stood under the shower. Once I had soaped up and rinsed off, I turned the arrow on the gauge to blue. The cold water beat down onto my chest and shoulders, reinvigorating me. I needed all the help I could get. As I towelled down, I felt a pleasant sensation, like thousands of tiny cold pins all over my body, and I wondered once again why I didn't have a cold shower every day. I dressed as if for work. Stu or no Stu, I needed to be Dr Stuart today.

I felt hollow at the centre of my stomach, utterly empty. I was not in pain, but I ached. It was as if I was physically yearning for something. The feeling was, I suspected, akin to what an alcoholic suffers when deprived of drink, or that experienced by a smoker when he realises that all the cigarettes have gone. But my yearning had no quick fix. It would not be satisfied until I had saved Tania, and the process I feared was going to be long and tortuous.

Solving problems was my field. Every day in my office clients, who risked losing a large chunk of their revenue or estate to various national taxing authorities, seek my advice, and my solutions, though I say so myself, are usually both subtle and original. Tania needed me now, and I would solve her problem too. But I was worried. I was not detached. The damn ache just wouldn't go away.

As I walked from my dressing area, Julianna met me with a mug of freshly brewed Blue Mountain coffee. There would be more in the kitchen. Good. 'What's up?' she asked with concern. Jealously did not enter our relationship. We had an understanding. Though let it be clear, her concern was for me, not Tania.

'You heard,' I said. 'Tania was arrested yesterday and kept in a police cell overnight.' I sipped my coffee. It should have been a luxury. Drinking good coffee should be an act in itself, not something done whilst doing something else. The coffee, as always, was rich and smooth, but today there was no pleasure in it. I just need the caffeine, and the heat. I sipped quickly. The hot coffee was dulling the ache.

'What's she been arrested for?' asked Julianna, lingering.

'Money laundering.'

'What's that?'

'Holding or processing the receipts of a crime. In this case, and in most cases, that crime is drug trafficking.'

'Did she do it?'

Wrong question. The difference between a right question and a wrong one is that a right question moves you forward. A wrong question just increases the pain. Wrong questions are also the more difficult to answer. More difficult, that is, if you tell the absolute truth. 'Of course she didn't,' I said.

'How do you know?'

'She told me.'

'Fine,' Julianna said slowly. 'And you believe her, but if nobody else does then what happens?'

'The maximum jail term for money laundering is 14 years.'

Julianna was choosing her words carefully, something that did not come naturally to her. It was clear she was trying not to offend me, lest I explode. Her caution was justified. 'So,' she asked avoiding eye contact, 'what are you going to do?'

That was the right question. I needed to get her a lawyer. I wanted to see her, if they would let me. Surely she would need a change of clothes. Food, would they feed her? I needed to tell others, her family. And I needed help. 'I'm going to call BB.'

Julianna's face visibly brightened. 'Good idea,' she said.

We walked down the stairs and into the drawing room together. I picked up the phone. This was going to be difficult. 'BB, its Andrew.'

34

'Hi Andrew.' His voice was stern.

Nothing to do but take the plunge. 'BB, Tania's been arrested.'

'I know,' he said.

How did you know?'

'She called me from the police station. I told her to call you.'

This was no time for pride, but I felt deeply wounded. I had assumed that she had only called me, that she had been allowed just one telephone call. I wanted to be the one person she would turn to in trouble, the one man who could fix anything, and who would fix everything for her. I wanted to be her white knight. But she had been allowed more than one call and she had called BB first. It was BB who told her to call me. And that hurt.

I swallowed hard. 'We need to get her a lawyer, BB, right away. Someone who specialises in criminal law. The best. I know lots of commercial and tax lawyers, but no criminal lawyers.'

'I know a guy. Billy Carver. They say he's good. He's looked after some of my boys from the Club when they get themselves into trouble. He's looked after a fair number of their dads too, and their mums.'

'It's Saturday BB, could you get hold of him today?'

'Already done so. Billy works 24/7. I've told him the whole situation and he can see us at 2.00. That good for you?'

'Sure,' I said. It felt good talking to BB; maybe Tania was right to call him first. There is a strength about him, a can-do attitude. That left me with a query and I had to address it. 'BB, why me? Why did you ask Tania to call me?'

'Because if I was in any kind of trouble and I was allowed only one telephone call *I'd* call you.'

Billy's law firm was located in Peckham, an area in south-east London that had seen better times. His offices were no more than a converted two-up, two-down terraced house, with a discoloured fascia bearing the name *'Carver & Co.'* BB pushed the doorbell and we were buzzed in without interrogation. If the building looked weary from the outside, the inside was worse. The front door opened into a drab office, no reception worthy of the name. The carpet was threadbare and dirty. The front office had two desks facing each other and two stained canvas chairs on the far wall. For the undiscerning clients, I thought. Sitting at one desk was a pale, thin woman of about 35 with orange hair and a pierced nose. Opposite her was a black man with a huge upper torso. He had either bulked up on steroids or he pumped iron out at every waking moment. Their personal incongruity was matched by the wallpaper, floral on one side of the room, striped on the other. BB announced to no one in particular, 'We're here for Billy Carver.'

'Up the stairs on the right,' replied the ageing punk rocker.

We mounted the narrow stairs and, as instructed, turned right at the top, straight into Billy's office. It reeked of cigarette smoke and whiskey, the floor was covered in files, boxes marked 'exhibits' and bundles of papers each held together by string. There were two old, unmatched wooden chairs in front of Billy's desk which itself was cheap, peeling and scarred with coffee cup rings. Billy himself was fat, sweaty and brown, possibly mixed race. We would have called him 'half-caste' many years ago, but the term is no longer acceptable in polite society, not that we appeared to be in polite society that morning. Billy wore an open baggy cardigan over an unironed pale blue shirt. His paisley tie was noticeably darker around the neck, as if he simply lifted the loop of the tie over his head at night and lifted it back on again the following morning, never worrying to undo the knot. I quietly buttoned the last holes on the sleeves of my suit.

There was something comic, and not unappealing, about Billy Carver, a seemingly slow man who overindulged in life's vices. He put me in mind of a brown Billy Bunter. 'Are you sure?' I whispered to BB.

'Sure he's sure,' answered Billy with a chuckle and he stretched out his arm. 'Billy Carver.' I shook his hand. It was moist and fleshy, but his grip was firm.

'Mr Carver,' I said.

'Call me Billy.'

'I am Dr Andrew Stuart,' I said, adding reluctantly, 'call me Andrew.'

'Hi Andrew, BB. Take a seat.'

In one athletic motion BB was seated. I almost tripped over an Exhibit

Box, landing uncomfortably in the other chair. This, I was convinced, was going to be a mistake. Just behind Billy, slightly to his right, I could see a litre bottle of Teachers whiskey, about a third full, but I could see no glasses. I wondered if he drank straight from the bottle. He pulled out a cigarette from a pack of Marlboro sitting on his desk and lit it with a cheap disposal lighter. No ceremony here. He inhaled deeply and blew the smoke in our direction. No manners either.

'Right, Andrew, BB's given me the background. One of my solicitors, Arthur, a good guy, is already at the station. He's seen Tania. She's OK, a little shaky. Nothing unusual. She's new to all this. Tania will be formally interviewed at 3.00 this afternoon. Arthur will be present. She will be advised to say "no comment" to every question put to her.'

'Won't that harm her subsequent defence?' I asked.

'Not at all. We have, at present, been given insufficient information by the police. As far as I am concerned there is at this time no case to answer. If there is no case to answer we should not respond to their questions.'

'But the courts may draw an inference from Tania's silence or her refusal to comment.' This was not my area of law but I knew enough to make myself useful.

'Technically yes. At this stage, however, she is acting on her lawyer's advice. Don't worry Andrew I know what I'm doing. I do, however, need some information based on what the police allege was found in her house when they searched it.'

I looked at BB. He looked at me. He said nothing. It was clear that I was in charge. 'What did they find?' I asked.

'Cash,' he said. 'Two hundred thousand in pound sterling, one hundred and fifty thousand in US dollars and one hundred and twenty five thousand in euros.' He smiled, revealing teeth stained and uneven. 'They say the money was under her bed.'

Silence. I looked back at BB; BB looked at Billy; Billy looked at me: each of us suddenly rendered mute. Billy seemed pleased with the reaction to his disclosure. He addressed his next comments to me. 'The point is,' he said, 'Tania told Arthur that the money was yours.'

I froze. The ache in my stomach grew tighter, my throat dried up. I could have used a swig of Billy's whiskey. I wanted to protest, to make it absolutely clear that the money had nothing to do with me. But I said nothing. Tania must have her reasons. This was a defining moment. Tania would have known that this question would be put to me, and she clearly expected me to back her up, or at least not to destroy her initial defence. I suppose she thought that I could explain such large amounts of cash, which suggested, of course, that she couldn't.

Billy continued, 'Now let me be clear here. This is what she told us. Nothing has been said to the police. At this stage nothing will. Technically we don't have to explain the cash at all. They have to link the money to drug trafficking.' "Them" and "Us," I thought, the predator in the bushes and the prey at the watering hole. And I was drinking with the prey. Tania was the woman I wanted and BB was my closest friend. Richard Nixon once drew a distinction between those who stayed loyal when the proverbial lions attacked and those who painted their asses white and ran with the antelopes. I would stay and fight. 'All I need,' said Billy, 'is to know that you are not specifically denying that the money is yours or that, if it is Tania's, it was gifted to her by you. I need to paint a preliminary picture Andrew, just for us, and I need to know that you are not going to take my canvas away.'

I could see Billy's point. If the prosecution's case against Tania was based solely on the cash, and we could suggest at this early stage that there was a perfectly sound explanation for the money, then the case might be dropped prior to a trial. The hollow ache started to abate as I made my decision, as I ventured into that place where it has been said that angels fear to tread. 'Paint,' I said.

'Good,' said Billy. 'Can you both be back here at 7:00 this evening. Tania's interview will have taken place by then and based on the questions posed I'll have more information for you both. In the meantime if you want to make yourself useful get Tania a change of clothes. You know, undies and things, maybe a sweatshirt and some jeans.'

'So you don't think she will be released today?' I asked.

'I doubt it.' Billy said. 'I suspect she will be charged.' He smiled again. 'That was an awful lot of money you gave her Andrew.'

When BB and I were back on the street I asked him what he thought of Billy. He paused, which was unusual for BB. 'Well,' he said, 'he doesn't have your polish or presence, but he has your brains and, like you, he wins. Tania could not be in better hands. I wouldn't take risks on something like this. We're talking my little sister here.'

And my love, I thought. 'Let's go shopping,' I said. 'We'll get some clothes for Tania. Do you know her bra size?'

'Her bra size? Why the fuck should I know her bra size?' Then, just as suddenly as he had flared up, he calmed down and smiled. 'I suppose I should be grateful that you don't.' He put his arm around my shoulder. 'Come on, I don't need to know her size, and we don't need to go shopping. We'll take the clothes from her house. I've got a key.'

As we made our way back to my car I said, 'BB, you do know I didn't give her that money don't you?'

'I know,' he said, 'but they don't.'

BB and I were back in Billy's office by 6.30. I was surprised to see the same two staff members, Ms Punk and Mr Work Out, sitting at their computers in the front office.

Billy was in an ebullient mood. 'BB, Andrew, sit down. Let me bring you up to date.' Behind him stood the whiskey bottle, only now it was three-quarters full. Either he was topping his bottle up or it was a new bottle and he had done over half a litre of whiskey in half a day. He displayed no outward signs of drunkenness. His voice was strong and steady and his mind seemed clear. 'The interview took place at three, or a little after three to be precise. Arthur was present throughout. Tania, as advised, made no comment to every question. The questions, however, were quite revealing.' He lit a cigarette and inhaled as if he were imbibing the elixir of life.

'Tania's arrest was part of a very large operation called Operation Chalice. This, Arthur ascertained directly from Detective Sergeant Greenley before the interview started. Tania was one of twenty-four people arrested that same night. Six of those arrested had cocaine on or about their premises. The total amount of cocaine seized by the police is 20 kilos, which they estimate has a street value of £5 million. Apparently four of the twenty-eight have been under close surveillance for over five months, with voice activated probes in each of their houses for the past three months.'

'Bugs,' said BB.

'Yes, bugs which start recording once they pick up a voice, well any sound really.'

'Was there a bug in Tania's house?' I asked.

'No, not as far as I know.'

'Then why was she arrested?'

'During the interview they asked her if she knew any of the other people who had been arrested. DS Greenley read out their names to her. Of course, she made no comment. We think one or more of the individuals may have been observed, say, visiting her home.'

'That's it? They've arrested her because some people who may have been involved in drugs visited her house. Have they arrested everybody else those people visited?' I was getting angry.

'It gets worse. At the end of the interview they formally charged her with money laundering.'

'This is bullshit,' said BB.

'Maybe. But I am troubled. Everybody else was arrested for trafficking in drugs or, that favourite catch-all of the Metropolitan police, conspiracy to supply. Only Tania was arrested for money laundering, which suggests that they knew the money was there. More than that, they knew that the money was not the proceeds of her trafficking in drugs. You see, the easiest path for them to take is to charge her with conspiracy to supply, they can always if they want tack on the money laundering charge afterwards. If they can place her in the company of cocaine dealers and then find large amounts of unexplained cash on her premises, a conspiracy to supply charge is a shoo-in. When the police don't take the path of least resistance you know that they know much more than they are letting on.'

'Like what?' I asked.

'Like I don't know yet,' he replied, clearly warming up to battle ahead. He rubbed his pudgy hands and almost bounced in his chair. 'But I will find out.'

My immediate concern was with the here and now. 'Meanwhile Tania's been charged.'

'Charged and detained'

'What happens next?'

'We apply for bail. The earliest we can get her before a Magistrates Court is Tuesday. We need to think about surety and security.'

This prompted a third interjection from BB. 'What's the difference?'

'As you know,' said Billy, 'they are both forms of bail. A security is a cash deposit put up by the bailor and held by the court. Should the defendant abscond or otherwise fail to adhere to the bail conditions the security may be forfeited. A surety is like a charge over property, which is subject to a promise to pay a fixed sum into the court in similar circumstances. Should a defendant abscond the person who has put up the surety has fourteen days to pay the full sum into court. Failure to do so may result in imprisonment. Interestingly the courts prefer sureties. Their reasoning is simple. If a man can afford to lodge cash with the courts, chances are that he can, *in extremis*, afford to lose it. But if a man puts up his home, well, he'll move heaven and earth to keep it - might even put the defendant under lock and key himself! Sureties, the courts believe, concentrate the mind.'

'How much will you need for her bail?' I asked.

'I don't know. Is there a figure over which you would not go?'

'No.'

Billy looked at me quizzically, as if to say then why ask the question. He had a point. Lighting up another cigarette, he said through the smoke, 'The police will object to our request for bail.'

'Why?'

'It's a big case. They will object to everybody's bail. We will present our best arguments. The decision will be in the hands of the magistrates. Do you know who will be prepared to stand bail?'

'I will,' I said.

'Anybody else?'

BB remained silent.

'It's good to have two or three,' said Billy. 'It shows ties to the community.'

When BB spoke it was with a pained regret. 'I can't do it Billy, you know that. I don't have nothing.'

'Not you BB,' Billy explained, in a voice so soft it would have placated a tiger. 'Someone else.'

In fact BB couldn't even attend the case on Tuesday. His commitments at the Boys Club had to take priority. So on Tuesday morning I drove to Croydon on my own. I punched in the address of the court on my car's satellite navigation system, affectionately known as Sally, and left the volume on. Sally would guide me to the court. It was one less thing to think about.

The Croydon Magistrates Court was a large modern building housing several different courtrooms each identified by number. Tania's case was known as Pendry and Others, after the alleged principal co-conspirator. I looked at the court listings for the day. The case was listed for 10.00am. It was 9.40. I hurriedly made my way to Court 3. As I looked around outside Court 3, Arthur identified himself and introduced me to Tania's counsel, Ms Ologbenla.

She was a large, impeccably attired black woman who looked to be in her mid-thirties, though her smooth round face may have hidden ten years. She wore clothes that complemented her size, a billowing white blouse separated from a long navy blue skirt by a patterned leather belt at least three inches in width. Tucked into the neckline of her blouse was a floral cravat. Her jacket was folded over her arm.

'Dr Stuart, I've been looking for you. Mr Carver told me you would be here at 9:30.' Her accent was English, upper middle class, evidence of an expensive education. Her manner was imperious, owing more, I thought, to her upbringing than her law studies. 'We have a lot to cover and little time in which to do it. Come with me.' She led me down the stairs into the open hall and made her way to an area of the wall farthest from any other people. Arthur followed. 'Ms Berkeley hasn't arrived yet so we will not be on at ten as listed. It happens all the time. The Securicor van from Holloway is late. That said, I wish to be ready at ten. Always work to your own standards, not those of the opposition. I understand you are prepared to stand bail.'

'Yes,' I said.

'What figures are we looking at? I was hoping for a mixture of surety and security of at least £75,000.'

'I can do that.' I said.

'On your own?' she enquired.

'Yes.' I said.

'I see. I understand you are her *close friend*.' She raised an eyebrow on 'close friend', her timing so perfect she must have practised it. 'I would have been happier with a father, husband, employer, neighbour, pastor or even her brother-in-law. I don't like 'close friend' Dr Stuart. It's too loose. When used between a man and woman it sounds like he's sleeping with her without commitment.'

'I would have thought standing bail for £75,000 indicated a pretty big commitment,' I replied. 'But, for the record, I am not sleeping with her. I am wooing her.'

'Woooooing?' she stretched the word out to breaking point. 'People still woo today? You surprise me Dr Stuart.'

I flinched. 'Is there anything else?'

'Yes, you have to be a fit and proper person in order to stand bail. Do you have any previous convictions?'

I hesitated. Billy hadn't asked me that, and I hadn't thought about it. I had been acting on pure emotion since Tania had called me on Saturday morning. I hadn't had time to think. I was Dr Stuart. I had erased my past.

'Tell me,' Ms Ologbenla stated firmly. 'Tell me all. Don't send me naked into the conference chamber.'

I laughed, but what warmed my soul was that she laughed too. Not loud and not full, but she laughed, and as I looked at her restraining her impulse to throw her head back and let it all out I wondered just how much of her natural self she had had to stifle to get to where she was today. As much as I had?

My past was my own. I had risen beyond it with hard work and sacrifice. I was a testament to deferred gratification. I asked for no help, no breaks, just my due. Even in my profession I had ploughed a lonely furrow. Though holding degrees in law and accountancy, I was neither a lawyer nor a chartered accountant. Why? Because to join the Law Society, Bar Council or any of the Accountancy Institutes I would have needed to explain a previous conviction, and I was damned if I was going to. So I took a doctorate instead. I became the best in the world at what I did, and what I did was international tax planning. I was answerable to no one but my clients. Certainly not to the Croydon Magistrates Court. Now was the time to walk out. Sorry, wrong guy, can't help. But that would have meant walking away from Tania.

'I have no previous convictions Ms Ologbenla, you may walk into the conference chamber fully clothed.' She looked straight into my eyes. I tried to transmit that it was OK and, if I read her eyes correctly, she was saying, it had better be.

'One last thing Dr Stuart, when I mention your name to the magistrates as the person who will stand bail for Tania Berkeley please stand up.'

I entered the courtroom and sat in the front row of the public gallery. The dock consisted of a glass cage at the rear of the courtroom, with two rows of five seats for the accused. I was to learn that of the 24 arrested only 10 had formally been charged at this stage. The rest were on police bail. A door to the dock opened from the inside and the prisoners were led in by guards. The Clerk to the Court, clipboard in hand, spent some time directing the guards as to where each prisoner should sit. This created some pushing and pulling and sharp language. Tania ended up sitting in the first seat on the front row. She stared straight ahead. I felt such pain on her behalf. I wanted to attract her attention, to wave to her, let her see that I was there for her, but I resisted the urge. She would see me soon enough.

After a hush of expectancy the three magistrates entered and we all rose.

The clerk to the court read out the names and addresses of each of the accused. Then they, in turn, each had to stand and acknowledge their presence: it was a penal roll call. I realised, as the names were called, why there had been such a commotion about the seating arrangements and why Tania was seated in the front row. The alleged nine conspirators and the alleged launderer had been arranged in alphabetical order. This was no doubt a reasonable arrangement, but I felt it was the start of the dehumanising process.

Shortly thereafter counsel for the Crown was on his feet. He informed the Chief Magistrate that the allegations against ten defendants were the result of a major operation involving detailed surveillance of the principal co-conspirators. He said that the transcripts of the voice activated probes in the houses of Rufus Pendry and Horace Bushel would reveal a pattern of conspiracy stretching over a six month period involving each of the accused co-conspirators. Turning to Ms Berkeley specifically, for she was the only one on a separate charge, counsel for the Crown stated that there was clear evidence that she was intrinsically involved with the co-conspirators and that when her house was searched the police had found a very large quantity of money in different currencies under her bed, which the Crown had good reason to believe to be the proceeds of drug trafficking. He concluded by saying that given the seriousness of the crimes, the large sums of money involved, the foreign origin or ties of those accused, and the consequent likelihood of the defendants absconding, the Crown strongly objected to the granting of bail.

When Ms Ologbenla rose she did so in a grand manner. 'Sir, I apply for bail on behalf of my client. She is 26 years of age with no previous convictions. She is in full-time employment and has been since she finished college. Indeed, she manages one of the most prestigious salons in Mayfair. She owns her own house. Her ties to the community are strong. Her own brother lives in London and runs a Youth Club in Lewisham, funded by the local council, and aimed at keeping young people engaged in worthy pursuits. I am troubled by my learned friend's reference to foreign origins or ties. I am sure he is not suggesting that by virtue of my client's Jamaican ancestry her natural home is in the slums of Kingston.'

'That will do, Ms Ologbenla,' said the Chief Magistrate.

'Sir, with respect, it will not do. How long does a black person have to live in the United Kingdom to be accorded the same rights as his or her white friends and colleagues? Miss Berkeley was born in the UK. She attended primary school, secondary school and college here. She bought her home here and built her career here. Sir, she is British. But my learned friend would have you believe that at the drop of a hat she would run to Jamaica. Why? Because in his mind, and in the mind of too many people like him, Jamaica is her home. Not Britain, Jamaica. Why? Because she is black and of Jamaican parentage. It is the reasoning of a bigot.'

'Ms Ologbenla, I urge you to withdraw that last remark.'

'I withdraw it, sir, and substitute it with this: It is the sort of reasoning that I feel confident will find no favour in this court.' She paused. 'May I continue?'

'With caution, counsel.'

'A close friend of Ms Berkeley is prepared to stand bail for her. He is a professional man with an unimpeachable reputation. A pillar of the community. Dr Andrew Stuart.' I stood up as I had previously been instructed.

The Chief Magistrate seemed surprised. 'There is no need to stand Dr Stuart.'

Muffled giggles surrounded me and I felt the level of embarrassment I thought I had left in childhood. I immediately sat down feeling suddenly hot and very small. Surely, Ms Ologbenla would have known that it was not necessary for me to stand. So why, I thought, did she put me through it. The answer came with a rush. Because I was white. She wanted the magistrates to see that the person prepared to stand bail for Tania Berkeley was white. And I felt both angry and sad.

The case ran on. Each defendant's counsel requesting bail, enumerating ties to communities, requesting more evidence, doing the soft-shoe shuffle. When all was done the magistrates retired to consider their decision. The defendants remained seated in their glass cage, and those in the public seats got up stretched and talked. Ms Ologbenla wandered over to me. I was ready for her. 'I didn't like that,' I said.

To her credit she did not feign ignorance, nor did she pamper to my sensibilities. 'My job,' she said, 'is to secure bail. I believe I have done that. If I am right, I will be pleased, Miss Berkeley will be pleased and so, I believe, will you. Dr Stuart, it's about winning.'

And she won. Bail was granted with minimal conditions; no need for surety or security. The Crown, however, immediately appealed and Tania was taken to Holloway Prison pending her next appearance in the Crown Court, where the appeal would be heard on Thursday.

My work schedule had been completely overtaken by events. Anita, ever competent, rescheduled my client work for the next four weeks. There are people who can work on many different things at once. I learned early on that I was not such a person. I can only concentrate on one task at a time and my work schedule reflects this with large chunks of time allocated to specific tasks for specific clients. Within these chunks of time I take no telephone calls. Anita takes detailed messages and I return the calls during what Anita and I call my "down-time." We allocate at least two hours down-time per day. I could not operate this system without Anita. Clients trust her and they know that to talk to her is virtually the same as talking to me. She doesn't understand international tax, of course. But then, neither do they.

Wednesday morning 8:00 to 12:00 had been allocated to Walter Charlton, aka Lightning. On his Tax Returns I describe him as a singer/songwriter. He is in fact a rap artist, but why stir up any latent prejudices on the part of Her Majesty's Inspectors of Taxes? Think of a singer/songwriter and one hears the gentle rhythms of a Paul Simon, the love songs of a Chris De Burgh, or the haunting melodies of an Enya. You know, decent music by decent people, taxpayers. Think of a rap artist and you are into the world of Dr Dre, Eminem or, heavens forbid, Niggers With Attitude. Now would a man who cheerfully raps about bitches, rape, murder and incest be minded, in the eyes of the Inland Revenue, to ensure that all of his income and gains are duly disclosed on his annual Tax Returns? I think not.

My singer/songwriter client's worldwide sales had reached a level where his overseas royalty income could benefit from some offshore tax planning. I had agreed to implement the offshore limited partnership strategy, a particular favourite of mine. Under this structure Lightning would enter into a partnership with an offshore company, say a company incorporated in Jersey or the Bahamas. I would choose the Bahamas for Lightning, it's sexier. The Bahamian company would be the general partner of the partnership, responsible for the management. Lightning would be the limited partner. This offshore partnership, let's call it Thunder LP, would own Lightning's copyright interests, ensuring that the royalties from his worldwide sales accrue to the Thunder LP rather than to him personally. The purpose of this structure is to transform Lightning's royalty income into a form that is taxed in the UK on a remittance basis only. That is, his income would be earned tax free in the Bahamas, and only fall in charge to UK tax to the extent that he transfers money from the limited partnership to the UK.

It would not, of course, be that easy. First, the structure would not work unless I could agree Lightning's non-UK domiciliary status. Under UK law an individual has only one domicile at any given time. It is the individual's natural or permanent home. At birth the individual acquires the domicile of his father, unless his parents are unmarried in which case he adopts the domicile of his mother. That domicile may only be changed by adopting a domicile of choice, by demonstrating a clear intention to establish a permanent residence in the territory of his new domicile. Now, Lightning's parents are Trinidadian and so, though he was born in London, he acquired a Trinidadian domicile at birth, which is ideal for UK tax planning purposes. What I had to establish was that he had not abandoned that domicile of origin for a UK domicile of choice.

Next I had to find a path through which I could avoid the royalties being subject to the deduction of tax at source by the countries in which the royalties arose. The US, for example, in the absence of a double taxation agreement, subjects royalty income arising within its jurisdiction to withholding tax of 30%. The problem is that Thunder LP would be resident in the Bahamas, a country with which the US has no double taxation treaty.

Thunder LP would have to sub-license its copyright interests to a company in a country with which the US does have a double taxation agreement. That country in turn would have to have a policy of no withholding tax on royalties, enabling the income to move from the US tax free under the treaty and then on to the Bahamas without deduction of tax. Traditionally, Cyprus has been an ideal location for such a conduit company, but I knew I could do better. And all this had to be achieved without falling foul of the stringent US and UK anti-tax avoidance provisions.

This was my pleasure: painting a picture that only I would see in its entirety. The US IRS would see part, the UK Inland Revenue would see part, but only I would see the sheer beauty of the whole. Even my clients would not see it all, because they did not understand it. They would look at the structure as a tourist, having fought his way through the crowds at the Louvre, looks at the Mona Lisa. "That's it then?" The only regret I have about my work is the absence of applause.

I was treaty shopping, reviewing the latest and most apposite double taxation treaties for the location of Thunder LP's sub-licencee, when Anita, breaking our strict code, buzzed me. I picked up the phone. 'I hope this is important Anita.'

'Andrew, I have a Detective Sergeant Greenley on the line.' My heart sank. He was Tania's arresting officer, pointed out to me briefly by Arthur at the Magistrates Court the day before.

'Put him on,' I said. 'Detective Sergeant, how can I help you?'

As he started to speak, I could picture his crumpled, sad face. 'Andrew, I wonder if I could stop by for a short chat. It should only take a few minutes.'

'Dr Stuart.'

'I'm sorry?' He seemed genuinely confused, but my guard was up. I responded with righteous indignation.

'My name is Dr Stuart, Detective Sergeant Greenley. I have no problem granting you your full title. I see no reason why you should have a problem granting me mine. I worked very hard for it. They don't give away doctorates at the local supermarket.'

49

'I see,' he replied, clearly feeling stung. 'You will shortly discover that I didn't get to be a Detective Sergeant by stacking shelves either. OK *Dr* Stuart, I was hoping we could be civil about this. I was mistaken. Will you be in your office for the next two hours?'

This was going badly, but it is difficult to climb down from a high horse. 'I may be, I may not. Just let me make this clear: I am not inviting you to my office.'

'I don't need an invitation, Dr Stuart. Will you be in your office for the next two hours – yes or no?'

'Criminal law is not my area of specialisation, Detective Sergeant. I need to take advice.'

'You need to take advice on whether or not you will be in your office for the next two hours?' He let out a little laugh. It was forced. It was done for effect, but it worked.

He'd won and we both knew it. 'Shall we say 1.00pm?' he asked.

'Yes.' I gave up gracefully. It gave me one hour and a half to prepare. Thunder and Lightning would have to wait. I could not allow Sad Greenley to wrong foot me again. Not that he had finished.

'One last thing, Dr Stuart. One word of advice. When you talk to a solicitor, as no doubt you will the moment you hang up the phone, do not use the same firm as Tania. Firstly, it could prove to be a conflict of interest for the solicitors; and secondly you could be seen to be tipping off a defendant, possibly perverting the course of justice.'

He should have quit while he was ahead. 'I assume you're referring to Miss Berkeley,' I said. 'Please address her as such. As regards your advice, I am sure you mean well, but it will be a very bleak day indeed when I turn to you for advice on professional ethics or operation of the criminal justice system'

There was a short silence before he said his barbed goodbye. 'As you wish Dr Stuart. I'll see you at one o'clock. You'd better decide whose side you're on. Tania's already made her choice.'

Chapter 3

I telephoned Carver & Co and was thankful to be put straight through to Billy.

'Hi Andrew. How's everything?'

'Billy, DS Greenley just called me. He's coming here at one o'clock. He said he wants to have a chat with me. What should I do?'

'Say nothing.'

'Realistically, Billy. I can't just say nothing.'

'Yes you can. What you do is listen. Find out what he wants. Greenley and his pals are trying to build a case against Tania. They are gathering facts. Think of each fact as a brick that they will use to build a prison cell around her. Some bricks won't initially fit, but they will turn them, chip them, maybe even break in half until they do. You talk to Greenley and you're giving him bricks.' He paused. He was drinking something. I hoped it wasn't whiskey. 'Andrew, when he called you what did you say?'

I thought back to the conversation. 'Nothing really.'

'Good,' said Billy. 'Keep it up, and call me when they're gone.'

At 12.55 Anita informed me that DS Greenley and DC Clarke were in the reception area. I asked her to show them into the boardroom. I prepared myself as if the officers were clients. I adjusted my tie in the mirror, repeating Roosevelt's *'The only thing we have to fear is fear itself'* and then played the *Eye of the Tiger* in my mind's stereo.

DS Greenley and his colleague were standing as I entered the boardroom reading one of my many articles framed on the wall. 'Gentlemen' I said.

'Dr Stuart,' replied DS Greenley. 'Let me introduce you to DC Clarke.'

Clarke was younger than Greenley, with a tailored dress sense that I suspected irritated the older man, whose suit appeared as tired as his face. I shook the hand of DC Clarke. His handshake was dry and firm. I reached out a hand to DS Greenley, just as he lowered his head and pulled a biro from his jacket pocket. An awkward moment; I withdrew my hand. Greenley looked up and smiled at my discomfort, pleased with his perfect timing.

'Take a seat,' I said. They sat alongside each other and I sat opposite to them. 'Would you like some coffee?' I was determined to be civil.

'No coffee,' said Greenley, answering for them both. 'We just want a short chat. Tell me Dr Stuart, what do you do here?'

Say nothing Billy had told me. Just listen. What do I say now, 'no comment'? That would be just plain daft. But I felt uneasy starting this dialogue with no clear idea of where it was heading. I decided to keep my answers short.

'I am an international tax consultant, a doctor of finance and comparative revenue law.'

'Very nice,' the forced chuckle returned. 'That's who you are, but what do you do?'

'I arrange the affairs of my clients, who invariably have income, profits or gains arising in more than one tax jurisdiction, in such ways as to minimise their overall burden of taxation.'

'How do you do that then?' smirked Greenley.

I could see that my answers were always going to be longer than his questions. Moreover he was giving nothing away. 'Detective Sergeant Greenley, I cannot see the relevance of these questions to my standing bail for Miss Berkeley. Please tell me why you are here and the purpose of this meeting.'

'As I said I just wanted a chat. Is that a problem for you? So tell me how do you save these clients of yours so much tax then?'

'I have nothing more to say until you explain the relevance of your questions.'

I folded my arms. We sat in silence, eventually broken by Greenley tapping his biro on my boardroom table. If a £50,000 a year client had done

52

this, I would have told him to stop (and made a mental note to raise his fees). In those circumstances I would have been in control. Today I wanted to avoid unnecessary confrontation. There was no rhythm to the tapping, no potential client here. The tapping stopped as Greenley leaned forward and said in a quiet voice, 'What I don't understand is why you have not distanced yourself from a case like this. Dr Stuart, we're talking money laundering here, and given what you do, I mean, think about it. Offshore this and that, and then you stand bail for a money launderer, what am I to think? I ask myself why would such a man do such a thing?'

'Ms Berkeley is a close personal friend who is innocent of the charges you have brought against her. I don't walk away from my friends when they are in trouble.'

'That's just it, you see. How do you know that's she's innocent? We found £200,000, US$150,000 and 125,000 euros in her house in cash. Now that's a lot of money. Where could she have got that amount of money from?'

I remained silent.

'Aren't you just a little bit curious? Or do you know? Did you give her the money to hold for you Dr Stuart – is that why you stepped forward? Is it your money?'

That was the rub. I paused to think, and Greenley didn't harry me. Billy had specifically asked me not to deny that the money was mine. It gave him choices. Not so much for the trial, but to head everything off before the trial. To enable him to say, we can explain the money. But a denial now from me would close a valuable avenue, and place another brick in the wall of the cell they were building around Tania. I look up at Greenley and maintained eye contact. 'I understand,' I said, 'that Ms Berkeley has said nothing about the money. It would be highly irresponsible of me to make any comments in those circumstances. Now, gentlemen, if you please, I think the meeting is over.' I started to push back my chair to emphasise my point. Greenley made no attempt to rise. Neither did Clarke, but then he'd hardly moved and hadn't spoken all meeting. The tapping resumed.

'If the money is yours Dr Stuart, just say so. You can save the police a lot of time and help your girlfriend. One simple innocent explanation for the money and the charges will be dropped. Tell me now and you can be celebrating with your girlfriend all night long.'

At last a reaction from Clarke. He laughed. Not a forced or done for effect laugh, a laugh rising from the belly with such honesty it made his eyes shine. I was sure the thought of Tania and me locked in an all night sexual celebration was too much for him. Try as I might I could not blame him. The thought was almost too much for me. I chose to ignore him.

'Ms Berkeley is a close personal friend, not my girlfriend, and I cannot help you about the money. I'm sorry.'

'Let me explain something to you Dr Stuart. Anything you subsequently say about the money in any court of law will be tainted by the fact that I've asked you today and you have chosen not to answer my questions. Let's try just one more time: is the money found at Tania's house yours – yes or no.'

I'd been waiting since the meeting started to make my next reply. 'No comment,' I said and smiled. It was my last smile of the day.

'I'll tell you what I think you really do here,' Greenley asserted in a low, aggressive tone. 'I think you hide money. You hide money from the taxman. You hide money from the Vatman. My question for you, Dr Stuart, is this: do you hide money from the police?'

Anger seared through me. 'Now hold it right there, right there. What the hell are you suggesting – and stop abusing my boardroom table with your cheap pen. I set up structures, complex structures aimed at tax minimisation. These involve companies, trusts and partnerships sometimes in offshore jurisdictions. Sure accounts are set up for my clients in the UK, the US, Switzerland and elsewhere –'

'Cayman?'

'Yes, sometimes Cayman, and Jersey and the Bahamas and the Isle of Man. Even Vanuatu. But I do not hide money. That is not the purpose. I might protect money – protect it from creditors, litigious plaintiffs or beneficiaries, to circumvent the rules of primogeniture. But I do not hide money, not from the Revenue, not from the IRS, not from HM Customs & Excise and certainly not from the police. Now if you want to mount a case against me because the judge ruled against you at the bail hearing go ahead. Tell me the charges and I'll have my lawyers here within the hour. Otherwise leave. No, let me put it more succinctly, get out!'

I pressed my hands hard against the boardroom table in an attempt to mask their shaking. I pushed myself up. The adrenaline surge subsiding, I quietly repeated, 'Get out, and don't come back without a warrant.'

Greenley pulled a folded document from his pocket. 'Sit down Dr Stuart.' He carefully unfolded the A4 document and smoothed it out on the table. 'I have in my hands a Production Order. It is a court order, as I am sure you understand, and it requires that you release to me every file, document, bank statement or other financial record that you hold pertaining to Miss Tania Berkeley and others. Here, have a read. Better still, pick up the telephone and read it to your solicitors. And while you're sorting that out DC Clarke and I will have that cup of coffee after all.'

I picked up the Production Order. 'Excuse me gentlemen,' was all I could manage.

Once I was in my own office I buzzed Anita and asked her to arrange coffee for Greenley and Clarke in the boardroom. I then read the list of names on the Production Order. I expected to recognise no names other than Tania Berkeley. The list was alphabetically arranged. As I read, my heart started to beat faster and my body temperature rose. Perspiration formed on my forehead. I had a problem. Two thirds of the way down the list nestled between Peter Lawrence and Fredo Oman was the name Giovanni Mazzinni.

I rang Billy Carver and filled him in. Billy was intrigued. 'It grows curiouser and curiouser.'

'What do I do about the Production Order?' I asked.

'You comply. Is there a problem?'

'Possibly,' I said. 'Can I claim client confidentiality? Surely my files are privileged. At the very least I need some time.'

'Read me the Production Order.'

'It says, "That you should give a constable access to and supply such originals and copies as may be necessary of the material to which the said application relates, namely all files, documents and accounts and other records"-'

'Cut to the chase, Andrew. Half way down the form it should give you the deadlines.'

'You're right. It says, "You are hereby ordered to give a constable access to the said material not later than the end of the period of 7 days from the date of this order."'

'And the order is dated?'

'Today.'

'So you have seven days.'

'I think they expect to get the files now.'

'You have seven days,' Billy insisted. 'I suggest you stall and use that time to talk with your own lawyer. A conflict of interest does not exist at present but, given the current sequence of events, I think one may develop and I feel you should have the same lawyer all the way through.'

I did not like this. 'All the way through what?'

'All the way through wherever this thing is going.'

'Billy I know all sorts of lawyers, but if your fears are justified I need a criminal lawyer. Can you recommend one – the best in the City, no expense spared.'

'I see.'

'Sorry,' I said. 'I meant no offence.'

'None taken. I'm going to call George Fairlow. He's a high profile, white, Oxford educated, white-collar crime specialist who knows his way through the woods and he charges by the minute. I will call him now. Call me when DC Greenley leaves and I'll give you his numbers.'

The reference to colour jarred. I did not ask for a white lawyer, I asked for the best. Maybe Billy thought I was talking in some sort of code. I would tackle him on this but not today. 'Thank you,' I said and hung up the phone.

When I returned to the boardroom Greenley and Clarke had finished their coffees. I resumed my seat. 'Where are the files?' asked Greenley.

'I have seven days in which to deliver them to you. That is clearly stated on the Production Order.'

Greenley was unimpressed. 'We were planning to take the documents with us today. I cannot see why you would need seven days to hand over the relevant contents of your files unless you were planning either to remove items or create items. That, I hardly need to remind you, would be a criminal offence. I want all relevant documents now Dr Stuart, not in seven days time, not tomorrow, now. Any delay, however minor, will lead me to conclude that you are engaged in a criminal conspiracy with Tania Berkeley and others. Do you understand me?'

'I understand clearly. You are demanding everything today. The court allows seven days. You are trying to exceed the powers granted to you by the court and you are doing so in a threatening manner.'

'I am not threatening you Dr Stuart, I am just explaining the consequences of your actions. I am in fact trying to help you, to prevent you from taking action that may later implicate you in a serious criminal case.'

'Thank you for your concern. You will receive all relevant documents within seven days. I will courier them to your station, if you care to leave the address and any reference number with my PA, Anita.'

DC Greenley rose from his chair as if it required great effort. DC Clarke, following Greenley's lead, tried to rise equally slowly but, lacking his colleague's sense of timing, he was up and pushing in his chair, before Greenley had even straightened his back. 'Don't courier a thing, Dr Stuart,' Greenley said with a hint of menace. 'Call us when everything is ready and we will return to collect it personally. We don't want anything going astray.'

'I'll have Anita see you out,' I said.

'We can find our own way,' replied DC Greenley, and he walked from the boardroom followed by DC Clarke, and headed for the stairs. No good-byes, no handshakes, no files.

Once back in my office I called Billy and filled him in on the encounter. He repeated my need for legal representation. 'I've already contacted

George Fairlow of Bellows & Bellows and he has some time available on Friday. That will suit you because tomorrow, Thursday, you'll be back at Croydon Crown Court. Shall we say 3:00 pm at his offices. I'll fax you over the details.'

I wondered why all lawyers seemed to think that their clients have nothing else to do but meet with them at their convenience. 'Fine,' I said.

The Croydon Crown Court sits next to the Croydon Magistrates Court so on Thursday morning I repeated my Tuesday journey. I put Sally on for company. The morning was crisp, cold and bright. The traffic moved easily and I made good time. I was feeling confident. Billy told me it was unlikely that Crown Court judge would overturn the magistrate's grant of bail. He felt that the worst case scenario would be the imposing of further conditions to the bail, though he did emphasise that this was a completely new hearing.

Once inside the building I made my way to court 7, noticing as I walked along the corridors that all of the barristers were wearing the traditional white wigs and black gowns. It was as if the first hearing was merely a run through in mufti; this was the real thing. Outside court 7 there was an array of characters: barristers looking superior, solicitors on mobile phones, defendants dressed in their Sunday best, friends and relatives chatting with false bonhomie and children seemingly oblivious to the whole grisly pantomime. I busied myself by looking at the court listing, which was pinned to the wall to the left of the entrance to the court.

'Dr Stuart, how are you this morning.' I turned to face DS Greenley and, two paces behind him, DC Clarke. My nervousness returned. I tried not to let it show.

'Good morning Detective Sergeant Greenley.' He managed a grimace. I looked behind him. 'Good morning Detective Constable Clarke.' Clarke nodded.

DC Clarke had chosen a dark grey suit for the occasion and a narrow, dark blue tie with white polka dots. DS Greenley was wearing the same suit and tie as yesterday. 'Confident?' he asked.

'Of course,' I replied. 'Justice will be done, just as in the magistrates court'

He feigned puzzlement. 'Which case are you referring to?'

I put as much irritation into my voice as I could manage. It wasn't difficult. 'Ms Berkeley's, of course.'

'Not yours?'

'I don't have a case DS Greenley.'

'You will have if you don't get those files to us on time.'

'I have seven days'

'Six days,' he replied, and as he turned, followed by DC Clarke, he almost bumped into the large woman marching toward me. I wish he had. She would have sent him sprawling across the floor. Resplendent in wig and gown, Ms Ologbenla was all business. She ignored his muttered apologies and confronted me in a voice aimed for everyone's attention.

'Why were you talking to the arresting officers on this case?'

I replied in the low voice of a chastised schoolboy. 'They have been to my offices. Billy Carver knows all about it. I did not discuss Tania Berkeley's case. They served me with a Production Order.'

She turned to the direction of Greenley and Clarke and said, ostensibly to me, but in a voice meant to carry to the far side of the room, 'This is most irregular.' She turned back to me and looked directly into my eyes. I saw concern. 'Come,' she said softly and led me down the corridor into a small private room furnished with a table and three plastic chairs and smelling of smoke. Barristers' privileges.

I sat down. Ms Ologbenla remained standing. 'I must assume that they are going to object to you standing bail on the basis that you are not a fit and proper person. Are you sure you want to go through with this?'

'There's nobody else,' I said. 'So long as their objection will not harm Tania's case, I'll stand bail. I am a fit and proper person. They cannot harm me.'

'You may be cross-examined.'

'Bring them on,' I replied. 'I can't wait.'

Ms Ologbenla's face brightened. 'Fine,' she said. 'Just tell me this, is there anything else I should know?'

'Nothing,' I said, with more confidence than I felt.

'Good. Now I need to take you through your background so that I can ask you those questions that present the best possible picture for the judge. After that you'll be in the hands of the prosecution.' She sat down and started to take notes.

'How is Tania?' I asked after she had finished.

'She is coping. I spoke to her just before I came up to the court. She's made some friends in Holloway, a murderess, a fraudster and a drug baroness.'

'Is that wise?'

'You don't have a lot of choice about your social circle in Holloway, Dr Stuart.'

'Of course.' I felt stupid.

'She's got a job, which will keep her out of the cells for long periods should we fail today.'

'What kind of job.'

'Cleaning the floors, I think.' She could see the pain I was feeling. 'It's good to have a job.'

'We've got to get her out.'

'I will do my best.'

The appeal hearing was delayed until 2:00pm. It was to be held in camera; that is, the public were not allowed in. That included me. Ms Ologbenla told me to wait outside the courtroom. The usher would call me when I was required. I had been waiting for some 40 minutes when a cheerful, chubby, robed gentleman pushed open the court doors and in a deep baritone called, 'Dr Stuart.' Game on.

I walked into the courtroom feeling quite special. Everybody was waiting for me, the judge, the barristers, the solicitors, the clerks, the court reporter, the defendants, Tania. She was sitting at the back of the court with her co-defendants. First seat, first row. There was no glass cage this time, just a sectioned off seating area. The courtroom was furnished in pine. It

60

looked clean, modern and efficient. The judge was in his forties, bespectacled and clean shaven. I was led to the witness box and, standing there, read the oath.

Ms Ologbenla was on her feet. 'Dr Stuart would you state your qualifications please.'

'Certainly. I have law degrees from Nottingham University, an LLB, and New York University, a JD. I have an MBA from City University specialising in accountancy and a PhD from the London School of Economics in international finance and revenue law.'

'And where do you work, Dr Stuart?'

'I have my own business A J Stuart & Co. It's an international tax consultancy.'

'And what is its turnover?'

'About £6 million per annum.'

'And its profits?'

'Including my salary about £2 million.'

'Do you hold any other positions?'

'Yes. I am a Reader in comparative revenue law at London City University.'

'And what does this position involve?'

'It is largely a research post, but I also give lectures to postgraduates and supervise doctoral students.' The judge was making notes and I was beginning to relax. This was going rather well.

'I understand that you are prepared to stand bail for Ms Berkeley, is that correct?'

'Yes'

'What is your relationship with Miss Berkeley?

'She is a close friend.'

The judge turned to me with a kindly smile. 'Are you aware of the consequences of standing bail Dr Stuart?' he asked.

I decided not to remind him of my law degrees. There is a time for everything and right now was time for humility. 'I believe I do, Your Honour.'

61

'You see,' the judge continued regardless, 'the prosecution is absolutely convinced that if Miss Berkeley is given bail she will abscond. Should that happen you would lose any security you were required to lodge with the court. As regards any surety you were required to supply, you would have fourteen days to produce the funds. Failing that you would go to jail.'

'I understand.'

'Very good. I assume you have no previous convictions.'

I believe I did not hesitate. 'No, Your Honour.'

The judge appeared satisfied. Returning to Ms Ologbenla he asked, 'Does the defence have any more questions?'

'No Your Honour.'

The judge seemed keen to move things along swiftly. 'The prosecution?'

A young, tall, bearded barrister raised himself awkwardly to his feet. 'Just a few, Your Honour.'

The judge seemed surprised. 'Very well,' he said and leaned back in his comfortable chair. I, of course, remained standing.

'Dr Stuart. Where will the funds come from should his Honour decide to grant Miss Berkeley bail?'

'From my own resources.'

'I see. So you have substantial cash resources in your own name.'

'In my name or in the name of my business.'

'Which is it Dr Stuart, in your own name or the name of your business?'

'The bulk of my money is in my business.' I felt the need to explain. 'It's more tax efficient that way.'

'Really? This is not my field, but surely a sole trader is taxed on his total profits whether he leaves the funds in the business or not.'

The judge intervened. 'Is there a point to this questioning?'

'Yes, Your Honour.'

His Honour was unimpressed. 'Well get to it quickly. Dr Stuart is not on trial here.'

Counsel for the Crown ploughed on unfazed. 'The point is that you do not own A J Stuart & Co do you Dr Stuart. It is owned by a company. That is why the tax planning works. Is that not so?'

Before I could answer His Honour intervened again. 'A perfectly legit-imate arrangement. What is your point?'

'Do you own the company that owns A J Stuart & Co, Dr Stuart?'

Everyone in the courtroom, including the judge, was silent. 'Not direct-ly,' I said.

'Not directly, Dr Stuart? I would suggest not at all. The company that owns A J Stuart & Co is called Rocart Trading Limited and –'

'As disclosed on my letterhead,' I said.

The judge turned to me. 'Do not interrupt counsel Dr Stuart.' His tone was pleasant and friendly. Then in a much more businesslike voice he said, 'Carry on Mr Swainsong.'

'Thank you, Your Honour. True, that much is on your letterhead, though in very fine print. What is not on your letterhead is who owns Rocart Trading Limited.' Nor did it need to be, but I assumed the judge already knew this and, whether he did or not, I felt it would be unwise to point it out. One interruption, I decided, was sufficient. Counsel continued. 'I have here a Companies House search which discloses that Rocart Trading Limited is owned by an international business company called FiscalPlan Limited, which has its registered office in Jersey. We searched the Companies Registry in Jersey to ascertain the beneficial owner of FiscalPlan. And what do you think we found?'

That was clearly a question, so I answered it. 'FiscalPlan is owned by Catmouse Limited.'

'Quite so. And Catmouse Limited is a company incorporated in the Cayman Islands.' He had reached a dead end and I knew it. 'Do you own Catmouse Limited, Dr Stuart? And before you answer that may I advise you that we've done our homework.'

The last part was a bluff. No one could find out who owned Catmouse Limited. 'I do,' I said.

'Really?' he asked, as if suggesting that he knew something different.

'Yes,' I said.

Like the white mouse in the experimental maze, he had run up the wrong path and found a dead end. No cheese. But unlike mice, barristers are resourceful creatures. Without acknowledging my declaration of ownership, he asked: 'Why such a complex structure, Dr Stuart, for a simple tax practice?'

'It's not complex at all,' I replied. 'My practice is owned by a UK company which in turn is owned by a Jersey company, which is owned by a Caymanian company owned by me. It's all perfectly legal and open. If I had wanted to hide something you wouldn't have found it.' And I immediately regretted my answer. It was as if I had reached into the maze and dropped a nice little piece of Stilton right into mouth of the mouse where he stood in the dead end.

'Your Honour,' he said, 'it took a little while but that is my point. If he wanted to hide ownership he could; it's his field of specialisation. We will never know who owns Catmouse Limited. Its very name implies game playing with the authorities. A company incorporated in a territory renown for money laundering, owns a Jersey IBC which owns a UK company, which owns the practice from which money will be taken for the bailing of a defendant who herself is charged of money laundering. For all we know she is being bailed with her own laundered money. Maybe she owns Catmouse Limited. Maybe that's why Dr Stuart is here.'

Ms Ologbenla was on her feet in a flash. 'Your Honour, this is outrageous.'

His Honour smiled. 'It is certainly novel. Does the prosecution intend to present any evidence that Catmouse Limited, a singularly unfortunate name in the circumstances, is owned by anyone other than Dr Stuart?'

'No, Your Honour.'

'Then I will take Dr Stuart at his word. Does the prosecution have any further questions.'

'I believe we have made our point Your Honour.'

'Indeed you have. Does the defence have any further questions?'

Ms Ologbenla was seething. 'No, Your Honour.'

'Dr Stuart, you may step down.'

As I walked from the courtroom I could not look at Tania. I felt I had let her down. The usher led me away. The cheerful, chubby man who had shown such deference on my entrance almost bundled me out of the doors.

I had been sitting outside the court for some half an hour when Ms Ologbenla flew through the door, gown flapping, and, without breaking stride, beckoned me to follow her. She headed for the same small conference room we had used earlier. I entered and, assuming some atavistic proprietorial interest, took the same seat. As before, Ms Ologbenla stood.

'The judge is minded to grant Miss Berkeley bail at £250,000. That is, £125,000 security and £125,000 surety. Is this acceptable to you?'

'Yes,' I said. 'It seems high. How does it compare with the other defendants?'

'Everybody else has been denied bail.'

The full enormity of the case hit me. 'Well done,' I said. 'Bail in spite of my performance.'

She looked down at me with more compassion than I deserved. 'Your performance, as you put it, wasn't that bad. The Crown had done their research. You were ambushed. The Crown tried to ruin your reputation in there.'

I was heartened by her kindness. 'And the judge didn't buy it,' I rejoined.

'Oh, he bought it,' she replied, 'to the tune of £250,000.'

Like a machete hacked through the small of my back: an execution without the ritual. I chose to make no response. The job was securing the funds. I was holding substantial funds on my company's business reserve account. 'Will they accept a cheque?' I asked.

'No,' she replied. 'When they say cash they mean cash.'

'I'll need to find a bank. Will they hold Tania here until I secure the funds.'

'I doubt it. Chances are she will be returned to Holloway, and once the funds are registered you can pick her up from there, probably tomorrow.'

'Not tomorrow – she will spend not another night in Holloway. This must be done today.'

Ms Ologbenla sighed. 'Then get a move on Dr Stuart. The banks close at five, and it's already three-thirty. I'll see you in the magistrates court in about an hour.'

I made it to the nearest branch of National Westminster Bank just before 4 o' clock. There were long queues at the tellers, but I approached the customer service desk and demanded to speak to the manager. The customer services clerk was well trained. She informed me that the manager was busy, but offered her assistance. 'I need to withdraw £125,000 in cash immediately.'

'Is this your branch?' she asked.

'No,' I replied.

'I'll get the manager,' she said.

Ms Customer Services asked me to wait, pointing to two tiny chairs designed more for wear rather than comfort. I decided to stand. After the longest five minutes, the manager appeared: a slim, harried woman of about forty, with the drawn, pinched face of a serious smoker. She led me into her inner sanctum, sat behind a large desk and enquired as to how she could help me.

'My name is Dr Stuart. I run an international tax consultancy called A J Stuart & Co that banks with NatWest, and I need to withdraw £125,000 from the business reserve account in cash immediately.'

'And your branch is?'

'South Bank Business Centre. I know you will need to call them. Ask to speak to Bertram Care. He's my business bank manager.'

'I know Bertram,' she said, 'Do you know his direct line number? It will save me looking it up.' I did and she dialled.

'Bertram, it's Kathy Street... Kathy from the Croydon branch... It's nice to talk to you again too... Listen, I have one of your clients with me, a Dr Stuart. He wants to withdraw £125,000 in cash... One moment, I'll ask him.' She placed her hand over the receiver. 'Dr Stuart what identification do you have?'

'My credit cards,' I replied.

'His credit cards,' she said removing her hand. 'Of course.' She offered me the phone. 'He wants to speak to you.'

'Bertram,' I said.

'Hi Andrew, just needed to confirm it was really you. What are you doing out in the sticks?'

'My clients are everywhere Bertram, even Croydon. Will you authorise the withdrawal? It's important.'

'One question, Andrew. In what year did your hero Dr Alekhine defeat Capablanca for the chess world championship?'

'1927.'

'Pass me back to Mrs Street.'

'Mrs Street,' I said handing her the receiver, 'Mr Care.'

'Very good… Talk to you soon then… Bye Bertram.' She returned the phone to its cradle. 'Right Dr Stuart. Please complete this withdrawal slip. I'll be back in one moment.' She handed me the slip and a pen and walked from the office, closing the door gently behind her.

When she returned I immediately sensed that there was a problem. 'Dr Stuart,' she said, 'I'm afraid we do not have £125,000 in cash at the bank. We do our bullion run at 4 o' clock and it has already left. Will a banker's draft suffice?'

'I don't think so. The money is needed to stand bail for a friend. The court specified cash.'

She raised her eyebrows, as if wanting to know more. After all, £125,000 was a lot of bail. I decided not to tell her it was only half of the deal. She walked round to her desk and resumed her seat and started short tasks of no importance, like lining up her stapler with her post-it pads and paperclip holder. Curiosity, in the end, got the better of her. She said, with as much humour as she could muster in the circumstances, 'What did your friend do, kill someone?'

'No,' I replied, 'the bail for a murderer is much lower.'

Now she was really interested. She held my gaze, willing me to go on. When it was clear I had said all I was going to, she became all business. 'A draft, you know, is essentially the same as cash. I am sure it will be acceptable to the courts. By "cash" they surely meant "cash or its equivalent" and that would include a banker's draft. Anyway, it will soon be 4:30. It's the

67

only choice you have unless you want to wait until tomorrow.'

'OK.' I said.

'To whom shall I make the draft payable?'

The question, so simple and so necessary, hit me hard. I had no idea. The Crown Court, perhaps; or The Court Service; or, maybe, Her Majesty the Queen, at whose pleasure Tania was presently being detained. 'I'm sorry,' I said. 'I don't know.'

Mrs Street smiled wryly. 'We must have a payee, Dr Stuart.'

'Of course,' I said, feeling slightly embarrassed. 'May I make a call?'

She motioned to the phone with a nod of her head. I called Billy, he told me, and I told her. 'Clerk to the court,' I said.

'Thought so,' she replied with a grin.

We went through the necessary paperwork and Mrs Street prepared the draft, signed it with a flourish and handed it to me. She then fixed me with her friendliest gaze. 'What has he done Dr Stuart?'

'She,' I said.

'What has *she* done?'

'Nothing,' I replied, and I put the draft in my breast pocket and left. It was raining outside and I had no umbrella. I lowered my head, leaned into the wind and walked briskly back to the courts.

Though the bail hearing took place in the Crown Court, the security had to be paid into the Magistrates Court. It was 4:50 when I walked into the Magistrates Court and 4:55 when the Assistant Cashier informed me that a banker's draft was not acceptable as security. In short, he said, it was not cash. I remonstrated, but was making no headway, when a familiar voice behind me enquired as to the nature of the problem. True to her word, Ms Ologbenla had made her way over. I explained the situation.

She took charge. 'I would like to inform you that my client, for whom this gentleman has stood bail, has been arrested, charged and detained solely on the basis that she holds a large amount of cash and knows someone who knows someone who may sell cocaine. Cash is suspect today. It is dirty. You, however, are demanding that this gentleman, who incidentally is better qualified in revenue matters than either of us, tears up a perfectly legitimate banker's draft and substitutes it with the same grubby paper that got my client into trouble in the first place. Well, I am not having it. You will accept the draft and that is the end of it.'

The assistant cashier actually took a step back as if to protect physically himself from the verbal onslaught. 'It's after five. The banks are shut. I need to confirm the draft's authenticity,' he explained, 'and I cannot do that until tomorrow.'

'What does it look like to you?' railed Ms Ologbenla. 'It looks like a draft, right? That's because that is what it is: a banker's draft, a cheque that cannot bounce.'

But the assistant cashier had his rules and rules must be obeyed. 'Tomorrow,' he said. 'We're only talking about twenty-four hours.'

Ms Ologbenla was having none if it. 'Have you ever spent twenty-four hours in pain, sir, twenty-four hours in despair, twenty-four hours in prison? If that period of time means nothing to you, stay here for the next twenty-four hours, don't go home to your wife or put your children to bed, and don't call them either. Let them worry about you. It's only twenty-four hours.'

'You're being unfair. I am only following my regulations'

'I understand, and I have a suggestion.' Her voice softened. 'You accept the bail now and authorise my client's release. You verify the banker's draft first thing in the morning. Any problems you notify the police immediately. They will re-arrest my client, and for good measure, this gentleman too, none other than Dr Andrew Stuart.' She uttered my name with such a flourish I almost bowed. And it worked.

'This is not right,' he said. 'This is not right.' He repeated the mantra as he put the draft in an envelope, as he prepared the supporting paperwork and as he gave me the relevant documents to sign. The mantra stopped only when he made the telephone call which would result in Holloway releasing Ms Tania Berkeley.

Ms Ologbenla walked with me out of the courthouse, and immediately disabused me of any thought that it was my name that secured the acceptance of the bail. 'It was my reference to his wife and children that turned it,' she said with the confidence of an assassin.

'How did you know he was married?' I asked.

'He is wearing a wedding ring.'

'And the children?'

'Two. One little boy, one little girl. The photographs are in his office.'

'They could be a niece and nephew,' I suggested.

'I've seen them remember, you haven't. They are his children all right.'

There was an awkward pause. Like lovers not wishing to say good-bye. We had been through a lot and won. We really deserved a drink or something. A day like today should not end like this, but the truth we both recognised was that my day had not ended.

'I suggest you make your way to Holloway,' she said 'Do you need an address?'

'Yes,' I replied. There were many menus in my GPS, including theatres, restaurants and shopping centres, but I doubted there was a menu for prisons.

'It's on Parkhurst Road, Holloway.'

'Thank you,' I said and meant it.

'Dr Stuart?'

'Yes.'

'My name is Yetunde.'

'Andrew,' I said.

She raised her hand. I bypassed it, leaned forward and kissed her on the cheek. She smiled and in her eyes I saw compassion. 'I hope you know what you are doing,' she said.

This was becoming the theme of my life. 'Tell me Yetunde, have you ever been in love?' I asked.

'Yes,' she replied. 'Have you?'

We walked down the steps of the court together. It had stopped raining but the sky was overcast and the grey clouds threatened more of the same. We hugged and said our goodbyes. She turned left towards the railway station. I turned right toward the car park.

I set my GPS to Parkhurst Road in the parking bay. I would follow Sally's instructions to the letter. I was in a hurry, but I did not feel adventurous. Too much had happened today. We had won but at what price? Moreover this was only the first battle in what I feared would be a protracted war. My thoughts turned to Tania.

How much did I really know about her? She was BB's sister and BB was a rock. That didn't carry me very far. I loved her. *Take the second turning on the left.* And I wanted her in my life, to be with me, my partner, my lover, my wife. But did I really know her? Did I know her fears, her aspirations, her likes and dislikes? Did I know how she would cope should the walls of her life come crashing in? *At the roundabout take the third exit.* Hell, nobody really knows anybody. We only know how people behave and usually, based on the knowledge of their past behaviour, we can predict their future behaviour. True, but did I even know her that well? She was not a drug dealer. I knew that. Neither was she a money launderer. She didn't have the tools. How much money could you launder through a hairdressing salon, even if the salon was just a front, which hers certainly was not. *Keep to the right ahead.* So where did the cash come from? Did it matter to me? Would my past matter to her? We all make choices. We decide whom to trust, whom to befriend, whom to love. I had made a choice to love Tania and I would stay with it. It felt right. I yearned for her like I have for only one other woman. And when it happens, as it must, I will for the first time make love, and I will at last understand the sonnets and songs written through the ages. Sex with love: my personal Holy Grail. *At the next junction straight ahead.* As for the cash, there would be an explanation. Come on, in the overall scheme of things it wasn't that much money. But why would she hold US dollars and Euros? And why did she need an offshore bank account?

I juggled with my thoughts throughout the journey. There was an absence of structure in my thinking, an absence of rigour. But I was very tired and emotionally drained. The traffic was heavy. I had caught the afternoon rush hour. A taxi driver once explained to me that there were really three afternoon rush hours. The first caused by those who leave early

71

to avoid the rush, the second caused by those who leave during the rush, and the third caused by those who leave late to avoid the rush. It was 6:30. I was in the third rush.

I was close now. The star on my GPS shone triumphantly, the top left hand corner of the illuminated map indicated that I had 0.2 miles to go and, as if on cue, Sally announced, *'Your destination is ahead.'* Then I saw her. She was standing ahead of me on my side of the road, back straight, tall, defiant. She wore the tight black jeans that BB had picked out for her and an overlarge blue university sweatshirt. No jewellery, no make up, no adornments. The gym bag, containing her belongings, rested on the pavement by her side. Her hair was roughly tied back, as if she had prepared herself for a morning of scrubbing the prison's floors. Yet despite all this her bearing was almost regal. And my heart broke.

I slowed down, pulled up alongside her and jumped out the car. I wanted to hug her, but the circumstances and her demeanour seemed to forbid it. Instead I opened the passenger side door and she quietly got in. We drove in silence. My earlier relief at seeing her gave way to an overwhelming sense of apprehension. Sally would guide the car home, but I did not know how to move our relationship forward. I did not know where it presently stood. I did not know that we had a relationship. I knew I was the white knight, the avenging angel, but he who wealds the sword seldom wears the crown. She broke the silence. 'Thank you Stu.'

'It's OK,' I said. It was not. 'Don't worry.' Be worried. 'It's going to be fine.' I had no idea.

Chapter 4

That evening she sat on my cream leather sofa, her legs tucked up under her. She held a cup of Earl Grey tea in both hands and sipped slowly. Her head was down and her eyes were without focus. She was somewhere else. She was back in Holloway. 'It was horrible in there.'

There was a level at which I didn't want to know. It had passed and there was nothing either of us could do about it. To re-live it would serve only to create a level of pain we could not relieve. Renewed pain for her; new pain for me. Sometimes it is best to just leave the past alone. 'Tell me about it,' I said.

Tania shifted uncomfortably, still not looking at me. 'They came in the night. I was in bed. The doorbell rang, followed by a pounding on the door. I ran downstairs in just my nightshirt, thinking there must be a fire or something. I shouted out, "Who is it?" And they said, "Police." I was confused. I said, "Who?" They shouted "Police, open up." I opened the door. There were about ten of them. They pushed in. They started shouting about drugs. One officer showed me some paper or the other and said that I was under arrest. The others began searching the house. They were all over the place. One of them had a video camera. Two of them had dogs. I was so frightened. I tried to go upstairs to get my dressing gown, you know. But I was restrained and told to stand still; they said that anything I wanted they would get for me. So I just stood in the corner of the hallway.'

'You didn't ask for the dressing gown?'

'No.' She paused. 'There were two policewomen. The younger one noticed that I was shivering and went upstairs and got it for me. It felt good to put it on. I suppose it made me feel less vulnerable. I did ask for a drink, but they said no. They said I could have a cup of tea at the station. It was only at that point that I realised that I was in serious trouble.'

I wanted to be gentle, but any deftness of touch I possessed deserted me. 'Tania, surely you knew you were in serious trouble the moment they started to search. You must have known they would find the money under the bed.'

There was a flicker of anger in her face as for the first time that evening her eyes met mine. 'The money wasn't under the bed, and anyway why should that bother me? The money had nothing to do with drugs.'

It also had nothing to do with me. But her sudden flash of emotion made it clear to me that now was not the time to tackle this question. I would return to that later. 'OK,' I said softly, 'what happened next?'

'It's a blur. I stood in my dressing gown while they searched. The dogs were sniffing everywhere. They frightened me. The police were talking to each other as they tossed my things around, making jokes. It was awful.'

'What sort of jokes?'

'You know, nice place this, how could she afford all this, her line of work must sure pay, that sort of thing.'

'It must have been hilarious when they found the money.'

'They got all excited, started asking me questions. The officer who seemed to be in charge told them to stop. He said all the questions that need to be asked would be asked at the station under caution.'

'What happened at the station?'

Her eyes returned to the floor. 'They locked me up in a cell until the morning. That's when I called you. And I'm grateful for all that you've done. I know I have things to explain, and I will, just not now, OK. Trust me.'

'Fine,' I said.

'They locked me in a cell. It was smelly and dirty. They held me overnight. I didn't sleep. They said I could call a lawyer but I didn't know anyone. In the morning I called you. The solicitor you got me, Arthur, he was very good. The police interviewed me - they taped it. Arthur told me not to answer any questions and I didn't. Afterwards I was charged with money laundering. They photographed and fingerprinted me. Then Arthur left. On the way back to the cell the police continued to badger me. They were saying things like, "Do yourself a favour, tell us about the money and we can get you out of this." They said that only they could help me. They said that I would not get bail and that in jail I would be a target for all the lesbians – because I was pretty, you know. They said that there were a lot of dykes in prison. You know what they also said? That all my friends would run away, that nobody stands by anyone associated with a drugs charge. When the sun goes down, they said, it's everybody for themselves. But I knew you wouldn't desert me Stu, I just knew it.'

I didn't let on that I knew she had called BB first.

'You know the worst part? Going to Holloway. I was handcuffed to a security officer on leaving the court and marched to the Securicor van where I was locked in a small cubicle. I don't know how fat people cope because the cubicle was just big enough for me. As we were driven to the prison the people in the other cubicles were shouting and taunting the guards. I remained silent but I was tainted with the same brush as the others. We were let off one at a time and handled roughly. Another set of handcuffs and I was led into a room where I was asked for my name, address and occupation. When I said hairdresser, they sneered at me. What's wrong with being a hairdresser?'

'You should have said you were a manager of a hair and beauty salon. It's all about status.'

'Thank you. I'll remember that the next time I get arrested.'

'There will never be another time Tania, I'm going to look after you. What happened next?'

'I was led into another room and strip searched.'

I felt the heat of shame. 'What did they do?'

'They made me strip and they examined me wearing rubber gloves. They squeezed some clear jelly on the fingers of the gloves and felt in my vagina and my anus. Then they gave me a paper towel to clean myself up with and told me to get dressed. The whole process was totally humiliating.' Tania shoulders hunched and she began to cry. I'd never seen her cry before and I went over to comfort her. I held her as her body shook and I vowed to myself that no one would ever hurt her again.

After what seemed like a long time Tania gently pulled away. 'You got mauled in the witness stand. I'm sorry.'

'It's OK,' I said honestly. 'We got the result we wanted.'

She looked at me and looked away. She wanted to say more. 'What was the name of the Cayman company again, the one that owns the Jersey company that owns the UK company that owns your practice?' She had clearly been paying a lot of attention to my cross-examination.

'Catmouse Limited,' I said.

'That's right, Catmouse Limited. Do you own it?'

'In a manner of speaking.'

'Bearer shares?' she asked, referring back to our conversation on the plane to Cayman.

'Bearer shares,' I confirmed.

Tania followed me into the kitchen. Julianna was in her room. I must confess that normally I grew irritated when I had to look after myself. I didn't know my way around the kitchen. I didn't know where things were. I didn't know how they worked. This evening, however, was different. I was entertaining Tania. And making a second cup of Earl Grey tea was simple, even for me.

It was a huge pleasure doing small things for Tania myself. One could have said this was a bad beginning to a romance, but I felt a quiet sense of pride. I had been tested. I had come through. Sure, I could have bought her anything she wanted and flown her to exotic places. We could have had the best tables in the finest restaurants and attended the first nights of the latest plays, operas and musicals. I could have introduced her to Hollywood actors and premier league footballers. I could have showered her with diamonds and gold. But what I did was more. When she was in trouble I had rescued her, at great personal risk to me and all that I had worked for. There was no greater act of love. We returned to the lounge and sat side by side.

'Can I stay here Stu? I feel safe with you. I don't want to return to my house. It's been violated.'

'You have to stay in your own house,' I gently replied. 'It's a condition of your bail.'

76

Tania moved closer to me, rested her head on my shoulder. 'The judge would love me to stay here,' she teased. 'You could keep an eye on me - safeguard your investment - prevent me from leaving the country.' As we spoke she caressed the back of my neck, which caused my pulse to quicken and a shiver to run down my spine.

'We would need to apply to the courts,' I said.

'So do it. I'm moving in today. I am not going back to my house. Ever. I'm going to sell the house and the furniture and start over.'

'You must stay at the house until we get the bail conditions changed.'

'What are they going to do? Lock me up for staying at the house of the man who stood bail for me, because I was too frightened to return home? I don't think so. Unless they come looking for me they won't even know I'm here.' She paused and snuggled closer to me, her head moving from my shoulder to my chest. 'Where shall I sleep?'

'In the guest room,' I said. 'I'll have Julianna make up the bed.' I got up. Tania remained on the sofa.

'What will we do tomorrow?' she asked.

'You will rest. I have a mountain of work to tackle in the morning and two meetings in the afternoon.'

'Who are you meeting with?' she asked in a tone too casual for the question to be wholly innocent. In fact I was glad she asked. I had something to tell her.

'At noon,' I said, 'I have a lunch meeting with Hugo Maximillian, a director of Coats Bank.'

'What's that about?'

'He wants me to join the bank.'

'Are you going to?'

'No.'

'So why go to the meeting?'

'Because he serves the best food in London.'

Tania smiled. 'I like your life,' she said. 'And the other meeting?'

Here we go, I thought. 'At 3 o' clock I'm seeing my new solicitor, George Fairlow of Bellows & Bellows.' I hesitated, remembering

Greenley's unwelcome advice about the rules regarding tipping off a defendant, but I felt she had to know. 'I was served a Production Order on your case. I have to supply every document and file I hold relating to you and the others.'

'You don't hold any files for me.'

'That is not strictly correct,' I said. 'Remember the reference letter to the Island Bank?' Tania nodded, her face expressing apprehension. 'It is covered by the terms of the Production Order. I should supply it.'

'Don't,' she said.

'If I don't I'm in contempt of court.' I paused. 'Is there a problem with the account?'

'Come on Stu, it's an offshore account. If I wanted everyone to know about it I'd have opened an account on the high street.'

There was a glibness to Tania's response that offended me. There was such a lack of concern for my own position. 'I've just stood your bail to the tune of £250,000. I remained silent on whether I gave you the money found by the police. You told the solicitors it was mine, remember. I've got police investigating my clients. And you're now asking me to break the law. You've explained absolutely nothing. And now you want me to lie for you too.'

'Please stop it!' she shouted, her head shaking, the palms of her hands over her ears. Lowering her head, she said very quietly, 'I just want you to protect me, Stu. You said you would. You said you were going to look after me.' She looked so vulnerable, like a fawn who had lost her mother. A gust of shame swept through me. Tania had been through enough over the last few days and I was making things worse. I sat back down on the sofa and embraced her.

'I will,' I said, 'I will.' I held her tightly and felt a trembling, but I didn't know if it was her body or mine. I kissed her on the neck and she turned away. I got up again. She remained in the same forlorn posture.

'Is that why you're going to the solicitors,' she mumbled, 'to find out what to do?'

'No,' I said, 'I have another problem. Among the names on your

Production Order was a client of mine.'

'Oh,' she said looking up.

'A new client, called Mazzinni. Ever heard of him?' I thought I saw a flicker of recognition in her eyes.

'No,' she said, and slowly turned on her side, pulling her knees up till they were pushing against her breasts and wrapping her forearms around her shins. She was making herself as small as possible. Just as a fawn would do when frightened.

The headquarters of Coats Bank was located in Leadenhall Street, close to Lloyds of London. I went to my own offices first that morning and dealt with some general paperwork. Then I caught a black cab to the bank. I arrived at exactly 12 noon. Hugo Maximillian, as ever, was running late. He always worked to his own timetable, which differed from the one scheduled for him by anything up to an hour. A corpulent man, Hugo moved a little slower, sat a little longer and ate a little more than the rest of us. His position at the bank owed more to his heritage than his abilities. His father had been a director of the bank, as had his father before him. The bank (and Hugo) were steeped in tradition.

I was shown into the dining room at 12:25. A butler greeted me at the door with a tray on which rested a flute of champagne, a tumbler of orange juice and a tall glass of mineral water. I took the water and thanked him.

Hugo raised himself out of his chair. He was in an expansive mood. 'Andrew, my dear, good to see you. How have you been?'

I thought: I've fallen in love, wooed my lady in Grand Cayman, after which she was arrested, sent to Holloway prison, leading me to stand bail, after which the police came to my office, threatened me and served me with a Production Order on which was listed the name of a new client. 'Very well thank you Hugo, and yourself?'

'Quite frankly, I could do with a holiday.' He took about four holidays a year.

'Pressure of work?' I asked.

'No,' he said. 'I could just do with a holiday. One doesn't need an excuse to take a break. Sometimes one just wishes to get away. That's how I feel now.'

'I always feel a little guilty when I take a vacation so I try to combine it with an assignment I'm working on.'

'That,' said Hugo 'is because you're far too immersed in the Protestant work ethic. You should find time to relax. Now take a seat. Let's have lunch. Always cheers me up.' The table was set for three. 'I've invited Francis Peartree, head of our trust department, to join us for lunch. He's a complete boffin; no small talk. Can't discuss cricket and rugger with this fellow. But he'll keep you up to the small hours explaining the nuances of the statutory fictions that arise under the deeming provisions of the Inheritance Tax Act. Dull chap; brilliant, but dull. He's the one I want you to take over from.'

We had ventured down this path many times before, each journey approaching this space from a different angle. Hugo had wanted me to join the bank for years. 'Not again,' I said lazily taking a sip of my water. 'I'm happy, Hugo, just as I am. I'm in charge. I answer to no one. I decide which clients to take on. I decide the level of fees, and I enjoy all the profits or, of course, suffer the losses. In short, I sink or swim by my own efforts.' I allowed myself an indulgent smile. 'Mostly I swim.'

'I know you swim but, if I may say so, you swim in a lake with the trout. You are a one-man outfit, no disrespect to the lovely Anita, with limited resources. We, on the other hand, have a market capitalisation of over £5 billion. We have offices in all the major cities in Europe and North America, and representative branches in every decent offshore financial centre. We have over 1 million customers worldwide, and our private client portfolio is second to none. Join us and you'll be swimming in the ocean - with the sharks.'

'What's wrong with Mr Peartree?'

'*Dr* Peartree. I told you. The damn fellow's a boffin. Can't talk to anyone, without boring them to death. He makes tax planning sound like funeral arranging. You make it sound like an act of seduction. Look, Peartree's fine with the established old money clients. But he could never

80

attract the new money: the popstars, footballers, dot.com entrepreneurs - your type of clients.'

'I see.'

'I want you and I want your clients. The bank will buy your practice. We'll pay three and a half times your gross recurring fees plus twice your one-off fees, based on the average figures over the past three years, duly verified by our auditors. We will offer you a five year contract at a substantial salary, with, of course, a non-competition clause should you leave - which you will not because, dear Andrew, you will love it here.'

Although I had no interest, I couldn't resist doing a quick mental calculation of what I would net in such a deal: £20 million. This was his opening bid. I felt confident I could push him to £25 million. But I didn't need the money and I didn't need the job.

Hugo's private restaurant was impressive. I looked at my elegantly hand-written menu. As befitted an international bank, the starter was Swiss cream of barley soup, followed by Latin America beef stew with a marinated red-onion salad, followed by chocolate crème brûlées. Hugo lunched here most days. It explained his ample girth. I usually grabbed a sandwich at my desk, if I ate lunch at all. I was thinking how life was more comfortable on the other side when Francis Peartree entered.

Dr Peartree was lanky and bespectacled. He had a high forehead. Such hair as he possessed was grey and wispy; his skin was pale, as if he had been hidden from the sun. His dress was conservative and his manner hesitant. He clearly was ill at ease with Hugo and, from his innocent perusal of the dining area, I deduced that this was not his regular watering hole. And at once it occurred to me that if I took his job it wouldn't be mine either. I was being courted. Marriage would be entirely different.

'Sit down Francis,' said Hugo. 'This is Andrew Stuart. You know of him, of course. Now let's eat and talk tax.' The food was excellent. Francis ate sparingly, Hugo with relish. I drank only a small amount of the very fine wine. My mind was on the next meeting, which to a small degree impaired my enjoyment of the lunch as a social event. As a business event the lunch was a non-starter. In reality the business had been concluded before the lunch started. The bank had offered to buy my practice and I had turned the offer down. So, as we ate and drank Hugo amused himself by encouraging Francis Peartree to explain the trust department's current research projects and then stifling yawns through his charge's protracted narrative.

After coffee, I declined the cognac, made my excuses and left. My next meeting would be without fanfare. I needed a clear head. I made my way to Chancery Lane, to the offices of Bellows & Bellows.

Billy had given me the number of the offices, which was just as well. There was no brass plaque outside the building or anything else to indicate that London's premier white-collar crime specialists were housed inside. I suppose their view was that if you didn't know the address you couldn't afford the fees. Passing trade had no place in the marketing of Bellows & Bellows.

The reception area was small. There was just enough room for a narrow oblong wooden desk and a black two-seater leather sofa. The man behind the reception desk was old and tired, probably a retiree eking out his pension. I don't think he liked his job. His greeting was gruff and unfriendly, barely on the right side of rude. 'And what can I do for you?'

'My name is Dr Stuart. I have a meeting with George Fairlow'

I received no reply from the man whose desk nameplate read 'Reception.' Instead, he picked up the telephone and dialled George Fairlow's number. And then a change occurred, a complete transformation. In a mellifluous voice I heard him say, 'Mr Fairlow, sir, a gentleman to see you. A Dr Stuart.' He listened. 'Yes Mr Fairlow, certainly.' My surprise must have showed on my face. He smiled but instantly returned to his disagreeable manner. 'Take a seat, he'll be with you when he's ready. He shouldn't be too long.'

I wondered whether Mr Reception was trained to behave in this way. It was just possible that this was the first stage in Bellows & Bellows letting the high and powerful who had fallen on criminal times, or *alleged* criminal times, know that the rules had fundamentally changed, that they were no longer in charge. Alternatively, Mr Reception may have simply despised the men and women who had everything he'd never had committing crimes to get even more. Men and women who could have behaved within the law and retired early, never having to don a silly uniform in old age to supplement their meagre income, yet choosing instead to take a little extra when they thought no one was looking.

I sat and waited.

There was a large window by the sofa and I could see the suited men and women outside, each going about their individual business, each dealing with their own personal crises. This is where the lawyers plied their trade in a manner not dissimilar to their predecessors a century before. So many clerks were hauling heavy books, when CDs containing the same information would have slipped easily into their pocket. Barristers rushed by dressed in wigs and gowns that served no purpose other than to distinguish the wearer from the laity. Should not, I thought, their intellect alone achieve the distinction. It would have been funny had I not been in a position whereby I had to rely on the book carrying clerks and bewigged barristers for my freedom.

'Dr Stuart,' said Mr Reception. 'George Fairlow will see you now. Through the double doors, it's the third room on the right. His name is on the door.'

George Fairlow had a presence that was cold and austere. Tall and slim, with a ramrod straight back, he had the bearing of an officer in the Coldstream Guards. His features were aquiline, and on the bridge of his narrow beak-like nose rested round spectacles in a thin mottled-brown frame. When I was at school we used to refer to such spectacles as National Health glasses. Strange, I thought, how the bleak and the ridiculed of yesterday can become the fashionable of today. The frames, I guessed, must have cost George Fairlow a small fortune.

I took a seat across from his sizeable desk and, at his prompting, told my story. He took brief notes as I talked, mostly in the form of short headings that would serve to prompt his memory when he later dictated the file notes. And it was the issue of files, or the police access thereto, that he correctly identified as my principal cause for concern.

'Tell me Dr Stuart, just what are the files you do not want to surrender.'

Sometimes you know that you have embarked on a course of action that will lead inexorably to certain consequences, and yet in some part of your mind you seek to resist those consequences. The moment I sought legal advice on the ambit of the Production Order, I would have no choice, but to tell my lawyer what only Anita and I knew, and yet I resisted.

'May I talk hypothetically?' I said.

'No you may not. Tell me about the files you do not wish to surrender.'

'Audio files,' I said.

George Fairlow's face remained deadpan. 'Explain.'

'All my meetings in my boardroom are taped. I am a poor notetaker. Anita types up the meeting notes from the tapes, but she does so leaving out anything sensitive.'

'Such as?'

'Any robust advice, anything clear from the context of the discussion that I had not heard, or chosen not to hear. Sometimes I say to a client something like, "I think what you are actually saying is" and rephrase what he actually said. My version ends up in the records.'

'Give me an example.'

'Let's say a client says to me that he has no intention of giving the taxman a penny piece. Let's say he says "bend the rules, break the rules, just save my money from those bastards and keep me out of jail." I might reply, "I think that what you are saying is that you would like to explore all available avenues to establish a suitable structure for minimising your exposure to taxation within the confines of the fiscal and criminal law." And my version would end up in the file note.'

'I'm not sure I see the problem.'

'We don't destroy the tapes,' I said. 'We archive them. We have archived Mazzinni's tapes. The question is: are the tapes covered by the Production Order?'

'Before we get to that let me ask you this: are your clients aware they are being taped?'

'Yeessss,' I said. It was one of those long drawn out yes's that really implies "no." George Fairlow waited for me to expand on my answer. 'There's a line in my letter of engagement, which is signed by every client, that reads something like, "meetings may be taped to aid notetaking."'

'I see,' he said. 'And I assume there is something on the Mazzinni tape that is not on his files that is worrying you.'

'It might be seen, wholly erroneously you understand, that I was coaching him in how to answer the money laundering questionnaire.'

'Oh dear,' said George.

'Quite,' I replied.

'You have the Production Order with you I assume.'

'I do,' I said, and handed it across.

'It says,' he said reading 'that you should give a constable access to all files, documents and accounts and other records used in the ordinary course of business of the company, whether those records are in written form, are kept on microfilm, magnetic tape or any other form of mechanical or electronic data retrieval mechanism etcetera. That would seem to me to include audio tapes, I'm afraid.'

'Let's say I agree with your analysis. What are my options?'

'They are limited. First, let me say that I cannot advise you to withhold or destroy the tapes. Of course if they were destroyed inadvertently without your knowledge or, for whatever reason, you could not locate them when you searched for them, that would be a different matter. You cannot produce what you do not have.' He paused. 'However, if you can produce them, you must. Now, the police will not know what is on the tapes and you have no obligation to make their life easy. If this taped meeting were, say, on a very long tape containing a wide variety of irrelevant conversations, you may care to give them the whole tape and let them seek to find the Mazzinni morsel.'

'That's it?'

'What did you want?'

'More.'

George Fairlow removed his glasses and maintained unnervingly steady eye contact. The gaze was no doubt pregnant with meaning. But I read nothing, sensed nothing and heard nothing. When he was done he replaced his glasses and showed me the door. The gaze alone probably cost me £1,000.

The weekend passed quickly. Tania was back and forth between her house and mine, on the Saturday, moving her things. BB lent a hand. I spoke to Billy and then drafted a letter to him from Tania in which she formally requested that he apply to the courts to change her bail residency address. He told me that he would instruct Ms Ologbenla on Monday. He saw no problem with the application.

Tania slept most of Sunday. Julianna was off for the day. She was visiting her newly arrived cousins who were staying with friends in Deptford. I spent the entire morning marking revenue law essays and the early afternoon reading the first three chapters of a particularly turgid draft doctoral thesis on the interpretation of treaties provisions of the Vienna Convention. That evening Tania and I had supper at a local Thai restaurant. We were both preoccupied and didn't talk much, but we were together and that pleased me enormously.

Monday morning I was back in my office working. I filled Anita in on my meeting with George Fairlow and gave her his business card. Anita had her own views on the pregnant gaze. 'He wants you to destroy the audio tapes.'

'All of them?'

'All of them.'

'But I can't do that.'

'Of course *you* can't,' Anita said and smiled.

'No,' I said, 'leave them. If this thing gets complicated, and it might, I don't want you implicated in any way. I'm serious. Leave them be.'

I went to my office and pulled out the files on the Lightning's tax minimisation plan. My phone buzzed around mid-morning and Anita announced that DS Greenley and DC Clarke were in reception. With a sense of déjà vu I asked her to show them to the boardroom. Anita hesitated. 'They want you to come to reception, Andrew.'

'Ask them why,' I said. Any matter that can be dealt with in reception can be dealt with by Anita. My domain was the boardroom.

I was placed on hold. When Anita clicked back there was a faint trace of impatience in her voice. 'They will not say. They just said you are to come to reception immediately.' Growing stronger she added. 'They are being quite rude actually.' I could visualise her holding DS Greenley's gaze with the last comment. You take on Anita at your peril.

Pausing only to comb my hair I made my way to the reception area. 'Detective Sergeant Greenley, what is this about?'

'Dr Stuart,' he replied grim faced, 'you are under arrest for conspiring with Tania Berkeley and others to launder the proceeds of drug trafficking. You do not have to say anything. But it may harm your defence if you do not mention when questioned something which you later rely on in court. Anything you do say may be given in evidence.'

The shock was debilitating. I had been arrested before, a long time ago, long before I became who I am today. This should not be happening to me now. I am a different person now. The fear of yesteryear returned. I just stood there. Slowly my stunned confusion cleared. 'I have no comment to make at this time.'

'From a man of your education,' said Greenley 'I was expecting better than that.' DS Greenley studied my face. DC Clarke, as always, was standing behind him. He smiled the smile of a vulture eyeing a wounded animal. I turned to my only visible means of support: Anita.

'Ring George Fairlow,' I said.

'Don't touch that phone!' shouted Greenley.

Anita calmly picked up the phone, punched three numbers. The wonderful Anita; she'd already punched the details of the business card into the telephone memory. What would I do without her? 'George Fairlow please,' she said. 'This is urgent.' A pause. 'Mr Fairlow, my name is Anita Hume, Dr Andrew Stuart's PA. Dr Stuart has just been arrested. He asked me to call you. The arresting officer is a DS Greenley. I believe you are familiar with him… Quite so…He is here now…Both of them… yes, one moment.'

She looked up at DS Greenley with defiance. 'Mr Fairlow would like to know what station you intend to take Dr Stuart to.'

He made no answer. Instead, he walked to the front door. He pulled the handle, but the door didn't budge. 'Open it,' he commanded, turning and glaring at Anita. She flicked the switch. Greenley pulled the handle again and the door clicked open. 'Come in,' he instructed unseen officers who immediately barged through the doors. Seven of them, all dressed casually, as if off to a football match. Greenley walked back to me, leaned forward and deliberately invaded my personal space. His breath smelt like boiled cabbages. 'We're going to search your offices, from top to bottom, and we're going to start with your client files. Where are they kept?'

I had to restrain my impulse to physically push him away. Instead I took a step backward and turned to Anita. 'Ask Mr Fairlow if this is legal, given the confidential nature of my files.'

Anita explained the predicament, listened, and then addressed DC Greenley. 'Mr Fairlow would like to speak to you.'

Greenley walked to Anita's desk and took the offered phone. 'Yes... We will conduct the search as we consider fit... How can I know what is privileged until I look at it... All the bags will be sealed in Dr Stuart's presence... Section 32... Bexleyheath... Not tonight, probably tomorrow afternoon... As you wish... Of course.' He turned to me. 'Your solicitor would like to speak to you. Don't be long. We've got a lot to get through.'

'George,' I said.

'What a pickle,' he replied.

'Can they do this?'

'Yes they can. Now listen to me. Sometimes in cases such as these it is worth letting the police do their worst at this stage. We can make lots of noise in the High Court when they overstep the mark, as they will. You have been sensible, I assume.'

'Yes.' I said.

'Good, give them the run of the place, be polite, don't lose your temper. Remember you are much more intelligent than they are, but this is no time to remind them of the fact.'

I stifled a smile. 'Thank you for your advice.'

'I'll see you tomorrow at the police station. That's when you will be interviewed. Of course you say nothing until then. You will be detained overnight. There is little I can do about that. The good news is they're taking you to Bexleyheath, one of the nicer sets of rooms offered by Her Majesty. If you need me at any time, call me.'

'Thank you again,' I said and hung up. 'Where would you like to start DS Greenley?'

'Where are the files?'

I led him to the chamber. All my client files were held in a separate room. The correspondence and tax compliance files, yellow and orange respectively, were stored together by client alphabetically. The tax consultancy files, green in colour, which contained the details of the tax minimisation structures or asset protection plans, were stored separately behind a false wall, together with the archived tapes. My purpose was clear. The yellow and orange files contained everything the Inland Revenue, HM Customs & Excise or, for that matter, the IRS knew. It was part of the game. The green files contained the thinking behind the disclosures made: that balance of the game known only to my clients, Anita and me. These files were not secret; they were confidential. They were not hidden; they were protected. The false wall represented the line between public information and private knowledge. And Greenley was no Joshua. The wall would not come a-tumblin' down.

'Are these all your client files?' Greenley asked.

'Yes,' I replied, making no mention of the small button discretely concealed by the jamb of the door.

Greenley grinned. 'I bet this is a veritable Aladdin's cave Dr Stuart.' He called for his football supporters and once they had appeared waved proudly at the chamber. 'You see these files, go through them. You have the lists. Bag any file containing any reference to any name on the list.' He turned to me. 'While they're doing that show me where you work..' He called for DC Clarke who attended to him dutifully.

Greenley followed me to into my office. 'Impressive,' he said. 'What are you working on today, Dr Stuart? Whose money are you hiding now?' I made no answer. 'See what the good Doctor is working on Martyn.' DC Clarke walked over to my desk and started flicking through the files. 'Anything interesting?'

'Yes sir. I think this file relates to Lightning.'

'What?'

'Who, sir, he's a rap artist, very explicit lyrics, very anti-police. He wrote the song *Bright Day in Brixton* after PC Miller got shot. It was in all the papers.'

I wanted to say that it was also in the charts, in the UK and the US. It represented a popular, if misplaced, general hostility to current policing methods in inner cities. Moreover the lyrics were clever and the music very good. But I decided it was not the time for a discussion of rap as a contemporary urban art form.

'You act for this sort of human garbage, do you Dr Stuart?' said Greenley with disgust.

'Lightning is a client of mine,' I replied.

Turning to DC Clarke he said, 'Bag up the files, we'll review them at the station.'

DS Greenley and I returned to chamber where he checked on how his search team were getting along. They had only found two files relating to any name on the lists they held, one yellow and one orange, both in the name of Giovanni Mazzinni. 'Bag 'em,' said Greenley.

It addition to the files, the police seized Anita's diary and all the accounting and banking records of the practice. On DS Greenley's direction and under his supervision I opened the practice safe. It held £15,500. 'What's this?' he asked.

'Petty cash,' I replied. He ordered his men to bag it.

It was difficult to keep track of everything they were taking. In the end I decided to rely on Anita whose eye for administrative detail was far keener than my own. I sat in reception and waited. Eventually, DS Greenley ambled back in. 'I think we're done Dr Stuart. Now we will go to your home and repeat the same process there.' I hadn't bargained on this. 'We can do it, you know, do you want to talk to your solicitor again?'

'That will not be necessary.'

'Good,' he replied. 'Now, are you a violent man Dr Stuart?' He was playing with me. 'If you are we'll have to handcuff you.'

'You are well aware that I'm not violent,' I rejoined, 'but do what you feel you have to. All your actions will later be examined in open court'

'Well, I'll take you at your word.'

As we left the building I wanted to say something to Anita to let her know that all this would pass, that we would soon be back to normal, that she should not worry. She beat me to it. 'Would you like me to re-schedule your telephone conference call with Colonel Gadaffi and Saddam Hussein?' she asked, with a face so deadpan, so utterly serious, I could have kissed her.

It was only when I was placed in the back of the police car and the door was slammed shut did the full enormity of my position hit me. I was under arrest for money laundering. I was an international tax consultant, in which capacity I set up offshore companies, trusts, foundations and limited partnerships. I had transferred or had overseen the transfer of millions of pounds all over the world, mainly into accounts held in offshore financial centres. Any number of my transactions could be open to misinterpretation. Could I be called on in a court of law to explain and justify every transaction? And if I chose not to because of client confidentiality, could the jury be asked to draw an inference that my reticence owned more to guilt than honour? After everything that I had done to move beyond the circumstances of my birth, and beyond my last involvement with the criminal justice system, was I, despite all, on my way to prison?

Chapter 5

Thankfully, we drove to my house in an unmarked car. I gave directions to the driver, a morose individual who clearly would have preferred to be somewhere else, doing something completely different. He must have been around fifty-five and, I suppose, if at that age your role in life is to drive around the likes of DS Greenley and DC Clarke your childhood ambitions had not been wholly fulfilled. DS Greenley sat in the front as befitted his status. DC Clarke was in the back with me. They referred to the driver simply as 'Smith'. No one smoked. I was grateful for small mercies.

I directed the driver to my home. Each request to turn left or right or change lanes was greeted with a huff. It was clear that Smith's preferred route to my house would have involved him in driving in a straight line door to door. As we pulled up to the gate I suggested that I get out to address the intercom. Greenley insisted on doing it himself. I was convinced Julianna would not let him in. I was right. He got back in the car. 'Get these gates open Dr Stuart.' I got out the car without a word. I hit the intercom.

'Julianna, it's me. Open up please.'

'Who was the other man. He said he was a police officer. No way he's coming in here. It's to do with Tania, isn't it?'

'Julianna, I've been arrested too OK. There are three police in the car and more coming. They are going to search the house. Open the gates.'

'Andrew,' she said in a loud whisper, 'is there anything you want me to hide?'

Bless her. 'No,' I said, 'just open up.'

I got back in the car. 'Who's that woman?' asked DC Greenley.

'My housekeeper,' I replied.

'I'll be talking to her when I get inside.'

The gates swung open and Smith drove toward my house followed by the second car carrying the back-up search team. My home was a large modern architecturally-designed detached house set in about two acres in Sevenoaks, Kent. The gardens were mostly laid to lawn, surrounded by some trees and shrubbery. The long curved gravel driveway led to a double garage, separate from the house, with electric doors. Additional parking spaces were available just to the left of the garage. Greenley ignored these and ordered Smith to stop directly in front of the house. The second car, following Greenley's lead, parked directly behind us.

The search team consisted of Greenley, Clarke and Smith and three of the plain clothed PCs, who might have moonlighted as comedians. On stepping inside the entrance hall one of the three asked Greenley, 'What're we looking for in here then?'

Greenley replied, 'Anything that provides evidence of unusual financial transactions.'

The first PC winked at me and whispered to the second, 'We should take the house then.'

'And the driveway,' the second whispered back.

I went to open the front door but Greenley insisted that I give him the key so that he could open it himself. Once we were inside, he said, 'Describe your house to me in detail.'

'If you can wait 15 minutes,' I replied, 'I'll call my property agent.'

'One more quip like that,' he said, 'and you won't be seeing your house again for a very long time. Now what rooms are here, who will I find and what will I find in each room. And be specific. I don't want any surprises.'

'You are presently standing in the entrance hall,' I said. 'To the left I have my study. This contains some business files, but mainly my personal and financial papers. There is, of course, a computer configuration in there, and an entertainment system. Before you get to the study you will pass what the agent calls the family room. It is furnished but largely unused.'

'No family, eh?' said Greenley unkindly.

'If you bear to the right you will pass the drawing room.'

'That's what we call the living room guv,' said one of the three. Greenley grimaced.

'Beyond that is the dining room, which leads on to the kitchen. Upstairs there are three bedrooms with en suite bathrooms and two further bedrooms. The master bedroom is, of course, my own. Julianna, my housekeeper, has one of the en suite bedrooms. I have a guest staying in the other. Only one of the two remaining bedrooms is furnished.'

'And the name of your guest?'

'That is none of your business,' I said. But, of course, it was. It was Tania's room and I wondered how long I would be able to keep that information to myself. The room would be searched and I didn't know if there would be anything to identify Tania as its occupant. Strictly speaking she was still obligated to sleep at her own house as a condition of her bail. I had asked Billy to apply to vary the condition and he in turn should by now have instructed Tania's counsel, the redoubtable Yetunde Ologbenla. But no formal application could have yet been made. The bail had been set by the court and only the court could vary it, and a breach of a bail condition is, potentially, a serious matter.

'I will ask you one more time,' said Greenley, 'what is the name of the person staying in your guest room?' He had made an issue out of it and I felt trapped. To refuse to answer now would look like concealment. It would look like I was harbouring Tania. Our defence to any accusation pertaining to a breach of bail would be that it was only a technical breach caused by Tania's need to feel safe, a breach that would have been rectified at her next court appearance when we applied for an order to vary the conditions. For this to succeed we needed to be open, certainly in response to a direct question from the investigating officer. Greenley was getting irritated. 'I will not ask you again.'

'Tania Berkeley,' I said.

His crumpled face lit up. 'Does she sleep here?'

'Occasionally,' I said.

'Has she slept here since she was granted bail.'

'Yes,' I said, and made a mental note that that I could have been referring to an afternoon nap. It was weak, but in the hands of Ms Ologbenla it might be enough.

'Well, well,' he said, 'let me speak to her.'

'She's not in. She was meeting with her solicitors this morning. I thought she would be back by now. Maybe,' I said, seizing an opportunity, 'she's gone back home.'

Greenley was unimpressed. 'How do you know she's not here. You haven't been up to her room.'

'Her car's not here.'

'What does she drive?'

'A Mercedes CLK.'

'Nice car for a hairdresser,' he said. 'We'll look out for it. Something tells me she'll be coming right back here to be with you this afternoon when she's finished doing whatever she's doing.'

'We'll see,' I said.

'We shall. Now, are any of the rooms locked?'

'Not to my knowledge. If they are, Julianna will have the keys.'

DS Greenley ordered the three PCs to search upstairs under the direction of DC Clarke. Greenley himself headed straight for my study and started rifling through drawers, papers and files. There was a degree of eagerness in his demeanour that was absent at the office, as if he felt that here was where he would find the incriminating evidence, the proverbial smoking gun. The study was basically an extension of my office, though rather than mahogany, black ash was the theme. The room was big, comfortable and high-tech. My computer was networked into the office system enabling me to access any office files from home and to transfer files at will. The study was also a playpen. I had a large flat screen TV recessed into the wall opposite my desk, and a state of the art surround sound audio system. A purpose built racking system contained my favourite CDs, which was aligned to a bookcase containing my most treasured works of literature.

Greenley was tugging on a filing cabinet. 'It's locked,' I said.

'Open it.'

'Open it yourself. There are two black metal strips along each side.

Place your fingers on the strips and push upwards. You should notice the strips move no more than two millimetres. The cabinet will then be open.'

Greenley positioned himself in front of the cabinet and located the strips by touch. He looked like he was about to dance with a small bear. He pushed up, and then tentatively pulled on one of the drawers. As it opened his face betrayed the satisfaction of a man who had just cracked a safe. But he was a man used to denying himself pleasures, however small. 'That wouldn't deter anyone,' he said.

'It deterred you,' I replied.

The cabinet contained a series of files each with a blue cover containing reports prepared by a private detective agency. There were thirty-two files in all, each hung in a separate divider, each divider identifying by a red tab the period to which the report in the file related. 'What have we got here then?' said Greenley to himself.

I fought to placate discomfort. 'They are personal files,' I said. 'They have nothing to do with my work and nothing to do with your investigation.'

'Let's just have a little read shall we?' he said and pulled out a file seemingly at random. 'Hmm, interesting.' He looked at me over the blue cover, then moved to one of the two leather armchairs and flopped himself down. He read intensely, turning the pages slowly. 'Well, well.'

Julianna entered the room. The door was open. She had changed into her maid's uniform. I hadn't seen her in it for over a year. She looked sexy and acted subservient, and I could see apprehension in her eyes. Studiously ignoring DC Greenley, she said 'Dr Stuart, sir, may I bring you some coffee?'

'No thank you Julianna, just some water.'

'Sparkling or still?' Oh, she was playing the part.

'Sparkling, please.'

'Wait!' said Greenley, without looking up from the report. 'Are you the woman who answered the intercom?'

'Yes'

'Why didn't you let me in?'

'You are not my boss,' Julianna replied with a hint of defiance. 'You can't tell me what to do.'

'That's just where you're wrong little lady,' rejoined Greenley. 'I am an officer of the law, don't you understand that?'

Julianna remained silent.

Now Greenley looked up. 'Where are you from?' he asked.

'I came here from the kitchen.'

'Don't play with me,' Greenley spat out the words. 'Where were you born?'

'Jamaica,' Julianna replied.

'And how long have you been here?'

Julianna looked at me and I nodded. 'Two and a half years,' she said.

'Show me your immigration papers.'

Julianna didn't move.

'Now!' he shouted.

Julianna flinched but made no attempt to comply.

'Go and get your immigration papers or I assure you that you'll be on the next boat back to Montego Bay.'

'Kingston,' she corrected and left.

'Was that necessary?' I asked Greenley.

'They must learn respect,' he replied.

'*They?*' I asked incredulously.

'Yes, they,' he replied without apology or explanation, and resumed his reading.

To my shame I let it pass. I needed to keep my priorities in focus, and my immediate concern was the blue files. 'DC Greenley, having read through the file you must now be aware that it has no bearing on this case. Please hand it back to me.'

'*Au contriare,* I think we may need to take some of these files.'

I lost it. 'You're out of your fucking mind. Those files are personal. You touch them and I'll make you suffer. They have nothing to do with anything.'

Greenley shouted for Clarke through the open door. When he arrived,

Greenley pointed to the cabinet. 'All those files, bag 'em.'

I watched as Clarke lifted out each file, each report, and place them in plastic bags. This was a violation. I walked to the door and closed it. One last chance. 'Look Detective Sergeant, those files concern only two people and those people do not know the files exist. It must be clear to you that this is an intensely private matter. It cannot have any effect on the case you are mounting. A man is entitled to privacy.'

'First you threaten, then you beg.' He spoke the words with utter contempt.

Clarke was kneeling down packing the files. He spoke kindly and with empathy, but his words weighed heavily. 'You have no privacy now.'

There was a knock on the door. It was Julianna with my water and a surprise. The tall glass of sparkling mineral water was sitting on a silver tray (a gift from a grateful client) that we hardly ever use. The surprise was that she had changed her clothes again. She now had on an overcoat and an old fashioned hat I had never seen before, and I noticed, just outside the door, a suitcase. She handed me my water and turned to DC Greenley, 'No papers,' she said. 'Where's my ticket home?'

Greenley looked up with great annoyance showing on his face. Julianna held out her hand. 'My ticket. I want to go home. I don't like England, all the rain, the cold weather. You want to send me back home. Good. Give me my ticket.' She smiled. 'And a little spending money.'

Greenley remained seated. He took out his trusty cheap pen and a notebook. 'Full name,' he said.

'Julianna Sawyer.'

He wrote it down. 'Right, Julianna, you'll be reported to the relevant authorities. They will contact you at this address and you will be sorted.' Now it was Greenley's turn to smile. 'Your bluff didn't work little lady.'

Julianna removed her hat and made her way to the door, where she turned and fixed Greenley with a rude stare. 'No bluff,' she said. 'I never bluff.' Once outside the door I saw her pick up the suitcase in the manner of those characters in the old black and white movies: too easily, as if there was nothing in it.

'Passport, bank statements, cheque books, paying-in books, credit card statements, the lot. Which drawer, Dr Stuart?'

I was retrieving the items requested from various lever-arch files when one of the second team of PCs poked his head round the door. 'Guv, we've found something I think you should see. It's in one of the bedrooms.'

'Whose?' asked Greenley.

'The en suite guest bedroom.'

'Miss Tania Berkeley's,' said Greenley with a smile of satisfaction. 'Martyn continue bagging up these files. Dr Stuart, come with me.'

Greenley mounted the stairs with enthusiasm and bounded into Tania's room. 'What have we got?' he asked.

'There, guv,' said the PC and pointed to the open drawer at the base of Tania's divan. A blanket appeared to have been pulled aside and under it lay bundles of cash in sterling, euros and US dollars.

'Is this your money?' Greenley asked me.

I needed to think, but I had no time. I remembered Billy's initial advice. 'No comment,' I said.

'No comment.' mocked Greenley. 'We've just found more cash under your girlfriend's bed and the best you can come up with is "no comment." What goes on in universities these days? In my day you had to be really smart just to get in to study. You teach there! "No comment." Your life hangs in the balance and you act like a criminal. Only criminals say "no comment," those who are frightened to tell the truth. Have another go.'

'There is something else I would like to say and it is this: I was not present when you claim to have found that money in this place.'

'What are you saying?' Greenley's tone was menacing.

'Just that.'

'Take out your notebook,' he said to one of the constables. 'I want you to write this down.' The constable took out a small wire bound writing pad from his back pocket. It was bent, dog-eared and clearly the worse for wear. A colleague handed him a pen.

'Now Dr Stuart,' said Greenley, 'say that again.'

'I was not present when you claim to have found that money in this

99

place.' The officer scribbled hurriedly.

'I want to be clear here: are you saying that you have reason to believe that I or any of my fellow officers placed this money here ourselves and then claimed to have found it?'

'No,' I said.

'Well, we've cleared that up then, haven't we?' We had not cleared it up at all. My statement and my response to his question were wholly consistent. I was not present when the money was supposedly found, nor did I have any evidence that the money was planted. I thought of making this point but I remembered George Fairlow's advice. This was no time to be clever. I remained silent. 'Would you like us to count this money in your presence,' asked Greenley, 'or bag it up in your presence and count it later?'

'You may count it later,' I said.

'Get the bags,' he said to his team. 'And watch closely, Dr Stuart. I don't want any possible misunderstandings.' Greenley fixed me with a hostile stare before returning downstairs.

The money was being sealed in transparent plastic bags when I heard the front door open. 'Stu, I'm back,' Tania shouted. 'I finished with Billy early so I went to the West End to do some shopping.'

I ran down the stairs and got to the entrance hall at the same time as Greenley emerged from the study. Tania was struggling with five large shopping bags, three from Harrods, two from Morgan de toi. 'Let me help you,' I said.

'You'll do no such thing,' said Greenley. 'Miss Tania Berkeley you are under arrest for the breach of your conditions of bail. You do not have to say anything. But it may harm your defence if you do not mention when questioned something which you later rely on in court. Anything you do say may be given in evidence.'

Tania dropped her bags on the floor. 'Stu, what's going on?'

'Don't worry,' I said quickly. 'I've been arrested too, for conspiring with you.'

'That's enough,' said Greenley.

'Money was found in your room,' I said quickly. 'Say nothing.'

100

'I said that's enough.' Greenley called for his team. 'Right, you take the lady, I'll take him. 'Cuff 'em.'

'Gov?'

'I said 'cuff 'em. They talk too much.'

As we were being handcuffed I said to Tania, 'It's only a technical breach, you'll be released in no time.'

'She might,' said Greenley, 'but will you?'

Tania was led out first. She kept trying to turn around to look at me, but a PC kept his hand in the small of her back. As she got to the car she stumbled and fell, first to her knees and then over to her side. As the PCs were helping her up the gates opened and BB's car swung into the driveway, scattering gravel as he skidded to a halt in behind the second unmarked police car. He got out in a rage and headed straight for the PC with his arms around Tania.'

'BB stop,' I shouted. 'It's OK. She just fell.' BB wasn't listening. He threw his arm around the PC's neck, hauled him back and held him in a firm headlock. Tania fell forward onto the car's bonnet. 'Let him go,' I yelled. I turned to Greenley. 'Let me talk to him, or you're going have a war on your hands. Take these handcuffs off.'

'Talk to him if you want,' said Greenley, letting go of my arm, 'but the handcuffs stay on.'

I walked over to BB with my hand secured behind my back. 'Enough, BB,' I said. 'You're making matters worse. Release him.' BB slowly eased his grip. The officer stepped back, rubbing his neck. Greenley walked over. 'This is BB,' I said to him, 'Tania's brother. He didn't realise the situation, and he's sorry.'

'No I'm not,' he said.

'Yes he is, and he runs a Boys Club in a socially deprived area aimed at giving youths an alternative to criminal behaviour. Without him there would be more crime on the streets. He's one of the good guys. You're both on the same side really.'

'No we're not,' said BB.

Greenley moved very close to BB, invading his personal space. BB's size and physique seemed not to intimidate the dishevelled detective sergeant. 'Now listen up,' he said in a low voice. 'You've just assaulted one of my officers. Assaulting an officer in the execution of his duty is a very serious offence. Jail time is a certainty. Now your friend here says you didn't know what you were doing, and I'm going to accept that, just this once. But when I get to the station I'm going to make a note of this incident, and if our paths ever cross again, and you so much as brush up against me or one of my men too closely, I'll have you. Do you understand?'

'He understands,' I said.

'Martyn,' said Greenley, calling DC Clarke over, 'get Dr Stuart in the car. Tania, are you all right?' Tania was now leaning with her back against the car. The side of her face was speckled with gravel that she was unable to brush away. She looked badly shaken. Nonetheless she nodded her assent.

Clarke guided me back to the first car, his hand on my arm, and pushed my head down as I got in the rear seats. He got in beside me. Smith arrived next, shortly followed by Greenley. As Smith turned the car around I saw Julianna tearfully waving from the front door. Standing next to her, defiant and stone faced, was BB. I knew that she must have opened the gates to let him drive in, but it was only when I saw them standing together that I realised she had asked him to come. She'd called him on learning of my arrest, just as I had called him on learning of Tania's, and just as Tania had called him from the South Norwood police station. BB, in times of trouble, everyone's first call.

'Why didn't you arrest him sir,' asked Clarke as we drove towards the electric gates.

'A man sees his beloved sister on the ground surrounded by three burly plain clothes coppers, one manhandling her, what do you expect him to do? When he realised the situation he stopped. He is, according to Dr Stuart here, a pillar of the community.'

'I think he understood the situation well enough,' said Clarke.

'Then let me put it this way. You have a major money launder sitting next to you and his accomplice in the car behind. How much paperwork do you want to do this evening?'

When we arrived at the police station I was ordered out the car by Greenley. Clarke escorted me into the police station; Greenley followed. Smith was left to park the vehicle. As we approached the glass doors, I turned and saw the vehicle containing Tania pull into the police car park. The Bexleyheath station was a relatively modern building. The doors led into a corridor and on to a large hall-like area with an enclosed oblong counter at the far end. Behind the counter was a ginger-haired wiry man in a white short-sleeve shirt open at the neck. Clarke led me toward him. It was Greenley, however, who did the talking. 'This is Dr Andrew Stuart,' he said to the desk sergeant. 'He's been arrested for conspiracy to launder the proceeds of drug trafficking contrary to -'

'Are the handcuffs necessary?' asked the desk sergeant. He had a broad Scottish accent.

'Not at this time, no,' said Greenley.

'Then take them off.' Greenley nodded to Clarke who swiftly retrieved and inserted the key, unlocking the 'cuffs.

'Thank you,' I said to the desk sergeant, but he ignored me.

Looking at Greenley he said, 'You were saying?'

DS Greenley explained the nature of the offence and the desk sergeant asked me for my personal details. These he recorded on a pre-printed form attached to a clipboard. He asked me questions relating to drug abuse, alcohol abuse and learning disabilities. When this was complete he handed me a sheet of paper explaining my rights whilst held in custody. He offered me a duty solicitor and I politely declined, explaining that I had already appointed a firm whose specialist partner would be present at my formal interview. I gave his name. Next I was asked to empty my pockets. My credit cards were itemised and my money was counted. Both were sealed in clear plastic wallets.

'What about his tie and shoelaces?' asked Greenley.

The desk sergeant sighed. I had never before heard someone sigh in an accent. Yet his was the most Scottish sigh I'd ever heard. 'Do you intend to kill yourself Dr Stuart?'

'No,' I said.

'Then you can keep your tie and shoelaces. But if you feel an urge for suicide coming on, please notify the nearest officer and we will take them off you.'

'That is very kind,' I said.

'Not at all.'

Greenley offered no more suggestions. This was the first time I had been exposed to the politics of the police station. I was surprised by the power of the desk sergeant in the face of a detective sergeant. Or maybe it was just this desk sergeant. Or maybe it was just Scotsmen.

When my processing was over I was led to a far corridor. I turned to see Tania standing in the company of the three plain clothed officers. Two of them were talking to her civilly and the third was behind her unlocking the handcuffs. Sensible move, I thought. The far corridor housed the police cells. I was led to the fourth one along on the left. I stepped inside and the door was locked securely behind me. The cell was small and grey with no natural light. In the corner was an uncovered toilet. The bed consisted of a thin blue plastic covered foam-like mattress on top of a solid concrete base. An old brown blanket lay folded on the floor. The walls were covered with graffiti, some of which protested innocence, in varying degrees of literacy, but most of which were pictorial in nature, usually of small men with huge sexual organs.

It had been a long day and I was tired. I lay down on the mattress. The plastic was cold to the touch. I turned on my back and looked up to the heavens, and I just had to chuckle. There, where I least expected it, printed on the ceiling was an advert.

> "Crimestoppers 0800 555 111. Call anonymously with
> information about crime. Your call is free. You do not have to give
> your name. You may get a reward."

I closed my eyes happy in the knowledge that if I could still laugh the light inside me had not gone out.

I drifted into a shallow sleep, which was disturbed by the sound of a door opening and footsteps making their way down the concrete corridor.

Next I heard the turning of keys. I opened my eyes to meet the opening of the cell door. DS Greenley and DC Clarke were accompanied by a senior uniformed officer, tall and smart, wearing a peaked cap. I stood up. 'Sit down,' barked Greenley.

'He may stand,' said the Commanding Officer. 'I'd like to get a good look at him.'

'Stand up,' said Greenley in a slightly more agreeable tone. I stood, more for myself than for them. I did not know why they were here. There was a sense of the ceremonial about the encounter. Clarke was standing with an almost military bearing, though he appeared uncomfortable. Greenley was triumphant. Turning to his Commanding Officer he announced with overwhelming pride, 'Sir, may I introduce you to the Laundryman.'

Chapter 6

The encounter was over almost as soon as it had began, and I was left alone in my cell to ponder its significance. I sat on the mattress and for some time went over the day's events in my head. I decided I needed more information. I got up and pushed the button near the cell door for assistance. After a minute or so the narrow eye-level panel in the middle of the door was slid open. 'Yes,' said an officer.

'I would like to speak to Detective Constable Martyn Clarke.'

'I'm sure he's busy but I'll see what I can do. It might be a while.'

'Thank you.' I said.

After about thirty minutes the now familiar pattern repeated itself: the footsteps, the key in the lock, the door opening. I was expecting DC Clarke. Instead a young WPC I had not seen before placed a large full black plastic bag on the floor, a bag normally used for garbage. 'Someone brought these for you,' she said.

'What are they?' I asked.

'Clothes and books, I think.'

'Who brought them?'

'A woman, well, two women, in fact. One very professional looking, and her …friend.'

'Their names?'

'I'll have to go and check.'

'Don't worry,' I said, 'I'll work it out from the contents of the bag.'

'OK,' she said and securely locked the door behind her.

I opened the bag. The clothes had clearly been taken from my home. Julianna. She had packed a towel, flannel and toiletries too. There were also two novels in the bag that were not from my library: Hard Times by Charles Dickens and An Evil Cradling by Brian Keenan. Both books were paperbacks, well worn and slightly dog-eared, the books of a reader. There was also a brand new book of crosswords. Anita. She was the profession-al one, and Julianna was her… friend.

An hour and a half later, following two further requests, Martyn Clarke finally got to my cell. He appeared smart and crisp, as if he had just stepped out of his house at 7:30 in the morning. It must have been nearly midnight. He wasted no time. 'What do you want?'

I matched him for directness. 'Who is The Laundryman?'

'You.'

'I don't think you believe that. DS Greenley does, but I don't think you do. But let's put that to one side. Maybe my question was wrong. Describe the Laundryman to me.'

Clarke's shoulders sagged a little and I could see, despite his appear-ance, that he was dog-tired. Without Greenley, Clarke was very different. 'May I sit down?'

'Of course,' I said.

He sat on the thin blue plastic covered mattress that I was pleased to call my bed. He pitched his fingers together creating the shape of a tent, one of the few stress reducing exercises that doesn't involve getting changed. Looking at the floor he began in a low voice. 'For some years now we have known of the existence of the Laundryman. We just don't know who he is. We don't know where he is. He is the man who processes the cash of the principal cocaine suppliers in London. He launders money. He turns dirty money into clean money and he transfers it to anywhere in the world. One man. We know this because we have successfully infiltrated a number of the large drug supplying organisations. Each undercover officer's report makes reference to the Laundryman and the terms used and the process of cash delivery leads us to conclude that he operates here in London. We don't know how he operates, but we know this: he is very clever, considers himself untouchable, is highly respectable, and has banking contacts all over the world. Think of him as a financial Professor Moriarty.'

'And DS Greenley thinks it's me.'

'Everybody thinks it's you.'

'Except you.'

He raised his eyes from the floor and looked at me. 'I could not possibly answer that question Dr Stuart. You fit the profile.'

'I am not untouchable.'

Clarke stood and stretched, then slowly sat back down again. 'That's not the part that bothers me,' Clarke sighed. He passed his hands over his face as if they contained a wet, cold flannel. 'You see,' he looked up, 'although you've got the book learning, the higher education and postgraduate degrees, and the like, you really don't behave like the Laundryman. I've thought about him a lot. I even have a picture of him in my mind. He is cold, methodical, precise and unemotional. The Laundryman would never have stood bail for Tania Berkeley.'

I ignored the slight. 'Can't the others see that?'

'People see what they want to see. Right now the powers that be want to see the Laundryman, so they see him: Dr Andrew Stuart.' He rose again. This time to leave. He walked to the cell door and added coldly, 'If you ever refer to this conversation, I'll deny it and I'll hurt you.'

The finality of my position overwhelmed me. I had to act fast. 'You want to catch him personally don't you?' Clarke remained still with his back to me. I added very softly, 'I can catch him.'

He turned slowly. 'What?'

'Get me out of here and I will catch him.'

'You wouldn't know how to start. Do you have any idea how many resources we have already thrown at this case? And remember we have caught him; he's you.'

'It will not hold DC Clarke, you know that. Right now you may be the only one, but you know it. They can charge me, but I'll walk, for the simple reason that I am innocent. Set me free and I'll deliver the Laundryman to your door. Think about it. What a coup.'

Clarke was interested but he couldn't show it. 'If we can't find him, why on earth do you think that you can?'

'Because I have the skills you lack. I understand international finance, offshore banking, the use of offshore companies and trusts, that whole arcane world. I know how to create a financial mirage. I can think as he thinks and can create a trap he will not see until he's ensnared. Moreover, I am not the police. He won't see me coming.'

'So you're Sherlock Holmes?'

'No, I'm Mycroft Holmes, Sherlock's smarter older brother.'

'I can't let you go Dr Stuart, I don't have the authority.'

'That's OK. My lawyer will get me out, just don't stand in the way.'

'Who's to say you don't abscond.'

'Monitor me. Move into my house if you like. If my ultimate freedom is dependent on finding the Laundryman, I will find him. One more thing: if I find him you have to let Tania go too.'

'You don't ask for much, do you?'

'That's the deal.'

'Forget it. You have nothing to deal with.' He got up again and walked to the cell door. 'I don't understand you. Here you are in custody. The top brass think you're the Laundryman. That means you're likely to get banged up for a very long time. And all you're concerned about is Tania Berkeley who, however you look at it, is as guilty as hell. What's the matter with you?'

'I love her.' There. I'd said it out loud, for the very first time.

Clarke opened the cell door. 'When will your lawyer be here?'

'Tomorrow morning.'

'I'll talk to DS Greenley,' he said. 'If you can find the Laundryman maybe, just maybe, we can do a deal for you, but not for Tania.' And he was gone.

I slept badly that night. It was the waiting that was killing me. I did not know what would happen next. Every hour I woke up bathed in sweat and disorientated. My home, my business, my reputation, my life could be snatched from me in the morning. I had long held the view that when it really mattered, when you stood to lose everything you had worked for, when your whole life hung in the balance, there would be one thing about which you could be absolutely certain: you'd be on your own. And I felt alone. Terribly alone.

I awoke at 5:30 and immediately pushed the assistance button. I tried to change my mental state by thinking of it as a room service button, but it required greater effort than I had at my command. Another WPC spoke through the locked door. 'Yes.'

'I would like to take a shower.'

'No you wouldn't. The heating system doesn't come on until 7 o' clock. The water will be freezing this time in the morning.'

'Perfect,' I said.

George Fairlow arrived at 11:00am. I was due to be formally interviewed at 12:30. We were allocated a room for a pre-interview conference. I took control.

'As I see it I have two problems. First, Tania has told her lawyers that the money she is holding is mine. I need to distance myself from any money laundering activities without specifically denying that I gave her the money. Secondly –'

'Before we get to the second point, let's examine the first. My obligation is to you, not Tania. My advice is that you answer no questions. However, if you wish to answer their questions then you should tell them that the money is not yours. I can see no point in harming your defence to support a comment made by Tania to her solicitors. It's not as if she has made this comment to the police, though even if she had my advice would be the same. Understand this: right now you are on your own and so is she.'

'This is a time for moral courage. I will not let her down.'

'What exactly do you think she is doing to you?'

'Whatever she's doing she's not letting me down. She knows I can handle it.'

'But can you?'

'Yes. Point two. Have you heard of the Laundryman?'

'I have practised criminal law for some twenty years and I specialise in the so-called white-collar division. Of course I've heard of him. If you could think of the criminal world as a vast ocean the Laundryman is Moby Dick.'

'They think I am the Laundryman.'

George leaned back, looking for comfort on the wooden chair. Finding none he pushed himself forward and rested both arms on the table. The room was silent for some time. George was either processing this new information through his vast knowledge of the criminal justice system or he was quietly reeling from the shock.

'Are you?' he asked.

'No,' I said.

'All the more reason you should say nothing,' he insisted.

I disagreed.

'Let me explain,' he said. 'Once you start answering questions you cannot stop, not without drawing attention to the question you choose not to answer. You are then telling them where you feel vulnerable.'

'If I say absolute nothing they won't release me. They will oppose bail. I need to be free.'

'I can understand that.'

'No you can't because I haven't explained it yet. You see, I'm going to catch him.'

'Who?'

'The Laundryman.'

George smiled. 'Yes Captain Ahab.' He looked at me for what seemed to be a long time. 'There is a third way,' he said.

'Let's hear it.'

'We make a statement at the commencement of the questioning, but refuse to answer any specific questions on the basis that they have yet to establish that there is a case to answer. In your statement you can address all the points you wish to make. It will be read into the record. You will have co-operated. But once the statement is read we sit on our hands and say nothing, which satisfies my concerns.'

'The third way it is,' I said. 'Let's get started.'

We worked on the statement for about an hour, replacing words, reversing the order of sentences, changing emphasis, and constantly making it more and more concise. When we were finished it was only five sentences long, but, I thought, it was enough to secure my bail. George Fairlow called in DS Greenley and informed him that we were ready for the interview. That is, we were as ready as we would ever be.

We were led into small windowless room. It contained an old table with four chairs. A large grey audio recording set sat on a shelf, with a double tape deck. DS Greenley invited us to take the chairs with their backs to the wall, leaving the chairs with their back to the door for DC Clarke and himself. We squeezed in uncomfortably. DC Clarke arrived with some brand new cassette tapes in their cases, which he asked me to check were properly sealed. He unsealed them with great difficulty, resorting in the end to the use of his car keys. Once the two of the cassettes were in the tape deck, DS Greenley commenced his well-rehearsed preamble. He stated the time and place, identified himself, DC Clarke identified himself and George Fairlow and I spoke our names for the record. With the tape running, I took charge. 'Before you put any detailed questions to me I have a written statement I would like to read.'

'Is the statement in your own hand?' asked Greenley.

'Yes it is,' I replied.

'Will you sign the statement and give it to us after you have read it.'

'Yes,' I said, 'provided I can have a photocopy.'

'Very good,' said Greenley, 'proceed.'

I read from my text. *'I am not guilty of the offence for which I have been arrested. I have not laundered money. More specifically, I have not conspired with Tania Berkeley or any of her co-defendants to launder money. You have provided me with insufficient evidence to establish that I have a case to answer. On that basis, and in accordance with the advice of my legal representatives, I propose to answer no further questions during this interview.'* I signed my statement and handed it to DS Greenley. He promised to give me a photocopy once the interview was over.

'Notwithstanding the statement that you have read, Dr Stuart, I still have some questions I would like to put to you. I invite you to answer them, but if you wish to decline please say "no comment" for the record. A

112

grunt, nod or a shake of the head will not suffice.'

'That last comment,' said George Fairlow haughtily, 'was wholly uncalled for.'

'It's a standard instruction.'

'It was gratuitously offensive. My client is a doctor of law, DS Greenley. Please remember that and treat him accordingly.'

'That leads me on nicely to my first question,' said Greenley with a smirk. 'Dr Stuart, what is your profession?'

I was tempted to grunt, but instead said, 'No comment.'

'Are you self-employed?'

'No comment.'

'Do you handle large volumes of cash in your business?'

'No comment.'

'Do you know a woman by the name of Tania Berkeley?'

'No comment.'

'What is the exact nature of your relationship with her?'

'No comment.'

And so it went on for about an hour. I was asked about the cash found at Tania's house, and the cash found in Tania's room at my house. I was asked about all of her co-defendants, and all the names on the Production Order, including Mazzinni. Greenley covered the nature of my work, the purpose of offshore companies and trusts and whether I had personal offshore accounts. He seemed to ask about everything except whether I was the Laundryman. At the end of the interview DC Clarke labelled the tapes and we were led from the room. I was informed that I was still technically under arrest and was escorted back to my cell by a police constable. Sitting in my now familiar grey surrounding, I hung desperately to the word "technically."

After about an hour and a half the cell door was unlocked and in walked DC Clarke. 'You're going to get police bail,' he said. 'That means that you will not be formally charged. You don't have to surrender your passport, but you do have to reside at your home address. You must surrender into custody again in three months. Then everything will be reviewed again.

113

There's some paperwork to go through which will take about an hour. After that you'll be free to go.'

'Thank you,' I said.

'There's more. Tania Berkeley has been released with a caution in respect of her bail infringement. She remains, of course, on court bail in respect of her money laundering charge. When her counsel makes the formal application to amend the residency aspect of those bail conditions the police will make no objections. This took some doing Dr Stuart. You'd better catch him. Heaven help you if you don't.'

On my release I called Anita, who was relieved, and then headed straight to the Boys Club to see BB. He was distraught. 'Have you heard of James Baldwin?' he asked me, taking two cans of beer from the fridge in the small kitchen area off of the main hall. Sure I had heard of James Baldwin. Black people think of him as a black writer. Baldwin to me was simply a writer full stop, one of the finest writers in the English language. I had read *Another Country* when I was seventeen and its searing language and poignant portrayal of the clash of cultures and sexuality remained with me to this day. I disliked the appropriation of authors by classes, races or sexes. Great writers belong to us all.

'I've read James Baldwin' I said.

'Well,' BB continued, 'there's this letter he wrote to Angela Davis – do you know Angela Davis?' Now he was really irritating me.

'I know Angela Davis.'

'Well, she was about to be arrested because of her revolutionary views and stuff. And James Baldwin writes to her and you know what he said?'

I knew but I didn't want to spoil BB's story. He was hurting. He had to talk.

'Tell me.'

'He said to her: "If they come for you in the morning, they'll be coming for me by

nightfall." That's how I feel about you. You stood up for my sister and now they are going to bring you down. You're a black man now. And when they've got you, they'll be coming for me.'

I was uncomfortable seeing BB in such pain. His face wasn't made for pain. Laughter, yes, and anger, but not pain. It lost its beauty in pain. 'They won't be coming for you BB. You haven't done anything wrong.'

'Neither have you,' he challenged.

I had done too much wrong. I got involved in a money laundering case when I should have stayed far away. I had made myself known to the police and once I had placed myself within their ambit they made their presence felt. In the process I had risked the security of my clients and the well being of my friends. And all for a woman I hardly knew, a woman I simply chose to love. I had done wrong; I could have chosen to love someone else. But our lives are the summation of the choices we make. I had made mine and I would stick with them. 'BB,' I said, 'I have a more immediate problem.'

'What's that?'

'I need to catch the Laundryman.'

'Who?'

I told him.

We drank our beers in silence, with BB quietly observing his boys. A row was brewing over the scoring of a table tennis match involving not only the players and the scorer, but also those who had gathered around the table to watch the game. 'Play the point again,' said BB, and it was settled.

'Impressive,' I said.

'Simple,' said BB. 'So how are you going to catch him?'

'The Laundryman? I don't know. I've got to identify him first.'

'How are you going to do that?'

'I don't know.'

'Let me get this right,' said BB. 'You don't know who he is, you don't know where he is, you don't know how he does what he does and you don't know how you're going to catch him.'

'That's right,' I said.

'And if you don't catch him they will assume he's you, prosecute, and if found guilty, and you will be, you'll go to prison.'

'For a long time.'

BB was a good friend. I felt that he was completely on my side. The obstacles had to be identified but they didn't deter him. 'Where do we start?'

'Ideally, I'd like to do some brainstorming.'

'What's that?'

'Knocking questions about in a small group until the answers begin to appear. Are you in?'

'Just tell me when and where.'

I went to the office next and raised the issue in the office with Anita. 'I want to gather together a small group of people,' I said, 'so we can thrash this out, a brainstorming group.'

'Who do you want?'

'BB,' I said. Anita raised her eyebrows. 'BB's not intellectual Anita, but he's smart, he's tough and he's loyal.'

'Who else?'

'We need a lawyer.'

'You know plenty of those.'

'No, a criminal lawyer.'

'What about George Fairlow?'

'He's too close to me.'

'One of his associates?'

'I need someone I know. How about Tania's solicitor Billy Carver?'

'Would he do it?'

'I can only ask,' I said.

'Anyone else?'

'Yes, and this one's tricky, DC Clarke.'

'The man who arrested you? Are you mad?'

'He believes in me and he wants to catch the Laundryman as badly as I do. He also has the inside information I will need.'

'If he colludes with you he'll be thrown off the force.'

'No, I'm not asking him to show me police records, just to share his views. If he wants me to catch the Laundryman he has to help. I don't know if I can do it without him.' I was not convinced I could do it with him either.

'Fine, we have BB, Billy Carver, DC Clarke and you. Four's a good number. Where will you gentlemen meet?'

'In the boardroom.'

'Bad idea,' Anita said. 'It's too formal, and certainly too official for DC Clarke. He'll be off duty, of course, if we can get him. You must meet him in an informal setting. And it will be better for the others too. The last time BB sat at a desk he was probably at school. He'll find the boardroom far too daunting. And Billy Carver, well, I'm sure he'd appreciate some time out of an office.'

'What do you suggest? I don't want to meet in a public place.'

'What's wrong with your home? It's big enough.'

'Agreed,' I said. 'And I want us to meet on Saturday.'

'You'll have to make the calls. This will need to be a personal invitation.'

'I'll do at least one invitation face to face.'

'BB?' she asked.

'You,' I said. She was genuinely pleased. 'I need you Anita. I need the best brains around.'

'It will be a sort of Brains Trust,' she said, and the name stuck.

When I got home Tania was waiting for me. She threw her arms around my neck and hugged me tightly. I put my arms around her waist and pulled her closer still. I felt the charge of a massive emotional release and I shook as I held her. After what seemed like an age we both reluctantly eased ourselves apart.

'You look so tired,' said Tania.

'I am. It's been a very rough day. I'm going to take a shower and go to bed.'

'A shower won't relax you. You'll still be tense. Let me give you a massage. I'm not only a hairdresser, you know, I'm also a qualified masseuse.'

'I'm not sure this is a good idea, Tania. We're crossing a line that I only

117

want us to cross when we're both ready.'

'We are not crossing anything. I'm a masseuse and you're my client.'

'You mean I've got to pay?' I teased.

'Funny,' she said. 'Where shall we do this?'

'In the bedroom I suppose.'

'Bad choice on two levels. The first is obvious. The second is that the bed will not be firm enough and I need to work around your body. Now do you have a large narrow table.' I looked at her helplessly. 'Forget it, lets use the floor. What room?'

'I have a small spare bedroom upstairs with virtually nothing in it.'

'Carpeted?'

'Yes.'

'Show me.' I led her up to the room. 'Perfect,' she said.

'What next?'

'You'll need some towels, a large one, thick, something like a beach towel, and a couple of smaller ones. You get those, I need to get some things from my room.' I got the towels and returned to the room before her. She arrived shortly after carrying a small array of bottles, which she arranged in the corner by the door. 'Right, put the large towel in the centre of the room, strip naked, lay face down on it. Roll up one of the smaller towels and rest your chin on it, and cover your bottom with the other one. I'll be back again in two minutes.'

I started to undress thinking of Tania's hands all over my body and the inevitable happened. I grew hard, rock solid, and it wouldn't go away. I willed myself to think of her in a different way. I thought of her being arrested, handcuffed and driven to the police station. I thought of her transfer to Holloway, and the humiliation of the body search. And that just made it worse.

When she returned the large white fluffy beach towel was on the floor. I, however, was not face down on it. I stood with my back to the wall with one of the smaller towels around my waist. 'I have a problem Tania,' I said.

'I can see,' she replied. Her eyes were dancing. She held out her hand. 'Give me the towel.'

'I don't want it like this. It's like a scene from a porno movie. I want it to be right.'

'OK, when shall I come back?'

'I don't know. What shall I do?'

'I've got no idea. Why don't you call Julianna?' I felt as if I'd been drenched in ice water. My proud erection, along with my ego, suffered an instant deflation. 'Well, that seems to have solved your problem,' she said. 'Shall we start?'

Tania's hands were warm on my back; they were also surprisingly strong given how slender her fingers were. The scent from the oils was seductive. 'Smells great,' I said. 'What is it?'

'Cedarwood and rosemary, I mixed them myself.'

'They feel so smooth on my skin.'

'That's the almond oil,' she said. 'Cedarwood and rosemary are the essential oils. That is what you smell. Almond oil is a carrier oil, you know, it carries the essential oils, that is what you feel.'

'Why do you need the carrier oil?' I said.

'Because if I put undiluted essential oils on your back it would irritate your skin like hell. Anything else?'

'No,' I said. 'You sure know your stuff.'

'This is my field,' she said. And as she worked my lower back, and to my subsequent astonishment, I paid her the greatest compliment you can pay to a professional masseuse, I fell asleep.

I worked hard in the office the following day. Anita fed to me piece-meal the work that had formed a backlog over the recent days. She seemed happy that there was a degree of normality back in our lives. As always, she allocated the downtime in which I returned my calls, insisting that as far as possible I limited each call to not more than five minutes. At her prompting, expressed as a concern for my health, I left the office at 5 o' clock.

'Coffee, please, Julianna,' I said as I entered the kitchen.

'Dark, strong, smooth and ready,' she said with an emphasised Jamaican

119

lilt. She rolled her shoulders as she poured my coffee, as if dancing to a Caribbean beat.

'Something sweet you?' I said in by best Jamaican accent.

She laughed. 'Andrew you shouldn't even try to speak patois. It doesn't suit you and you're no good at it.'

'What's the good news?' I said.

'No good news; it's bad news really. But, you know, I'm trying not to let it get me down. The police were here today.'

'What did they want?'

'Stu!' Tania stood at the door, legs apart, hands on hips. She was wearing faded blue jeans and an orange tanktop cut off and frayed just below her braless breasts. She had sneakers on her feet and a baseball cap on her head. She looked like $5 million. 'The bastards have frozen my assets.'

I realised at once that what had caused her anger was equally responsible for Julianna's sassy merriment. 'How do you know?'

'They served a restraint order on me today. I gave it to Julianna and told her to show it to you as soon as you got in.'

'See it here,' said Julianna picking up a four-page legal document from the breakfast bar.

I took it from her and started reading. 'Has Billy Carver seen this?' I asked without looking up.

'No,' said Tania. 'What do I need Billy for when I'm living with you?'

'He's your solicitor and an expert in criminal law. You need to fax this over to him right away. It says that you cannot deal in your property in any way. You no longer have access to your bank or building society accounts. You cannot sell or re-mortgage your house. You can't even sell your car.'

'Can I drive it?'

'Yes, of course you can drive it. The purpose of this order is to stop you depleting your assets.'

'Why?'

'Because, if you lose the case, not only do you go to prison, the Crown will also confiscate your assets to the value of your alleged benefit from the crime.'

120

'Bastards, bastards, bastards. And I've done nothing wrong. Nothing!'

'They're allowing you to draw out £300 per week.'

'Bastards.'

'Do you know how to use my fax machine?'

'They're just bastards.'

'I'll do it myself.' I went to my study, typed out a brief cover note and faxed the restraint order to Billy. When I returned to the kitchen Tania was still petulant and Julianna was still happy, gay even, in the old fashioned sense of the word. I could see trouble brewing and I sought to head it off by asking Julianna to prepare the dining room for dinner. It at least got her out of the kitchen. After five minutes the phone rang.

'Bastards,' said Billy.

'What are you still doing in the office at this time?' I asked.

'I'm a humble legal aid criminal lawyer, Andrew, I don't earn George Fairlow's hourly fees, or yours for that matter.'

'What are we going to do?'

'Vary the restraint order. £300 per week is piss. We need to get Tania access to as much of her money as possible. You can help here. What I need is some iron cast expenditure that Tania must incur. Something that the Crown Prosecution Service would be heartless to refuse. I'm talking violins playing, handkerchiefs out stuff. What have you got for me?'

'Nothing yet. Do you want to speak to your client?'

'Does she want to speak to me?'

'No.'

'Then no, call me back.'

I relayed the conversation to Tania and we put our head together. I called Billy back in five minutes flat.

'Tania needs to pay a year's fees in advance for a course. She also needs a computer and some very expensive books.'

'I see,' said Billy. 'This can be substantiated can it?'

'Sure, she's going to do a law degree at London City University, as a mature student.'

'She's got a place has she?'

121

'Yes, I've just interviewed her.'

'Law school fees,' said Billy. 'I'd love to see the CPS try to turn that down.'

'We have a result,' I said to Tania having hung up. 'Let's eat.'

Julianna served us dinner. There was still a lightness in her step. She served us fried fish, rice and peas and callaloo. We were eating more West Indian dishes since Tania arrived. This suited Julianna. It played to her strengths, but she refused to give Tania any credit for the change in the culinary emphasis. Tania was the enemy, and each of her misfortunes was to be celebrated with a dance.

The following day at the office I had a decision to make. At its essence the question was simple: do I surrender the Mazzinni tapes or not? The surrendering of his yellow and orange files was no longer an issue. The police had seized them as part of the search of my offices on my arrest. They contained the sanitised version of our professional discussions. The tapes were a different matter. The decision had to be a political one. I recalled a book by Professor William Twining, an eminent jurist. He created a character that he called the Bad Man of Boston. The character did not evaluate what was right or wrong according to the laws of the day. He determined his actions on the basis of benefits and detriments. In my case he would have determined the consequences of sending the tapes against those of not sending them.

To send them opened me up to misinterpretation. Added to the Tania business, it could be the final nail in the coffin. I could be re-arrested and detained and the Laundryman would go free. Moreover, if I gave them one tape I feared they might demand all of my tapes and my confidential discussions with my clients would be in the public arena. Alternatively, if I omitted the tapes, who would know? If the worst came to the worst, and they found out, I'd be in contempt of court. That was not to be taken lightly, but there were more serious charges. And so my decision was made, I had surrendered the files, but would withhold the tapes. It was a gentleman's decision, I thought, and a reasonable one. Who doubts the value of a good liberal education? The Bad Man of Boston had nothing on the Wizard of Wigmore Street.

Chapter 7

Setting up the Brains Trust was easier than I thought it would be. BB was in, Anita was in. DC Martyn Clarke wanted to take part, but he made it clear that he would be there unofficially and in his own time. Last on the list was Billy. I called him. I explained the composition of the Brains Trust and its purpose. 'Billy,' I said, 'I want you to join us.'

'No.'

'Why not?'

'Let me count the reasons. One, I am a criminal lawyer who only acts for the defence. Two, I would lose all credibility with my clients if they ever knew I had worked together with the police. Three, I assume I would be doing this for nothing and if I wanted to do pro bono work I would join a law centre. Four, this is a financial crime and my accountancy skills are zero. Five, there is a potential conflict of interest; this Laundryman could be a client of mine. Do you want me to go on?'

'Come on Billy, this is going to be fun. You will not be acting as a lawyer per se. You will not be helping the police, you will be helping a friend, me. And remember I'm a defendant. So you don't get paid, so what. You don't do anything with your money anyway. As regards your lack of accountancy skills, it couldn't be less relevant. What we need I have. Look Billy, this is a chance to do something really meaningful, to catch Moby Dick. And he's not a client of yours – you know that. This guy is the top of the tree, sophisticated, connected, professional and almost certainly white. He would not use a firm in Peckham run by a chain-smoking alcoholic who looks forward to death the way a child looks forward to Christmas.'

'Steady on. What you really mean is, he wouldn't use a black lawyer.'

'That's true,' I said.

'Why ask me, why not George Fairlow?'

'You're smarter than George,' I said.

'That's true too.'

'So you're in?'

'I don't know Andrew.'

'You're in, Saturday night, my house, 8:00pm. You'll have to bring your own cigarettes, but I have a bottle of 12 year old malt whiskey which I will break open for the occasion.'

'Just one bottle?' he asked dejectedly.

Anita arrived first. She was dressed as if for the office: a classic navy blue suit, cream blouse and a single string of pearls. Her hair, as always, was tightly drawn back from her face and secured in a bun. Martyn was dressed casually, but in name only; that is, he was dressed in casual clothes, but the slacks were pressed and his open-neck shirt was crisp. Billy just looked a mess, and reeked of cigarette smoke. BB wore a thin, white polo neck jumper and tailored brown corduroy trousers. He looked the most comfortable, at ease in his clothes, at ease in his body. My quest for casualness led me to don a Versace tie, which I found a mite garish. As Tania observed, as I sat in her salon, I'm fairly conservative in appearance.

My drawing room did not reflect my conservatism. It contained a four-seater green leather sofa with a buttoned seat effect, three brown leather armchairs each on a swivel base. In the centre of the room sat a low antique Chinese tea table. Then there was a stool covered with thick chenille, which didn't seem to match anything. Nor was I fully aware of its purpose. On the far wall hung a striking modern oil painting by Andrew Galitzine. It was original and expensive and I liked it, but I didn't understand it. Everyday I thought it was about something else.

The whole effect was a tribute to a German interior designer whom I engaged when I bought the house some four years ago. For me, the room lacked comfort and intimacy. But it looked the part and, for good or ill, looking the part was important to me.

BB and Billy sat at either end of the long green sofa, Anita and Martyn each sat in an armchair. I stood to begin with, but, as the meeting progressed, I would alternatively sit, kneel and perch on the thick chenille stool.

Julianna arrived with a large tray of sandwiches, which she placed on the oval table, next to the previously arranged plates and napkins. 'What would everyone like to drink?' she asked.

'First bring the whiskey, the good bottle, for Billy, and the Chablis for me,' I said. She set the Chablis in a large ice bucket, and placed a smaller ice bucket with tongs next to Billy. She opened the whiskey bottle and started to pour generously into the wide mouth Edinburgh crystal whiskey glass.

'You can take the ice away, but leave the bottle,' Billy said and smiled at the hesitant Julianna. She looked across to me. I nodded.

Martyn requested Perrier. 'With ice,' he added pointedly.

'Beer please,' said BB. 'No glass.'

'Miss Hume?' said Julianna, turning to Anita.

'I think Anita would be pleased to share the Chablis with me,' I said.

'Two glasses,' said Anita.

Remaining on my feet, I opened the meeting. 'We all know why we're here,' I said. 'You are my Brains Trust. Together we will identify and catch the Laundryman. This is a brain-storming session. There are no rules. Let's all express our views, ideas and opinions openly. I'll pull the strands together as we progress. Who would like to start?'

BB opened. 'This money laundering, I understand it's a crime, but I really don't understand what it is. Someone explain it to me, because we're never going to find this guy if I don't even know what he does.'

Surprisingly, it was Billy who spoke next. 'You know, BB, in the 1920's alcohol was prohibited in the US. It was as unlawful to distil, sell or consume alcohol then as it is to process, supply or take cocaine today. Can you imagine?' He lifted his glass to his lips and took a large swig of his whiskey, keeping his eyes on Martyn Clarke as he did so. 'So the bootleggers were the drug traffickers of yesterday, from the uppercrust Joseph Kennedy, future Ambassador to the Court of St James and father of a president, to the working class Al Capone, future jailbird.'

'Your point?' asked Martyn clearly getting irritated.

'Plus ça change, plus c'est la même chose,' replied Billy.

'What?' asked BB.

'The more things change, the more they remain the same,' I translated.

'Having made my point,' Billy cut back, 'I will now explain the term money laundering to BB.' He lit a second cigarette from the softly burning butt of his first and inhaled deeply. 'Bootlegging, like cocaine dealing, generated a lot of cash, but as bootlegging was a crime this money could not legitimately be banked. Large sums of cash were a pain to store and easy to steal. Banks were safer. So Capone and his gang set up a series of fake businesses and they deposited their illicit cash into banks as if it were the income of these businesses. One of the business fronts they used was a chain of laundrymats. Hence the phrase "money laundering."'

'Right,' said BB very slowly, as if he understood enough to move forward but not enough to pounce.

'Wrong,' said Martyn. 'Billy's given you the romantic explanation. In truth money laundering is called what it is because the phrase precisely describes the process involved in changing dirty money into clean money. The money is washed, it is laundered.'

Billy Carver and Martyn Clarke, the criminal lawyer and the detective constable, the black defence solicitor and the white law officer, they would lock horns all night, but that was OK. This was a brain storming session and I needed creative tension. BB needed more information. 'Why is this money laundering such a big deal? I mean, the main crime, the drug trafficking, has already taken place.'

'If you knock out the money launderer,' explained Martyn, 'you seriously harm the drug dealer. Without the launderer the dealer simply could not spend the proceeds of his crime; at least not without drawing attention to himself. Nobody legitimately transacts business in large amounts of cash these days.' I thought of the Croydon Magistrates Court, but let it pass.

'So you hit the launderer to hurt the dealer,' concluded BB.

'As far as I'm concerned the launderer is usually a bigger criminal than the dealer,' corrected Martyn. 'Certainly the Laundryman is much bigger than any of his clients. Let me give you some idea. It is estimated that over US$600 billion is laundered annually worldwide.

BB let out a low whistle. Billy just lit another cigarette. I had some idea of the magnitude of money laundering activities, though Martyn's figure was higher than my guesstimates. I am suspicious of figures given for the quantification of illicit activities, when the huge resources of the Treasury are unable to quantify legitimate trade figures with any great accuracy. That said, even if one halved Martyn's figure it still revealed a massive global financial industry.

'All done through Laundrymats?' asked BB. He was deliberately being obtuse. He knew much more than he was letting on. Was this an act for DC Clarke, and, if so, why?

'Oh no,' said Martyn rubbing his hands. 'Let me tell you the ways. First the deposit: you've got to get rid of the cash. You can pay it into a bank or carry it abroad and then pay it into a bank. We've picked up hundreds of simpletons at Heathrow with suitcases of cash, usually unemployed black women on social security.'

BB and Billy bristled.

'No offence,' Martyn added. 'The more sophisticated find a way to deposit the money in the UK. Fine. They're now in the banking system but they're not problem free. If they spend the money the question still arises as to where they got it from. So they need transactions that obscure the source of the money. The most common is the offshore loan back scheme. After depositing the money in the UK, they set up offshore shell companies. The money is transferred to the offshore bank accounts of these companies and then loaned back to UK companies owned by the UK principals. They spend the money. Asked where they got it from, they will inform you, quite honestly, that it was a loan. Dr Stuart could explain it better.'

'Don't defer to me after you've insulted my friends,' I said with good humour. 'I've met plenty of white male simpletons in my time.'

'Usually in uniform,' added Billy.

'Gentlemen,' said Martyn, on the retreat, 'I really meant no offence

But there is a cultural divide here. I have found that the less sophisticated white criminals in this field often use high value items to wash their cash. They will buy diamonds or antiques for cash, sell them in return for a cheque or draft and deposit the same into the UK bank – no questions asked. Cash to Jamaica, or wherever, in suitcases is the black man's game and he usually uses poor black women as the couriers. I'm telling you the truth and the truth is important. I don't want to start a war with you guys.'

I sought to deflect an unnecessary argument. 'I assume the Laundryman uses none of the techniques?'

'High value items, cash in suitcases? No. The Laundryman is the ultimate sophisticate.'

'Then let's talk about how he does it,' I said.

'We don't know a lot,' confessed Martyn, 'but here goes. The Laundryman needs to do three things. He needs to enter the dirty money into the financial system. He needs to wash the dirty money. He needs to deliver the clean money to his customers.'

BB leaned forward. 'Let's slow this down. I'm no college boy. One stage at a time. Entering the dirty money into the financial system, you mean paying it into the bank right?'

'Usually, yes, but not necessarily. The cash can be used to buy foreign currency. A few years ago there was a man in Birmingham who, over the course of 13 months laundered £64 million through bureaux-de-change in London. Several times every week he would pack suitcases full of cash and travel to London. I spoke to a Customs officer on the case who told me that at one stage he was changing more Sterling into Dutch Guilders than the amount that would normally be changed in the whole of Britain.'

'And no one noticed?' asked BB.

'Not for 13 months,' responded Martyn matter-of-factly.

'I still don't understand,' said BB. 'Surely you're only exchanging a suitcase of cash for a suitcase of cash. You've still got to deposit it at some stage whatever currency it's in.'

'Good point.' There was no condescension in he voice. 'Let me address that on two levels. Firstly, crisp high denomination Swiss Francs are a lot cleaner, easier to transport and deposit than suitcases of grubby five and ten pound notes. Secondly, and more importantly, the fact that you have changed pounds into Swiss Francs does not mean that you are walking out of the bureau with a full suitcase. You could be walking out with a small envelope.'

'A foreign currency cheque,' said BB and smiled.

'That's right, which you could deposit anywhere in the world, no questions asked.' Martyn continued, 'The casino wheeze is a variation on the same theme. You walk in, buy a large number of chips for cash, play for a few hours, usually cautiously, cash in your chips at the end of the evening requesting a cheque. Net result: you have a cheque from a reputable establishment of entertainment. Why? Because you won at the tables. Clean money.'

'Small fry for the Laundryman,' said BB.

'Not if he owns the casino,' said Martyn.

'Do you have a lead?' I asked.

'No, no,' he replied. 'I'm just running through a couple of ideas. BB in fact was largely right. In most instances "entering the dirty money into the financial system," means paying it into the bank.'

Julianna knocked on the door and entered. 'More drinks?' Martyn asked for some more water and BB wanted another bottle of beer. Julianna refilled Anita's glass and then mine. She glanced at Billy's whiskey bottle, down by a third, and turned to me. I shrugged. She emptied Billy's ashtray and made her way to the door. I watched her tightly clad bottom as it swayed slowly out of the room.

'Once the Laundryman has got the dirty money into the financial system,' continued Martyn, 'he needs to wash it.'

'OK,' said BB, 'you've got to give more details. Maybe the others know what you're talking about, but I'm really not sure that I do. What do you mean by *washing*?'

'The money became dirty in the first place because it formed the proceeds of criminal activity. By *washing* I mean engaging in transactions that serve to disassociate the money from the crime that gave rise to it. Take Dr

Stuart here, he could send money all over the world through offshore companies and offshore trusts and other offshore structures I don't begin to understand. When he was finished, who would be able to identify where the money started off? And when you can't identify that, the money is clean. It has been washed.'

'So you're saying that the Laundryman is an international tax consultant.'

'Not necessarily, though he may have many of Andrew's skills. The wash can take many forms. I've already talked about the offshore loan back scheme. As another example, let's take commodity futures.'

BB waved his hands. 'I'm not going to understand this part but carry on anyway.'

Billy was determined that BB not get left behind. 'Actually,' he explained, 'it's not difficult to understand at all. A commodity is a standardised product like wheat or coffee, and a futures contract is an agreement to buy or sell the commodity at some date in the future at a price agreed today.'

'I couldn't have put it better,' said Martyn.

'You could have put it as well,' said Billy.

'Let's move on gentlemen,' I said. 'How does that help the Laundryman wash through comodities?' They all looked at me as if I was being disingenuous. 'For the sake of this discussion,' I added, foolishly.

'A futures contract is a zero sum game,' said Martyn. 'That is, for every seller there is a buyer. The broker in whose name the transaction is registered charges a commission. The Laundryman uses the futures exchange by being on both sides of a single transaction and liquidating both positions before the contract expires. Dirty money in, buying a futures contract to liquidate his first position; clean money out, selling the other side of the same futures contract to liquidate his second position. The perfect wash.'

Almost perfect, I thought.

'So the Laundryman could be a commodities futures trader,' said BB.

'Or a metal futures trader, or financial futures trader, or a broker, or a lawyer, or a banker, or an accountant, or a tax consultant, or an independent financial advisor, or any damn thing,' said Martyn, tired and under strain.

'Or a casino owner,' said BB. 'I like that one.'

Suddenly the drawing room door swung open. My guests turned expecting, I thought, to see Julianna, but I knew she would have knocked. I was gripped by fear: another arrest, another search, another police cell. The fear was irrational (how would they have got into the house?), but my pulse raced and my stomach turned over. My relief, however, was immediate. Dressed in one of my own white shirts, the sleeves rolled up, the tails tucked into the small waist of her tight jeans, entered Tania. 'Hi Sis,' said BB.

Tania walked over to me and I stood up to greet her. She held the attention of the room. Her confidence was total. I drank in her sheer physical beauty. Emotionally, I was under her spell and she knew it. 'I've come to join the Brains Trust,' she announced.

'No way,' said Martyn.

BB moved himself forward so that he appeared to perch on the edge of the sofa. He raised his hand, palm open, and tilted his neck slightly to the right. His face took on a puzzled expression, but there was no hiding the menace. 'Why not?' he asked.

'Because it would not be appropriate,' Martyn replied.

'Stu,' purred Tania, 'you're in charge. Can I join the Brains Trust?'

'Stu?' said Anita. 'Who the hell's Stu?'

'Tania calls me Stu,' I said softly.

'Well tell her to stop it,' said Anita.

'Tania,' I said.

'Yes Stu,' she replied, looking at Anita.

'Let's discuss this later.'

Tania picked up my glass of Chablis, now half full. 'Is this yours?' she asked.

'Yes,' I said.

She raised the glass to her lips and without taking her eyes off mine took a long slow sip of my wine. I grew hot, and hard. She put the glass back in my hand. 'Later,' she said and walked to the door. I raised the glass to my lips in a silent toast to my love and drank the rest of the wine.

'You were saying DC Clarke,' said Anita in a frosty tone.

'Yes,' he replied but he'd lost his train of thought. He paused. 'Yes,' he said again, as a holding measure.

'What happens after the wash?' said Anita sharply.

'Right,' said Martyn grateful for the prompt, if not the manner of its delivery. 'After the wash the Laundryman needs to deliver the clean money to his customers. This is not as simple as it sounds. He must deliver the money in such a way that his clients have a perfect answer to any questions pertaining to how they finance their lifestyle. You see, it is often the case that we arrest traffickers who have little or no contact with the drugs sold under their direction. We secure convictions based on their associations with others who have been convicted and having the jury draw an inference that their lifestyles could not be financed in any other way.'

'OK,' said BB, his earlier anger subsiding, 'give me an example of a clean delivery.'

'Profits from trading activities are best, but a clean delivery would also include loans from UK or overseas banks, legacies, verifiable betting winnings, gains on the sale of capital assets, things like that. The key thing is that when we start to push at the explanation, it has legs. Everything the Laundryman does has legs.'

'So how do we catch him?' I asked.

'You said you knew how,' reprimanded Martyn. 'Something about a financial mirage.'

'I know how I would do it.' I replied. 'But this is a brainstorming session. I am interested in how each of you would catch him.'

'Well, you can count me out,' said Martyn. 'We've been looking for him for years. Some of us think we've already found him.' He looked at me with wry amusement. I thought for a moment that he too had not fully made up his mind.

'I know how I would do it,' said BB. We all turned to him. 'It's easy. Look, the drug traffickers found him didn't they? We just have to think like them.'

Now we were moving. 'Go on,' I encouraged.

'Right, I've got 100 kilos of coke. After I've cut it with some bicarbonate of soda and cooked it a little I've got an asset with a street value of £15 million. Now everybody's got to take a cut, the mules, the safe houses, street sellers etc. OK, I end up with say £5 million in cash. I could get more but I'm a generous guy. A happy worker is a loyal worker, am I right?'

'You seem to know a lot about this,' interjected Martyn. To be fair even I was getting a little worried.

'I watch TV, OK,' was BB's quickfire response. 'Fine, this process takes three months, and my supply is reliable, so I know I'm on £20 million in a year. I've got a problem. What do I do with the cash? Who can I talk to?'

'Great,' I said. 'Who would you talk to BB?'

The enthusiasm waned and BB seemed suddenly sheepish. In a tone dripping with apology, he said, 'I'd talk to you Andrew.'

'Me too,' said Billy.

'And me,' said Martyn.

Anita just looked at me and smiled. She'd seen it coming.

'But I couldn't help any of you,' I remonstrated.

'Maybe not,' said BB, 'but I bet a dollar to a dime that you'd know a man who could.'

'If your analysis is correct BB, please explain to me why I do not get a stream of drug barons knocking on my door.'

'Easy again,' said BB. 'They do not know you exist. I do, which is why I would go to you but they don't, so they wouldn't.'

It was a fair point. 'Fine,' I said. 'If you didn't know me BB where would you go with your wheelbarrow full of cash?'

After some hesitation, BB glanced across at Martyn. 'I'd rather not say. I don't want some unsuspecting brother to get a knock on his door tonight.'

'It was all right for me though BB?' I retorted.

'You can look after yourself,' he said.

134

I turned to Billy. 'And how would our ace defence lawyer find the Laundryman?'

'I'd take out an advert.'

'Billy,' I said, 'don't be daft.'

'I'd take out an advert,' he repeated with emphasis. 'It would read something like: investor with substantial portfolio previously in pharmaceutics, now mostly liquid, looking for asset manager for purposes of reinvestment in more diversified stocks and shares.'

'Where would you put this advert?' I asked incredulously.

'In the Financial Times. I know the Laundryman read the FT and I know DC Clarke and his colleagues do not. Even if they saw the advert they would not think there was anything suspicious about it. The Laundryman, however, would recognise it immediately.'

'Billy, be serious,' I implored.

'I am serious,' he replied. 'Do you have a better idea?'

Anita interrupted. 'I do,' she said

'Let's hear it,' said Billy.

'Well, my understanding is that the police know of the existence of the Laundryman because they have infiltrated cocaine cartels here in London. Is that right?'

'Yes,' said Martyn guardedly. 'Infiltrated, directly or indirectly,'

'So you know people, *directly or indirectly*, who know the Laundryman. Is *that* right?' Anita seemed to be mocking the off duty detective constable.

'We know of people engaged in drug trafficking who we have reason to believe have had contact with the individual known to us as the Laundryman.'

Anita removed her glasses and rubbed her eyes. She looked at Martyn with what must have been blurred vision. 'In other words, "yes"?' she asked.

'Yes,' he reluctantly replied.

'Good,' she said and replaced her glasses. 'Go get them, and torture them until they tell you who the Laundryman is.'

The room went silent. My interpretative skills were clearly required.

'What Anita is saying is this: would it not be an idea to round up two or more persons whom we believe have had contact with the Laundryman and interrogate them with such vigour that they would consider the whole exercise torture?'

'I mean nothing of the sort,' Anita said sharply. 'I mean torture them. Electrodes to the testicles, all that sort of thing. They'll soon tell you who the Laundryman is.' The room fell into an uneasy silence. 'What?' Anita asked, the sharpness of her tone becoming more acute. 'What?' She looked around the room, with increasing annoyance, focusing separately on each of us. Four men suddenly rendered mute. 'What?'

'It's against the law,' I said quietly.

'Oh, I see,' said Anita. 'Silly me. I thought you were serious. I thought you really wanted to catch him.'

Martyn was bushed. He stood up and stretched. 'I must make one thing absolutely clear,' he said. 'I may be off duty, but I remain a police officer. Should I become aware that your attempt to catch the Laundryman involves any criminal activity I will immediately inform my superiors, and recommend that one or more or all of you are prosecuted to the full limit of the law.'

Anita was scathing. 'This is why I don't like committees. Sooner or later everyone becomes preoccupied with protecting their position, or as my father used to say, covering their ass. Well, DC Clarke your comments have been read into the record. Can we move on?'

'No, the meeting's over for me. Just remember what I said Miss Hume, and the rest of you. I'm deadly serious.'

I rose too. 'I think the meeting's over for us all,' I said. 'I would like us all to meet the same time next week.' I stifled the protests. 'This has all been hugely valuable. Next week I will set out how we will catch the Laundryman,' I looked at Martyn, 'within the confines of the law.'

'Tell us now,' said Martyn.

'The man said next week,' said BB.

'It'll be worth the wait Martyn,' I promised. He nodded. Everyone was now standing. 'Anita,' I said, 'let me call you a cab.'

136

'I'll give her a lift,' said Billy.

Anita looked him up and down. 'I don't think so,' she said. 'Could you drop me at an underground station DC Clarke?'

'Of course,' he replied.

I showed Billy, Anita and Martyn out. BB held back. As I closed the front door, he said, 'Do you fancy a game Andrew?'

'Sure,' I replied.

BB quickly set up the board in the kitchen and took a beer from the fridge. I sat down, my mind only partially on the game. After brief opening moves, BB launched a ferocious attack on my king's side. He sacrificed a bishop to weaken my pawn defence. This, I thought, was a mistake. I could still defend my king adequately and my piece advantage would be critical in the end-game.

'Anita surprised me,' BB said as I paused to consider my move. 'She's a real hard ass. She also had a problem with Martyn Clarke. What was all that about?'

'Can't be certain,' I said. 'Her father, the man who presumably never "covered his ass," was an officer in the army. He fought in the Second World War. He was wounded and never fully recovered. He regaled her with war stories, of a time when he was whole. He died when she was fifteen. She never got over it. His photograph, in full uniform, is the only personal item on her desk at work.'

I moved and BB immediately brought his second knight into the attack. Some would call it a bold move. I considered it rash.

'Maybe,' he said, 'she sees a humble detective constable as one of the troops.'

'No, I don't think that's it. Anita never married. I think no one matched up to her idealised picture of her father. Her only social activity outside of the practice is her volunteer work for the Just In Case Veterans Homes. The Homes provide shelter and recreational activities for any veteran of World War II. There is no discrimination on the basis of rank, and if there were I do not think she would tolerate it.'

I moved my king out of harms way and BB brought his rook into play.

'You're not suggesting that Anita disapproves of discrimination, surely. Did you see how she looked at Billy when she turned down his offer of a lift.'

'Yes, the look was scornful, not because Billy's black, but because he drinks.'

'Then what has she got against Martyn?'

'I think he's just a little too cocksure for her taste. Young men, without the scars of battle, should not, in her opinion, hold any rank at all.'

BB started to involve his queen in his attack. I continued to maintain a strong defence.

'Did you have to throw my little sister out of the meeting?' he asked softly.

'Yes,' I replied, without looking up.

I won the game, as I thought I would. When BB's attack collapsed he did not have the pieces or the formation to resist my assault. We shook hands and he saw himself out. The day was over and I was restless. I poured myself a large whiskey and drank it quickly, feeling the warmth flow into my stomach and I immediately felt heady. How, I thought, does Billy drink bottle after bottle of this stuff without any effect? I turned off the kitchen lights and went to bed. As I was drifting off to sleep I heard a faint tapping on my door. 'It's me.' Julianna. She had the loudest whisper in the world.

'It's not locked,' I said, switching on the bedside light, 'come in.'

She entered wearing her thick towelling dressing gown. She swiftly untied the matching belt and let the gown fall to the floor. Naked, she moved to the far side of the bed, her heavy breasts swaying. She didn't pull back the covers; she tunnelled under them head first, like a sexual mole, and, finding her prey, she devoured it. When she emerged from the covers, smiling and wiping her lips with the back of her hand, she put her fingers in my mouth. They tasted of her. 'We both came together,' she said and snuggled up to me closely. The body warmth, sexual release and, I suppose, the wine and the whiskey, gave me a light-headed contentment, and sleep came easily.

138

I woke with a start at 3:00am and shook Julianna. 'What's the matter?' she asked.

'You've got to go to your room.'

'Why?'

'We're not alone in the house.'

'You mean Tania,' she said as she sat up.

'Yes, Tania.'

'I don't like Tania,' she said, begrudgingly getting out of bed.

'Why not?'

'She's dodgy.' With that Julianna picked up her dressing gown from the floor, tightly tied the belt, and left my bedroom firmly closing the door behind her.

The following morning was fraught with tension. Julianna had made scrambled eggs for breakfast and Tania was not impressed. I was sitting at the breakfast bar with Tania. Julianna was busy doing what housekeepers do, cooking, serving, clearing and tidying up. 'How was this cooked?' asked Tania.

'I don't know,' I replied, 'ask Julianna.'

'Julianna, how were these eggs cooked?'

I knew there was going to be trouble, and that it had nothing to do with the eggs. This was a power play. Tania wished to assert her authority. She now considered herself the woman of the house, and considered Julianna to be staff. I felt considerable apprehension. Julianna did not know that I loved Tania and wanted her in my life forever. Tania didn't know that I slept with Julianna. I wanted to be somewhere else.

'They are eggs,' Julianna replied, 'scrambled.'

'Scambled with what?' asked Tania.

'A little water.'

'Water? Not milk? Milk would make them creamy, not this runny yellow stuff you've served up.'

'Dr Stuart likes them as I serve them, don't you sir?' said Julianna with ice in her voice.

'Perhaps,' I said, aiming for conciliation, but, I feared, sounding weak, 'perhaps we could try a little milk next time, if that's how Tania likes them.'

'OK,' said Julianna, 'you must tell me how Tania likes everything, and we could try a little of it next time.' The reference, I was sure, was sexual. This, I hoped, passed Tania by. Julianna looked at me. Her eyes said, "Are you sure?" Had it not been Sunday I would have excused myself, grabbed my briefcase and headed for the office. I remained in my seat fearing the worst. I was not disappointed.

'You'd better get used to me, Julianna,' said Tania. 'I'm not your typical houseguest. Stu and I are romantically involved. These are early days, but I intend to make changes. I want to make his life better. I think that too many people are taking advantage of his good nature. Both he and I are going through difficult times, but that is no reason to let standards slip. With his permission,' she looked at me and smiled, 'I'll be taking over the running of the house, and that includes the kitchen. And from today eggs will be scrambled with milk.'

'If you are not a typical houseguest,' countered Julianna, 'how come you sleep in the guestroom and I –'

'That's enough!' I said. 'Tania, let's take things a little more slowly. Julianna, I will not tolerate rudeness. I want to be clear here. One word out of place and it's curtains. This conversation is at an end.' We ate our scrambled eggs in silence. After a decent interval I announced, 'I have to go into the office.'

'It's Sunday,' Tania and Julianna replied in unison.

'I know,' I said. 'No rest for the wicked.'

But I didn't go to my office. I went to a bedsit in Shepherd's Bush.

140

Chapter 8

From the time I decided to catch the Laundryman I knew I had to go to Shepherd's Bush. I took the underground. I always take the train to Shepherd's Bush. It wouldn't be right to drive. I had to be in the right mindset. Twelve year olds don't drive. I got off the train and walked to Goldhawk Road. I stopped at the familiar house, walked up the crumbling steps and put my key in the lock. Once inside I faced a number of locked doors, each a bedsit, and I descended the stairs to mine in the basement. The corridor smelt of cooked Caribbean food, jerk chicken mingling with curried goat. Things were improving. The dumplings from my childhood carried no smell at all.

I unlocked the door and entered my room. Minimal furniture. Minimal, not minimalist. There was no art to it. The room contained the furniture we could afford. I had preserved the room as best I could. This was not the original furniture, but it closely resembled that of my childhood. My prize acquisition was the paraffin heater. Such a heater had kept us warm when we couldn't afford the money for the meter. And we could cook on the paraffin heater too. We cooked dumplings. We needed only flour, water and salt. I never talk about my childhood. It's nobody's business. I come here not to reminisce; there is no nostalgia. This was the place where I first learnt to dream. I would sit and dream with an intensity that induced physical pain, and my dreams had come true.

When I was troubled, this is where I would come. It was not quiet, it was not calm, but here I could regress and capture that space that linked me to the infinite dimension of universal intelligence. Here I could find that door through which I had once passed to create a future far beyond the circumstances of my birth. Usually, I would come here when my office had failed me. Sometimes it was to unravel an abstruse point of revenue law.

Occasionally a personal problem would require some attention. Today, I came in search of the Laundryman.

I sat on my straight back chair in the corner of the room and remembered the familiar noises of my childhood. My mother yelling at me for things I had not done, the raised voices of her ever-changing boyfriends. My mother yelling at those men for things they had done, things that a son should know nothing about. I remembered the noise of my neighbours, all West Indian, reggae music, the smash of dominos on rickety tables, babies crying, the quiet moaning of rhythmical sex, and the dull thudding of domestic violence. I sat and smelt the seductive aroma of marijuana, insufficiently pungent to mask the stench of the damp and rot in our room, our home.

And as I sat the door opened to the land of infinite possibilities, and I slept and I dreamed. I slept and dreamed for hours. I awoke emotionally and physically drained; intellectually, however, I was satisfied. The Laundryman: I did not know who he was and I did not know where he was, but I knew how I would catch him.

Monday morning I was back in my office and wholly without focus. I asked Anita to hold all my calls, no downtime. The files of the work scheduled for the day sat on my desk untouched, and time moved forward very slowly.

I have this thing about time. I believe I can make time stand still. When I have an important project that must be completed under an impossible deadline, I work through the night. But first I cover all the clocks and put my Rado wristwatch in the drawer out of the way. I turn off all the lights, and delete the time bar on the computer screen. The telephone system is switched to voice mail. I am left with the glow of the VDU in a dark, timeless environment. And I enter the zone and work until the project is finished. When I emerge from this cocoon and re-enter the normal world of petty demands, tired eyes, lower back pains and toilet breaks, time has hardly moved. More precisely, time has moved but only slowly. Say twelve hours work has been completed in four. I meet my deadlines every time.

I once made the mistake of mentioning this phenomenon to BB. He told me that if I really stopped time wouldn't it be more fun if I didn't cover the clocks so that I could see time slow down before my very eyes. Think about how slow the second hand would go round. He laughed out loud. 'You could videotape it,' he said, 'and send it in to those TV programmes. I hear they pay £100 per tape.' He was enjoying himself but, seeing my discomfort, he put his arm around my shoulder good-naturedly. 'Andrew,' he said, 'time doesn't slow down. You just work faster in the dark.' Time had slowed down this morning though; perhaps, I thought, I should give him a call.

Anita knocked on my door. She wasted no time getting to the point. 'This has got to stop.'

'What?'

'You're not working, and I can tell that you're not going to work. Not today, not tomorrow, not all week. Don't ask me how I know, I just know. It's in your demeanour, your voice, your actions. Now listen to me, and listen good. Bad news travels ten times faster than good news. You've been arrested. Given the profile of our clientele, some clients will know that already. The rumour mills are grinding out stories, helped no doubt by your competitors. You can't stop that. But you can let your clients see that it's business as usual. You can take their calls, or at least return them. You can do their work. Anything else will confirm their worst fears. You'll be seen as damaged goods and they will walk, one by one.' I tried to interrupt her, but I'd have had more success trying to interrupt Margaret Thatcher in her prime. 'Do you know who called this morning? Sheikh Khalifa. I told him you were not available. What do you think he's thinking? Are you going to let him down while you alternate between hiding under your desk and chasing after a brown-skinned dolly bird? Stu, indeed! What's the matter with you?'

'Anita –'

'In life we have choices. You've always impressed me Andrew, but now you're making bad choices. All round. This Laundryman, for instance, why do you have to find him? That's the job of the police. Why give yourself an impossible task?'

'It's not impossible,' I said.

'Then how on earth are you going to do it?'

I did not tell her of my trip to Shepherds Bush, or my communing with the forces of universal intelligence. That would have received very short shrift from Anita. But I did lay out my plans in detail. When I had finished I asked her, 'What do you think?'

Anita paused for a long time. Finally she said, 'I like it.'

'Good. I'll put it to the Brains Trust on Saturday.'

'No,' she said, 'the sooner the better. Let's all meet tonight. I'll arrange it.' She got up to leave.

'And Anita,' I said.

'Yes Andrew.'

'Don't you ever refer to Tania like that again.' She bristled, muttered a muted apology and left.

How Anita got everyone together at such short notice, I do not know. But they all came: Martyn, Billy, BB and, of course Anita herself. Julianna had laid out another spread of sandwiches and proceeded to serve the drinks. Everyone, in a curious demonstration of the human need for consistency, sat in the same places as before. Except me. I chose the third armchair instead of the ridiculous thick chenille stool. Tania, I assumed, was in her room. 'Gentleman,' I said, 'Anita and I have a plan.'

'We all have plans,' said Billy generously pouring his first glass of the evening.

'Yes,' I said, 'but the essential difference between my plan and your plans is this: you are all going in search of the Laundryman; I will wait for the Laundryman to come to me. You see, you all want to identify him at the cash stage. It makes sense of course. This is the most difficult stage, when he is at his most vulnerable. But it is also the stage when he is most alert. I want to identify him when he is more relaxed. After he has deposited his cash and he enters the market for the latest offshore financial vehicle, the cutting edge one, the one with bells on, the financial equivalent of the Maserati. I will design it personally. I will call it the Mycroft plan. When the Laundryman buys it I will know him because he will buy it from me.'

'And how will he know this Mycroft scheme exists?' asked Martyn.

'Good question,' said Billy. 'He'll have to advertise it in the FT. This is just another version of my own suggestion. You could give me some credit Andrew.'

'No credit is due,' I said. I leaned back in my chair, comfortable at last. This was my domain. 'The marketing of offshore tax minimisation schemes is an arcane art. There are no press releases, no launch parties and certainly no advertisements. The process is a gentle one: a discrete word with a city solicitor here, or a chartered accountant there. There is the obligatory round of dinners at banks, of course. Quiet references are made to the product in the gentlemen's clubs where the great and the good congregate, the old money. A little more noise is needed at the high profile music and sporting events favoured by the nouvelle riche. I call this the placing. If the product is cleverly placed, people feel privileged to have the information. It soon becomes the essential secret that just has to be shared. And when the process is done everyone who needs to know knows. They know whom, they know where and they know how much.'

When the gathering was over I went upstairs to see Tania. I was conscious that she felt she had been unfairly excluded from the Brains Trust and I wanted to make it up to her. Music with a disco beat flowed from her room. I knocked on the door. 'Who is it?' she shouted over the music.

'It's me,' I hollered back.

'Music too loud?'

'No, can I come in?'

'Sure.'

Tania was standing with her arms outstretched, turning her torso to the right and the left. She was wearing a red leotard, which revealed every curve of her body. Her matching headband was damp with perspiration.

'I'm working on my tum, thighs and bum,' she said. She grabbed a towel, placed it around her neck and walked over to the hi-fi and turned the volume down. 'Meeting over?'

'Yes,' I said.

'Are you any closer to catching him?'

'I think so.'

'But you don't need my help, right?' Tania sat down on the bed, removed her headband and ran the towel over her face.

'Of course I need your help, just not in those meetings. You're far more valuable to me one on one.'

'Flatterer,' she said. 'What do you want?'

'I would like to take you to the opera.'

'On a date?'

'Yes.'

'So ask me.'

'Ms Tania Berkeley, will you accompany me to the opera this weekend on a date?'

'Of course, if it will make you happy I'll go.'

'Excellent,' I said. 'I have tickets for The Pearl Fishers.'

'What's it about?' she asked.

'It's about two men, two close friends, who fall for the same woman.'

'So it's about true love.'

'And danger and jealousy.' I said. 'It's written by Georges Bizet, the same man who wrote Carmen. You've heard of Carmen?'

'Who hasn't?' she said, but her reply sounded too glib.

'You do like the opera?' I asked.

Tania stood up and rubbed the towel over the back of her legs and then, taking a deliciously long time, slowly dabbed the inside of her thighs. I waited for her answer. 'No,' she said.

'But you said you would be happy to go.'

'I said I would be happy to go if it made you happy. There is a difference.'

'Where would you like to go?'

146

'To an R& B concert, but would that make you happy?'

It would not have been my ideal choice. 'Can we meet somewhere in the middle?'

'Like where?'

'At a musical perhaps?'

'Keep going.'

'Les Misérables?'

'Tell me about it.'

'It's a very popular musical based on Victor Hugo's novel. There are many plots and subplots. In essence a zealous police officer called Javert pursues a prisoner called Jean Valjean, but many more issues are raised involving love, honour, cruelty and redemption.'

'Not unlike our own lives then?'

'True, but it's set in 19th century France.'

'I'll give it a go. Can you get tickets?'

'Always,' I said.

The following morning I sat at my desk in my office. Directly in front of me was my keyboard and PC, my laser printer was on my right. A neat vertical, narrow handmade mahogany tower rack rested on the floor to my left. It held the CDs which contained the transcripts of every tax case, statute, revenue ruling and double taxation treaty relevant to my work. In book form they would fill a large library. My Mont Blanc pen lay on a plain writing pad which sported the small AJS logo in the top left hand corner. That was it. The screen was on, the pad was blank and I was prepared for work.

I was ready to create the Mycroft plan. The objective was impenetrability. I decided to start with a simple offshore trust. A trust is a thing of beauty. At its essence lies the separation of the legal ownership of property from the power to enjoy that property. It is part of the rich English common law tradition, originally used to protect family wealth. In short, it is a way of having something that no one can take away. I don't explain the detailed operation of a trust to all my clients. One has to judge the degree of detail the client can handle. This is particularly pertinent to sportspeo ple and entertainers. If I start a sentence like, "As the beneficiary of thi offshore discretionary settlement," and I see the client's eyes glaze over, keep it very short.

Next I sprinkled around some European offshore companies, using th jurisdictions of Luxembourg, Monaco and my trusty old standby, the Isle o Man. These I married to Caribbean offshore companies, incorporated i Bermuda, the Netherlands Antilles and the British Virgin Islands. Some o these companies were in a group; that is, where A owned B who owned C some were in a consortium, say, where A, B and C owned D.

Next I needed to build in what I called the title tango, a dance wit names. At a fixed point in time all the companies in the group or consor tium would change their names or, more accurately, they would swa names. So, put simply, Red Limited would change its name to Blu Limited and Blue Limited would change its name to Red Limited; Gree Limited would change its name to Pink Limited and Pink Limited woul change its name to Green Limited and so on. The underlying companies their purpose, assets and liabilities remained the same. Only the name changed. The unique identifying factor of a company is not its name, it i its registration number. So the title tango really alters nothing. It jus makes it rather difficult for the uninitiated to follow, particularly if one titl tangos with different partners every month. What is crucial is that the relat ed paperwork is faultless and the timing impeccable.

I always found that the title tango worked particularly well with corpo rate cloning. This involved creating companies with the same name. It i true, of course, that no two UK companies can have the same name. The Registrar would not permit it. However, one could have, say, one Orange Limited incorporated in the UK, another Orange Limited incorporated in Belize, another in Hong Kong and yet another in the Turks and Caicos same name, but different companies.

This was all good, but fairly standard for A J Stuart & Co. The Mycrof plan required something special. I had just closed my eyes to picture the complex matrix of offshore companies and trusts when the internal line buzzed.

'It's Lightning,' said Anita. 'He says it's very important.'

I was surprised. It was very unlikely that he would want to talk to me about his tax affairs. Once the concept of an international tax plan had been sold to a client like Lightning, let us say one of the less technically sophisticated clients, I am left to get on with it. The fees had been agreed, fifty percent paid in advance. I was at a loss.

'Lightning,' I said. 'Talk to me.'

'Talk, sure, I'll talk. The police have just left.'

What trouble, I thought, had Lightning got himself into now. 'I'll help in whatever way I can,' I said, 'but you'll probably need a criminal lawyer.' I thought of Billy. 'I can recommend someone good. What are the issues involved?'

'The issues are you.'

'I don't understand.'

'They came to talk about you, man. Two of them, in plain clothes: an old fart and his mate.' DS Greenley and DC Clarke, I thought. 'They said you'd been arrested and charged with money laundering relating to drug trafficking. They wanted to know if you were a pukka businessman. They said you were in real trouble. They suggested,' he said mimicking Greenley, 'that in the circumstances it might be wise if I found another firm to represent me.'

'What did you say?'

'I told them to fuck off. Then they got heavy. They said,' he mimicked again, 'that my attitude led them to conclude that I was probably implicated in the conspiracy and that they would now investigate me too. I don't need no investigation Dr Stuart. What's going on?'

'It's not a bad as it appears,' I lied.

'Yes it is. It's one thing for the police to hassle me. They've been doing it for years. But when they start on the likes of you, a white, middle class, professional badass, then I start to get worried, and I don't worry easily. I'm on your side Dr Stuart. I might be able to help you. Tell me all about it and don't leave nothing out.'

It was an honest offer of help from a man I knew only as a client. I a
normally very guarded about my personal life, but Lightning had caught m
at a time when I was both vulnerable and very tired. Maybe he could hel
I started to recount the tale starting with the call from Tania, leaving out th
fact that I was in bed with Julianna at the time.

'So you're hunting the Laundryman.'

'That's right. Have you heard of him?'

'Nope, but I'll find out who has.'

'How will you do that?'

'By rap. I'll call you later. I need to select some samples.'

I returned to the Mycroft plan. I now had a range of vehicles, each wit
professional directors, trustees or partners, each with interlocking owne
ships. I had mixed them up. Some companies were serving as trustee
some of the trusts owned some of the companies. It got better. Some of th
trusts can operate like companies and some companies were effectivel
trusts. There were limited partnerships too, and a couple of joint venture
thrown in.

I had allocated a designated bank for each entity. I held account oper
ing forms for over 100 international banks at my office. These had bee
built up over the years. I had visited each bank, met with the principa
executives and supplied references on myself and A J Stuart & Co, usuall
from other financial institutions and sometimes the university. The bank
over time, relied on their due process of me to open accounts for my client
without, initially at least, any due process of them. This was invaluable t
me. It meant I could implement my structures with the minimum of delay

When a client buys one of my tax minimization or asset protection plan
he is purchasing not only the offshore vehicles that make up the structur
and the related banking facilities, he is also buying speed. He is purchas
ing the time of an entire network of professionals in offices around th
world. He is buying all the paperwork necessary to enact the transactions
and the exquisite timing of the same. He is purchasing the execution of th
title tangos, corporate cloning and other benevolent mischief. Most of al
he is buying the intellectual and technical aptitude and the creative thinkin

behind the plan. He is buying me, and my reputation.

That is why I sat at my desk dissatisfied. The Mycroft plan wasn't good enough. I spent hours refining the intricate edifice, but there was still something missing.

I was still searching for that elusive feature late the following morning, when Anita buzzed me.

'Lightning again,' she said with a hint of exasperation.

'Dr Stuart, you've got to come down to the studios, man, I've done it.'

'I'm very busy Lightning. Done what?'

'I'm going to lay down a track and put it out to the clubs.'

'You want my artistic approval?' I said.

'No, I just want you to listen man.'

'Why?'

'It's about the Laundryman.'

'Where are you?' He gave me the address and directions. 'I'll be right over.'

I took my jacket from the hanger, went down the stairs and headed for the door.

'Why are you going?' asked Anita.

'I'm going to Lightning's recording studio. He has, to use his words, laid down a track, about the Laundryman.'

Anita was unimpressed. 'I've scheduled out your work for today. It was difficult enough accommodating this Mycroft plan, without you running off to listen to rap music. You have clients, Andrew. They are depending on you. You have to stick to the schedule or no proper, professional work is going to get done. Forgive me but I think you should be upstairs working. Get Lightning to send you a tape or CD of the track. You can probably have it by tomorrow.'

'You don't understand,' I said. 'I'm going over there to stop him.'

When I arrived at the studio I was shown into one of the lounges by a pretty teenage girl dressed in designer casual wear. I said that I was there at Lightning's personal invitation and she went to check. The room was yellow and bathed in light. From speakers recessed into the wall aggressive rap music pumped out at some volume. The furniture was attractive but lacking comfort. This was no place for the slow or the sleepy.

The door opened and a young bearded man in a white T-shirt and denim entered and announced that he was one of the engineers. He led me into the control room. Through large thick panelled glass I could see Lightning, alone in the adjoining recording studio. When he saw me he waved and spoke into a microphone. His voice, amplified, bounced off the control room walls.

'Dr Stuart, you're gonna love this.' He put on his headphones. 'Ready man. Here goes.' Music flooded into the control room, an insistent beat overlaid with a short repeated melody. The music was catchy; repetitive, but melodious. It sounded good. Then came the words. *'They want to kill the niggers/ They want to kill us all.'* The beat became more dominant and Lightning hit his stride. *'On a dark cold night/They arrest twenty-four of us/ Hunting for the fox/That they call the Laundryman./ Is the Laundryman a nigger?/ No, he's a white man/ A motherfucking colonel/All part of a scam/ To take the money from the ghetto/ That's the motherfucking plan/All the niggers hand their money/ To the fucking Laundryman.'* Jesus Christ. I looked around. No one shared my horror. As I moved toward the glass, the engineer put a friendly but restraining hand on my shoulder.

'They arrest a tax consultant/ He's my motherfucking man/Beating down the doors of Babylon/Working all he can/Tax he says is wickedness/He's smarter than the rest/ He screws the Queen of England and the IRS.' No, please God, no.

'Listen up my brothers/Listen up real good/There's a man called Greenley/Loose in the hood/He'll bust up on your business/He's busting up the town/ And if you don't move fast/ You'll end up going down/ If you don't move quick/ Ten years of sucking dick.'

The short melody returned. It was faintly recognisable. Lightning had sampled well. The music was so at odds with the lyrics that the effect was both jarring and enticing. Pornography as art. There was more.

'Greenley is a pussy/So is the Laundryman/Let them fight it out together/ It's time that we ran/ Our businesses together/Black on black – you

know we can/And our first fucking move?/ Give up the Laundryman. Give him up, give him up, give up the Laundryman.'

The melody returned and faded out. As those in the control room were congratulating themselves, Lightning walked in grinning, headphone round his neck. 'What do you think?' Lightning asked me eagerly. It was clear that the others thought it was great. 'I know it needs some work,' he continued. 'But I like it. It's relevant, you know. It's now.'

I took a deep breath. 'You're not going to record that song, Lightning. It's libellous.'

'Of course it's libellous,' he replied. 'All rap is libellous. Rap hits hard. It hits you where you live. I've been waiting for an issue, you know. Enough of bitches and guns. I'm moving into new territory now. Social comment. A call to arms. Revolution.'

'First,' I said, 'I don't think any record company would release it. Secondly, if one did you would find yourself arrested on some pretext or the other. Thirdly, if it was released and you were not arrested, I would probably sue you myself.'

'OK, let's see. One, it will be released. Two, any arrest would only boost sales. And three, I don't believe that you'd sue me. You'd only draw attention to yourself and you'd look ungrateful. Remember, I'm trying to help you man.'

'Not like this.'

'Yeah, just like this. This is what I do. You want to catch the Laundryman, right? You do it your way and I'll do it my way. We'll catch him Dr Stuart. Just wait and see. Gotta go.' He turned towards the door.

'Just one thing,' I said. 'If you go ahead, how long would it take for this thing to get radio play?'

'Maybe one or two months,' he said and left. I was grateful for small mercies. I checked my watch. It hadn't taken so long. If I got a taxi right away I would have been out of the office for just under an hour. I could save Anita from rescheduling.

The engineer was between me and the door. 'Excuse me,' I said.

'Sure,' he replied, moving aside. 'Tell me, why did you ask Lightning about the release date?'

'I just wanted to know how long it would be before people actually heard the track.'

'Then, my friend, that is what you should have asked him.' I was halfway through the doorway. I turned around. He continued, 'The release of the single would normally trigger radio play. That may not be for one or two months, but the white label will be playing in the clubs within the week.'

I stood still in the doorway as the small mercies, for which I had been so grateful, floated away.

Anita was pleased that I had returned so soon, though she didn't say anything. She just handed me the pink slips on which she records the phone messages. I flicked through them, handed them back and went straight to my office. I looked at the Mycroft matrix on the computer screen and, as so often happens after a break, knew immediately what was wrong. The matrix, though full of labyrinthine complexity, remained penetrable. I needed a change, at the very top of the structure.

I decided I would use the Anstalt. Known only to the cognoscenti of finance, it was the black hole of asset protection. The Anstalt was unique to the Principality of Liechtenstein. It had no members, no participants and no shareholders. It was, in essence, the corporate embodiment of the rights of its founder. It was like a charity with no charitable purposes. Under the laws of Liechtenstein an Anstalt could conduct businesses of any kind, engage in non-trading activities and, best of all, serve as a passive holding company for businesses anywhere around the globe. There was no obligation to reveal the beneficial ownership of an Anstalt to any regulatory authority in Liechtenstein or anywhere else. Moreover, as a passive holding company, the Anstalt did not need to file profit and loss accounts. The Anstalt was the perfect body into which would disappear all of the strands of multiple and separate ownership of the varied offshore vehicles in the Mycroft complex. It was the most secret and secure offshore entity in the world.

Anita was right. The Mycroft plan had consumed all my energies, causing me to leave client work untouched. I needed to put it to bed. I resolved to work through the night. When it got to 8:00pm I covered all the clocks, put my wristwatch in the drawer and deleted the time bar on the computer screen. I turned off all the lights, leaving me with the glow of the VDU in a dark, timeless environment. And I entered the zone where time stood still. The Mycroft plan was completed by daybreak.

I got home just before 6:30 am. I went to bed, feeling mentally and physically exhausted, having first set the alarm for 12 noon. My plan was to be at the university for a 2:00 pm meeting with the Dean of the Law School and then travel back to the office in the mid-afternoon. I fell into a deep sleep and dreamt disturbingly of Tania and Julianna wrestling in a huge auditorium in front of a violently baying crowd. They were both naked. Several times I tried to get into the ring to stop the fight but on each occasion I was pushed back by guards dressed in prison uniforms. I was about to make one last determined foray when my dream was shattered by the ringing of the telephone. Rolling over to my side, I reached for the phone and without sitting up, put the receiver to my ear. 'Hello.'

'Andrew, it's Anita. I'm sorry to disturb you. I know you stopped time last night. It's just that Detective Sergeant Greenley's been on the phone. He wants to see you this morning at the office.'

'Why?'

'It's not good news. He wants to talk to you about the green files.'

'The tax consultancy files. He doesn't know they exist.' They remained securely stored behind the false wall, along with the archived tapes.

'Apparently, he does.'

I felt my stomach tighten with fear. If he knew of the files he would know that I had been less than honest with him during the search. I was certain these files had nothing to do with the criminal case. I just did not want them in the public arena. The taxing authorities would have a feast. 'This is very disturbing.'

'I know.'

'OK, let's move it forward. I'll shower and come in. Anything else?'

'Yes, he said he also wants to talk to you about P and M. He said you would know what he meant.'

'I do.'

'Don't do it Andrew.'

'Don't do what?'

'P and M.'

'What are you talking about?'

'Plea and mitigation, that's what P and M stands for isn't it? We worked together a long time, and shared everything. Don't hold out on me now. We'll fight this thing together.'

'When did Greenley call?'

'Nine o' clock on the button.'

I looked at the clock. It was 9:50. 'And for the better part of an hour you've been fretting because you think I may have cracked up, and looked for a deal with the police. Anita, if I were ever thinking of throwing in the towel you'd be the first to know.' And I realised at once that that's what I should have done in the dream. Instead of trying to climb into the ring, I should have thrown in the towel.

'Then what does P and M stand for?'

'They are initials taken from the private files I kept only at my home, until the police seized them. They refer to an intensely private matter.' I remembered Martyn Clarke's words as he knelt down to bag up the files. *You have no privacy now.* 'If the police are interested in P and M, I need to talk to someone. I'll tell you all about them when I get to the office. I will need your wisdom and your guidance.'

Chapter 9

I arrived back at Wigmore Street at 11:15. DS Greenley was sitting in reception. 'Dr Stuart,' he said, rising, 'working half days?'

'No,' I said, 'full nights. Would you like to come up?'

'That's why I'm here.'

DS Greenley sat in the boardroom and sipped his coffee. He said nothing. I suppose he was hoping that I would fall into the empty space, and start defending myself before I had been accused. I decided to tackle the detective sergeant head on. 'I am here at your request. May we get on with it please?'

'I was just thinking,' said Greenley, 'coming into these offices, looking around this room, you have a lot to lose.'

He was right and I sensed danger. 'I am here in the spirit of co-operation. I do not wish to have a general conversation with you about what I may or may not have to lose. Ask me specific questions. I may choose to respond to them; I may not. My solicitor is a phone call away.'

'Let's not talk about solicitors at this point. You're an intelligent man. I'm going to give you some inside information about this meeting. Ready? For the purposes of evidence gathering it's virtually meaningless. It is not being taped and I do not have an officer with me to corroborate your answers. I am here because I am puzzled. You can enlighten me, and then I can decide how much further I wish to take this formally. Do you understand?'

'Yes.'

'Good, where would you like to start, with the green files or P and M?'

It was the choice from hell. 'The green files,' I said.

'Where are they?'

If one has something to protect the simple questions are the most difficult to answer. 'Your question,' I replied, 'presupposes that the green files exist.'

'Do they?'

'No.'

'What puzzles me is this. When we searched your personal office we seized the files that were on your desk. They related to the client you were working on at the time, Walter Charlton, better known as Lightning. There was a yellow file containing correspondence, an orange file containing tax documents and accounts, and a green file containing detailed tax planning notes. However, when I spoke to the officers who conducted the search of your filing room, they told me that the slings contained only yellow and orange files. So I ask you again, where are the clients' green files?'

'Let me put it this way. There are no green files that have any bearing on the criminal case that you are investigating.'

'Is there a green file for Giovanni Mazzinni?' He held up his hand to prevent me from answering. 'If there is please go and get it and give it to me. I'll wait here.' I didn't move from my seat. 'Right now the only client of yours that concerns me is Mazzinni. DC Clarke believes that you're not the Laundryman. He is working with you, unofficially of course, to catch the Laundryman. I do not want to get in the way. But if you get in my way I will crush you. I will contact every client you have and make their life a misery. Everyone's got something to hide, particularly I would suggest those who need your services. Am I getting through to you? You give me Mazzinni's green file or I shut you down. For good.'

'You've already started going to my clients,' I said.

'You mean Lightning? We went to see Lightning because he's a public nuisance. You gave us an excuse, that's all. We just wanted to shake him up.'

'Well,' I said, thinking of the forthcoming single which featured Greenley by name, 'you did that all right.'

'The file.'

'Before I see whether I have a green file for Mazzinni, I have a question for you, as we're talking informally and off the record. Was he one of those arrested as part of Operation Chalice?'

'No.'

'Why was his name on the Production Order?'

'I cannot tell you the nature of the evidence we have against him. But I can say that I am not interested in any legitimate tax planning scheme you may have set up for him. My sole concern is whether Mazzinni was involved in drug trafficking, or laundering the profits of the same, whether on his own, in conjunction with Tania Berkeley or yourself, whether separately or together. Now, and for the very last time, may I have his green file?'

'Yes,' I said. I left Greenley in the boardroom and as I made my way downstairs to instruct Anita, I heard Mazzinni's voice in my head. *I have heard it said that when you hide money God can't find it.* I returned to the boardroom with the file and handed it to Greenley.

'Thank you,' he said, 'shall we turn to P and M?'

'They,' I said, 'have nothing to do with anything.'

'You have gone to a lot of trouble to keep tabs on them. Who are they?'

'As if you haven't worked that out.'

'I want to hear it from you. Who is P and who is M?'

'P is Patsy Smith, you could call her my childhood sweetheart. M is Michael Smith, her son. And mine.'

'I'm going to have to interview them.'

'Please don't. You've read the reports. You know what M does. He has absolutely nothing to do with this case. To involve him, however tangentially, would damage him. Are you a father Detective Sergeant?'

'Two daughters.'

'Then I ask you, father to father, please leave my son out of this.'

'As father to father,' Greenley repeated and smirked. 'I saw my daughters when they got up this morning. When was the last time you saw your son?'

'I've never seen him.'

'Then you're asking bad father to good father and the answer is no. I am duty bound to see him, and Patsy. They may have information pertaining to the case.'

'Of course they don't. Patsy hasn't seen me in 23 years.'

'I need to satisfy myself of that, and other things.'

'Like what?'

'Do you support P and M?'

'Yes, well, indirectly. Some years ago I set up a trust fund for them.'

'I see. Another of your fanciful financial shenanigans.'

'No, a simple offshore trust.'

'Cayman, I suppose.'

'No, Jersey.' I said.

When Greenley left, I sat in my office staring at the phone. I knew I had to call Patsy to warn her of his visit. I had learned her number from the private detective reports, but I'd never called it. What do you say after 23 years, hi Patsy, it's Andrew? I nervously reached for the receiver and dialled.

'Hello.' Her voice was just as I remembered it.

'Hi Patsy, it's Andrew.'

'Andrew?' I could hear her smile. I could hear her beauty.

'Yes,' I said.

'The police have been here.'

'What?'

'A detective sergeant, Greenley his name was, came here yesterday and asked Michael and me questions about you. I'm glad you called. I was worried. What's going on?'

'I'm coming to see you. I'll tell you all about it then.'

'When will that be?'

'Soon,' I said. 'Goodbye Patsy and don't worry.'

I was enraged. I wanted to physically hurt Greenley. I wanted to smash his face. I dialled the Boys Club and told BB what had happened. 'So he tells me that he's going but he's already been! I thought we were being open. He deceived me. And for what? What did he gain? I just don't know why he did that.'

'I do,' said BB, 'he's playing with your mind.'

'But why lie?'

'All coppers lie. They lie, they cheat, they plant and they steal. You should know. You teach law.'

'I don't teach that.'

I feared that my anger and my lack of sleep were a bad mix for a meeting with the Dean of the Law School, who was infuriating at the best of times. I rang his secretary, Miss Keen, made my excuses, and re-booked the appointment for the following Monday. The intervening weekend proved to have been an interesting one for my students. As I made my way along the broad hallway towards the Dean's office, many of the students I passed seemed to be smiling at me. Others made an exaggerated gesture of getting out of my way. Something had changed. I thought of the grades I had awarded to the postgraduates on the revenue law option on the LLM course. I am a fairly generous marker, and was particularly so this year. The students were bright (no one took tax law as a soft option), the essays well thought out and some of the exams scripts were quite outstanding. But the marks had not yet been posted. The previous month I had won the staff student debate arguing against the motion that 'all tax planning schemes are intrinsically immoral'. It was good knock about stuff, but these events are forgotten almost as soon as they are over. It was something else. Up ahead I spied Marcus, black, insolent, arrogant and brilliant. Could have been the best student in his year, if only he had tightened up his writing style. As he walked toward me, in his affected ghetto gait, seeking out eye contact, though making no attempt to stop, I heard him rap sotto voce, 'They arrest a tax consultant/ He's my motherfucking man...' The students knew of my celebrity clientele, and they'd made a leap of faith. The record was out.

The Dean of the Law School was nearly sixty, though he looked ten years older. It was rumoured that he became head on the Buggin's turn principle. He had simply outlasted his colleagues. He taught company law and, I suppose, he was competent. But his accountancy skills were minimal, and given that accountancy was the language of business, I always considered this an unforgivable weakness. In my view he taught company law in an academic vacuum, giving credence to those critics who describe

161

academia as an ivory tower. I was not alone in my low opinion of Professor Givens. Law School Dean was largely an administrative position, and his administrative skills were worse than mine, which took some doing. I had heard it jokingly suggested that Miss Keen, the law department's fifty-five year old senior secretary should be made department head. It was not, in fact, such a bad idea.

It was Miss Keen who greeted me in the Dean's outer office. 'Professor Given's will be back in fifteen minutes Dr Stuart. Please take a seat.'

'I'd rather come back then,' I said. 'I've got a lot to do.'

'Take a seat, Dr Stuart,' she said firmly. 'It wouldn't do for you two to keep missing each other.' She moved back behind her desk. Miss Keen was my favourite person in the law department. Miss Keen, mind, not Ms, I made that mistake once, only once. I took a seat, as I had been told, and waited for Professor Givens.

After twenty minutes I pointedly looked at my watch and sighed heavily. When I looked up Miss Keen's eyes locked on mine. She didn't say anything; she didn't have to. It took all my will to refrain from saying sorry. Professor Givens arrived eight minutes later. Tall, thin, gangly and hesitant, he seemed apologetic without actually saying so. Books and folders under arms, he made his way to his office whist verbalising a stream a consciousness. 'Andrew, yes, well, yes, indeed, we must talk, come through, bad day, committees and all that, running late, well, yes, come through.'

I followed him into the office where he dumped the books and folders on the floor. Later he would look for one of these folders and be unable to find it. I knew this because he was never able to find anything. It was Miss Keen who created the order out of chaos, but usually not before he had had one of his "I can't find it" tantrums, during which he would literally wave his arms and stamp his feet. I had witnessed only two of these and each time I was reminded on the poem "Not Waving, But Drowning." Fortunately, it looked like he needed to refer to no papers for my meeting. 'We have a problem,' he said.

I thought of the record, but concluded quickly that it was highly unlikely that he had heard it. Marcus was one thing, Professor Givens was quite another. Never defend until you are accused. I waited.

'I've had a visit,' he said, 'from a Detective Inspector Greenfield.'

'Is that not Detective Sergeant Greenley?' I suggested.

'Might be,' he said and started patting the papers which covered his desk. 'He gave me a card.'

There was no point in allowing him the time to lift, shift and shuffle his papers until the card fell out. We'd have been there all day. Chances were he'd used it as a temporary bookmark in a tome since returned to the library, complete with the business card. 'What did he want?' I asked.

'He wanted to know all about you I'm afraid Andrew.' He was still patting his desk, but I felt this now had less to do with Greenley's card than avoiding eye contact. Without looking up he said, 'He told me you had been arrested for money laundering, that you are currently on police bail.'

'I see,' I said. I did not know where this was going but I knew I was not going to help it on its way.

'Where's that card, we need to make sure we're both talking about the same thing, wouldn't do if you're talking about one case and me quite another. Have you, er, been arrested for money laundering? Are you, er, on police bail?'

'Yes,' I said.

He looked up. 'Then it must be the same case then.'

'Quite so,' I said.

'Well, what have you got to say? You must appreciate the seriousness of this. You've placed this department in a very difficult position, the university even. Come on, say something, what have you got to say? This can't go on, we've got to do something. I could get Stephen on it I suppose.'

'Don't do that,' I said. Stephen Malt taught criminal law. He was a pure academic, fine on the niceties of mens rea and actus reus, but utterly divorced from the real world. On the list of people you would ring on being faced with a serious criminal charge he would rank just above Jonathan Aiken. Just.

'Then what do we do?'

'First,' I said, 'we need to determine what is at stake here. Do we need to do anything?'

'The issues, right, good point, what are the issues, or, as you put it what is at stake?' Slowly his administrative brain, which was a mess, gave way to his legal brain, which, if not first class, was certainly competent. 'I'll put it this way: is it acceptable for an individual who has been arrested for a serious financial crime to teach students international revenue law at a prestigious metropolitan university?'

I preferred him when he was rambling. 'I think,' I began, slowly, 'that there is a difference between an arrest and a charge, as there is between a charge and a conviction. To start at the furthest end of the spectrum, it would be unacceptable for a person convicted of a serious financial crime to teach revenue law, or anything else, at a prestigious metropolitan university, or anywhere else. To turn to the beginning of the spectrum, I don't think an arrest should have any effect whatsoever on a person's teaching position. I think only the middle of the spectrum poses a problem; that is, determining the correct course of action where a person has been charged with a serious crime, and is awaiting trial. That does not apply to me. I have only been arrested.'

'Oh Andrew, I was hoping you were not going to be difficult.'

'Do you disagree with my analysis?'

'It is too narrowly legalistic,' he said. 'From where I sit it is not enough to do the right thing, I must be seen to do the right thing. Caesar's wife and all that. If I let you continue to teach it would not look right. You might, er, consider resigning.'

'I will not resign,' I said.

'Then I'm sorry, but I feel I have to suspend you.'

'What about my research interests, access to the university library and the doctoral students I am supervising.'

'To be frank, I hadn't thought about that. Think about it for me Andrew. Present me with a paper justifying why I am prepared to allow those things. Something for me to tell governors should they ask.'

'Thank you,' I said.

'But the teaching is suspended as of today.' He returned to patting his desk. I got up to leave. 'One last thing Andrew, does this business have anything to do with that song?' he said.

Here we go, I thought. 'What song is that, Edward?'

'Well,' he said, shaking his head, 'I don't know. I haven't heard the thing, but I've been told that you feature in a song about this wretched Laundryman.'

I wanted to get away from the university as quickly as possible. I felt I had been profoundly wronged. As I walked briskly through the department Anton, a post-graduate law student, fell in step with me. Anton was in his late twenties, but looked older. His face was heavily pockmarked and his hair was thinning. He had a small frame, and his extra weight hung unkindly about his body. His chin had all but disappeared. Though of modest intellectual ability, Anton had the confidence of the affluent middle classes. His father was an eminent surgeon, though Anton preferred to see himself as self-made man, which he patently was not. This delusion was probably helped or induced by his well-known cocaine habit. 'I know who the Laundryman is,' he said to me.

I stopped. 'Who is he?'

'It's a secret,' he said and smiled.

I had just been relieved of my teaching responsibilities and there is an upside to everything. 'Fuck off Anton,' I said. 'Everyone sees you for what you are, a jumped up little shit who snorts coke at his father's expense. You know nothing. You'd love to know because you crave respect, but you'll never get it. Now excuse me, I am very busy.'

'I do know,' he said. 'How much is it worth?'

'What's happened? Has daddy cut back on your money?'

'I am suffering some cashflow difficulties at the moment if you must know. So how much Dr Stuart?'

He couldn't even negotiate with any sense. 'Let's just say you did know and let's just say I was prepared to pay for the information, how much would you want?'

'£1 million.'

'Fuck off Anton.'

'Half a million.'

I walked away.

In the cab back to the office I called BB on the cell phone. 'Maybe he does know,' said BB.

'He's a cocaine abuser, not a dealer. He doesn't know anything.'

'It's a lead, Andrew.'

'It's nothing,' I said.

'Let me talk to him.'

'No.'

When I got back to the office I was in no mood to work. I didn't even go straight to my office. I lingered in reception, picked up The Times from Anita's desk. It was folded to the crossword page. Only two clues were unanswered. She'd get them by the end of the day. I waited until she had finished the paperwork she was dealing with and said, 'The university has suspended me.'

'Do you blame them?' said Anita. 'If you're not careful your clients will start suspending you too. You're not concentrating on what is important: your work, your practice, your clients and your students. You've got this bee in your bonnet about the Laundryman. It's all nonsense.'

'I've got to catch him.'

'Why? Look at what it is doing to you. Let it be. Leave it to the police.'

'I'm better placed to do it than they are. I have the tools, the knowledge and the intellect.'

'This is not a game, Andrew, not some Holmesian puzzle. You are talking about real criminals who, I suspect, will stop at nothing to protect themselves. Are you ready for that?'

'No,' I said, and I wasn't. I had my strengths but they were mainly of the mind: inner powers of resilience and laser beam concentration. I was not, to be fair, a crime buster. I felt physically weakened and feared the onset of depression. 'I feel that my life is no longer my own,' I said. 'I am caught up in something that is not of my own making. I am not saying that

166

sometimes, during my professional life, I haven't been a little cute at the edges. You know I have. But this is different. This is organized crime and I stand accused. I could lose everything I have worked for, and I've worked harder than you can imagine. A long time ago I had to reinvent myself and I did this by sheer force of will. But that reinvention is about to unravel and when it does I will lose my rudder, I will lose all sense of direction.'

Anita was not taking this journey with me. 'It's started already, Andrew, just pull yourself together and you can get out of this and your life can return to normal.'

'I'm not so sure,' I said.

'Then,' Anita replied, 'it is just as well that I am. Now, let's sort out this business with Tania.'

'What business?'

'Your infatuation.'

'I am not infatuated, Anita, I love her.'

'How can you love someone like that?'

'Like what?'

'A tart.'

'I've warned you before Anita, I'm not going to warn you again. You will not use that language about Tania. Just get used to this fact: Tania is now and will remain part of my life.'

'Madness.'

'Listen to me. We've been close for such a long time, I want to explain.' I was not used to exposing my vulnerability, but I felt that for all of her antagonism to Tania, she was on my side. I could trust her. 'There has never been much love in my life,' I said, 'not as a child and not as an adult. I always thought it never bothered me. In fact, I thought it spurred me on to achieve, and maybe it did. I have possessions, qualifications and status, but now I know that nothing can substitute for love.'

'That's a speech about love, Andrew. I was talking about Tania.'

'Anita –'

'And something else bothers me. It's silly, I know, but it bothers me. Her name.'

'Tania?'

'Yes, it's an anagram of mine.'

She was right. In fact, you turned "Anita" into "Tania" just by moving the "T" to the front. I'd never thought it, but then I don't do The Times crossword every day. 'Does it really bother you?' I asked.

'Yes,' she said, 'but let's move on. You worked through the night on Thursday, made time stand still.'

'That's right.'

'So you've finished the Mycroft plan.'

'Yes.'

'Good, I'll discretely put the word out as soon as possible. How much are you going to charge?'

'It will be expensive to put together and expensive to maintain. I was thinking of £150,000 for the plan and £75,000 per annum thereafter for maintenance.'

'Are you mad? You'll have every two-bit launderer knocking on your door.' Anita was always more bullish on fees than I was. 'Remember DC Clarke's figures? You have to pitch this high; high enough to deter the rest. You only want the Laundryman.'

'OK, how much?'

'Let's front-end everything, no annual fees, just a one-off charge for a five-year plan paid up front. Say, £1 million.'

When you have worked closely with a PA for a long time, her thinking becomes part of your own. She becomes in a literal sense your alta ego, only to be challenged when you know she is wrong. This was not such a time. '£1 million it is,' I said. 'Now let me tell you about P & M.'

'I know all about P and M.'

'How?'

'You were in the boardroom. I recorded the conversation and listened to the tape. And I have no wisdom for you Andrew and no advice. Not on that matter, but I have some advice for you on Tania.'

'What's that?'

'You can't tell her about the Mycroft plan. She might be part of the problem.'

'Anita,' I said, 'stop it.'

'I'm serious. What do you really know about her other than that she got you into this mess in the first place? Has she explained her money to you? No. I've heard that love is blind but this is ridiculous. The woman is a criminal. I'm not insulting her. I'm just being descriptive. She's committed a crime – a big one, and she's dragging you down too. I know her sort.'

'What sort is that Anita?'

'The me, me, me and bugger the consequences sort.'

'Enough,' I said.

That evening as I lay face down on the large white beach towel with Tania massaging my back, and the scent of cedarwood and rosemary in the air, I told her everything about Mycroft. My reasoning was simple. If she was part of the problem, so was I.

Chapter 10

The interest in the Mycroft plan was immediate. The first serious purchaser was an African emissary, a Colonel Mansa Mussa. Anita arranged the appointment for Monday of the following week and the meeting took place in my boardroom. I had expected a figure of considerable military bearing. Mansa Mussa, however looked like a successful civilian businessman. He was tall and thin, with skin the colour of charcoal. It was difficult to determine his age, but his skin had begun to sag and his eyes were yellowing. He was well dressed in a light grey Savile Row suit, which he wore with a bright red cravat.

I took charge. 'I understand you have expressed an interest in the Mycroft plan. Perhaps you would be so kind as to tell me a little about yourself and the purpose you believe will be served by the Mycroft plan.'

'Certainly, Dr Stuart. I represent an African ruler, a military dictator if you like. His name is unimportant. He wishes to divert a small portion of his country's resources overseas as a personal insurance against a military coup.'

'Forgive my next question, Colonel Mussa, but in your opinion is this legal?'

'Of course it's legal. He's the head of state. He has absolute power. His actions could not be successfully challenged in any court in his country.'

'And the purpose of the Mycroft scheme?'

'To burn away the paper trail.'

'The reason being?'

'Because, though it is legal today, it may not be legal tomorrow. When my principal is himself subject to a coup, as he surely will be, everything he has done during his rule will be judged illegal. The incoming regime will brand him a traitor one second after he has been deposed. He will be a thief whether he's taken anything or not. And your Western governments, who are presently happy to do business with him, will treat him as a pariah, whilst currying favour with the new president. There will be calls from the US and the EU for all his foreign held assets to be repatriated, but you can't repatriate what you can't identify. Is that not so?'

'It is so,' I said. This was hiding money, pure and simple. This is what Greenley had accused me of doing in this same boardroom less than four weeks ago. But the underlying concept, which I had encountered several times before, was an interesting one. If an absolute ruler can deem the raiding of his country's Treasury as lawful, it must surely follow that subsequent transfers of the same money does not involve money laundering, because the funds transferred did not arise from a crime.

'Have I amused you?' asked Mansa Mussa.

'No,' I said, 'I was just thinking of a legal conundrum. Please continue.'

'The Mycroft plan, I understand, is ultimately controlled in Liechtenstein.'

'Yes, by an Anstalt. Is that important to you?'

'Very important. You remember General Abacha, the Nigerian leader. They claim he embezzled $3 billion during his five-year rule. On his death, while his body was still warm, they started seizing his assets all over the world. London, Paris, New York, even Switzerland froze his assets. Switzerland! Our confidential friend. When the Swiss start freezing assets, it's time to move to Liechtenstein.'

'Liechtenstein froze his assets too,' I said.

He seemed surprised. 'You know this case well?'

'Let's just say Sani Abacha wouldn't listen.'

Colonel Mussa considered this response thoroughly and he took some time before posing his next question. 'How did he move his money?'

'He used a number of methods. He would sometimes award government contracts to bogus companies and pocket the money. More often he would get legitimate companies exporting goods to Nigeria to over-invoice for them. The government paid the inflated price and the premium was transferred, by the exporting company, to a designated bank account under General Abacha's control. Alternatively, when Nigerian state industries exported they would sometimes be encouraged to under-invoice. The difference between the true price and the discounted price again being transferred, this time by the importing company, to the good general's accounts. You will be aware, I'm sure, that he collaborated with two of his ministers to transfer over $1 billion from the Central Bank of Nigeria for the refinancing of a giant steel mill. Only the steel complex got nothing. The money was transferred directly to private bank accounts in London. Everything traceable.'

'You tried to sell him the Mycroft plan?'

'I don't try to sell my plans to anybody. My clients come to me, as you have. But, for the record, the Mycroft Plan did not exist then.'

It is my experience that the more important a client's question, the more carefully he phrases it. He poses it more slowly and in a softer voice. Mansa Mussa's next question was barely audible. 'Had it existed and had he used it, would they have been able to seize his assets?'

I spoke equally low. 'They never would have found them.'

Colonel Mansa Mussa bought the Mycroft plan. We completed the necessary paperwork and he promised to send me an international money order in the sum of £1 million by registered post the following day. (It arrived two days later.)

When the meeting was over, Anita came up to see Mansa Mussa to the door. We had completed a very serious business deal so as he rose to leave the boardroom I aimed for levity. 'I have a friend whose name is Bryon Berkeley. We all call him BB. Do your friends call you MM?'

'No,' he said.

Anita's glare at me indicated her total disapproval of my attempt at humour. She showed Colonel Mussa out and then joined me in my office. 'While you were in that meeting,' she said, 'we've had another enquiry about the Mycroft plan.'

'Good,' I said, 'see if you can book him in before the next Brains Trust meeting.'

172

'Already done,' said Anita. 'The meeting's set for 2:00 pm tomorrow. And it's not a him, it's a her. A Miss Kay Frisk.'

'Intriguing.'

'I thought the same. All you men looking for the Laundryman, and the Laundrywoman walks right past you unnoticed.'

At 1:55 the following day Anita buzzed me in my office. 'She's in the boardroom waiting for your entrance. Shall I introduce you.'

'No,' I said, 'I'll do that myself. What's she like?'

'Prim, educated, polite and well spoken.'

'Anything else?'

'Yes,' said Anita. 'She's very attractive.'

Anita was right. She was attractive, in an English rose sort of way. She was slim and pale. Her hair was auburn and she had faint freckles across the bridge of her nose. She was dressed in a light grey suit, her skirt falling to just below the knee.

'How can I help?' I asked. She looked up at me, her eyes were hazel, and then down again, as if she was shy. I thought this was affected. Not many shy people buy international asset protection schemes at £1 million a pop. 'Miss Frisk?' I said.

'Mycroft Holmes,' she said and reached hesitantly into her handbag and took out a cheque book.

'Miss Frisk,' I said, 'I suspect you have not done this before. I need to ask you some questions.'

She put the cheque book back in the handbag which she placed back on the floor. She crossed her legs and put her hands in her lap, one over the over. With her head slightly tilted to one side, Kay Frisk maintained eye contact for the first time. It was as if she was bracing herself. 'Go ahead,' she said.

She seemed vulnerable and I didn't want to frighten her away. Not, that is, until I was certain that she was not in any way connected to the Laundryman. I thought this would not take long. I was wrong. 'First,' I said, 'are you here on your own account or are you representing another?'

'I'm representing another,' she said.

'And your principal is?'

'A newspaper baron. He likes the structure. He says it's better than the financial matrix Bob Maxwell established, and it cost the DTI £20 million and took them over ten years to unravel that after Captain Bob's suicide.'

'They never fully unravelled it,' I said, 'and I, for one, never subscribed to the suicide theory. An accident, perhaps, or murder, but never suicide. He just wasn't the suicide type. What is the name of your principal?'

'Charlie Parnell.'

This would have made sense. Charlie Parnell's media interests were global, his financial affairs were shrouded in secrecy and he could easily afford the Mycroft plan. The problem was that I knew Charlie. I had set up a tax minimization scheme for him some two years ago. He was still paying me annual fees for its maintenance. If Charlie wanted the Mycroft plan he would have called me himself. I chose the direct approach. 'Why are you lying to me?'

'Because you ask too many fucking questions,' she said. Her head was now shaking slightly from side to side. She was either very nervous or she had an involuntary tremor. Or both.

'One more time, Miss Frisk, why are you here?'

'I want to buy your Mycroft Holmes.'

'Why do you need it?'

'I need to put my affairs in order.'

'Your own affairs?'

'Yes. And I need to do it quickly.' The tremor began to affect her neck, and it occurred to me that she may have been keeping her hands firmly in her lap to stop them from shaking too.

'Why the urgency, Miss Frisk?'

'Isn't it obvious, Dr Stuart?' she said, her eyes moistening, 'I'm dying.'

I did not respond immediately. I averted my gaze and, looking for something to do, I picked the blue folder containing the Know Your Client questionnaire. After what I judged to be a decent interval I said, 'I'm sorry.'

'No need to be sorry,' she said. 'My life now has new meaning. I know what's important. I see life with a clearer focus. We all die. I just know

174

that I will be dying sooner than you.'

'Not necessarily,' I said and, as I looked up, she was smiling, revealing white even teeth. Her shaking was slightly less pronounced. She looked vulnerable and sad and beautiful, and I felt protective. 'How can I help?' I asked.

'Sell me Mycroft Holmes.'

'Let's move to first name terms,' I said. 'Just call the plan Mycroft.' Her laugh was soft, like gently running water.'

'Sell me Mycroft,' she said, and lowered her eyelids as if we had exchanged a moment of intimacy.

'I can do better than that,' I said. 'It would appear that you really need some inheritance tax planning. I can put together a bespoke structure that addresses your specific needs and it would be far, far cheaper than Mycroft, which is really for asset protection. If you need an element of asset protection, I can incorporate it into your bespoke structure.' I opened the blue folder. 'Let me take down some details.'

'Close the folder Dr Stuart. I know what I want and I intend to give you the minimum amount of information necessary to implement Mycroft. Are you ready?'

'Yes,' I said. I took down the information. She had £25 million to shelter, initially at least. She said there may be more. I arranged for payment, not by cheque, but by wire transfer to the Island Bank in Cayman. Paul Canolla, I thought, would be pleased with my recent transactions. When I had finished imparting my banking details I walked Kay to the front door.

'Why did you see her out yourself?' asked Anita, once Kay was on her way. 'I hope this is not going to be another of your conquests. I've told you about sleeping with clients, but you never listen. And remember this is all about catching the Laundryman. Please don't lose sight of that. Come on, what's the story?'

'She's dying Anita.'

'Me too,' she said.

On Wednesday afternoon I called BB. 'Are you busy?' I asked as soon as he picked up the phone.

'I'm always busy. What do you want?'

'There's another purchaser of the Mycroft plan. I'm going to see him. Do you want to come?'

'You need muscle?'

'Hardly, he's a wheelchair-bound recluse.'

'So what do you need me for?'

'It's Joseph Feingold.'

'Holy shit. When are you leaving?'

'Tomorrow, 8:00am.'

'I'll be there.'

Joseph Feingold had that sort of effect on people. He was a self-made billionaire. Like many others of this exclusive club, he started young. At grammar school in the late 1960s he created cassette tapes of his record collection and sold them to his fellow students. He had not heard of the laws of copyright, and when teachers pointed them out to him he studiously ignored them. He soon worked out that he could recover the cost of a record by selling seven copies of it. He then simply catered to the tastes of his classmates. If he knew he could sell more than seven copies he brought the record. As he recalled years later, 'I was copying all sorts of crap.' He skipped university in favour of an articled clerkship with a medium-sized accountancy firm. He never qualified, taking instead an accounts position in a small record company that his firm audited. Five years later he was running the company and two years after that he executed a management buy-out. Feingold had the knack for finding talent or, more accurately, finding acts that would sell. 'More sophisticated recording equipment,' he once quipped, 'same old crap.' Unlike Gerald Ratner, however, such remarks never damaged his business. His catchphrase became: 'I give the public what they want.'

And the more they wanted, the more he gave, and the more profits he made. He started putting on concerts, first of his own acts and then those signed to other labels. He used his financial muscle to book up concert halls for large tracts of time. Soon if you wanted to put on a major concert in London you had to deal with Joseph Feingold. He controlled the fly-tippers, turning a blind eye to the tactics employed by his charges in dealing with the competition. His public face was all smiles. Mr Entertainment, he had a talent for getting positive publicity. Though short and craggy in appearance, he dated the top film stars and supermodels, most of whom towered above him. His marriages were public, lavish and short-lived. His lifestyle was one of unabashed conspicuous consumption: mansions, yachts, Rolls-Royces and the rest. He upstaged his own artistes.

Then some five years ago, at he height of his fame, a helicopter he was piloting crashed leaving him paralysed from the waist down. His fifth marriage failed shortly thereafter and he withdrew from the limelight. He continued to manage his businesses with much reported success, but to judge from the society pages his party days were over. In a rare interview, shortly after his sixth marriage, this time to a 23 year old starlet, a journalist on the Observer had the temerity to ask him about his sex life. He said, 'I eat pussy better than anyone in the world.' This was vintage Feingold on three levels. One, he didn't duck the question. Two, he refused to acknowledge there was a problem. And three, he was the best in the world at what he did. Joseph Feingold. Always the best.

BB arrived at my house at 7:30. Julianna showed him into the kitchen where I was having breakfast with Tania, eggs scrambled with milk. 'Keen,' I said.

'I just want to meet him,' said BB.

'Who?' asked Tania.

BB looked at me. 'I haven't told her,' I said.

'Who?' she repeated.

'Joseph Feingold,' I said. 'He wants to buy the Mycroft plan.'

'When are you leaving? She asked, rising.

'In half an hour,' I said.

'I'll be ready,' she replied.

When she was gone BB said, 'You could have said no.'

'I've been saying no a lot to her recently.'

'True,' he said.

Joseph Feingold now lived in a remote castle in Scotland. I had chartered a private plane for the journey, a Cessna CitationJet, through RB Aviación SL, the Andorra registered company I had set up for my client Robin Brocklehurst. Robin had offered to leave the warmer climate of Spain and France to pilot the jet for me personally when I explained that I was meeting Mr Feingold ("Yes, Joseph Feingold") and that he had his own runway. Indeed, as he lacked any superstition, he had his own heliport too.

BB, Tania and I drove to the small local airport and were greeted by Robin and one of the assistant pilots, each impeccable attired in navy blue uniforms, almost looking as if they had just stepped off a movie set. I was not, I mused, the only one who recognised the need for a little theatre in providing business services to high net worth individuals. As we walked to the plane I said to Robin, 'Oh, by the way, I must thank you for the client you introduced.'

'Who was that?' he replied.

'Giovanni Mazzinni.'

'Never heard of him.'

'You never recommended a Mr Mazzinni to my practice? Think hard Robin.'

'Don't need to think at all. Haven't recommended anyone to you recently. Not with your fees!' We both chuckled politely, but I was troubled. If Robin wasn't the pilot who introduced Mazzinni to me, who was?

We boarded the plane and settled into the comfortable seats. Before take-off Tania insisted on swivelling around in hers and seeing how far the seat would recline, but she had satisfied her playful curiosity in time for take-off. 'I could get used to this,' said Tania once we were airborne. 'Why don't you buy a jet, Stu. You can afford it.'

'I don't know how to fly a plane,' I said.

'Take lessons, you're smart.'

It wasn't such a crazy idea. It would get me out of the office and learning something new. 'When all this is over,' I said, 'I'll take flying lessons.'

'And when you've passed,' she teased, 'as a present, I'll buy you the sexy uniform.'

She'd lifted my spirits and for the moment made me forget about Mazzinni. 'Can't wait,' I said.

The flight was surprisingly smooth and the journey took just over two hours. Mr Feingold's butler greeted us as we disembarked and led us into his castle. It was a real castle. There was a disused moat and drawbridge and the external walls were crumbling with age. Inside, however, was warm and comforting. We walked through many archways until we reached a large double door. The butler knocked. 'Come in,' said a booming voice, and we entered into his presence. The room was huge and contained modern Italian furniture and high-tech appliances. Joseph Feingold, as one would have imagined, was in the centre of the room being tended to by three very attractive secretaries. 'Dr Stuart, right?' His voice was unnaturally loud. 'And?'

'Business associates,' I said, 'Bryon Berkeley and Tania Berkeley.'

'Husband and wife?' he enquired.

'Brother and sister,' I said.

'So I'm in with a chance, hey Tania?'

This was a bad beginning, but Tania knew how to play the game. 'Mr Feingold, you've got a head start.' BB looked at me and I wondered whether he or she was aware of the Observer article.

Mr Feingold was delighted. 'Call me Joe,' he said. 'And sit down, all of you, let's wear this furniture out. I don't use it!' And he roared with laughter. Tania took the seat closest to him.

'You have a lovely castle,' she said.

'It's crap,' said Joe, 'but it's out of the way. After the chopper thing I needed to get away. It serves its purpose, but it cost me half a mil just to get rid of the draughts. You wouldn't believe how draughty an old castle can be.'

'I suppose you pay for the authenticity,' said Tania.

'You're right,' he said, 'of course, you're right. But it wasn't authenticity I was looking for, it was solitude.'

'You could have found solitude on a yacht,' teased Tania.

'I wanted to be on solid ground,' he replied. 'I like you, you got a boyfriend?'

'Yes,' she said.

'Does he buy you diamonds?'

'Set in caymanite,' said Tania.

'That's good, give the man some credit. But does he tend to your every need?'

'No, he works too hard.'

'Dump him. I'll be in London next month. Have you eaten at the Belvedere? It's a Marco Pierre White restaurant, Holland Park. It's the business.' He rang a small bell. There were several dotted around the room. One of the secretaries returned within 30 seconds. 'Jackie, get my diary, I'm taking Miss Berkeley here to dinner. And why not?' I was quietly uneasy; BB was quietly fuming. Tania was quietly assured.

'You're married,' she said.

'I am?' His voice was like thunder. Joe was centre stage and he was loving it. 'Jackie, am I still married?'

'I believe you are Mr Feingold,' said Jackie.

'Why, in heavens name? Who's my wife this time?'

'Fiona,' answered Jackie.

'And where is she?'

'She flew to Paris this morning.'

'Then she is not my wife until she comes back on bended knee,' he declared. 'Jackie, my diary. I feel an *affaire du coeur* coming on.'

'Business before pleasure,' said Tania softly.

'Business is pleasure,' said Joe. 'But I take your point. Jackie, get me Lucky Sucky.'

Jackie hesitated. 'You want her to blow you?'

'No,' he said, 'I want her to bring me some coke.'

Joe said to no one in particular, 'Can't feel a thing, but I like to watch.'

'And why not?' mimicked Tania, with such openness that it caused Joe to chuckle loudly.

Lucky Sucky arrived with a mirrored tray of white powder with a silver knife and several straws at the side. She could be described unkindly as a blonde bimbo, and it would take a little while to think of a kinder description. Six foot two, lots of hair, almost certainly dyed, huge breasts, almost certainly implants, and tons of make-up. Her clothes were skimpy and a size too small. She fixed the tray to the arms of Joe's wheelchair. As she turned to leave Joe said, 'Would either of you guys like a blowjob?'

'No thank you,' I said. BB just buried his head in his hands.

As she closed the door behind her Joe said, 'She used to be a man.' He lined up the cocaine with the knife and with a finger over one nostril, inhaled deeply through straw into the other. 'Go figure,' he said, and repeated the process reversing his hands and nostrils. Satisfied, he laid his head back and closed his eyes. 'Help yourselves,' he said.

'We're fine,' I said.

'I'm not,' said Tania and walked the few yards to Joe's tray. Picking up the knife and a fresh straw, she made her up her two white lines and, more swiftly than Joe's, they were gone. I looked at BB who shrugged as if to say, "you didn't know?"

Turning to me Joe continued a conversation he must have been having in his head, 'I hear this Mycroft scheme costs £1 million. How do you guys justify those sort of fees? Could have been an accountant myself, you know. It bored me shitless. Mind you, what I learnt, I've used. So any money I put into Mycroft cannot be traced, am I right? You'll guarantee this, right? I mean if it fails I want some recompense, big time. I'll be walking down the street thinking I've got my clothes on and everyone will be looking at my bare arse.' Tania giggled. 'It's a nice arse, Tania, the best, but if I've paid one million quid for it to be covered, it should be covered, right? In gold.'

'You're right Joe.'

'Of course, I'm right. So how about it Dr Stuart.'

'Call me Andrew,' I said.

'Yeah, yeah, how about it? What have you got for me?'

I explained the Mycroft plan in detail. I got the feeling that Joe was only half listening, but when I had finished the questions he asked would have put most of my PhD students to shame. Joseph Feingold, always the best. He bought Mycroft, arranged payment by wire, gave Tania his telephone number and we flew back to London. BB, who hadn't said a word during the meeting, slept for most of the flight. As we were preparing to land he spoke, though his eyes remained closed. 'I've just flown to Scotland to meet an icon only to discover that he's an asshole.'

'He's sweet,' said Tania.

'And smart,' I said.

'He's an asshole,' said BB.

'The question is,' I said, 'is he the Laundryman?'

'Oh no,' said Tania.

'Just an asshole,' said BB. 'And one more thing. No one saw any cocaine at that castle. You two are enough trouble as it is without admitting that you've been to a cocaine party. Are you with me on this?'

'Yes,' I said.

'And why not?' giggled Tania.

The purchasers of the Mycroft plan were the primary focus of discussion at Saturday's Brains Trust. As only I had met all three of the purchasers I gave my impression of each of them and relayed as accurately as I could the substance of each encounter. I then invited comments.

'I like Feingold,' volunteered Martyn.

'Why?' asked BB defensively.

'It's a perfect fit. He's got the businesses. He'll launder like Capone. He'll just add the illicit income to his legitimate income and bank it.'

'Cash?' said BB.

'Yes, cash. This man is responsible for more concerts in the UK than any other. He turns the drug money into his cash takings. Whose going to question him?'

'He'd need to involve other people within his organization,' I suggested.

'So he involves them, and pays them well. I don't see your issue. Look, this man has been sticking his figures up at the Establishment his entire career. He thinks the rules do not apply to him. He also publicly insults his own artistes. Maybe he knows that what is keeping them afloat is his second business rather than their talents, but he can't come out and say so, so he berates them instead.'

'Too far fetched,' said BB.

'Not at all,' continued Martyn. 'Think about it. The entertainment business, the drug business: they're two peas in a pod.'

'That is a prejudice,' announced Anita, 'but a prejudice I happen to share. I've seen it up close.'

'That's enough, Anita,' I said.

'Do you want me to be part of this committee or not Andrew?'

'I do,' I said.

'Then I must speak my mind. DC Clarke is right. I'm surprised Mr Feingold didn't offer you a line of coke when you met him.' The comment was addressed to me. BB and I exchanged glances, but remained silent. Anita was one step ahead. 'And if he did I hope you turned him down. You have enough problems as it is without turning into a cokehead. Mr Berkeley can do what he pleases.'

'Thank you,' said BB.

'He's our man,' said Martyn. 'What's the next step?'

'We wait,' I said. 'Anyone for Colonel Mansa Mussa?'

'Our African plenipotentiary,' said Billy. 'Not really. He seems to have his hands full.'

'If you believe his story,' said Martyn.

'How many laundrymen are we looking for?' asked Billy. 'I thought you had settled on our disabled impresario.'

'I'm keeping my options open,' said Martyn. 'Andrew you should have made him name his principal then we could have checked.'

'And how would we have done that?' I countered. 'The African continent is littered with dictators and they are all moving money to the West.'

'Which makes it the perfect cover,' said Martyn.

'It's not Mansa Mussa,' said Billy. 'He's all wrong. For a start the Jamaicans would never use him.'

'Why not?' asked Martyn, 'I'd have thought he had an advantage being black.'

'He's African,' said Billy. 'There is distrust between West Indians and Africans.'

'You're thinking too small,' said Martyn. 'Race, creed, religion are irrelevant. The stakes are too high. The cartels use the Laundryman not because they like him. They use him because he delivers.' Billy grunted. 'What was your assessment of Mansa Mussa Andrew?'

'I thought him a gentleman,' I said.

'Chou En Lai was a gentleman,' said Billy. 'I read that he could kill you with his bare hands and walk away calmly smoking a cigarette. Is our Mansa Mussa a gentleman in the same mould?'

'I don't think so. He'd get someone else to do the dirty work.'

'He's a launderer though, isn't he?' said Billy.

I thought of my legal conundrum. 'It all depends on the existence of a predicate offence,' I said. 'As far as he is concerned his principal has committed no offence. No crime, no laundering.'

Martyn Clarke showed his exasperation. 'I'm not interested in whether he launders money. I'm interested in whether he is the Laundryman.'

'No,' I said.

'No,' said Billy.

'I don't think so,' said Anita.

'No he's not,' said BB. 'Neither is Joseph Feingold. I like the woman, what's her name?'

'Kay Frisk,' I said. 'Why do you like her?'

'She's a drama queen. She tells you she's dying, you offer her a better structure –'

'Not necessarily better,' I said, 'just one more suited to her needs.'

'Same thing,' he said, 'and, more importantly, what you offer her is considerably cheaper, and she doesn't want it. She turns you down flat. The question is why. And the answer is because she's not dying. She has another agenda. She puts on the shakes for sympathy. She probably gets her men the same way.'

'Seduction by tremor,' said Billy, 'that's a new one.'

BB turned to Billy. 'OK then, what do you think?'

'I haven't seen her, of course, but it sounds like Parkinson's disease to me, which is not necessarily a killer. You're right, I think, about her having her own agenda, but I don't think she's the Laundryman.'

Martyn was more adamant. 'The Laundryman is not a woman. It just doesn't feel right.'

'I am a great believer in feeling and instinct,' said Anita, 'but they must be checked by reason. I fear that your views are driven by the fact that you could not abide to learn that a mere woman had outmanoeuvred you and the entire Special Crimes Unit.'

'I'm not sexist,' said Clarke.

Billy laughed. 'Of course you are. You're sexist, racist, anti-Semitic and homophobic. You're a policeman.'

'Enough,' I said. 'Let's re-focus. We have one vote for Joseph Feingold.'

'And one against,' said BB.

'One vote for Kay Frisk.'

'And one against,' said Martyn.

'Billy?'

'I don't like any of them.'

'Anita?'

'I'm keeping my powder dry.'

'Now we have the names,' said Martyn, 'I can do some research. I'll run them through the police computer. Technically, I shouldn't share the results with you, but I'm sure I can find a way to usefully impart relevant information.'

'Sometimes,' said BB, 'you talk like Andrew. Are you going to tell us what you find out or not?'

'He will,' said Billy. 'He just will not tell us officially. Isn't that right, detective constable?'

'Yes,' said Martyn. 'Look, I'm in a difficult situation here. My presence is not official. I am here as a private citizen. I do not wish to compromise my ethical standards.'

'Relax,' said Billy, 'no one's going to say a word.'

I felt for Martyn. He was putting a lot on the line. 'I think we all understand that these meetings are strictly confidential,' I said. 'I too will be researching these names using Lexis-Nexis and other databases. If they've been in the press at any time here or abroad, if they have served as an officer of any company or been a member of any professional or trade association, I'll know about it. Let's have a short ad hoc meeting early next week.' I turned to Martyn. 'We can compare notes.'

'Any other candidates?' asked Martyn.

'Not at this time,' I said, but I lied. There was another candidate, one that made me feel distinctly uneasy, one I could not lay before the Brains Trust. Shortly before leaving the office on Friday, after my meeting with Kay Frisk, Anita received another request for the Mycroft plan. Anita took the details, told me and we both stood in silence. "What are we going to do?" I asked her. "Keep it to ourselves," she replied. And we did. So in answer to Martyn Clarke's question I made no mention of the fourth purchaser of Mycroft, my solicitor, George Fairlow.

Chapter 11

We met again on Tuesday evening. I took the lead. 'Mansa Mussa is a very busy man. He holds directorships in a wide range of companies, mostly international in nature. Companies such as Trunxworld Engineering (Finance) Inc, Foldgold Futures Ltd and Minx Brokers GmbH.'

'Do they mean anything to you?' asked Martyn.

'Once I found out his association with the companies, I did a full database search on the companies themselves. The P & L figures are large but the disclosed principal activities are vague. The companies are private so the amount of information available is limited. At a guess they seem to be conduit companies, middle-men, collectors of commissions.'

'For money laundering?' Martyn asked.

'Who knows? They could be money launderers, arm sales intermediaries, facilitators of bribes to Third World countries – '

'Or,' said Billy, 'just plain honest traders.'

'That too,' I said. 'Moving on to Joseph Feingold, his activities are well known and in the public domain. I could find nothing on Kay Frisk.'

'I could,' said Martyn. 'You described Miss Frisk as a prim and proper, butter-wouldn't-melt-in-her-mouth type. Seven years ago she stood trial for embezzlement from her employer, a large pharmaceutical company. She got off largely due to the tricks of her legal team. She was guilty as sin.' I expected Billy to object to this damning indictment of our judicial system but he remained strangely silent. 'Two years later she was caught with enough cocaine in her house to supply a small army of cokeheads. Went to trial again. This time she pleaded guilty. Lawyers argued that she used the cocaine medicinally, that there was no intention to supply it to others for commercial gain. They did concede that there might have been some element of not-for-profit social supply among her friends. She got six months, served three. I've done some digging. You may be interested in who represented her.'

Billy spoke into his glass. 'George Fairlow of Bellows & Bellows on the embezzlement charge.' I felt like a knife was piercing my guts. 'And me on the possession charge.' Disembowelment completed.

'Quite so,' said Martyn.

'Billy,' I said, 'why didn't you say something before?'

'Client confidentiality,' he replied and downed his drink in one.

'Can you tell us anything about her?'

'Nothing.'

'Off the record?'

'Nothing.'

Wednesday was a bad day. I just sat at my desk staring into space. The work allocated to me in such tidy parcels of time sat neglected. Anita was unmerciful. 'I thought we were up and running. Now what's the matter?'

'I just can't face it,' I said. The truth was the magic had gone. I remembered one of the very few pieces of advice my mother gave me. "Don't let the light go out," she had said. She explained that all of us were born with a light shining inside us. It was the light that bought us joy. We could be poor and in crappy jobs but the light enabled us to see the funny side of everything. The light made us laugh. We could be in pain and the light made us draw strength from the pain. The light taught us to see that most pain was good. However bad things were today, the light made tomorrow better. But when the light when out, crap was crap, pain was pain and tomorrow didn't exist. "Don't let the light go out," she said. "When the light goes out you die. You may walk, eat and sleep, but you're dead. Dead inside."

'I can't deal with this now, Anita. If I tried, I'd make a mess of it. I have no focus, no passion, no light.'

'And how long is this going to go on for?'

'I just don't know.'

'I do,' said Anita, 'and I'm going to give you some advice. First things

188

first. Sit up straight.'

'What?'

'Sit up straight. You will feel better.' I had not realised I was slouch-
ing. I straightened my back and squared my shoulders. It made me feel
more in control though I feared the feeling was temporary. 'You know what
you lack today?' Anita asked.

'Self-discipline,' I suggested.

'No,' she said. 'Routine. Your success here is based on routine. The
minutes of every day are allocated to specific tasks. I know because I allocate them. And as far as possible your days are similar. Each client's affairs
are different, of course, but when you come in, when you develop your tax
planning schemes, when you take or return calls, when you hold meetings
and when you go home, all these things are subject to a routine. There is a
reason for this: your power of concentration is awesome, but you can only
concentrate on one thing at a time. You still have focus, you still have passion, and you still have light, only not for your business. You are wasting
them on a wild goose chase. So you have a choice: A J Stuart & Co or the
Laundryman.'

'We have to catch him.'

'No we don't.'

'I could go to prison.'

'We'll fight it in the courts.'

'I want to catch him.'

'That's what I feared. You're on the road to hell, Andrew, and I'm not
going with you.' Anita got up and returned to reception. Five minutes later
I walked past her on the way to the door.

'I'm going for a walk,' I said. She did not reply. I was breaking with
routine. I stepped into Wigmore Street, walked south down James Street
into Oxford Street, then turned right and headed for Hyde Park. The park
was peaceful in comparison with the mêlée of shoppers on Oxford Street,
but it nonetheless had an energy of its own. The people here, I thought,
were trying too hard to relax. In the countryside the pace of life is genuinely slower. You cannot, however, slow down the pace of London life by

stepping into Hyde Park, any more than New Yorkers truly slow down by strolling through Central Park. The businessman eating his sandwiches in a city park is all too well aware that the next crisis, real or imagined, is not very far away. The park serves as neutral ground, the place of a temporary truce. My crisis had arrived and Hyde Park seemed a good place to be. I eventually found an unoccupied park bench under the shade of a tree and I sat there for hours.

When I returned to my office Anita wasn't in reception. No doubt the voicemail was on. I walked to my office and saw a hand-written white envelope lying in the centre of my desk. The handwriting was Anita's. I tore the envelope open and read the letter.

> *Dear Andrew*
> *This is the most difficult letter I have ever had to write. I wish to inform you that I will leave your employment today with immediate effect.*
> *Technically I am in breach of my employment contract in that I have given you no notice. I hope that you will overlook this in light of my long service. I have left you detailed notes on every ongoing case. You will find them in my office file.*
> *I am leaving because I just cannot take it anymore. I cannot stand what this case is doing to the business, to the clients and, most importantly, to you. You have lost all professional focus, interest and drive. And for what, or should I say, for whom?*
> *Working for you has been my life for the past eight years. You have taught me so much. We have had such fun. But I cannot stand by and watch the man I respect more than any other self-destruct in front of my eyes.*
> *Regards*
> *Anita*

I held the letter in my hands for a long time. I knew I needed to reply, but I had to let the anger and sense of betrayal subside. Anita had been my rock. It was not my practice, as much as our practice. She possessed all the administrative skills I lacked. She also had emotional balance. How could she leave now, when I needed her most? The answer, however, was clear: she'd had enough. Me too, I thought. I sat down at my WP to draft a reply, and changed my mind. This letter I would write by hand.

> *Dear Anita*
> *I accept your resignation. The absence of notice is of no consequence in the circumstances. I will, of course, provide a glittering reference to any future employer.*
> *You will be an asset for whomever you choose to work. They will be getting a precious gem. For my part, I do not know how I will ever replace you. I do not know if I am even going to try.*
> *Love*
> *Andrew*

My next letter was to Coats Bank in which I suggested a meeting to discuss the sale of A J Stuart & Co. I had several false starts. I'd turned Hugo down so many times and now I was approaching him. It was important that I do so from a position of strength. I knew he would seize on any perceived weakness and use it as a basis for knocking the price down. I decided that, rather than state that I was looking to sell, I would refer back to his offer at our last breakfast meeting, and ask for clarification. Once the letter was drafted I felt better. I printed it onto my letterhead, but I did not sign it. I wanted time to think.

I leaned back in my chair and closed my eyes. My mind, however, would not stay on the task at hand. I was completely out of sorts and I knew of only one way to deal with it. I called the agency.

'Kingsway Associates'

'Hello,' I said, 'this is Mr Brown.'

'Mr Brown, good afternoon. I assume you're looking for an evening appointment?'

'No, can you do something for me this afternoon?'

'That's rather short notice, let me see.' The line started playing classical music. I recognized Dvorák's 9th Symphony. After 30 seconds she was back. 'Possibly Mr Brown, what are you looking for?'

'Do you have a pen?' I said. 'My instructions are rather precise.'

'As always, Mr Brown. What are the instructions this time?'

'I would like her to come to the same office as the evening appointments, the address is on file.'

'Yes.'

'She must be dressed in a conservative business suit and wearing glasses. She should also carry a slim briefcase.'

'Very good.'

'When she gets to the office I will open the door. I am here alone. She is not to say a word. I will lead her upstairs to a separate office and stand in front of a desk. She will get on her knees, unzip my trousers, take out my cock and give me a blowjob for about five minutes. During the blowjob she should keep her glasses on and avoid eye contact. After that she will get up and bend over the desk. I will lift up her business skirt - so it shouldn't be too tight - and pull down her knickers: French, please, any colour. I will then enter her from behind. After I am done, I would like her to rearrange her clothes so that she is as smart as when she arrived and, again without saying a word to me, allow me to show her to the door.'

'Do you have a particular choice of girl?'

'Yes, she should be white, older and plain.'

'None of our girls are plain, Mr Brown.'

'Then she should look plain. Hair pulled back, no make up, that sort of thing.'

'Let me see what I can do.' Dvorák returned. 'We do have someone. She's new. Eastern European with slightly accentuated English.'

'Go back to my instruction,' I said. 'If you hadn't told me about her accent I never would have found out. She is not to speak. She's fine.'

'Four o' clock?'

'Agreed.'

'That will be £3,000, Mr Brown.'

'There will be two envelopes on the reception desk marked Kingsway Associates: one containing your fees, the other a tip for her. She may collect both when she arrives.'

'Both cash, of course?'

'Of course,' I said.

After I had hung up two thoughts occurred to me. One, I hoped the newly arrived guest to our shores got the street number right, or one of my neighbours would be in for an unexpectedly entertaining afternoon; and two, I hoped that no bespectacled, conservatively dressed potential new client called on me at 4:00pm.

I had time to kill. I went to the drinks cabinet and poured myself a large whiskey; large by my standards, not Billy's. With Billy on my mind, I decided to give him a call. We agreed to meet socially one evening later in the week. I sat at my desk and picked up my letter to Hugo Maximillian and re-read it. It would do. I signed it with a flourish and retrieved an envelope from my drawer. In fact, I retrieved three envelopes: a small one for the letter, a large one for the fee and a medium one for the tip.

That evening I prepared to relay the day's events to Tania over dinner (omitting, of course, my 4 o' clock visitor). Dinner now always took place in the formal dining room. This was another of Tania's changes. In the past I'd eat dinner at the kitchen table or breakfast bar, often alone. Sometimes BB would call to say he was coming over, sometimes I'd tell him to stop by. It was always informal. Julianna would serve us, but within an atmosphere of closeness and good humour, a family atmosphere. Now Julianna was staff, so classified by Tania, staff who served in a formal setting.

Tania insisted on proper place settings. She actually taught Julianna one morning when I was at work. So that evening as I sat down to dinner I was faced with a dinner knife, fish knife and soup spoon on my right; a fish fork, dinner fork and salad fork on my left. Three goblets sat diagonally above the knives, one for red wine, one for white wine and one for water. The dessert spoon and cake fork lay horizontally above the dinner plate, on which rested the soup bowl and plate. Top left was a bread and butter plate, and butter knife. The setting was completed with a large, thick, folded white napkin to the left of the forks.

'You need to get your logo embroidered onto these napkins,' said Tania as she unfolded hers and laid it on her lap.

'Perhaps not,' I said. 'The logo may be sold along with the practice.'

Tania was shocked. She was about to quiz me when Julianna entered the room carrying our first course on a silver tray. Tania raised a finger to her lips, indicating silence. Julianna saw it. I think she was intended to see it. After our soup had been served and Julianna had departed, Tania said, 'You're going to sell the practice? Why?'

I told her of Anita's resignation.

'Bitch,' said Tania.

'That's a little strong,' I said, but in truth it was no stronger than "brown-skinned dolly bird."

'She's a bitch. Think of all the things you've done for her, and I bet you paid her too much. That's why she can afford to leave. If you'd kept her on a short leash you wouldn't be in this trouble now. Of all the times to go. Couldn't she wait until the case was over at least. Anyway, good riddance. You don't need her.'

'But I do,' I said. 'Without her there is no A J Stuart & Co. That's why I'm selling.'

'You're crazy –'

Julianna entered and removed the soup bowls and plates.

'You're crazy, you're the one with the brains. You just need to find a good secretary.'

'Anita was more than a secretary. She ran the business.'

'You make her sound like the boss.'

'Funny that, I suppose in some ways she was.'

Julianna wheeled in the main course on a serving trolley. She served us in silence. Tania had clearly used the time to think. 'I could take her place,' she said when Julianna had left. I put down my knife and fork. 'I could, Stu. It would be great. I would organise your clients, fix your appointments, represent you at functions, everything. I'd need a secretary, of course, and maybe a clerk to do the running around.' She hadn't even got the job and she had already doubled my staff.

'No Tania,' I said. 'It wouldn't work.'

'Yes it would.'

'No it wouldn't, and anyway the timing's all wrong. You have been charged with money laundering. I have been arrested for the same offence. The police think we conspire together. They will know you are working for me within a week of you starting. Andrew Stuart and Tania Berkeley setting up offshore companies together on behalf of themselves and their clients. The police will arrive at fantastical conclusions. We don't need it.'

'Are you always worried about what other people think?'

'When those people have the power to lock me up, yes, I am concerned about what they think and so should you be.'

Tania had hardly touched her food. I suggested we eat and return to the subject at another time. Tania, however, was reluctant to let go.

'Can I work with you after you've caught the Laundryman?'

'The circumstances would be fundamentally changed,' I said. 'Yes, I would certainly be prepared to consider it.'

'So catch him.'

When I arrived in the office the next morning there was a fax from Hugo.

> *Andrew*
> *Letter received this morning. Glad you've come to your senses.*
> *No point in delaying matters. Is 3:00pm good for you?*
> *Hugo*

I scribbled, "3:00pm good for me," on the bottom of his copy, initialled it, and faxed it back to his private office. Unusually for me I arrived at the bank half an hour early. Even more unusually for Hugo, he was waiting for me. 'This way Andrew,' he said, leading me into one of the executive meeting rooms. The room was spacious and airy. A broad window at the far end of the room supplied ample natural light. The net curtains were very fine and rather than lose the effect of the light with heavy curtains, embroidered silk had been simply draped around the window frame. A large oval highly polished mahogany table surrounded by twelve Chippendale chairs dominated the room. In front of each placing was a pad and pen.

'I thought this was just a preliminary discussion,' I said.

'Quite so,' said Hugo, 'but I like this room.' I wondered if the room was meant to intimidate me or whether Hugo was simply emphasising his position within the bank. On balance, I considered both thoughts ungenerous. Hugo simply liked the room. So did I. We sat at the far end of the room, by the window, opposite each other where the table was narrowest.

Once seated Hugo fixed me with a benevolent stare. 'Shall we cut through the normal preliminaries, Andrew. We've known each other a long time. We have no reason to waste time on a coy courtship. When would you like to join us?'

'I don't want to join you.'

'Andrew,' said Hugo lazily 'do we have to do this dance? I want you to join us. You want to join us. I have a package in mind. You have a package in mind. May I suggest that you show me yours and I'll show you mine?'

'I appreciate your frankness and I intend to be equally frank. I truly don't want to join you. I want to sell you my practice.'

'Oh, your letter said you wanted clarification of my last offer. That was not an offer for your practice, was it?'

'It was not, but as you said let's cut through the usual preliminaries. Are you interested?'

Hugo leaned back on the hard wood of his Chippendale chair. The stare returned without the benevolence. 'I have an idea that may suit us both. We buy the practice and as part of that deal you sign a two-and-a-half years consultancy agreement with us. It's a big climb down for us. Remember, originally we were talking about a five-year renewable employment contract. We'll meet in the middle. You started at zero, we started at five. We'll settle on two and a half. Now this will affect the price we pay for the practice. It's less valuable without you, obviously. We will also need a non-competition clause. All the more so now that you're only going to be with us for two and a half years.'

'Hugo, you're not listening. I do not wish to join the bank: not as an employee, not as a consultant, not as a director –'

'Not on offer, dear boy.'

'– not as a doorman. I don't want to join the bank. I want to sell my practice and walk away.'

'I see,' said Hugo, 'would this have anything to do with your recent difficulties?'

'What difficulties are you referring to?'

There was a hard edge to Hugo's manner that I had never seen before. 'Your arrest Andrew. Money laundering, wasn't it? I thought you wanted to come here where you could disappear into a bland corporate structure. We could have looked after you, assuming you were not convicted of course. But, once again, you want to go it alone. Sell the practice and go your own way.'

'It's a business proposition, Hugo. Let's not get personal.'

'It's not a business proposition. It's a rescue mission. Given your current difficulties I'm sure your clients are deserting you in droves.'

'I have not lost a single client.'

'Yet.'

'Are you interested in purchasing my practice or not?'

'Slow down Andrew,' he said. 'I've ordered a pot of tea. It should be here shortly. Remember, we are discussing an international tax practice not a second hand Ford Fiesta. Relax a little. If I may say so, you are a little too eager.'

'I am just trying to establish whether in principle we are discussing a sale. If we are not I will skip tea and make an appointment with someone else.'

Hugo looked at the closed door, then raised himself out of his seat and leaned forward towards me. His voice was low and harsh. 'You're in shit Andrew. Nobody is going to take on a clientele that the police are crawling all over looking for money laundering activities. You have nowhere to go. No appointments to make.' He sat back down, and in his normal avuncular tone he said, 'but if you're very nice to me I might be able to work something out to our mutual benefit.' There was a knock at the door. A middle aged black woman entered with a huge tray containing a china pot, cups and biscuits. 'Ah, tea,' Hugo said cheerfully. 'Put it down Mrs Reynolds. We've been waiting for this, haven't we Dr Stuart?'

Over tea we discussed the general composition of the deal. All my clients would become the clients of the bank (subject to one condition). The bank would honour all existing contracts with clients, subject to a liability indemnity from me, and enjoy the annual renewal and maintenance fees. I would provide the bank with details of the composition and operation of all of my tax minimisation and asset protection plans, which the bank would be free to market as their own. I would sign a non-competition agreement under which I was prevented from operating in the same profession for three years in Europe, the USA or Canada. The sale price was to be paid to me in twelve quarterly instalments over three years, with adjustments to the instalments by an agreed formula should any of my clientele leave the bank.

It was the fear of losing my clientele that worried Hugo the most. 'We need to put out a line to these clients,' he said, 'and have everyone in the bank stick to it. Remember, they signed up to a personal and professional service from you. Next thing they know they're being looked after by Francis Peartree. Good God. There's not even a hint of continuity.'

'I can offer some continuity,' I said. 'My PA, Anita, will be looking for a job. She knows all the clients. They know and respect her. She is very loyal and I'm sure would support the bank's line regarding the changeover. She would, I think, be a tremendous asset to you. Her salary level would probably break the bank's pay norms for administrative staff, but I would say that she's worth every penny.'

'Ask her to give me a call.'

'May I suggest that you call her.' I wrote her number on the bank's pad with the bank's pen. 'She would appreciate it.'

198

'What about this condition you mentioned?'

'You have probably heard of my Mycroft plan.'

'I have. How do you do it? £1 million a shot. I love it. Do you have any idea how much money we would have made together. Come on Andrew, buckle up for the ride, if only for a couple of years. We'll turn the Chancellor grey.'

'I said no and I mean no. I have four purchasers of the Mycroft plan. I wish to continue to look after these clients on this project. Everything else, including the Mycroft plan itself, passes to you.'

'Do I get the files or just the standard information on each client?'

'If you take on Anita you get the files, subject to my right to access information in response to any legal action. I would point out that Anita knows her way around those files better than I do.'

'Then we have the beginnings of a deal subject of course to the price. I think the bank would restrict me to paying only one quarter of the original price in these circumstances.'

'Then we do not have a deal,' I said and started to get up.

'It's not me, Andrew, it's the bank. My hands are tied.'

'Then I'll go elsewhere.'

'No one else will buy it.'

'Then I won't sell it.'

'One third. They told me I could go to one-third, tops.'

'When they let you go to one-half, call me.'

'I have an idea,' said Hugo, 'let's draft the heads of agreement on the basis that the price will be one-half of the original price and I'll see what I can get past the Board. It will not be easy and I make no promises, but I will try my best. We've known each other too long not to part as friends.' He was getting the deal of a lifetime and he knew it.

Back in on Wigmore Street I felt a tremendous sense of loss. I rang Billy to cancel our evening together. I told him I was low. He said that's the best time for friends to get together. He told me to drop everything and get over to Peckham. I did not find this encouraging, but I did it. Some two hours later I was sitting across from him on a grubby chair in a grubby pub. It was the closest pub to his offices, which accounted for why he had chosen it as his local. I was drinking a pint of lager. Billy, surprisingly, was drinking a pint of bitter. 'Just what has brought you so low?' he asked.

I told him about Anita's resignation, the negotiations with Hugo, the sale of the practice to Coats Bank and my overwhelming sense of loss. 'I handed him my practice,' I said. 'I just gave it to him.'

'You are wrong,' said Billy. 'You negotiated the best price you could achieve given your precarious legal position and the rigid constraints of time.'

'That is a very kind interpretation of the day's events.'

'Kind and true. You're concentrating too much on what a good deal he is getting and forgetting that you've achieved the better half of the deal.'

'The better half?'

'Yes, he's getting your clients but you're getting out,' said Billy, adding quietly, 'I wish I could get out.' He downed the rest of his bitter. 'Drink up,' he said. 'Let's go back to the office. I need some whiskey.'

'They have whiskey here.'

'Not in my measures.'

There were no comfortable chairs in Billy's office. Billy, it seemed, derived all his comforts from alcohol. He was sitting behind his desk. I was sitting on one of the visitors' chairs. On the desk were two tumblers, each filled with whiskey, poured generously by Billy's own hand. I had never been good at small talk. There was something about Billy I wanted to understand. So I just asked. 'Billy,' I said, 'George told me that you were top of the law school, a 'first' no less. George said he got an upper second. So how come he's the one who now earns the big bucks?'

Billy drained his glass in two gulps and reached for the bottle. He replenished his glass almost to the rim. I had never seen anything like it. He could have been pouring mineral water. He took another swig and, pleased with its effects, placed the glass on the table by his chair, leaned back and closed his eyes. When he spoke it came from a dark place deep within his being. 'In my final year, I thought I'd do the rounds of the top firms of solicitors in London. I was top of the law school and president of the student law society. I was a star. The first firm I secured an interview with grilled me with a passion. That was fine. I was up for it and technically equal to their questions, no problem. Then they started to ask me about my background. Technical ability, they said, was only half the story. They said that their clients had a certain standing in society and that they were interested in candidates who will maintain the social milieu of the firm. Well, they shot my cock off right there.' He reached for his glass and drained it.

'You're killing yourself, Billy.'

'I know,' he said. 'Guess where I ended up doing my articles? In a local authority. I was the beneficiary of their equal opportunities policy. I was not alone. Most of the trainees in the law department were black. It seemed that once an honest choice was made on the basis of abilities, the councils were picking black law graduates every time. This is not because black law students were better, of course we weren't. It was because, unlike our white counterparts, the best of us were not getting picked off by the prestigious law firms, so we were still in the water when the local authorities came trawling by.'

'How come you specialised in crime? You could have become a major player in local government.'

'I couldn't stand the office politics. I wanted to be on my own. I joined a small firm as an assistant solicitor and as soon as I felt able I set up on my own, first from a small serviced office then I bought this place.'

'Do you enjoy your work?'

'I defend the poor, the weak, the downtrodden and the dispossessed. It's a noble calling.'

'You also defend the guilty,' I suggested gently. 'You defend criminals.'

'Most crimes now are drug related. If drinking and smoking were illegal, and let's face it that's drug taking too, I'd be a criminal myself.'

'No, Billy,' I said. 'You're a lawyer. If it were illegal you would stop.'

'I would not,' he said, and he looked suddenly sad. 'Can't.'

'When did you start drinking?' I asked with genuine sympathy.

'When the pain started.'

'When was that?'

'A long time ago.'

Billy slouched back in his chair, all of his energy draining from his body. His eyes moist, his mouth drooping, he was beyond sad. He was forsaken. Lost for anything appropriate to say, I looked around his shabby office and noticed for the first time the absence of any family photograph or personal artefact. We sat in silence for several minutes.

I felt sorry for Billy and sensed the need to share something personal with him. 'I was supposed to have been born black,' I said. He looked at me with a mixture of amusement and bewilderment. 'It's true,' I said, and proceeded to tell him about the circumstances of my birth.

My mother was living with a black man at the time of my conception. Egbert, or Eggie to his friends, was handsome and very dark. He worked as a labourer, but he had plans and he studied at night. When my mother fell pregnant they were, after the initial shock, both happy about it. They both wanted a boy. Eggie was very attentive to my mother when she was pregnant. Her condition brought out the gentler side in him. My mother enjoyed the thoughtful attention. "I lapped it up," she once told me. She had forgotten the drunken one-night stand (the "fling down" as she called it) with a bar hand at the Rose and Crown. She'd never given it a thought. Until I was born.

Children were delivered at home in those days. When the interval in my mother's contractions fell to twenty minutes, Eggie ran down the street to call the district midwife from the public phone. Mrs Nolan, a small cheerful woman, took control the moment she arrived. She ordered Eggie to boil copious amounts of water, while she tended to my mother, talking all the time in a soothing Irish lilt. She rubbed her back and held her hand, and encouraged her to breathe in the gas and air through the mask attached to the small portable unit. From the large midwifery bag, Mrs Nolan removed her sterile towels, scissors, clamps and other instruments of childbirth, all in preparation for my arrival.

If, on my entry to the world, Mrs Nolan knew from looking at me that

202

I could never be Eggie's son she never let on. Maybe that was part of her training. Her job, after all, was to deliver babies, not to determine parentage. So after the umbilical cord had been clamped and cut, and I had been washed down, Mrs Nolan called for the father and cheerfully offered me up into the arms of Eggie who, on peering into my face, almost dropped me.

My mother is unclear about the exact sequence of the events that followed. She knows I ended up in the arms of Mrs Nolan. She can still feel the blows as Eggie punched her about the arms, head and stomach as she lay on the bed just minutes after giving birth. She knows the police arrived, brutally restrained him and took him away. She remembers he was crying and kept asking her, 'Why?' And she will never forget the pain. The physical pain and the emotional pain. The day I was born, my mother never grew tired of telling me, was the worst day of her life.

'Can't beat that,' said Billy who seemed cheered up by my story. 'What happened to Eggie?'

'Eggie,' I said, 'was prosecuted and convicted for Grievous Bodily Harm, and the presiding judge, dismissive of all claims for mitigating circumstances, handed down a very heavy custodial sentence. My mother wrote to him in jail. She wanted to explain. She wanted to apologise. She wanted to say she'd wait for him. She wanted to try again. But he never replied.'

'Damn right!' said Billy, now positively buoyant, as if set free by a story worse than his own. He took a swig from his tumbler and then leaned forward conspiratorially. 'The Laundryman,' he whispered, 'it's not Kay Finch.'

'Breaching client confidentiality?' I teased.

'No. I could never do that. It's just that she's not smart enough. Sure, she's got the confidence, and the moral issues wouldn't bother her. But I talked to her a lot. She just hasn't got the smarts.'

'She's smart enough to amass £20 million,' I said.

'I've given you my views. I can say no more, other than that it might not be her money.'

'True,' I said, and reflected for a while. 'Tell me. Just one last thing, when you knew Kay Finch, did she have a tremor, did she shake?'

'She never moved a muscle.'

As the evening drew to a close we talked of love. 'I have loved,' he said, 'but always unrequited. Always unspoken.'

'You've never told them?'

'I'm not a loveable guy Andrew. Can't take any more rejection.'

'Do you love someone now?'

'Yes.'

'Then tell her.'

'Can't.'

'Yes, you can.'

'Let's just say that it would be professionally unwise.'

He looked at me with such concentration that I began to feel uneasy. Then it hit me. Tania! Damn! 'Tania's mine,' I said.

'I know,' he said, pushing himself up out of his chair. 'More importantly, you are hers.' Billy stretched and yawned. 'Let's have one last drink and forget this conversation ever happened.' He poured me a large one, for which I was very grateful.

I arrived home feeling the worst effects of alcohol. That is not to say that I was drunk, just depressed. Alcohol does that sometimes. It caresses you first, then it smacks you in the mouth. I had hoped to come in, have a long hot bath and go straight to bed. I ended up watching an arts programme on BBC2, and was glad I did.

It was Tania who brought the programme to my attention. Presented by the ubiquitous Merlin Bowater, Performance was the channel's leading highbrow programme for the appreciation of the arts. Usually it would feature profiles of classical musicians, avant garde painters, unfathomable poets or self-indulgent actors. Merlin, himself, had an irritatingly ingratiating manner. There was no rubbish his guest could speak that he would not fail to treat as the most profound wisdom. His guests, after all, were the good and the great.

Yet every so often Merlin would "slum it," choosing as his subject a popular artiste, but emphasising that there was more to his or her art than could be appreciated by the masses who bought their works. Such artistes were treated by Merlin with his same unique brand of reverence. I suppose he knew no other way. His featured artiste that night, Tania excitedly told me, was Lightning, with a special cameo appearance by a mystery guest.

Chapter 12

'Let's watch the programme in the family room,' said Tania. 'We never use the family room.'

This was true. As DS Greenley had unkindly intimated, I have no family. The room was furnished with a soft floral patterned three-piece suite. A Bang & Olufsen TV, finished in black lacquer, sat in the corner of the room. The deep pile carpet was the colour of an overripe tangerine. This was not the work of my interior designer. A short-lived girlfriend, a Tudor loving American history professor, had taken charge of the room some years ago. I'd hardly been in the room since she left.

'You may want to re-model this room at some stage,' I said to Tania. 'I don't really like it. Here's the remote, put the TV on; when does it start?'

'In ten minutes.'

'Good, then I've got time to get myself a large whiskey. I feel I'm going to need it.'

'Haven't you had enough?' she asked.

'No,' I said.

The programme opened with its familiar signature tune, Rachmaninov's "Rhapsody on a Theme of Paganini – Variation 18." Not entirely appropriate for what is to follow, I thought. Next the face of Merlin Bowater filled two-thirds of the screen, leaving just enough space over his right shoulder to show the silhouetted figure of Lightning sitting in the far background waiting to be interviewed. Merlin launched into his opening monologue.

'There is a form of music that is engaging the minds of our young called "rap." At a superficial level the attraction of this music rests in its harsh, though relatively simple and easily absorbed melodies, overlaid by iconoclastic and wholly irreverent lyrics, usually couched in what some would call vulgar and obscene language. Others view this language as the poetry of the street. An American professor of literature has likened the best of the genre to William Blake, the lyrics containing as they do a complex structure of rhyme. We have with us today Britain's premier exponent of the art of rap who, with his latest release, has moved the art form from its hitherto primary focus on the often violent nature of personal relationships in our deprived urban communities, to a new level. *The Laundryman*, the first track of a forthcoming album of the same name, is a rallying call for economic self-sufficiency within Britain's ethnic communities. And it is more. It calls on those communities to surrender their dependency on the financial institutions whose failure to reinvest locally serves to stifle the growth of local enterprises, and thereby the general well-being of the community as a whole, whether or not those enterprises are within the established legal norms of contemporary society, recognising that such norms are built on the ever shifting sands of public opinion.'

'What did he say?' said Tania.

'He said that Lightning is a rebel.'

'Then why didn't he just say that?'

'Because his name is Merlin Bowater.'

'Tonight,' continued Merlin, 'we examine this new development in the art of rap and ask whether this is just a small aberration in the multi-million pound mass market or whether Britain is once again at the forefront of a fundamental and potentially cataclysmic artistic transmogrification serving to bring this popular but infant musical form into a formidable adulthood. After the round-up of current exhibitions and events I will be talking to Lightning in the studio.' Merlin faded from the screen to be replaced by an Anglo-Asian presenter who ran through those principal cultural events of the week that should not be missed by any self-respecting member of the intelligentsia.

'Lightning,' said Merlin once the round-up was over. Both Lightning and Merlin were sitting in black canvas director's chairs. Between them was a small oval pine coffee table on which sat two plain glasses of water. The backdrop to the set was plain white.

'Yo,' said Lightning.

'Now would it be fair of me to say that rap music has received much negative press in the mainstream media, notwithstanding the huge commercial success that it has enjoyed with the young?'

'Not just the young Merlin,' said Lightning. 'Rap is reaching people of all ages. It's also getting to both black and white, man and woman. But you're right, the press is down on us big time and the politicians.'

'Why do you think that is? I have a view –'

'Why doesn't he let Lightning answer the question?' said Tania.

'Because it's Merlin's show,' I replied.

'– and my view is this: rap is an art form that challenges cosy middle class assumptions. All things new challenge the status quo until over time they are absorbed into the mainstream. What you are experiencing happened to Elvis Presley, the Beatles, the Rolling Stones and the Sex Pistols, each of whom are now wholly respectable, with the possible exception of Johnny Rotten, but even he is no longer reviled.'

'True,' said Lightning, 'but I never wanted to join the mainstream. I want my work to be in a state of permanent revolution.'

'I hear shades of Leon Trotsky. I hear the understated rumblings of a socialist transformation of society, perhaps the internationalisation and globalisation of the process of social revolution. But we have limited time –'

'Thank God,' I said.

'– and I want to move on to your new single *The Laundryman*. What was its genesis?'

'Its…?'

'That is, where did you get the initial idea that led you to conceive of the concept for the single?'

I thought to myself, what's the matter with this man? It wasn't a love of words, I concluded, it was a love of self.

'Right,' said Lightning. 'there's this person called the Laundryman –'

'A metaphor, I assume, for all those financial institutions and intermediaries who you feel effectively rob ethnic communities of their economic independence.'

'No, the Laundryman exists. He is a money launderer, the biggest money launderer in Britain. He is the daddy of all launderers. All the dealers must launder their proceeds –'

'That is,' said Merlin, 'those engaged in the supply and distribution of recreational drugs, which, though, at present, unlawful, is a widespread and lucrative activity, must disguise the proceeds of, what today I suppose we must call, their crimes.'

'Right, and the big players use one person. I'm not talking about people who think they're big. I'm talking about those who are really big. The cartels. They use one person. One person, for all their needs. And that person is known as the Laundryman. And the problem is that the police can't catch him. Well, they've caught someone who they think is him, but he's not.'

'Who have they caught?'

I held my breath. 'I can't say, but just because he's really smart, and they can't find the Laundryman, they're trying to pin it on him.'

'Why him? We are, of course, all aware that we live in a time when expediency has replaced integrity as the motivation for most political acts. Would you say the arrest of this man was a political act?'

'Certainly. He takes on the Establishment by preventing them from stealing too much of people's money through taxes, and Bam!' Lightning brought his fist down on the coffee table upsetting both glasses of water. 'Sorry,' he said.

'No,' said Merlin clearly shaken by the suddenness of Lightning's strike, 'it is fitting…' Merlin was struggling, 'fitting that the order in this studio is upset just as you wish to upset the order in society.' He found his feet 'Let no one replace these glasses during the poetry interval. I wish them to remain upturned. Their symbolism is significant.'

'They didn't come for him first, they came for his girlfriend –'

'Me!' said Tania. 'We're famous Stu.'

'Only for 15 minutes,' I said, 'hopefully.'

'– she was one of twenty-four arrested on the same night and that where

209

the track starts,' Lightning started to rap, *'On a dark cold night/They arrest twenty-four of us/ Hunting for the fox/That they call the Laundryman.'*

'What would you say was the principal objective of this track? Would you, for instance, say that the record was a call to arms?'

'It's a call to catch the Laundryman,' said Lightning. *'Give up the Laundryman. Give him up, give him up, give up the Laundryman.'*

'We now take a short break from this week's theme to listen to the fourth finalist in this year's Performance Poetry Prize. When we return we will go straight to a satellite link up in Scotland for a rare live interview with the managing director of Lightning's record company, none other than Joseph Feingold.'

'Joe!' said Tania.

I felt wretched. 'Can it possibly get any worse?'

After the poetry reading, there was Joe beaming into the camera. The link-up had been set up in the same room as Tania, BB and I had met him in. He had positioned himself, once again, in the centre. He appeared to be alone. His entourage, I thought, must be just out of the camera's view.

'Mr Feingold,' said Merlin as the picture panned out leaving Joe on a large screen in the studio and Merlin in the foreground, 'we are honoured that you have chosen this time and this arts programme to give your first television interview since your unhappy helicopter accident some five years ago. May I first ask you, before I turn to Lightning's radical development of the phenomenon of rap music, how you are personally? We have missed you.'

'Well Merlin, I find it hard to believe that you have missed me at all. I am the antithesis of everything you promote and hold dear to your intellectually superior bosom. That said, hey, you miss a headache after it's gone; am I right? So I'll accept you at your word. How am I? I'm great and excited about Lightning's work. This is going to be big. You watch.'

'It is pleasing to hear you compliment one of your artistes. You are on record as being less than kind to some of your biggest artistes. In your opinion what makes Lightning different?'

'I've never been unkind to an artiste yet. The word "unkindness" implies a degree of cruelty on my part. Never been cruel in my life. If I call someone's work "crap" it is because that is what it is. I still market it. I still sell it. I still make millionaires out of the singers, the musicians and the producers. What you have to understand is, people like crap. They love it. That's why there's so much of it about. Now Lightning's work is different. It is bold, direct and dangerous. You know what, he really wants to catch this Laundryman. When was the last time popular culture took the lead in hunting down a criminal? Not just any criminal now, a financial mastermind, a frigging genius. This is going to be huge.'

'What, Mr Feingold, do you think of the wider sociological impact of Lightning's departure from the hitherto primary concerns of rap music? Will rap now become the voice of the dispossessed?'

'Why do you always ask two questions at once?' A tall busty blonde came into view as she placed a glass of water on the tray fixed to Joseph Feingold's wheelchair.

Tania said, 'That's Lucky –'

'I know,' I said.

'One question at a time will do,' continued Joe. 'Now what do I think of the wider sociological this and that? Nothing at all. Will rap become the voice of the dispossessed? No. Rap will crawl back into the hole it came out of. It is a base art form. However, today and for a brief period of time it will dominate the arts, it will dominate the news, it will dominate politics. *The Laundryman* will become the anthem of our time. Trust me. It's going to be humongous.'

Joseph Feingold was back, and talking up a storm. The media loved it. The Guardian took a line similar to that adopted by Merlin Bowater in Performance, treating Lightning as a radical rap artist with a new message. The Telegraph was utterly dismissive of Lightning and his message, suggesting that even a cursory analysis of his lyrics revealed a third rate mind operating in a fourth rate medium. The Sun, some two days after the programme, featured a topless Lucky Sucky on page 6 under the caption, "What keeps Joseph Feingold's spirits up." She was pictured holding aloft a long football-type scarf embroidered with the word "Give up the

Laundryman." Two days later in a "world exclusive" the same paper revealed that Lucky Sucky used to be a man. To illustrate the story they ran the same picture. Joe was at it again, giving the public what they wanted and making a mint. One week after its release *The Laundryman* entered the Pepsi charts at No1.

The merchandising served to keep the issue of the Laundryman before the public. There were T-shirts with "The Laundryman" written on the front and "Give Him Up!" written on the back. The Laundryman logo was used on baseball caps and mugs. This was all the work of Joseph Feingold, supporting the song and exploiting the market. Within days the cottage industry end of T-shirt screen printing were making up their own slogans, ranging from "Keep the Laundryman safe" to "I am the Laundryman." The internet very quickly developed chat rooms focused entirely on the Laundryman. Conspiracy theories developed overnight linking the Laundryman to such diverse figures as Gerry Adams, The Duke of Westminster and Lord Lucan, who apparently was still alive. "The police today," said a chirpy Radio 2 DJ, "have enlisted the help of cat burglars. Why? To catch the Laundrymouse!" The Laundryman had become a phenomenon, a *cause célèbre*. He had entered the national psyche.

I had put off going to see Patsy for as long as I felt I could. There were no more excuses. The recent sequence of events had forced me to confront my past. My Wednesday afternoon was free and I made my way to Ealing. I drove at first in silence. The route map was on but I had muted Sally's voice. My mind was on Patsy.

She had lived with her father, the pastor, in the best of the rooms in the large house in Shepherds Bush. Their rooms were at the top of the house, ours were in the basement. This also reflected the difference in our status. We were both at the bottom of the socio-economic scale, but the pastor and Patsy ranked slightly higher than my mum and me. So, though we lived in the same building, the pastor never spoke to my mum, and Patsy never spoke to me. I learned early on that black people, given the opportunity, were as class conscious at white people.

212

I only got to know Patsy when she started secondary school, by which time I was in the third year. She was beautiful. She had the smoothest brown skin and the whitest teeth I had ever seen. Her hair was always shiny and worn in two long, thick plaits. Always so neatly dressed in her school uniform, she stood out from the rest of the girls, most of whom sought to buck the dress code in an attempt to assert their individuality. Yet by staying within the rules, even celebrating them, Patsy, to me at least, was the most individual girl in the school. Ever cheerful, always helpful, she got the reputation of being a teacher's pet. To the girls she was a goody-two-shoes. To the boys, as she never flirted, she simply didn't exist. To me she was everything, and I loved her with a passion that only a 13-year-old can feel.

I never saw her mother and Patsy never talked about her. She never stopped talking about her father or, more accurately, her father's rules. He was the strictest of men. At home she did all the cooking and cleaning, and washing and ironing. Her homework took second place to her chores. I joked once that she was like Cinderella and took to occasionally calling her Cindy. She didn't like it. One evening, walking home from school she explained that her father had stood by her. He could have had her adopted, fostered, put into care or palmed off to relatives, and got on with the rest of his life. Instead he had raised her himself, even though he was wholly ill suited to the task. She said he was a good father; an inadequate man, but a good father. I never called her Cindy again.

I needed a diversion. I punched on the radio and flicked through the preset channels, stopping and listening only briefly to Classic FM and Jazz FM. My CD's were Andrea Botcelli, the Beatles, a collection of Baroque, Courtney Pine and the latest demo by the girl band Truce. Nothing seemed to fit the mood. I needed the human voice in dramatic form. I had a number of plays and poetry collections on cassette in the car and was about to stop to choose something appropriate, when I noticed the time. It was almost three o' clock. Radio 5 Live would soon be broadcasting Prime Minister's Question Time direct from the House of Commons. Half an hour's unscripted verbal cut and thrust from the mother of parliaments. Just what I needed. I hit the mode button on the steering wheel, which switched the radio back on and choose the station by hitting the preset button for the AM band.

The commentator was setting the scene and trying to guess the likely topics on which this Wednesday's questions would be based. In my mind's eye I could see the crowded House of Commons, MPs squeezed together on the green leather government benches (so-called, they were more like very long sofas), less so on the opposition benches. All the men wore shirts and ties; some were smart, some were scruffy. The women wore a variety of outfits; some were colourful, some were plain, but all were smart.

'Questions to the Prime Minister,' announced the Speaker of the House.

The first question, as always, asked the Prime Minister to list his official engagements for the day. The Prime Minister responded, 'This morning, I had meetings with ministerial colleagues and others. In addition to my duties in this House, I shall be having further such meetings later today.'

The follow-up question, was from a Conservative backbencher, was: 'Does the Prime Minister agree with me that today's increase in interest rates is yet another indication of the failure of his government's economic policy?'

Tony Blair was on his feet and smiling. 'It may have escaped the honourable gentleman's notice that the operational responsibility for setting interest rates has rested with the Bank of England since 1997.' Laughter rose from the Labour backbenchers. 'The rise in the interest rates today is fully in accordance with the government's objective of maintaining a level of price stability which is the envy of the last five Conservative Chancellors.'

The second follow-up question, from a different MP related to drugs. 'Is the Prime Minister aware that in the last month alone four of my constituents have died from drug overdoses? Given the increasing prevalence of drugs in British society, what specific measures does the Prime Minister intended to implement to root out this cancer which is destroying the lives of too many of our young?'

Tony Blair was immediately back on his feet. 'As I am sure the honourable gentleman is aware the availability of illegal drugs is a worldwide problem. It was discussed at the recent G8 summit. The global market for drugs is now estimated at up to $500 billion a year. We need to see the international cartels of organised crime for what they are: major international businesses with the same need for banking facilities, working capital and investment funds as any other business.'

'What are you going to do about it?' yelled an animated Conservative backbencher, 'That's the question.'

'If the honourable gentleman can restrain himself for thirty seconds,' retorted the Prime Minister, 'I will tell the House. The G8 has agreed a further clampdown on money laundering, tax evasion and banking secrecy. That will be underpinned by the eight standards developed by G7 Finance Ministers in a new report that we published, setting out the measures that offshore financial centres will need to comply with to avoid sanctions in the future.' Tony Blair's voice softened. 'As regards the deaths my honourable friend mentioned in his question, my sympathies and I am sure the sympathies of this whole House, go out to their families and loved ones.' This was greeted with a loud chorus of 'Hear, hear!' from Labour, Conservative and Liberal Democrat members alike.

Another backbencher caught the Speaker's eye and was called. 'Moving from the global to the local, would the Prime Minister advise the House on exactly what measures the government has put in place to catch the Laundryman?'

The radio commentator interrupted to describe the scene. 'The Prime Minister appears wrong footed. He is talking to colleagues on his front bench.' I bet he is, I thought. 'He's rising now.'

'I would say to the honourable gentleman that I consider drug trafficking to be the scourge of modern times and that money laundering is its partner-in-crime. Money launderers are criminals, plain and simple, and they should be subject to the full rigours of the law. As regards the measures we have taken to deal with this and other crimes, I would remind the honourable gentleman that this government has allocated more money to the police over the last three years than was allocated in the last three years of the previous government.' The car stereo filled with a mixture of cheers and jeers, as the Prime Minister moved on to question 2, which as usual was identical to question 1. 'I refer the honorable gentleman to the reply I gave some moments ago.'

I turned the radio off. So the Laundryman had received the ultimate accolade. He had been the subject of a question to the Prime Minister in parliament. He was no 1 in the singles charts, the subject of numerous articles in the newspaper and magazines, and programmes on the TV. It would not be long, I thought, before some enterprising postgraduate student proposed a doctoral thesis on the subject. Something like, 'A critical examination of the effect of the Laundryman on the social and economic morés of contemporary Britain, with comparative analysis with the effects of the Jackal on France.'

My mind returned to the Prime Minister's answer. It was a bland answer, but as the commentator said the PM was wrong footed. Something was bothering me, and I couldn't place it. I drove through Knightsbridge, taking the Brompton Road, passing Harrods, Tania's store of choice. Ealing was not far away now, and my sense of apprehension returned.

When I was 16 and Patsy 14 we were boyfriend and girlfriend. We were "going out together," as we used to say at the time, though we never really went anywhere. The problem was the pastor, who knew nothing about our liaison. We still never talked in the house. We walked to school together and walked home. And when we walked we held hands. It was delightful. There are those who believe the early Beatles' song *'I want to hold your hand'* is a euphemism for 'I want to make love to you.' They are wrong, or I hope they are. Holding hands is simple and wonderfully intimate. Well, it was then. And, following my trip to Cayman with Tania, I can confirm that it is now. But then, as now, it wasn't enough.

Every Wednesday evening from 6:00 to 8:00 the pastor attended counselling classes at a local college, and every Wednesday evening from 6:30 to 7:30 Patsy came down to our basement bedsit. My mother, at this stage of my life, was hardly ever around. She bought the food and washed my clothes, but basically I looked after myself. I was closer to Patsy than anyone else.

I never raised the subject of sex. Each time we kissed, I let my hands wander further. Of course Patsy resisted, as all good girls were supposed to, but the next time I could resume where I left off. No ground gained was ever lost. I became adept at kissing and caressing, kissing and unbuttoning, kissing and unzipping. One evening when I had my hand in her panties and my tongue was tracing lines down her neck, she whispered, 'Are we going to do it?' And we did. And she got pregnant. And all hell broke loose.

As I turned into Church Gardens, and my conscious mind focused on the ordeal ahead, I realised what had bothered me about the Prime Minister's answer. Though he chose to address his answer to money launderers generally, he did not actually deny the existence of the Laundryman.

I parked the car, badly, at the end of the street. My heart was beating fast. I was sweating. My hands were shaking. I searched for reasons to go back home. There were plenty, but none was good enough. I got out the car and walked up the street, checking the door numbers as I went. I had never seen the house before. It was terraced, with a small front garden. I pushed the gate, walked up the neat pathway and rang the bell. As the door opened, there was Patsy, and twenty-three years melted away in a second. 'Andrew,' she said. 'I've been expecting you.'

'May I come in,' I asked. 'I assume the pastor's not here.' The pastor, her father, a man I'd heard preach of fire and brimstone, hell and damnation, but never of love and compassion.

'He's back in Jamaica. A conference of churches, I think. He's going to make a speech.'

'Heaven help them,' I said.

Patsy led me past a row of coats in the hallway, into the lounge. The room was clean and tidy, and amply furnished, but with too many contrasting colours for my own comfort. I wondered whose taste would have prevailed if we had been able to make a life together.

'Well,' she said and clapped her hands together as a child might.

'Yes,' I replied, equally at a loss.

'Tea,' she suggested and pointed towards what I assumed was the

217

kitchen.

'That would be nice.'

I watched her every move as she made her way to the kitchen, and felt an overwhelming attraction to her. She was still petite, and she still had that buttoned-down allure of sexuality. Her hair, as before, was thick and long and shiny, black without a trace of grey. She now wore it in a simple twist that reached the small of her back. She wore a cream blouse with white buttons. It was tucked into a skirt that reached to the knee but accentuated the round curves of her bottom. How I wanted her. Our inexperienced fumbling of yesteryear was all wrong. When we did it I just wanted to fuck. My focus was on me, not her, and I never got the chance to make it right. I wanted to make it right, now. In the kitchen, on the living room floor, anywhere.

'How do you take it?' she shouted from the kitchen.

'White, no sugar.'

'Do you want a mug or a cup?'

'A mug please,' I said.

She returned carrying a bright yellow mug, one hand on the handle, the other forming a sort of cradle around the other side of the mug, not quite holding it and not quite leaving it alone. She had a faster gait than I remember, almost a light trot, which seemed out of place in a house. Maybe I was making her nervous. Maybe she was nervous all the time. 'Here you are Andrew,' she said.

'You're not having one?'

'Yes, yes, it's in the kitchen. I'm going to get it now.'

She moved back to the kitchen in a canter. She returned with her own mug, carrying it in the same way. 'Are you OK Patsy?'

'Yes,' she said with a smile that dazzled. 'I'm glad you came. It's so good to see you. It's been so long.'

'Twenty-three years.'

'I never thought I'd see you again. Look at you,' she said eyeing me up and down. I suppose it was the first time she had seen me in a suit. It was almost the first time she had seen me out of school uniform. 'You're very

218

'successful aren't you?'

'Always said I would be.'

'I know, and I always believed you.'

'You did.'

'But now something's gone wrong.'

'Yes.'

'And it affects Michael and me.'

'No, not directly.'

'Yes it does, that's what the detective sergeant said. He said – how did he put it? – that we were intrinsically involved. Michael was furious.' I bet he was, I thought. 'What's going on Andrew?'

'What did Detective Sergeant Greenley tell you?'

'He didn't say a lot to me. He spoke mostly to Michael – and father.'

'Your father was present.'

'Yes Michael, I'm sorry.'

'What did he say?'

'You really want to know?'

'Yes,' I said and prepared for the worst.

Patsy got up and smoothed down her skirt. She tilted her head back and started shaking her shoulders. She had done this before many, many years ago, and had me convulsed in laughter. Today it would not be funny, but the act would still be startling: Patsy mimicking her father. Hands outstretched, palms turned upwards, she started in a voice powerful, trembling and full of rage: 'He was bad, bad to the core. I called on the good Lord then, I call on him now. Turn this sinner back to the path of righteousness. The devil entered his soul at birth. At birth the devil saw his wayward mother and knew he had found a disciple, knew that the apple would not fall far from the tree, and from that day the boy has been doing the devil's work. You think you come with news detective sergeant, but you have no news for me. I am surprised only that this boy walks free in the world to do his evil deeds. He knows of no morality, knows of no right or wrong. There was no one to teach him. His parents left him to root about in the gutter. He would not let the Lord into his life. Heaven knows I tried. He wanted only gratification, gratification of his base and corrupt desires.'

'He never tried,' I said, 'He never even spoke to me.'

Patsy remained in character. 'You tell me of money laundering. I am not surprised. The love of money is the root of all evil. Andrew is a son of Satan, a man who will burn in hell. Fire and brimstone.' Patsy was shaking, almost levitating, 'Hell, death, damnation and destruction. And I, a poor misguided sinner, who still believes in the power of redemption, I, now, at this late hour, call and plead with the Holy Ghost to save the soul of this tormented Andrew John Stuart Singley.'

I froze. 'He gave Greenley my full name?'

'Yes,' said Patsy, breathing deeply, trying to regain composure. 'Is that a problem?'

'I changed my name by Deed Poll. Stuart is my surname now. I dropped the Singley twenty years ago.'

'Why?'

'Why do you think?'

I heard the key in the door. 'That's Michael,' she said and I was filled with dread. He entered the room like an athlete, looked at me and stopped dead still. He was taller than both Patsy and me, with a solid build. He was brown, of course, but his facial features owed more to European than African ancestry. His hair was cropped very short, and his eyes were the clearest blue. He was strikingly handsome. Though my pride in his physicality was complete, I found it impossible to disregard the uniform. I knew about it from the reports, but it was different to see him in it in front of me in the circumstances of the day. Here was my son, a policeman.

Chapter 13

Patsy was over-animated. 'Michael, darling, look who's here.' Her whole body moved jerkily as she talked. 'You'll never guess. Come on. Shake his hand. Let me take your jacket and hang it up. It's your father, darling. He's come to see us. Isn't that nice?'

Michael just stood and stared.

I stood up. My legs felt weak. I tried to keep my voice strong. 'Hello Michael,' I said.

'Get out,' he replied.

Patsy stepped between us. 'Now Michael, that's no way to talk to your father.'

'I don't have a father. I have a mother and a granddad and that's it.'

'If you want to blame anyone for that,' I said, 'blame him.'

'You mean granddad?' Michael was immediately defensive. 'Granddad has always been there for me. You may have paid the bills, but granddad taught me right from wrong, something you appear not to have learnt.'

I couldn't chastise my own son. I was twenty years too late for that. But I could challenge him as a man. 'Your granddad robbed you of a father.'

'I don't want you as a father. You raped my mother.'

So that was it, that was what the man of God had been peddling to my son for twenty years. I had always made it reasonably easy for Michael to find me, but he'd never tried, not even out of curiosity. Now I knew why. 'So that's what the old bastard told you!' I moved to the dining table and placed a hand to steady myself. I tried for calm. 'Your mother and I loved each other. Your mother was 14; I was 16. We made love.' No, it was sex, it was teenage discovery, it was irresponsible fucking, but I was talking to my son. 'Your mother was underage. She got pregnant. When she told her father and he went to the police. I was charged with statutory rape. That's not rape, Michael. That's underage sex. They are worlds apart. I longed to be with your mother with all my being. I wanted us to raise our child - you - together.'

'That's true Michael,' said Patsy.

He ignored her. 'Why didn't you come back?'

'I tried, believe me. After the case, to which I pleaded guilty, I was placed on juvenile detention. I was treated as a sex offender. Your grand-dad had no difficulty in obtaining a restraint order to prevent me coming anywhere near Patsy and you. After a while, I had to cut off physically and emotionally, or I would have destroyed myself. I always sent your mother money. It was only a little during my student days, but I worked every vacation and did library duties during term time to help. Later on I estab-lished the trust fund.'

'And you appointed a private investigations company to spy on us. DS Greenley told me. He even showed me some of the reports. Professional courtesy, you know.'

'I needed to know that you were OK. I needed to know Patsy was OK. It was the only way I knew how, other than re-entering and disrupting your lives.'

'Then the reports should have said, "They're OK." Instead they went into detail about where we went, who we saw, copies of my school reports, who mummy was dating. You invaded our privacy.'

'I just wanted to live a little with you both. Vicariously, if you like.'

'You're sick.'

'No, Michael, I'm wounded. Is there a place where we can talk?' I needed to get away from Patsy.

'Upstairs,' he said, and led the way.

It was a three-bedroom house. Michael had the small bedroom on the turn of the stairs. I assumed Patsy had the master bedroom and the pastor the second bedroom, but it may have been the other way round. Michael's room was in stark contrast to the living room downstairs. His walls were white and his pillow and duvet were cream. There was a complete absence of the avalanche of colour favoured by his mother. My genes, I thought. The room was also unusually neat and tidy for a man, but I assumed it reflected the discipline instilled in him by his police training, or by his granddad. He sat on his bed and motioned for me to pull out the seat by his computer desk. I did so, sat down and waited.

'So you're a money launderer.'

'I am your father,' I replied. 'Professionally I'm an international tax consultant, though I have recently sold my practice. Is that what they teach you at Hendon these days, that a man arrested for a crime is automatically guilty of that crime? I haven't even been charged for Christ sakes. Haven't you heard of the due process of law, or have you already been corrupted by the canteen mentality of the Metropolitan Police Force?'

'DS Greenley says you're the Laundryman. Can you imagine the effect that will have on my career? I don't know my father. Never meet him. Then boom, a senior officer knocks on my door and tells me that my dad is the most wanted criminal in London. Thanks a bundle. I was doing just fine without you, now I would appreciate it if you would quietly disappear.'

'I'm not the Laundryman,' I said. 'In fact I'm moving heaven and earth to identify, find and catch him.'

'How are you doing?'

'I've got some leads.'

'I think it's you. It confirms everything granddad told me about you. He said you were bad, from bad stock. Your dad was a drunk, your mum was a whore. You turned your back on God, so you never had a chance.'

'Your granddad is a bigoted asshole.'

Michael was shocked. 'He's a man of God.'

'OK, a God loving bigoted asshole.'

He leapt from the bed and grabbed me by the shoulders, forcing his forehead roughly against my own. 'Get out, and don't come back.'

'What?'

'I don't want you in my mother's life.'

I was badly shaken. I thought he was going to thrash me – my own son.

I said, 'Don't you think that's your mother's decision?'

'No I don't. She not good at making decisions.' Like granddad, like grandson. 'I mean it,' he said, pushing me away. 'If you ever come back I'll arrest you, personally.'

'What for?'

He eyes were menacing. 'You don't want to know.'

I made my way down the stairs. To be arrested and fitted up by my own son. I suppose I deserved no better. Life has a way of paying you back when you least expect it.

'One last thing,' he shouted from the top of the stairs as I reached the door. 'No more money. Break the trust fund. We want no more money of yours.'

'Why not?' I asked lamely.

'Because we don't know where it's been.'

'Patsy,' I said, 'I'm leaving.'

She didn't come out. Clearly the men ruled in this house. 'OK Andrew, take care.' I closed the door behind me and trudged slowly back to my car.

Thursday afternoon BB came round to the house. He seemed in a buoyant mood. He was dressed in black jeans and a black short sleeve shirt open at the neck. There was a light sheen of perspiration on his forehead. 'Been working out?' I asked.

'Sort of,' he said.

'If it's a woman I don't need to know the details.'

'I wouldn't give them to you.' He stretched his arms and yawned. 'Actually,' he said, 'I think I've progressed our case a little this morning. You remember Anton?'

'My student, Anton?'

'Yeah, the cokehead who reckoned he knew who the Laundryman was.'

'I told you to stay away from him BB.'

'I know you did, but I didn't.'

'So you've spoken to him.'

'Up close and personal.'

224

BB was grinning. I assumed this meant he had good news. 'And?' I said.

'And he's going to tell me everything.'

'When?'

'Now, he's outside in the car.'

'Bring him in,' I said.

'No,' said BB, 'you'd better come outside.'

The wind slapped against my face as I walked down the driveway to BB's old but well maintained BMW. As I approached the car I strained to see inside. 'He's gone,' I said.

'He's in the boot,' said BB. I turned on my heels and walked back towards the house. BB grabbed my arm before I got to the door. 'Now listen, he doesn't know where he is or who we are. You're Dick and I'm Tracy. You don't talk in case he recognises your voice. I talk to him through the boot. He gives us answers. I drive him away. Easy.'

I wanted no part of this and tried to pull my arm away from his grip without success. BB swung me around to face him. Grabbing both biceps he squeezed until it hurt. His expression was fierce. 'Have I got your attention?'

'Yes,' I said. He eased his grip.

'Right, now I have gone to a lot of trouble to bring this overeducated, puffy little shit to your house and now I'm going to talk to him.'

'Just tell me how. Amuse me BB. How did you get a postgraduate law student of mine, a man you had never met before, into the boot of your car?' BB explained that he knew all he needed for the task: the target's name, his location and his habits. He had gone to the university's canteen and ordered a coffee. He sat by himself and read the Guardian, which he had brought, he said, to look the part. He needn't have bothered, a lot of the students were reading the tabloids. Most of the conversation about him featured football, personal relationships and just plain gossip. BB was surprised. He had expected loftier discourse. Eventually he overheard two girls discussing a paper the taller of which was writing on intellectual property. He approached them. "Hi'" he said. "Law students, right." "Yes," they replied together. "I'm looking for Anton, a postgrad, do you know him?" "You obviously don't, he's sitting over there," said the taller of the two girls pointing. "Who are you?" "I'm new here," said BB, "a research post." The girls looked dubious. "If you like," said BB, "I'll give you some help with your intellectual property paper. That's my field." "Oh, please," she said, and BB took her phone number. "He's the puffy looking one in the designer tracksuit." "Call you later," promised BB.

He approached Anton, sat down and got straight to the point. "I hear you're the main man here. The guy that makes things happen." "Who have you been talking to?" asked Anton. "Everyone," said BB. "I've got some very good stuff I need to shift, large margins, credit terms, if you can handle it." "I don't deal," said Anton. "I'm not asking you to deal," said BB. "I'm asking you to introduce me to someone who can deal. But first you'll want to try the stuff right? To make sure it's the business. A free sample." Anton followed BB to his car, left in an NCP car park. "Have I got something to show you!" BB opened the boot. "I'm really trusting you here Anton, open the case, it'll blow your mind." As Anton leaned into the boot to open the case BB grabbed his testicles and squeezed. "Get in," he said, and squeezed a little harder.

'BB,' I said, 'let's look at the crimes here: kidnapping, false imprisonment and assault, and that's just off the top of my head.'

'Do you want me to talk to this guy or not?'

'Not like this.'

'I'm sorry.' BB's eyes widened. 'Did you want me to invite him to dinner? Maybe I should have sent him one of those fancy little cards with RSVP in the bottom corner. You know, black tie only, and maybe he'd have told you all about his cocaine supplier over cheese and biscuits. But I don't think so. I don't think you're to get any information out of this worthless turd without him being scared.'

I didn't answer.

'And right now he's scared shitless. Come on.'

BB made his way to the car. I reluctantly followed. BB kicked the boot. 'Anton.'

226

'What?'

'My friend Dick here wants to ask you some questions about your cocaine habit.'

'Fuck off.'

'Come on, show the man some respect, Anton.'

'Let me out of here then. I won't run anywhere. Look, I've got cramp in my legs. Let me out and I'll talk.'

'No way,' said BB. 'You sound real good to me right where you are.'

'Do you know who I am? Do you know who my father is? Do you know what is going to happen to you when this is over?'

'Yes, yes and yes,' replied BB. 'You are a cokehead, your father's a doctor and when this is over I'm going home to sleep with my wife, Mrs Tracy.'

'Not if I fuck you first.'

'That's it,' said BB. 'I'm leaving now. Dick, I'm gonna drive this car to Lover's Lane, you know, the place with the sheer drop. I'm gonna get out, admire the view, then release the handbrake and push this piece of junk off the fucking cliff.'

'You wouldn't dare.'

'I wasn't talking to you I was talking to my friend Dick here. Shut the fuck up. You're no longer part of this conversation. What do you think Dick?'

It was just as well that I had a non-speaking part. I was speechless.

'What's that Dick? Set the car on fire to get rid of any prints. Steady on my friend, Anton would be fried alive. That aside, good idea though. Couldn't use Lover's Lane, though. Oh? You know a place Dick, an auto scrapyard? Sounds good to me.'

'You're just winding me up.'

BB turned to the talking trunk. 'I said shut up.'

There was a long silence. BB looked at me. It was as if he was counting down. I was thinking about how best to die. When the voice came it was soft, barely audible over the rustle of the bushes in the breeze. Had I not known there was a man in the boot I would have missed it. 'What do you want to know?'

BB knelt down at the back of the car so that the boot was eye level. He too spoke softly, as if in recognition that the threats were no longer necessary, 'Who supplies the coke Anton?'

'Lord Baxter,' he said.

BB looked at me to see if I recognised the name. I nodded. Lord Baxter was one of the governors of the university. 'Thank you Anton,' he said.

'Happy?' asked BB having led me some ten yards away from the car. I just shook my head at the bizarre nature of the exchange that I had just witnessed. 'One favour deserves another right?'

'Sure,' I said.

'I need you to help re-write a paper on intellectual property.'

The girl in the cafeteria, I thought. 'Isn't she a little young for you?'

'She didn't seem to think so.'

'So you're going to pass off my work off as your own.'

'No, I'll come clean as soon as I meet up with her, but a promise is a promise, right?'

BB drove off with Anton in the boot and I walked back to the house drenched in sweat. Julianna greeted me in the hallway. 'What was going on out there?' she asked.

'Nothing,' I said.

'I was looking from the upstairs window. You and BB seemed to be talking to his car.'

'BB was talking to the car. I was just listening.'

'Why would BB talk to a car?'

'You know BB,' I said and went upstairs to take a cold shower.

BB called Rebecca, the intellectual property studying law student, and they went out on a date. The next day BB brought her essay to me for suggestions for improvement, which I gave by writing extensive notes in the margin of her paper. A promise, after all, was a promise.

'Where does Lord Baxter live?' asked BB.

'Nottinghamshire,' I replied.

'Been there before?'

'Yes, but not to see him.'

'You were seeing his daughter?'

'No, no.'

'His wife?'

'No,' I said, 'his home.'

'His home?'

'You'll see,' I said.

There are those who would say that my house was impressive, but it looked like a granny annex compared to Baxter Hall, one of England's great Elizabethan houses. Built by Lord Baxter's great- great- great- great- great- great- great- great- grandfather, who was well rewarded for the many bloody favours he performed for Queen Elizabeth I, it dominated the view for miles. Though Lord Baxter owned the property and lived there, it had for many years been registered with the National Trust. It was open to the public from March until October, and one summer I was dragged around it by an overexcited American history professor, who swore that she would live in England forever. I now get the annual Christmas card from California.

'Impressive,' said BB as he looked across the countryside at the Hall from some five miles out. 'Too big to live in though.'

'True,' I said. 'Think of it as a museum. It houses huge tapestries, which hang on the walls, together with priceless 16th and 17th century embroideries. It has a Battle Room containing arms and armour from the Tudor period. The art collection is quite famous. The Hall also has a Great Kitchen with a full display of the original copper and brass cooking utensils.'

'And people pay to see this stuff?'

'I did,' I said, which wasn't exactly true. I'd paid because the professor had wanted to see Baxter Hall and I had wanted to sleep with her.

'Maybe I'll appreciate the old pots and pans when I see them.'

'You won't,' I said, 'because you're not coming in. I'm doing this on my own.'

I drove, as directed, to the small private car park in a secluded part of the grounds close to the house. The only other parked vehicles were a ten-seater minibus, two saloon cars and a white van. BB put up only a token protest to being excluded from my meeting with Lord Baxter. I think he understood that I had to win the Peer's complete trust and to do that I needed to be alone. BB did not actually concede the point. He simply ended the discussion by asking me to leave the car keys so that he could put his seat into recline, relax and listen to some jazz while he waited.

So I made my way to the private entrance of Baxter Hall alone. I was formally greeted by a butler in traditional livery, who led me into the surprisingly modern private quarters where Lord Baxter was seated in a comfortable leather armchair. His ample girth was clad in a bright red waistcoat. The choice of colour may have had to do with his own ruddy complexion. Maybe he thought that his own face would look paler in contrast. If so, he was wrong. The overall effect was that of an off duty Santa Claus, minus the whiskers. Santa's jolliness, however, was very much in evidence. 'Dr Stuart, so good to see you,' he said getting up and extending his hand. 'Take a seat. I really don't get a lot of chance to meet with the staff of the university. Of course you also have a private practice, as I do. Your secretary spoke to my staff, said it was urgent, and here we are.' He paused. 'She mentioned Anton Bickley-Smythe. Should his name mean anything to me?'

'I understand you supply him with cocaine,' I said.

'Me?' he said with mild surprise. There was no outrage in his voice or demeanour. The mention of cocaine had not shocked him, nor had the accusation that he supplied the drug. The slight, if he felt one at all, was that I had suggested he had supplied cocaine to Anton.

'Yes,' I said. 'He told me himself.'

'Did he now. That was very naughty, and totally untrue.'

'Why do you think he would tell such a lie?'

'Why indeed? Where are we going with this Dr Stuart?'

'I need certain information from you. I mean you no harm and your transactions with Anton or others will remain confidential. The information

I need does not concern the business of cocaine dealing. My interest is solely limited to money laundering. Let me share something with you. I have been arrested for money laundering and, if charged and convicted, could face a very lengthy term in prison.'

'Deary me.'

'I am innocent of the crimes for which I have been arrested-'

'But of course you are.'

'- and in order to establish my innocence I need to understand much more about the money laundering process. I thought you may be able to help me. If you need a greater level of comfort I can give you the names of reputable people who can vouch for my integrity, and we can meet again in a few days time.'

'Well said and wholly unnecessary. Your reputation precedes you. Tell me Dr Stuart, do you like wine?'

'Yes,' I said.

He leaned toward me conspiratorially. 'I have a case of Chateau Lafite-Rothschild in the cellar.'

'Which year?'

He virtually bounced in his chair. 'This very year,' he said. 'It's an amazing wine, Dr Stuart, simply amazing. It will be the wine of the vintage, I'm sure. Some people believe that over time the Chateau Margaux will prove the more superior, but I doubt it, I really do. You'll see, wait there.' As he rose from his chair joy seemed to radiate through his body. He was almost light on his feet.

We were on to our second glass, and Lord Baxter consequentially more mellow, before I broached the subject again. 'So who does your laundry?'

'Laundry? Dear boy, you are out of date. Only the street vendors need to launder their proceeds. With me there is no laundry at all. My clients are from the upper crust. What's the vulgar phrase you people use – high net worth individuals? That describes my clients, from the lords and ladies to the minor Royals; stately homes and inherited wealth, old money: the best.

'And businessmen?' I asked.

'All my clients are businessmen, even though many of them do not have a business. Tax planning, you see. Look, what can you deduct for tax purposes from investment income? You should know. Nothing. Am I right? So their accountants set them up in business. For example, those with a little land become market gardeners. Sure, to sustain the image, they need to grow some vegetables, or their gardener does. This poses no problems. It may be a little inconvenient, but the prize is substantial. The effect of being in business is that they can write off all of their expenditure.'

'Such expenditure as has been wholly and exclusively incurred for the purpose of the trade,' I corrected.

'Same thing,' he said nonchalantly. 'They write off their staff costs – maid, butler etc. – travel costs – someone has to pay for the Bentley – interest on that part of the mortgage pertaining to the land – reducing their financial costs – oh, and of course the cost of the gardener.'

I'd done this for clients so many times myself that I could not understand my newfound sense of moral disapproval. I just sat in silence.

'They also write off the cost of my little supplies.'

'What?'

'I submit an invoice, dear boy, for management consultancy services.'

I was stunned. 'How does it work?' I asked.

'It's really quite simple. I supply the young charlie, along with an invoice. They pay the invoice by cheque or credit card.'

'You accept credit cards?' I asked incredulously.

'But, of course. Precious little cash among the nobility. My merchant agreements with Visa and Mastercard, not forgetting American Express, serve, I suspect, to triple my turnover.'

'Your clients get a statement indicating that they have purchased consultancy services.'

'Moreover, they get a tax deductible expense, and I get income I do not need to wash.'

'Taxable income,' I said.

'Yes, yes. But I too have deductible expenses. I'm a management consultant. There's the cost of my offices here at home, and my not inconsiderable travel. I deduct the cost of my secretary, my lovely daughter; my bookkeeper, my expensive wife; and my clerical assistant, my cheeky little French mistress. They don't do anything, but I pay them, of course. And they, in turn, pay tax on this income, after their own deductions and personal allowances.

'My accounts are prepared by my accountant and submitted to the Inland Revenue annually in the usual way. I've never had any problems from Her Majesty's Inspectors of Taxes. I can account for every penny I have in the bank, or under the stairs for that matter. My financial affairs are in impeccable order, as befits a management consultant to the good and the great.'

'What about value added tax?' I asked. He was way over the threshold limit.

'I charge VAT to my clients. Those of my clients who are registered for VAT deduct the charge as input tax on their own VAT returns. It poses no complications. I even had a VAT review by two young things from HM Customs & Excise some three months ago. Passed. Flying colours. Dr Stuart, I am very good at what I do.'

'I'm impressed,' I said and I was.

'I keep it simple, Dr Stuart, that's the key.'

'Have you ever heard of the Laundryman?'

'Who?'

'Never mind.'

We fished the bottle of wine between us while we talked of his art collection, the declining academic standards at the university, and his passion for fine wines. He was right about the Chateau Lafite-Rothschild. It was excellent.

As I made my way to the door, thinking of the Greenley raid, I asked him: 'What about your files containing the advice you have given to your clients over the years?'

'Every client has a file which consists of their name, address, contact details and the nature of their business. It also contains a letter of engagement signed by the client which stipulates that, given the client's position in society and their sensitivity to publicity, no permanent record is to be maintained on the specific advice I give on the management of their business.'

I resisted the urge to ask for a copy of the letter for my own use. 'Finally,' I said, 'just for the sake of completeness, is Anton a client?'

'No, I didn't even recognize his name at first,' said Lord Baxter. 'It is his father, the surgeon, Sir Percival Bickley-Smythe, that is the connection. He's been a client of mine for years.'

I walked back to the private car park where I had left BB. The same parked vehicles had been joined by a Land Rover containing three men, each with a beer, sharing a joke. Labourers or farm hands, I thought, laughing about the work they were being paid to do whilst they sat in their car having a drink. As I approached my car, it was clear that BB had indeed reclined the seat, but he was not comfortable. Someone was holding a knife at his throat. 'Just keep walking Dr Stuart,' said the voice behind me as I felt the sharp point of a blade at my lower left side. He steered me with the point of his knife to the back of the white van. 'Open it and get in,' he said. I did as I was told, and the door was locked behind me. The interior of the van was cramped and windowless. Old rags lay on the floor. They smelt of horse manure. There was a thick wire mesh separating the rear of the van from the front where a driver sat. He was thick set with long dirty blond hair. He did not turn round. I knelt down, sat on my heels and waited.

Someone was pounding the doors of the van. 'Here comes your friend, Dr Stuart, one false move and we slit his throat. I'm opening the doors now.' One of the double-doors opened, sunlight flooded in and BB, head lowered, was pushed into the van. He turned and sat with his back to the wire mesh, facing the door. Our captors proudly stood side by side. There was the thin, greasy-haired, side-kick who I had seen in the car holding a knife under BB's chin. Next to him was my own knife-wielding assailant, Anton Bickley-Smythe. He stood exultant in a long black trench coat.

'Expecting rain?' asked BB.

The door was violently shut on us and securely locked. Anton got in the

234

passenger's seat. 'Chico will be driving your car,' he said turning in his seat and looking through the wire mesh. 'Your friend, Tracy here, kindly gave us the keys. I suppose you're Dick.' Dick, I remembered had a non-speaking role. I stayed in character. 'In any event, Dick or not, I bet you're dying to know how I staged this little coup.' It was not so much that we were dying to know, but he was certainly dying to tell us.

'I'm sitting at home. My father says to me, Lord Baxter's called him about some professor who wants to talk to him about me. He asks me what it is about. I say I don't know, but I start thinking.'

'Steady on Anton,' said BB.

'I start thinking about the gorilla who grabbed me by the balls, threw me into the boot of his car and threatened to kill me unless I gave up the name of my supplier. And then I think, hold on, what connection could he have with one of the professors at the university? I think back to our little conversation Dr Stuart, you know, about the Laundryman. And bingo!'

'Your head exploded, right?' said BB. 'Too much thinking.'

'Tell your friend to shut up Dr Stuart or I'll do him right now.'

'You tell him,' I said.

'Anyway, I ask my father when the meeting's taking place, and he tells me. So I arrive before you. I know all about the private car park. I've driven my father there many times and sat in the car until he returned with his purchases. I wait, with my collar turned up. I wait for about half an hour. Then you arrive, with the gorilla.'

'Strike one,' said BB. 'Three strikes and you're out.'

'You don't even notice me. You go inside, leaving your friend to mind the car. You know what he does Dr Stuart? He starts playing with the seat, messing with your stereo, and, to cap it all he falls asleep. My boys arrive and it's so easy. Chico gets in the back seat of your car and puts a knife to his throat. The man who you'd left to mind your car hadn't even locked himself in!' Anton had clearly amused himself. He convulsed in laughter.

BB looked at me. 'I thought,' he said, 'that I'd be safe in Tudor England.'

'Then,' said Anton, 'wiping his tear streaked face with the palm of his

235

hands, 'then, then all I had to do was wait for you. I knew which way you'd be coming out. I just waited in the shrubbery, and you walked right past.' Anton's laughter subsided into a snigger. 'And now it's your turn to take a ride. Yours and the gorilla's.'

'Strike two,' said BB.

Chapter 14

We had driven for over an hour, mostly through lanes, when the driver turned off the registered road network altogether and drove across a field. We came to a stop next to some isolated farm buildings. Anton and the driver sat in their seats for a few moments in silence. I heard two other cars approaching. 'Now,' said Anton, and they both got out of the van and walked to its rear. When they opened the doors, they were both holding knifes. Behind them I saw Chico getting out of my car, and three young farm-hand types getting out of the Land Rover I had last seen in the private car park by the private quarters of Baxter Hall. It became clear that the joke they had been sharing had been on me.

As I stepped into the sunshine my body ached. The poor suspension on the van, unassisted by a cushioned seat, had taken its toll. Anton and the driver positioned themselves behind us and told us to make our way to the thatched barn some fifty yards ahead. I hobbled as I tried to walk off the cramp that seemed to affect my whole body. BB walked as if leaving the gym after a light workout. How, I wondered, does he do it?

'Anton,' said BB, 'you compliment me.'

'How's that?' he asked, needlessly.

'I double you up all by myself, two balls and one sorry dick all in one hand. When you take me on you bring five of your mates. What's that Anton, two guys for each ball and you and sissy Chico here holding my dick?'

'Sissy? Who you calling a sissy?' said Chico with much animation. 'Your mouth wasn't so big in the car. No, you were very quiet in the car. Frightened I would slice you up.'

'Chico, you couldn't slice bread.'

'What you say?'

'You were holding the blade all wrong. I felt sorry for you. In fact at first I thought you were a girl.'

Chico pulled out his knife and started waving it tauntingly in BB's direction. The knife had a double-edged blade of some ten inches. Its handle was ornamental. It looked like a ceremonial dagger that would not have been out of place in Baxter's Battle Room. It looked lethal.

'Put it away,' said BB, 'before you hurt yourself.'

'Nigger,' said Chico.

BB ran toward Chico. Chico tightened his grip around the dagger.

'Come on,' said BB. 'Let's see what you've got. You're a baad man, right, so take me.' They circled each other slowly, both slightly crouching. 'Come on, pussy man, come to daddy.' Chico started to sweat. He eyes darted in every direction. BB's eyes never left the knife. Suddenly Chico lunged forward. BB swayed back and in one swift motion grabbed Chico's wrist with his right hand and, pulling it toward the space just over his shoulder, punched the palm of his left hand to the back of Chico's elbow. I heard the sharp crack of bones snapping, followed by the high-pitched, animal-like screech of Chico as he dropped the knife and fell to the ground.

BB turned to Anton. 'Pick up your friend,' he said. 'Take him to a hospital. Do it now, don't look back and I'll do my best to forget that any of this shit ever happened.'

Chico was squirming in the grass, his broken arm lying at an unnatural angle to the rest of his body. He was whimpering pitifully, tears rolling across his face. I wanted to pick him up and take him to the hospital myself.

The farm-hands and the driver were at a loss. They looked to Anton who struck a pose that I assume he had seen in the movies. He stood motionless, his hands inside the trench coat. His stare was directed exclusively at BB. Anton, the hard man. It was laughable. Until he pulled out the gun. 'I was hoping this wouldn't be necessary,' he said.

'Wow,' said BB. 'Do you mind if I have a look at that thing.' BB dared to take a couple of steps toward him. I stood still. So did the farm-hands.

So did the driver. Chico twisted in the grass, squealing and moaning, his face contorted in pain. 'That is a serious piece you've got there Anton. Let me see. Clearly a revolver. Barrel three inches, maybe three and an eighth. I'd say a .44 Smith & Wesson Special. Am I right?' BB took another step forward. 'What's the material Anton? I mean, it looks like stainless steel, but some models are made of an aluminium alloy frame with a titanium cylinder.' Another move forward. 'Let me get a closer look.'

'One more step and I'll put a hole in your throat. That should shut you up.'

'Point taken,' said BB innocently stretching out his arms. 'Your move.'

'Pete,' Anton said to the driver. 'Put Chico in the van and get him to a hospital. Fast. Call my father if you have to. Tell everyone he had an accident.'

'What kind of accident?'

Anton looked heavenwards. 'I don't know. Say he fell from a tree.' Just get him out of here.'

Pete, the driver, reversed the van to where Chico lay, got out, opened the back doors and scooped him up and in as if he were some farm produce. Chico screamed in pain. Pete locked the doors, jumped back in the driver's seat and sped away, throwing up a shower of mud from his tyres. The piercing sound of Chico grew dimmer the closer Pete got to the country lanes.

'Into the barn,' said Anton, who now maintained a safe distance from BB, as did the farm-hands. The barn had long been deserted. It smelt damp and musty. There were rusty disused agricultural equipment along one side of the barn and abandoned furniture piled up the far corner. And it was draughty.

'Tie them up,' said Anton to the farmhands. Not one of them moved. 'I said tie them up. Don't worry, the nigger will behave himself. I have a gun.' Reluctantly, first one then the other two walked toward us. They tied us, each in a standing position, to an old tractor with thick rope they had brought with them for the purpose. I did not resisit. Neither, strangely, did BB.

'My part is done,' said Anton. 'I have some friends who are not as, shall we say, squeamish as I am. They will be here later. I don't know exactly what they will do. I didn't ask for the details. But once they have started their fun you will beg them to kill you. Nobody fucks with Anton Bickley-Smythe. Good day gentlemen.'

'Anton,' said BB, 'what's it like to have such a small dick? I mean, seriously, do you go out with midgets to compensate? What's the story?'

'Just wait till my friends get here,' said Anton. 'You just wait.' He put his gun back in his trenchcoat. 'Come,' he said to his "boys" and he was gone.

'Was that necessary?' I said.

'No,' said BB, 'but it was fun.' After some consideration he added, 'If we get out of this I hope you give him an F.'

'I've been relieved of teaching duty.'

'Give him an F anyway.'

I strained against the rope without success.

'All you're doing is making the knots tighter,' said BB.

'OK,' I said, 'what's your idea?'

'I don't have one.'

'I'm not trying to be critical,' I said, 'but you know he would never have used that gun don't you?'

'I know he wouldn't have used it; not on purpose. That was my problem. If a man has a gun and he knows what he's doing you can predict his behaviour when you attempt to disarm him. Your friend Anton was a complete novice with a powerful firearm. That is a dangerous combination. If you attempt to disarm an expert and fail he might shoot you in the leg to make his point. If it had gone wrong with Anton he might have blown both our heads off by accident.'

'Fair point,' I said. 'Do you believe him about his friends?'

'I think that it's safer to work on the assumption that he's telling the truth.'

'Me too.'

'On the subject of which,' said BB, 'you know that thing you do with time?'

240

'You mean covering the clocks, working through the night, making time stand still.'

'Yeah, that thing, the last part.'

'What about it?' I said.

'Do it now.'

Nothing happened for hours. It grew dark and, with the darkness, grew fear, and the fear amplified each sound. The sparrows sounded like eagles, the rats sounded like jaguars and when the barn door opened it sounded like a thunderclap. A torch shone toward us. Behind the light, in the darkness the footsteps were heavy and the movement clumsy.

'I'm too old, too fat and too tired for this stuff.'

The figure stumbled around us in the dark. I pulled my head back to avoid the familiar potent smell of his breath. 'And too drunk,' I said.

'You should be grateful I've had a few drinks. A sober person would have left the two of you here till morning. It's what you both deserve,' said Billy. 'Anton told me to bring a knife. He was not wrong.'

Painstakingly, with the torch as his spotlight, Billy tackled the knots with a small penknife. Both he and the knife were less than effective. As he cut, he explained. 'Anton is a client of mine. He's not as stupid as he behaves. On leaving you here, he telephoned me and told me what he'd done.'

'Why?' I asked.

'Because I'd told him to keep me informed after he'd told me about the kidnapping.'

'You knew about the kidnapping?'

'Yes.' There was no point in asking him why he didn't tell us. Client confidentiality.

'You knew he was going to do this?'

'No, but I thought he was going to do something. I wasn't worried. He's harmless. But I told him that he must inform me if any other incidents arise, whether he is at fault or not. That way, I said, I can protect him. I remember thinking at the time, it's not only committees that cover their ass.'

241

'I wouldn't have thought Anton would be a client of yours.'

'He wasn't originally,' said Billy. 'His father took him to Bellows & Bellows. George Fairlow referred him to me. George felt a case of possession was more in my line.'

'Not for the first time,' I said.

Eventually we were untied, and we made our way, guided by Billy's torch, out of the barn and into the night. My car was still there. Billy handed me the keys, said his goodbyes and headed back to his own vehicle. When he opened his car door, the internal light illuminated his passenger. Anton. I have never seen BB move so fast. He was at the car door in seconds, yanking Anton out off his seat and hauling him across the grass.

'Stop it,' said Billy. 'Right now.' BB held Anton by the scruff of the neck. 'I wouldn't have found you without him. He guided me here. You should be grateful.'

'Oh I am,' BB said and dragged Anton back to Billy's car, then helped him to his feet. 'Let me show you how grateful I am.' The punch was fast, accurate and merciless, right to Anton's solar plexus. He slid down the side of the car and crumbled in a heap on the ground.

I helped get Anton back into Billy's car, offering apologies amid Anton's groaning. Billy said he would address matters later. I followed the taillights on Billy's car back to the country lanes. Then I put on Sally. It felt good to be going home. I ached, I was cold and I was bruised. But, all things considered, I was fortunate. I thought of the pain Anton would be in on his drive back. BB was looking out the side window. 'Strike three,' he said softly.

Billy arrived late for the next Brains Trust, the first without Anita. As he entered he was clearly unsteady on his feet. He almost fell into the armchair. His whiskey and glass stood on the side table awaiting his attention. 'Whose lives are we going to attempt to ruin today?' he said, his speech slurred. For all the whiskey I had seen Billy consume, this was the first time I had seen him truly drunk.

'Billy, are you OK?' I asked.

'Yes, I'm OK. I just understand now why I've always worked for the defence.' He opened the bottle and poured. 'You see, I just don't like fucking up people's lives. I don't like selling people things they don't need so that I might, just might, catch a money launderer. I don't like kidnapping students and threatening to kill them because they might know someone, who knows someone who knows a money launderer.'

'What's he talking about?' asked Martyn.

'I don't know,' I said.

'I don't like walking in on eminent peers of the realm and accusing them of serious crimes. I don't like rescuing my friends from disused barn houses because they intimidated my clients. I had a simple life. I defended the accused. I saw myself as a shepherd. Now I'm running with the wolves.'

'Slow down,' said Martyn.

'It's nothing,' I said.

Billy pointed a finger at me that he could not stop from shaking, whether from anger or alcoholic poisoning. 'Look at how many innocent people you are climbing over to find a single guilty one. The police do it all the time. It doesn't bother them, but it bothers me. It taints me. It makes me feel dirty.' He paused. 'Like a pig.'

'That's it!' said Martyn rising.

'Sit down,' I said. 'Billy, you're drunk. Go home.'

'If he gets back in his car in his state,' said Martyn, 'I'll arrest him.'

'Oh mummy, mummy, please protect me. The big policeman's going to lock me up,' Billy responded in a childlike voice. Looking over to me, he asked, 'If DC Clarke arrests me, Andy Pandy, will you come and visit?'

'Billy,' said BB, 'you're cracking up.'

'No, no, you lot are. I've found what I've been looking for,' he said holding up the bottle. 'You can't find the Laundryman.'

'These meetings are getting nowhere fast,' said Clarke. 'You've lost one member, now it looks like you've lost another. We should have made more progress by now.'

'Hold on,' said BB. 'How long did you say you've been looking for him? I think we've made a lot of progress. We've got suspects, Mansa

Mussa, Kay Frisk, and so on. Are you ready to give up on Joseph Feingold already?'

'No, not at all, but I need something substantial, something I can arrest him for.'

'Just give me time,' I said.

'You don't have time. You know that. You have to surrender into custody in what, six weeks?'

'Are you really going to charge Andrew?' asked Billy.

'If necessary.'

'Take me instead,' said Billy holding out his wrists as if to be handcuffed. 'I'm sure you'd prefer that.'

'You're right there,' said Martyn.

Julianna knocked and entered. 'Same again?' she asked.

'Julianna,' I said, 'I'll have a small whiskey.'

'An ally,' said Billy.

'A friend,' I replied.

'I'll have a whiskey as well,' said BB.

'And me too,' said Martyn, 'with a little water.' Martyn, in fact, added so much water to the whiskey that he diluted it away. But I was touched by the gesture and so, I think, was Billy who raised his glass in Martyn's direction in a silent toast.

BB drove the rest of the meeting. He had an idea.

The Laundryman, he argued, must network. 'Why don't we go and watch him at work?'

'Where?' asked Martyn.

'The London Arena,' he replied.

'I don't understand,' I said.

'Me neither,' said Martyn.

Billy was quietly snoring.

'It's easy,' said BB. 'Next week Lennox Lewis defends his World Heavyweight Championship against Frans Botha. The fight takes place at the London Arena. We will be at ringside.'

'I still don't understand,' I said.

'People do not pay £1,500 to sit at ringside in order to watch the boxing,' said BB. 'Ringside at a world championship fight is an exclusive club peopled by those who have business to transact. Big business. Sure you get your celebrities. They are there to be seen, and just in case they're missed, their presence is announced from the ring just before the main event. But the rest is about deals. This is the ideal environment for the Laundryman.'

'If the celebrities and the dealmakers are sitting at ringside, where are the true fans?'

'It's like the opera, Andrew. The true fans are in the cheap seats.'

'I like it,' said Martyn.

'You can get the tickets?' I asked.

'If you've got the money, I've got the contacts. How many do we need?'

'Let's see, you, me, Martyn and Billy. Six.'

'Six?'

'Yes, us four, and I need two more.'

'Make that five,' said Martyn. 'I'm a police officer. I don't need a ticket.'

A cough and a splutter announced Billy's return to consciousness. He wiped a light dribble from the corner of his mouth and tried to straighten up. To be fair, straightening up in an armchair is not easy for anyone, but Billy looked like he was wrestling with an octopus. He eventually gave up the struggle, settling for a semi-dignified slouch. 'What's the plan?' he asked, clearly back in the fold.

'Billy,' I said, 'we're going to a boxing match.'

That evening, as I dressed for a dinner party, I thought about the Laundryman. Was he really so clever, or just lucky? A no brainer. He was clever. It takes serious intelligence to operate successfully outside the law. He must also be seriously wealthy. How much did he launder? £10 billion a year? More? And what was his commission? Five percent, ten? I wondered whether the media hype was annoying or entertaining him.

'Stu?'

Or her.

'Come in,' I said. Tania was wearing the haute couture gown I had given her the money to buy for the evening. It had a light sheen and looked luxurious. She told me it was made of jersey (not inappropriate, I thought). The gown, light gold in colour, hugged her body, and the draped neckline revealed the perfect curves of her breasts. Adorning her ears were the diamond studded elongated caymanite earrings I bought for her in Georgetown. She looked enchanting.

'Do you need help with your bow-tie?' she asked.

'Always,' I said.

She stood in front of me and, as she created the perfect bow, I said casually, 'Do you like boxing?'

She made a face by wrinkling her nose. 'Well, you know BB used to box, but I find it barbaric. Why do you ask?'

'I have ringside seats for the Heavyweight Championship next week.'

'Barbaric,' she said, 'but fascinating.'

'So you want to come?'

'Of course.'

BB reported back the following day. 'I've got five ringside tickets, but I couldn't get them all together. I've got three and two. How shall we do this?'

'I'll sit with Tania and Billy,' I said.

'Leaving me with the mystery guest. Who is he?'

'I don't know yet,' I said, 'I haven't asked her.'

That afternoon I drove to Greenwich. I had not been there for a while. I noticed that the historic building I knew as the Dreadnought Seamen's Hospital had become part of the ever expanding campus of Greenwich University. I passed the Royal Observatory and hoped that it would remain safe. I pulled up outside a house on Maze Hill that would have had a perfect view of the beautiful Greenwich Park, had the park not been walled in. I rang the bell and heard the brisk, no nonsense steps to the door.

'Hi,' I said as the door opened.

'Hello Andrew,' said Anita.

'May I come in?'

'Of course.' She led me into the lounge. I had only been to her house a couple of times before and what struck me again about the room was its manifestation of the phrase, "a place for everything and everything in its place." The room was beyond neat and tidy, the room was in order. 'Take a seat, Andrew, tea perhaps.'

'That would be nice,' I said.

'Assam or darjeeling?'

'Assam will be fine, thank you.'

Anita returned after five minutes, as I was looking at the picture of her father in uniform in an ornate frame on her mantelpiece. She carried a tray containing a large teapot, two cups and saucers, and a plate of biscuits..

'Let me help you,' I said.

'I can manage,' she replied. And, of course, she could, and did. 'Are you still looking for the Laundryman?'

'Yes, that's partly why I'm here. But first, how are you?'

'I'm very well, thank you Andrew. I was astonished to get the call from the bank. I never thought you would sell the practice.'

'Did Hugo call you himself?'

'Not at first, no. It's a big bank Andrew. I can't expect that sort of personal attention at my level.' How we adapt, I thought. 'But I spoke to him as part of the interview process. Even now I don't work with him that closely. My boss is a man called Dr Francis Peartree.'

'Yes, I've met him,' I said. 'Hugo said he made tax planning sound like funeral arranging, whereas I made it sound like an act of seduction.'

'We all have our strengths and weaknesses,' she said. 'In fact Dr Peartree is a very kind and decent man –'

'I was suggesting nothing else.'

'– and the clients are taking to him.

'I see,' I said. There was an uneasy silence.

Anita filled the void. 'I'm glad you stopped by,' she said. 'I have been asked to serve as a trustee of the charity for which I do volunteer work, the Just In Case Veterans Homes.'

'Congratulations.' I said.

'To tell the truth,' she said, 'one of the former officers who used to serve had a stroke a couple of weeks ago. He can't serve anymore. They just need a replacement.' However, she was obviously pleased to have been asked. 'They gave me the Trust Deed to review, but I don't really know what I'm looking at. I don't want to let anyone down, but you can't be too careful. I was going to ask Francis Peartree to have a look at it for me, but as you're here perhaps you could cast an eye. I value your opinion more. You know that.'

She took the Inocace Trust Deed from the sideboard drawer and handed it to me. The document ran to fifty-eight pages. The stated purpose of the trust was: "The Relief and Assistance of Veterans of the Second World War in Need." Its beneficial area was the United Kingdom. The Deed, which set out the constitution of the Trust, was unnecessarily wordy. More lawyers earning more fees. In this and all other respects the Trust Deed was fairly standard. 'Is there anything you're particularly concerned about?' I asked.

'What are my duties?'

'Primarily to act in the best interest of the beneficiaries; that is, the veterans. This usually means their best financial interest. You must also safeguard the assets of the Trust. The role is largely one of stewardship. It is ideally suited for you. Take it.'

She picked up the photograph on her mantelpiece and said, 'It would have made father proud.' She turned back to face me and, I think, regretted her display of sentimentality.

'How's everyone doing?' I asked.

'I can hardly discuss that now, can I? You understand client confidentiality better than anyone.'

'Generally I mean, personally.'

'Not generally, not personally and certainly not professionally. No, no, no.' She put the empty teacups back on the tray. 'Would you like another biscuit?'

'No thank you.'

'Then I'll clear these away.' When she returned from the kitchen she said, 'You walked away from them, Andrew. They didn't walk away from you.' She sat down. 'Now, what did you want to talk to me about?'

I took the ticket BB had given me from my pocket. 'I would like you to come to a boxing match with me.'

'Don't be daft.'

'You're right,' I said and got up. 'Thank you for the tea. I'll see myself out.'

Anita followed me to the door. As I opened it she said, 'Andrew, I do miss it, you know: you, the practice, Wigmore Street, the clients, the strategies, the excitement. It's not the same at the bank.'

'You walked away from me, Anita. I didn't walk away from you.'

'You were falling apart. I couldn't help you.'

'You can help me now. Come to the fight,' I said, and placed the ticket in her hand. 'I'll explain when you get there. I'm going to catch him.'

'You're doing it all wrong. This is not your battle.'

'Come. Please. I need your instincts.'

'You're going to get hurt.'

'Just be there,' I said and walked to the car.

London Arena is located in the heart of London's Docklands. It is not an architecturally attractive building; it looks not dissimilar to a large warehouse, but it is functional. I had been to the London Arena only once before, and then only to attend a tax conference in the Glengall Room. This was my first sporting event at the venue, and my first boxing match ever. As BB had suggested Tania and I arrived early, secured our parking space and familiarised ourselves with the arena. A morose and preoccupied Billy arrived about an hour later.

It took even longer for the ringside seats to fill up. BB had explained to me that the undercard was a good one. Adrian Stone, he said, was fighting Geoff McCreesh for the light-middleweight IBO championship, and Scott

Harrison, who he described as a plucky little Glaswegian featherweight, was fighting Boom Boom Johnson, a former world champion. The ringsiders, however, were not interested.

There was the odd spattering of American celebrities. I saw Jerry Springer make his way through the arena. Spontaneous chants of "Jerry, Jerry" rang out from each section of seating that he passed, like a verbal Mexican wave. He acknowledged this with dismissive gestures, but he was smiling and seemed to take the most circuitous route to his ringside seat. Primarily, however this was a British affair, footballers, singers and soap-stars.

And dealmakers. I overheard a short, swarthy man, expensively over-dressed, pitching a bejewelled Indian lady. 'Just tell me how many cartons you want. You can have them in 48 hours. No questions asked, all the sup-porting paperwork; but I've got to know now.'

'Can you handle 250,000?'

'Does Bill Clinton like a cigar?'

A more domestic conversation was taking place to my left, between a plump English lady and her wafer thin Italian suitor. 'I hope you're enjoy-ing this,' she said, 'I'd rather be somewhere else.'

'Where, where you wanna be?'

'Somewhere romantic.'

'This is romantic. You watch. Boxers put you on fire. You watch. Make you hot all over. I put fire out later.'

'How Achilleo?' she asked demurely.

'How? How? I piss in your mouth, that's how. Now watch the fights.' The plump lady cuddled up to her lover. As Joseph Feingold would say, go figure.

In front of me they were actually talking about the main event. 'Who do you fancy?'

'Lennox in seven. You?'

'I'm looking for an upset. Lennox leaves his chin open, Botha tags him. Remember Botha looked good against Tyson.'

'Until he got knocked out in the fifth.'

250

I got up. It was time to go walkabout. 'I'll be back soon,' I said to Tania.

'And what am I suppose to do while you're away?'

'Watch, listen,' I said. 'And observe. If all else fails talk to Billy.'

'I'll try,' she said in a low voice, 'but he hasn't uttered a word to me all evening.'

I made my way over to where BB was seating. The seat to his right was empty. 'Your mystery guest hasn't turned up,' he said.

'No mystery,' I replied. 'It's Anita. I'm sure she'll be here.'

'Why did you invite her? She's stuck up and she left you in the lurch.'

'She's smart and her instincts are good. I've been relying on them for years. Seen anything?'

'I've seen Martyn Clarke. He came over with the other one.'

'DS Greenley?'

'That's him. I was tempted to brush up against him, see what happened.'

'You didn't?'

'No, he was quite pleasant, started talking about the fight.'

'Knowledgeably?'

'Not really. He thinks Lennox will win. Who doesn't?'

'A guy sitting in front of me,' I said. 'He reckons Lennox will leave his chin hanging out.'

'No way.'

'Anything else?'

'Yes,' said BB. 'What's an Anstalt?'

'It's part of the Mycroft plan.'

'I thought so. You were talking about that to Joseph Feingold weren't you?'

'Yes,' I said impatiently. 'Have you heard the term here?'

'They were talking about it,' said BB pointing.

'Who?'

'Them, the fat man and the black guy.' My eyes followed BB's pointed finger and rested on Lord Baxter in earnest conversation with Colonel Mansa Mussa.

I made my way back to my seat in time for the main event. The MC introduced the celebrities to the crowd, as BB told me he would, each receiving cheers to varying degrees. Most of those introduced I had already seen at ringside. The biggest cheer, however, was reserved to last. 'And entering the arena just in time for the main event,' announced the MC, 'none other than the biggest musical sensation from these shores for years. Let's big it up for Lightning, ladies and gentlemen, Lightning.' The crowd erupted. I had no idea he was present and I couldn't see him from where I was sitting. I turned and twisted without success.

'He's up there,' said Tania. And there he was, dressed in a huge white fur coat, on the highest tier, Lightning holding his hands aloft. In a dramatic act of inverse snobbery he sat down at the end of the row of the cheapest seats in the house.

'He must be a fan,' I said to Tania.

'He's a rebel,' she replied excitedly.

The lights dimmed and Frans Botha made his way to the ring as the partisan crowd jerred and whistled. Then the lights went down again and the rhythmical beat of Bob Marley's Crazy Baldhead filled the arena. It was not appropriate but my mind immediately pictured Julianna in a pose of total sexual abandonment. I put my arm around Tania and she responded by leaning into me. In that moment, despite my troubles, I felt I was a lucky guy. 'Dem crazy,' sang Marley, 'Dem crazy, we're gonna chase dem crazy baldheads out of town…' We were all on our feet, some standing on chairs, swaying to the reggae beat. The heavyweight champion entered the arena surrounded by a human phalanx made up of his team: conditioners, dieticians, trainers, family and friends, Lennox Lewis towering above them all.

The main event itself proved to be a short-lived affair, with Lewis knocking out Botha in the second round. There were whoops of delight around the arena, and the muffled sounds of deals being concluded at ringside. As the TV and radio interviewers, who invaded the ring, were pushing microphones in Lewis' face, with considerably more success than Botha's punching, I sought out BB.

I fought my way through the crowds of people who had invaded the ringside area, now that the event was over and security relatively lax. Fans chanting the name of the heavyweight champion jostled against each other as I tried to push by causing the least offence. Spirits were high and I thought it wouldn't take much for one of the more rowdy supporters to invent a slight and then try to emulate Lennox's performance in the ring. So with a bag full of "excuse me's" and the moderate use of my shoulders and elbows, I pressed on through the largely unresponsive horde. At one stage I almost fell. It was then I saw him, sitting alone dressed in a pin-stripe suit, chin up, back straight, oblivious to the noise around him. He seemed utterly detached from his surroundings. 'George?' I said.

'Andrew,' he replied.

I dropped into the seat next to my solicitor. 'Didn't know you were a fight fan.'

'Does one have to be a fan to be here?'

I wondered if George Fairlow ever allowed his brain to relax. 'No,' I said. 'Business?'

'Perhaps,' he replied. He was looking into the far distance. 'Perhaps.'

So, I thought, George is at the fight. On its own I could make nothing of it. It was just another piece of the puzzle. There would be nothing to gain by probing. George, I knew, would give nothing away. 'Well.' I said rising to re-enter the fray, 'I'm looking for my friend BB. Wish me well.'

'I need to see you,' he said, and suddenly I absorbed all of his attention. He fixed his gaze on me and said, 'Monday good for you? Two o' clock?'

These days, with no practice, I no longer had to consult my diary. 'Sure,' I said.

'My offices. Any changes I'll call you.'

'Fine,' I said, and seeing a temporary gap in the mêlée, darted in the general direction BB.

He was sitting alone. 'Where's Anita?' I asked.

'She off talking to someone. She said if you don't catch her she'll call you tomorrow. I think she's got some news. By the way, it's not over yet,' he said. 'I've got us some tickets to the post-fight party.'

'Where's that?'

'At a nightclub near Whitechapel.'

'How many have you got?'

'Four, we'll have to leave Anita behind.'

'That's OK,' I said. 'I don't think it will break her heart.'

Then I saw Anita in the distance. BB was right, she was off talking to someone and there was no reason for him to recognise her companion, but I did. It was her new boss, Hugo Maximillian. As I tried to catch her attention, without enjoying any success, a very firm hand squeezed my shoulder. 'Make that two-thirty,' said George Fairlow.

Chapter 15

On the following Monday afternoon, as I walked down Chancery Lane, I could see it was business as usual at Bellows & Bellows. From a delivery van, illegally parked outside the offices, two men dressed in casual grey uniforms, were carrying, in relay, white cardboard boxes form the van to the reception. I held the door open for one of them before I entered. Inside, Mr Reception was not happy. About twenty boxes were stacked up by the side of his desk, and more were coming. 'They can't stay here,' he said to one of the relay team, clearly not for the first time.

'Look, we're paid to deliver to Bellows & Bellows. This is Bellows & Bellows right? Job done.'

'They need to go into our Exhibit Room.'

'So move them.'

The relay team continued carrying in their boxes and Mr Reception, defeated, picked up the telephone. 'Sir,' he said, 'I need two articled clerks to move the Watchley Fraud boxes to the Exhibit Room... I know, sir, I asked them... Yes sir...Thank you.' Two articled clerks in a blue-blooded City firm would soon be doing the work turned down by the deliverymen. Billy, I thought, you didn't miss much.

'Hello,' I said when Mr Reception had hung up.

'Yes?' he said as if he hadn't seen me before.

'My name is Dr Stuart. I have a meeting with George Fairlow.'

'He's expecting you. Go through, you know where it is.'

I walked through the double doors, to the third room on the right, and knocked. George Fairlow called out for me to enter, which I did. He was not alone. Sitting opposite him was a thin man dressed in a loosely fitting three-piece suit, complete with fob and chain. He turned his drawn, gaunt face toward me as I entered. 'Dr Stuart,' said George Fairlow, 'I would like you to meet Sir Kenneth Llewellin; Sir Kenneth, Dr Stuart.'

The name was faintly familiar. We shook hands and I took a seat. 'Sir Kenneth,' continued George Fairlow, 'as you may know, is an executive director of the Bank of England and a member of its Monetary Policy Committee. What a coincidence the two of you should be in my office at the same time. Maybe you would like to talk about areas of mutual interest, informally of course, while I attend to important work elsewhere. I'll be back in half an hour.'

As set-ups go it was not elegant, but it was effective. Here was a man who clearly wanted to talk to me. I waited.

'I understand,' said Sir Kenneth, 'that you are interested in the Laundryman.' His voice was a pitch higher than I had expected. 'There is something I would like to do for you.' He crossed his legs and leaned back on his chair. 'I would like to show you the big picture.' This was going to be a tutorial.

'More money,' he said, 'is spent in the UK on illegal drugs than is spent on food. Moreover, it's all cash.' I chose not to mention the management consultancy business of Lord Baxter. 'If all the supermarkets only accepted cash, and failed to deposit this cash in our banking system, what do you think would happen to the economy?'

'On that sort of scale,' I said, 'it would stifle the multiplier effect, which would restrict the money supply. The result would be deflation.'

'In short, Dr Stuart, it would bugger the economy. In purely economic terms the same applies to the proceeds of drug trafficking. The proper stewardship of the economy demands that cash is regularly deposited in the banking system. From this perspective the Laundryman is our friend. He ensures that the Treasury model of the economy actually works. Sure, from a crime enforcement point of view money launderers should be caught and prosecuted. But if money laundering was wholly stamped out by noon tomorrow, cash would languish in basements, interest rates would increase, businesses would fail, unemployment would rise, the Governor of the Bank of England would be sacked by the Prime Minister, who in turn would be

256

'thrown out by the country at the earliest available opportunity.'

'So you want to curtail the activities of the police in this area.'

'Not at all. We want the police to do their job, but not too well.'

'If you need the cash in the system,' I said, 'why not simply make it easy for the launderer.'

'But we do. In essence there are two approaches to detecting money launderers, one employed by America, and the other by us. Both are virtually guaranteed to fail. In the US all cash transactions over $10,000 must be reported to the central authorities. You can imagine what happens. The quantity of reported transactions is so enormous that there is no possible way they all can be followed up. The entire investigative process is buried under a mountain of paperwork. Result: money laundering flourishes. Our approach here in Britain is, I think, a little more subtle. We insist that only unusual transactions need to be reported. Any decent launderer would know how to render a transaction usual: you simply repeat this week what you did last week. We have far less cases to investigate and we only catch the clowns who shouldn't be in the business in the first place.'

I was surprised by Sir Kenneth's casual manner to criminality. 'And morality?' I asked.

'Global or national morality really doesn't work. Morality is a personal matter. I am faithful to my wife, I do not steal and, when they were alive, I honoured my mother and father. You remember Jimmy Carter's disastrous term of office. Was there ever a more moral president? And what of our own dear Labour Government's ethical foreign policy; how long did that last: two weeks? I do what works, Dr Stuart, as I believe do you.'

'I used to,' I said. 'I recently sold my practice.' Adding with good humour, 'I'm thinking of going straight.'

'Go to the Bahamas, my friend, and lie on the beach in the sun until all such irksome thoughts drift out with the tide.' He got up and stretched his lean frame then pulled his fob watch from the pocket of his waistcoat to check the time. 'We don't have long,' he said. 'Let me complete the picture by talking about your area of expertise: offshore tax planning, I understand.'

'You've done your homework,' I said.

'We know more about you than you can imagine,' he replied. 'I know you think you have an adversarial relationship with the UK tax authorities, and to some extent you're right. It would however be more accurate to say that you too are part of the Treasury model. Not necessarily you personally, of course, but offshore tax consultants generally. You make use of offshore financial centres and believe that we are powerless to stop you. You are wrong.

'Let's take the Cayman Islands, for example, a familiar haunt of yours I believe. The islands, as you know, are a British Crown colony. We appoint the governor. We appoint the attorney general too. The defence of the islands and its foreign affairs are the sole responsibility of the British Government. If we wanted to close down the Cayman Islands as an offshore financial centre we could do it tomorrow. Why don't we? Because we don't want to. I'll tell you something else. For all our political control, in reality the Cayman Islands are an American dependency. Grand Cayman is less than 500 miles from the coast of the United States. The Caymanian dollar is fixed to the US dollar, not the pound sterling. US dollars are accepted throughout the islands. The economic pressure the US could exert on the Cayman Islands is enormous. Why don't they? Because they don't want to.

'All the offshore financial centres in the world have a host nation in the developed world, be it politically or economically. The OECD countries could shut down most, if not all, of these centres. Do you know why they don't want to?'

'The right to levy or not to levy tax,' I said, 'is one of the basic tenets of sovereignty. Offshore financial centres are usually small island economies competing fiscally for goods and services with the developed countries. Just as the developed countries compete on technological advancement and physical infrastucture. You can't close a country down because you do not like the competition.'

'Yes we can, if the competition is harmful to our national interests. Let's be mature about this Dr Stuart. Have another go.'

I felt like a graduate student in front of a particularly demanding professor. The analogy, however, was false. This was not academia. Sir Kenneth was a practitioner of financial governance at the very highest level. 'From a fiscal perspective,' I replied, 'offshore financial centres encourage tax avoidance; that is, legitimate tax planning on an international scale. This can always be countered by anti-tax avoidance measures by the legislature and courts of the developed nations. However, without these centres criminal international tax evasion would become more widespread with the consequent severe damage to the fiscal administration and economic regulation of the West. Offshore financial centres, I suggest, serve as a sort of economic safety valve.'

'Better,' said Sir Kenneth, 'but still weak. You're missing the main point. Let me help you. When money is deposited in an offshore financial centre what do you think happens to it?'

'A portion of it is loaned to other customers of the bank.'

'And if the demand for loans does not equal the supply of funds?'

'The surplus is placed in the international money markets.'

'Which means?'

'It becomes available to the developed countries.'

'Precisely. We get it back Dr Stuart. Jersey alone contributes enormously to our balance of payments. The Cayman Islands and the Bahamas do the same for the US. When you host an offshore financial centre it is simply good business for the nation. We compete for such centres. If they didn't exist, we would set them up.'

'If they didn't exist at all it would be a zero sum game.'

'True, but they do, and we're not going to get rid of ours until the other nations get rid of theirs, and they feel the same, so offshore financial centres will I suspect be with us for ever.'

'Even to launder dirty money.'

'I am a banker, Dr Stuart. There is no such thing as clean money or dirty money. Only money.'

'So we live in a land of illusion,' I said.

'Always have done. Do you think that Mrs Jones knows that her £3,000 life savings are not actually at the bank; that her money has been loaned to a corrupt Latin American government? I accept that if she came in we would find £3,000 to give her, but if all the Mrs Jones came in at once we wouldn't have a chance. We rely on the fact that they will not, and they sleep peacefully knowing that their money is safe in the bank. An illusion, but it works.'

'This is more serious,' I suggested. 'You're playing games with the criminal law.'

'Only because, to paraphrase Mr Micaber, the criminal law is an ass. Most drugs should be legalised. Then they could be regulated and taxed and the money launderers, in this field at least, would not have a job to do. Every politician knows this but they lack the political will to do anything about it. They would have you believe that they are winning the war on drugs. That is the greatest illusion of all.'

'You sound like a radical.'

'I'm a realist, Dr Stuart. I have to be. It comes with the job.'

'There is, I suppose, a point to this conversation, notwithstanding that it sprung from a supposedly chance encounter in the offices of my solicitor?'

'Only this: we're on the same side, you, AJ Stuart & Co, me, the Bank of England. We all do what we do and the economy, subject to a little guidance here and there, works exceedingly well. It now appears, however, that you've stopped doing your job and instead have turned into an amateur sleuth intent only on identifying and catching a man with whom we have no argument. In the process you are doing serious damage to the smooth running of the economy. Have you seen the latest statistics?'

I had. Interest rates were up and predicted to rise further. Unemployment was growing. Inflation was down, which sounded good, but when the general price levels decrease, you may be heading toward deflation, which posed fundamental economic problems of its own. Yes, I had seen the latest statistics. I nodded.

'It's going to get worse unless something is done. You understand?'

I did not understand. I remained silent.

'You'll understand,' he said. 'You're in the middle of a judicial process, though remember that you haven't been charged yet. If you are charged you will be in the capable hands of George Fairlow. He's really quite extraordinarily able. I accept that you have been, and will be, subject to some discomfort. That, quite frankly, is about what you deserve for some of your antics. But it will all pan out well in the end. You're not the Laundryman. You will be found not guilty, and the Laundryman will exist to fight another day, which is in the interest of all of us.'

I was beginning to understand and I did not like it. 'Listen,' I said, 'the Laundryman has become a temporary national obsession. He's a celebrity, and everyone wants to know the man behind the name. I can't stop the hunt for the Laundryman. It's beyond my control. But just so that I leave you with no misunderstanding, let me also say this: even if I could stop it, I would not stop it. The small discomfort you refer to includes the loss of my business, the complete contempt of my son and the likely imprisonment of the woman I love. I will catch the Laundryman, and if that buggers up the economy, so be it.'

We sat in silence until George Fairlow returned. He immediately sensed the atmosphere in the room. 'It would appear,' he said, 'that the meeting was not a great success. Just as well it never took place.'

How they arranged it all in the one and a half hours it took me to get home I will never know. But Detective Sergeant Greenley and Detective Constable Clarke were waiting for me as I arrived home, sitting in their unmarked car parked outside the gate of the driveway leading to my house.

'I'll come straight to the point,' said Greenley once he'd made himself comfortable in one of the visitors' chairs in my study, Martyn Clarke sitting by his side. 'There has come into my possession an affidavit signed by a client of yours claiming that you have at various times boasted about your money laundering abilities. He also states that you told them that you enjoyed the title of The Laundryman. Do you have anything to say?'

'Name the client,' I said. I should have said nothing. I knew that, but I was very angry.

Martyn was looking down at the floor. Greenley was looking straight at me. 'I am not at liberty at this time to name the individual who has signed this affidavit, but I can assure you that he is a client of yours.'

'I cannot rebut accusations from an anonymous accuser, other than to say this: I have never boasted about money laundering abilities and I have never enjoyed the title of Laundryman.' My voice was shaking. There was nothing I could do about it. I was enraged.

'Any chance of a coffee?' said Greenley. I reluctantly picked up the internal phone to call Julianna. 'And biscuits,' he added.

It was only ten minutes before Julianna knocked on my study door, but it seemed like an hour. We had sat without talking, Greenley occasionally chuckling to himself, Martyn avoiding all eye contact. Julianna was brisk in her manner, laying the tray with the coffee pot, cups and saucers (and biscuits) on my desk without saying a word. As she turned towards the door Greenley, without looking up, mumbled, 'Still here then?'

'Waiting for my ticket,' she replied and left.

Greenley leaned back in his chair. He was relaxed and confident. He had his smoking gun. It was stolen and it was planted, but it was smoking. Fear and anger mixed within me creating such panic, I could no longer trust my judgment. I decided, for the moment, to say nothing more. Greenley dipped his biscuit in his coffee. 'You know what really surprises me?' he said, biting through the moistened half, 'You haven't called your solicitor. Last time out nothing could stop you. What's changed Dr Stuart?'

And there it was. Today I could no longer trust my own lawyer. I could not help but link Greenley's presence in my study with my "chance" encounter with Sir Kenneth Llewellin at George Fairlow's offices. *"You'll understand,"* Sir Kenneth had said. I did now. I was being set up so the Laundryman could stay free, resume his massive money laundering operation and save the economy from collapse. And my own lawyer was brokering the deal. This was not something to be shared with Greenley. I didn't trust him. Who did I trust? 'Nothing's changed,' I said.

'So call him.'

'I'll call him when I'm ready. Do you intend to arrest me?'

'There's enough here to arrest you again, charge you, take you to prison and deny bail. You'd be on remand, locked up until your trial.'

'You don't determine bail,' I said. I wanted to puncture his smugness. 'It's a matter for the courts.'

'No judge would grant bail to a man of your skills and wealth in a case of this magnitude. Why would you risk a conviction? You'd abscond. You could set up anywhere in the world. No, no, we'd have to lock you up. Now what are your comments on this affidavit?'

'Fuck the affidavit and fuck you.' I stood up. Rage seared through me. 'You find a fucking liar - no, no - you make a good person lie. What did you promise him? Or what have you got on him? Or how much hell did you put him through till he told you whatever you wanted to hear?'

'Calm down Andrew,' said Martyn, speaking for the first time. 'Calm down and shut up. You're not listening. We have evidence which is quite damning to your case. We have to act on that evidence. Under normal circumstances we would have arrested you on sight. We have not done that. We have come into your home and politely asked you to respond to the evidence that we have. If you can tell us anything that would cast doubt on the evidence that we have, we would have to consider that too. That would delay and possibly avoid an arrest and a charge. So, as DS Greenley just asked you, what are your comments on the affidavit?'

I was spent. 'Who is the client?' I asked wearily.

'Can't tell you that,' snapped Greenley. 'Not yet.'

'OK, where is this conversation supposed to have taken place?'

'At your offices.'

'I can prove his allegations are wrong.'

'How?'

'Tapes.'

'Tapes?'

'Audio tapes. I tape all conversations in the boardroom.'

It took a while for this information to sink in. The DS and the DC just looked at each other, as if communicating without speaking. I pressed on, 'But I can only supply the tape if you give me the names of the client who signed the affidavit.' Check mate, I thought.

'All conversations?' asked Greenley.

'All conversations,' I replied.

'Including Mazzinni's?'

Oh shit! My heart sank. 'Yes,' I said.

'Was that tape not covered by the Production Order?' Greenley asked with something resembling a wry smile.

'This is an area of considerable legal uncertainty. There is one school of thought which holds -'

'When can I have the tape?'

'Tomorrow.'

'As for the tape relating to he who signed the affidavit, I will need to confer with colleagues.' Greenley got up in his usual slow and languid manner. 'You did yourself a favour today. There will be no arrest and no charge and no lock up on remand.' He straightened up. 'At least for now.'

As soon as they'd left I picked up the telephone and called Billy at his offices. 'I need to talk to you confidentially,' I said. 'And urgently.'

Billy no doubt could hear the desperation in my voice and he displayed a lawyer's caution. 'Think before you talk Andrew. If this concerns Tania, remember she is my client. I have responsibilities to her. Don't tell me anything that you may later regret saying, or that I may later regret hearing. Subject to that, go ahead.'

'Not on the phone. I need you to come to my home.'

'My desk is covered with client work, I have a full schedule and I don't like exercise. Tell me now. I'm sitting down and comfortable.' And drinking, I thought.

'Come here, Billy,' I said, 'please.'

'Why?' he asked slowly.

'Because I'm falling apart.'

'I'll be right there,' he said

When I hung up Julianna was standing at my study door. 'Why have they come back? I thought it was over.'

'I'm beginning to think it will never be over,' I said.

264

Her eyes were sad. 'You need some loving,' she said.

We were alone in the house. Tania was at work managing Shadowlands. It would have been perfect, but I felt drained. 'No, not now.'

'OK, I need some loving.' She tilted her head and pouted. 'You worry too much, y'know. Sometimes I think you forget who you are. You need to chill. Bad things don't happen to big men like you. Come.'

She turned in the frame of the door and walked toward the stairs, swinging her hips for my benefit. I experienced a sudden surge of sexual energy and I followed her without protest. She was wrong, of course, but she was strong, and so sexy.

Julianna had to jump from the bed and grab her clothes when the front door chimed. I dressed more leisurely as I tried to order my thoughts. Billy was standing in the drawing room when I got downstairs. I apprised him of the meeting with Sir Kenneth Llewellin in the private office of George Fairlow, and the subsequent grilling in my study by DS Greenley and DC Martyn Clarke. 'I'll need to change my lawyer,' I said.

'Why?'

'Why?' I asked incredulously. 'Because he's part of the conspiracy to set me up, that's why.'

'No, I couldn't disagree more,' said Billy. 'George is working the system to your advantage. He's totally Establishment. You couldn't be in better hands. If, and it's a huge if, George had any role in Greenley's visit, say to fulfil his wider obligations, you can be certain of this: he'll have left you a way out. George never enters a building without knowing where the fire exits are. It's just the way he is.'

And, of course, Billy was right. George had left me with a neon-lit, double-doored way out. George knew that all my boardroom conversations were taped. It was the very first issue I consulted him on: should I give up the Mazzinni audio tapes under the Production Order that had been served upon me.

I told Billy. He was pleased but not delighted. 'Audio tapes, in a case like this, are difficult,' he said. 'Normally tapes are used to prove somebody *did* say something. "Look," his lawyer can say, "it's on the tape!" You, however, will want to use the tapes to prove that you *didn't* say something. Not an easy task. How do you prove that *everything* you said was taped?' I was deflated. 'No,' continued Billy, 'it's an exit. It's not neon-lit and it's not double-doored, but it's an exit. It is the sort of exit that requires an expert, highly paid, advisor to get you through, the sort of exit George Fairlow specialises in.'

'What did you mean,' I asked, 'when you referred to George's wider obligations? He shouldn't have any wider obligations. He should only have an obligation to me. I'm his client.'

'Listen to yourself. We all have wider obligations. For a start every solicitor has a duty to the Law Society and the judicial system. George also has an obligation to the Establishment.' Billy lit up a cigarette. 'Any whiskey?'

'Sure,' I said, 'Julianna will be back in a minute.'

Billy made himself comfortable in one of the armchairs and then looked around helplessly for an ashtray. It would have made more sense for him to have looked for the ashtray before lighting up, but for Billy lighting a cigarette was not a conscious action. I think he only knew he was smoking when he needed a receptacle into which to flick the ash.

'Here,' I said.

'Thanks.' Billy inhaled deeply on his cigarette. 'I've studied the Establishment over the years, ever since they locked me out. Its members exist to protect the status quo. They actually believe they are responsible for the order in society. In your case maintaining order means not allowing the pursuit of justice to get in the way of the smooth running of the economy.'

'And in the process I could go to jail.'

'Unlikely. OK, let's say you get charged. Chances are, you won't get convicted. Anyway, George will hold the case up for years.'

'I didn't think the defence could do that under the new rules.'

'They can if the prosecution co-operate.' I looked at Billy in disbelief. 'As I said, George is Establishment. Your case will be settled over fine wine and canapés. That is the part of the operation of the criminal justice system in this country that I totally despise.'

Billy was about to enter that melancholic state in which he seemed to spend much of his time. I hauled him back. 'But I *could* get convicted.'

'Sure, at the end of the day there's no telling what a jury might do. That's the only beauty left in the system, and they're trying to take that away.'

'And I could go to jail.'

'If convicted, going to jail is a certainty.'

'And I could be locked up before trial. I could be put on remand.'

'A bit strong, but possible.'

'I can't go to jail Billy.'

'Nobody likes –'

'No, really, I can't go.' And I told him why.

Chapter 16

After Billy left I regretted that I had exposed so much of my inner self, that I addressed the source of my overwhelming fears of prison. I sat alone in my drawing room on the thick chenille stool feeling wholly detached from the beautiful furniture surrounding me. The room had been designed for Dr Stuart, and at that moment he wasn't anywhere around. Dr Stuart, as I explained to Billy, was my own creation. He was confident and in control, a master of his field. A brilliant man, a solver of problems, a designer of fiscal illusions. Yet in many ways Dr Stuart was a puppet. And the puppeteer was Andy Singley, the hesitant unloved little boy I used to be. The boy I tried so hard to leave behind.

I had always thought Dr Stuart was built from the inside out. I had studied law, tax, finance and accountancy with an intensity that induced physical pain. I would be the best. I got my degrees. I became a doctor of international revenue law. Yet I never really felt like I was Dr Stuart until I was dressed. The double cuffed made-to-measure shirt, the AS gold cufflinks, the designer tie, the highly polished brogues, these were not merely desirable accoutrements. They formed a necessary part of the character's attire; his costume, if you like. The clothes enabled me to play the role. They were my stage-wear.

This is what my persecutors do not understand. They think I am the person they see. They think I am the perfect fit. They want to charge someone to take the heat off the Laundryman, and a conviction would be even better. That would add sparkle to the wine and canapés. What they do not know is that a conviction would be an execution, the killing of that persona that enabled me to assume my place in the world. When they take me down and drive me to the prison, thinking that they've got Dr Andrew Stuart, they will be wrong. So wrong. With all of his support system gone, Dr Stuart will die of asphyxiation in the Securicor van. The person who will walk through the prison gates will be Andy Singley, unhappy and alone, once again abandoned and utterly terrified.

I would not let them do that to me. I could not let them do that to him.

Far off, breaking into my trance-like state, I heard keys opening the front door, followed by muffled voices. Tania was back and she was talking to Julianna. I could not hear what they were saying, but from Tania's tone it was clear that she was growing increasingly agitated. Suddenly Tania was in the drawing room standing over me. Well, it seemed to be suddenly, but then my world that afternoon was moving more slowly than everybody else's.

'What happened, Stu?' she said, hands on hips. 'Talk to me.' She spoke with authority, without sympathy or concern. I motioned with my hands for her to sit down. I was somewhere between her world and my own, and the divide seemed too far to breach.

I continued to sit in silence for some time. When I spoke I was not addressing Tania as such. I was more airing my thoughts aloud, thinking back to my discussions with Billy. 'There is a jurisprudential dilemma,' I said, 'known to every first year law student and it is this. The revered president is shot. As a consequence riots ravage the land. There is burning, looting and shooting. Innocent people are dying. You can stop this mayhem by finding and executing the assassin. But you have a problem: you have no idea who he is. And you have an opportunity: anyone will do. So do you accuse and execute one innocent man to save the lives of thousands of innocent men, women and children who are dying in the riots?'

'No,' said Tania without hesitation.

This was the usual instinctive reaction of the young and the idealistic, those who would never have to make such a decision. 'Why not?' I asked instinctively.

'Because it's wrong.'

'You would save thousands of lives.'

'You would be taking one innocent life.' She looked at me with a worried expression. 'I'm right, aren't I? That is the right answer?'

'There is no right answer,' I said. 'The utilitarian view would be that you execute the innocent man. Others adhere to the words of Ferdinand I: "Let justice be done, though the world perish."'

'And you, Stu, where do you stand?'

'I've always answered the question by saying that provided it is certain that the rioting would stop and the thousands of lives would be saved, I'd execute. But now I'm not so sure.'

'Why's that?'

'Because I have a feeling that today I'm that innocent man.'

Tania did not try to hide her sense of exasperation. 'What happened?!'

'I've been set up.'

'Who by?'

'Good question.' I did not elaborate.

'OK, then, why?'

'Because, unwittingly, we have set in train a series of events that have served to raise the profile of the Laundryman. Lightning, with his record, and Joseph Feingold, with his promotion, have celebrated his existence, under the guise of hunting him down. So what has he done? He has stopped laundering money. Everyone's looking for him. He's being very cautious. Even the two-bit launderers have stopped laundering money, and for the same reason. The effect on the economy will be devastating. Over a very short period of time we're heading for deflation. Money is simply not circulating through the economy. And the Treasury has to do something about it.'

'They should help catch the Laundryman.'

'No, you're wrong. They *want* the money laundered. They need the money back in the banking system.'

'So what should they do?'

'The need to take the pressure off of money laundering activities. So, you're partly right. They must catch someone and tell the world they've caught the Laundryman. Then the real Laundryman can go about his normal business. And guess what? Anyone will do.'

Tania paused and then asked very softly, 'You?'

'Me.'

I moved close to her, held her in my arms and told her about the events of the day.

After dinner Tania and I sat in the family room watching a movie on Sky TV. I was watching far more television since Tania moved in. It was what she liked to do. As we nestled together on the sofa, the chimes of the front door rang through the house. It was late. I feared the worse. Tania place hers hands in mine, a kind and reassuring gesture. Julianna responded to the chimes and then knocked and opened the family room door. 'It's Mr Carver,' she said.

'Billy?' said Tania, raising herself from me. 'What does he want?'

'He wants to see you Andrew,' said Julianna with a cutting edge in her voice aimed directly at Tania.

'He's my lawyer,' said Tania petulantly.

This gave Julianna an opening she couldn't resist. Addressing me she said, 'He did ask if Tania was here and I said yes, but he insisted that he only wants to see you.' She smiled.

Smiling was OK, I thought, just don't dance. 'Show him to my study,' I said.

'No, he doesn't want to come in.'

I got up and went to the front door which was ajar, Billy standing outside with his hands in the pocket of his overcoat.

'Are you all right?' I asked.

'Yes I'm fine. I want you to come by my office tomorrow at 7:00 pm.'

'OK,' I said.

'Listen carefully.' Billy's tone was aggressive. I put it down to the drink. It seemed to be affecting him more recently. 'Listen, tomorrow, 7:00 pm, no earlier, no later. I have some important information on the Laundryman. If you don't follow my instructions it will ruin it.'

'Fine, Billy, calm down, your office, Monday, seven, I've got it.'

'Here's a key,' he said removing his right hand from his pocket.

'You're not going to be there?'

'I'll be there, but you'll need a key.' He placed the key in my palm. His hands were cold.

'Come inside,' I said.

'No,' he replied and started making his way unsteadily back down my driveway.

I called out to him. 'Billy, come in and relax for a bit. I've got a case of 12 year old Lagavulin, bought in just for you.'

He stopped and turned around. I could not make out his features in the shadows, but his voice seemed to break when he said, 'I've had enough.'

I awoke on Tuesday morning thinking only of Billy's strange request. Would this, I wondered, be the day I discovered the identity of the Laundryman and, if so, would Billy have enough information for Martyn Clarke to make an arrest? I wanted to call Billy, but his instruction had been exact and his manner strict: 7:00 pm, at his offices, any earlier and I would ruin it.

Fortunately, I had a meeting that morning with Hugo Maximillian of Coats Bank. Fortunate, in so far as it would help keep my mind off Billy. Hugo and I had signed contracts and I had achieved my minimum rebated price, one half of the figure originally discussed before the troubles. But as Hugo had moved from his "final" offer of one-third, I myself had to make a concession. Instead of the totally clean break I had originally envisioned, I had agreed to one consulting day per month for the first year. This was the first such day. So I got up, showered and dressed as Dr Stuart, but I didn't really want to go.

I suggested to Tania over our light breakfast that I call the salon on her behalf and say that she was sick and that she call the bank and do the same for me. I said we could go into London and do the touristy things that Londoners never get round to doing. She was having none of it. 'With all that's gone on,' she said, 'I'm glad I've still got a job. I'm not going to jeopardize it now. I'm going to work,' adding playfully, 'and so should you!'

I arrived at the bank at 9:30, which is a respectable hour for bankers. I was not surprised that Hugo did not greet me himself. No doubt he was running late. I sat in the plush reception area until Dr Francis Peartree, the head of the bank's trust department, came to get me. He, too, was in no hurry. When, at last, he appeared, his lanky frame seemed more stooped than I remembered, and his wispy hair more white than grey. Maybe the increased work load had taken its toll.

'This way,' he said, as we exited reception. 'You have been allocated a small meeting room. That shouldn't inconvenience you. After all, it's only one day a month.' Francis seemed resentful of my presence. It really shouldn't have bothered him. Had it been up to me I wouldn't have been there at all. We walked down a flight of stairs and along a narrow corridor. We stopped at about the fourth door along. 'Here,' he said.

The room was indeed small. It was also windowless. The only furniture in the room was a round wooden table surrounded by four black plastic chairs. On the table sat a white phone with its long cord carelessly extending over one of the chairs and leading to a point in the far corner of the room. Next to the phone was a white writing pad, blue folder and a biro. 'You shouldn't have gone to so much trouble,' I said.

Francis ignored me. 'There's a schedule of work in the blue folder. It's mostly what Hugo calls "hand holding." You are to ring those clients highlighted on the schedule and reassure them that they are in safe hands here at the bank. A file note should be prepared of each conversation.

'Any problems call me. I'm on extension 1314. Dial 9 for an outside line. All external calls are monitored. And at the end of the day the trust department receives a print out listing all calls by phone number, duration and cost. Each external call must have a job number allocated to it. This is a large, strict and structured organisation Dr Stuart. Cavalier practices are frowned upon.'

I picked up the telephone and started working through the list. The calls mostly resembled each other, hearty exchanges, jokes at the expense of the tax man, their regret at the move to the bank, my praising of the bank's huge network and expertise, and a concluding "understanding" that I would continue to take a special interest in their tax affairs.

There was a knock at the door. 'Come in.'

'Andrew.'

'Anita.'

She was dressed just the same as when she worked for me and she had the same air of order, efficiency and control. She was carrying a thin red folder. She looked around the room with disdain, but her loyalty to her new employers prevented her from making any comments. Instead she said, 'How are you getting on?'

'Fine,' I said. 'But you could have called some of these clients.'

'I have, but they all ask for you. I confirm that you're a consultant to the bank, but they want to know that you are still personally monitoring their offshore tax structures. They trust you Andrew. They need to hear your voice.'

'I understand, but there were no fires to put out.'

'That's because you're working the "B" list, those clients who are safe but need reassurance. I have here the "A" list, those clients we are in serious danger of losing. Francis suggested that I sit in while you talk to these clients so I can take notes.'

And what else, I thought, to prevent me from re-pitching those clients wholly disgruntled with the bank's services? When would they understand that I just wanted to get out?

'OK,' I said, 'who's the first on the list?'

'Giovanni Mazzinni.'

Anita briefed me on the bank's contact with the client and I called him. The phone was picked up on the third ring. 'Hello.'

'Mr Mazzinni, good morning. It's Dr Stuart.' I pictured in my mind's eye the dapper little man with the fluttering hands and the £20 million to protect.

'Dr Stuart?' He was surprised. 'Hello.' And cautious.

'I was reviewing your file. As you know I now serve as a consultant to Coats Bank, who have now taken over my practice. They are able to provide a more comprehensive service than I could offer because of their -'

'I don't need the service anymore.'

'I will remain deeply involved in -'

'That's not it. Things have changed. Keep the deposit. And -' he hesitated, '- and I'm sorry.'

There was something about his apology that unsettled me. It was genuine. But if I was keeping his £50,000 deposit and providing no services, why would he apologise? He was not obligated to give me professional work. I was not out of pocket. Then it hit me, and I took a chance. 'Why did you sign the affidavit Mr Mazzinni?' He was silent. I lowered my voice. 'It's OK, I can handle it, just tell me why.'

'I'm sorry but, how you say, they were squeezing my balls.'

'Who?'

Anita was looking at me strangely as the line went dead.

'It's personal,' I said.

There was a gentle rap on the door. 'Come in.' The door opened slowly and Hugo Maximillian ambled in.

'Andrew, my dear fellow, they put you in here? What were they thinking?' "They," I thought, were following his instructions, but I played along.

'It's adequate Hugo.'

He turned to Anita. 'You might wish to take a break,' he said. Anita got up and left, taking her red folder with her.

Hugo pulled out one of the plastic chairs and slowly lowered his expensively clad, ample frame onto to it. 'She's doing well, your Anita.'

'Thank you,' I said, though she was hardly my Anita anymore.

'How are you getting on with the clients?'

'Fine,' I said. 'It seems to me that most will stay on board. You're going to lose a few. It's inevitable, and the agreement provided for it.'

'Quite so.' He paused. 'Have you had coffee?' Hugo, I thought, was marking time, waiting for an opportunity to say what was on his mind. It came after Mrs Reynolds had served the coffee and left. 'There's an excellent corner office on the third floor, very spacious with tall windows and Georgian furniture, looking for a permanent occupant.'

'No,' I said.

I worked, largely alone, Mazzinni never far from my mind, until 4 o' clock, the end of my working day as a banker. As I drove home I tried to piece it all together. Someone had intimidated Mazzinni. He signed an affidavit saying, in effect, that I was the Laundryman. Mazinni, himself, was on the Production Order served on me by DS Greenley at the commencement of the case. Why? I didn't know. What was his connection to the case? Whatever it was he had enough at stake to lie about me. Did they offer him immunity from prosecution? Possibly. And when Greenley asked for the Mazzinni tape, which I then supplied to him, it was serving two purposes. First, it would highlight whatever the police were pursuing him for, and secondly (though I didn't know this at the time), it would demonstrate that I did not boast to him about money laundering activities or revel in the title of The Laundryman. A double whammy. I smiled, but I remained troubled. Who leaned on Mazzinni? It wasn't Greenley. *There has come into my possession an affidavit signed by a client of yours,* he said. So he didn't interview Mazzinni. Who did?

The closer I got to my house the more my thoughts of Mazzinni gave way to thoughts of Billy. I got home with enough time to shower and change before jumping back in the car and driving to Peckham. I arrived at 6:30 and parked the car across the road from the Carver & Co. I wanted to honour Billy's request of arriving at exactly 7:00 pm, whilst at the same time hopefully gaining an advance preview by recognising who was entering and leaving his offices. The key to his front door was in my breast pocket, which I tapped with my hand for comfort. The time passed slowly. By 6:55 no one had entered or left the building. Give it three more minutes, I said to myself. Billy was so precise in his instructions. When the time had passed I got out of the car, locked it, walked to Billy's front door, turned the key and stepped in.

The offices were dark and silent. The staff must have been sent home early. I didn't see them leave. I walked to the stairs. 'Billy,' I shouted. No answer. The offices smelt more musty than usual. No, they smelt more pungent. 'Billy,' I shouted again. 'I'm coming up.' I mounted the now

276

familiar stairs, turned right and saw Billy hanging by his neck from the light fitting at the centre of the ceiling of his office. Attached to his brown cardigan was a fifty pound note on which he had written in a black felt tip pen "The Laundryman."

'Billy,' I whispered and, with an honesty of feeling too rarely honoured in my life, I began to cry.

I walked back down the stairs hands on the wall feeling with my feet for each step like a blind man. There was a voice in my head chanting "Don't touch anything." I picked up the phone on the desk of Mr Steroids and started dialling BB's number. *BB, in times of trouble, everyone's first call.* I hung up. Too many people had dialled the wrong person at the wrong time in recent months giving rise to complications that should have been foreseen. No more. I dialled DC Clarke's private mobile number.

'Hello.'

'Martyn,' I said, 'it's Andrew. I'm at Billy Carver's offices. I think he's hanged himself.'

'You're in the building?'

'Yes,' I said and gave him the address.

'Right, stay where you are and don't touch a thing.'

'Can't I cut him down?'

'Is he definitely dead?'

'Yes, I think so.'

'Is he dead or not?'

'Yes.'

'Then leave him where he is.'

'OK,' I said and hung up.

I went back upstairs to Billy's office and reached up to the body. 'You're not the Laundryman, Billy,' I said softly, unpinning the fifty pound note from the cardigan. 'You're my friend, a wounded human being who never came to terms with his own genius.'

I heard police sirens, faint at first then louder, then deafening, as cars screeched to a halt outside the office. As I got to the bottom of the stairs, the police were pounding on the door. This was way too soon for Martyn

Clarke. I opened the door and three uniformed officers entered. The tallest one said, 'We have received a call that a homicide has taken place at these premises. Identify yourself.'

'I am Dr Andrew Stuart. Who called you?'

'Is the victim dead doctor?'

'I believe so; yes he is. But, listen, I'm not here in any official capacity. I'm not a doctor of medicine. I am - was - Billy's friend.'

'Where's the body?'

'Up the stairs on the right. I called DC Clarke. Did he call you?' The three officers exchanged knowing glances. Two of them bounded up the stairs, one remained with me.

'What's your name?' I said.

'PC Dias. Did you touch anything?'

'No.' I put my hand into my pocket and screwed Billy's fifty into a tight ball.

The two officers returned after some five minutes. The tall one said to PC Dias, 'Take him to the station and get a full statement.'

'I don't have to go anywhere,' I said. 'If you want a statement I'll give you one here. I'm waiting for DC Clarke.'

'I said, take him to the station and get a full statement. If he resists, arrest him on suspicion of murder, then take him to the station and get a full statement.'

PC Dias opened the front door. 'Dr Stuart?'

'I'm not going,' I said.

'Please,' he said.

'No,' I said. He was nervous and I decided to push my advantage. 'Moreover, if you choose to arrest me make sure you have good cause. As I said I'm not a doctor of medicine, but I am a doctor of law. Moreover you are about to make an arrest in the offices of the best criminal lawyer in London. So be careful.'

'Very careful,' said Martyn Clarke stepping through the open door. He identified himself, took control, viewed the body, issued instructions and led me outside. It had started to rain, very lightly. 'Where's the note?' he said.

'What?'

'Don't play with me Andrew, where's the suicide note? Billy's dead. You can't protect him. Nothing can hurt him now. Give it to me.' I took out the crumpled £50 note and handed it to Martyn. 'A literal note,' he said as he smoothed it out. Then he read aloud, 'The Laundryman.'

'He'd pinned it to his cardigan.'

'Why did you take it?'

'Because he's not the Laundryman.'

'That is your opinion and it's not a good reason for removing evidence from the scene of a potential crime. Anyway, how can you be so sure?'

'I met with the Bank of England yesterday. The Establishment are protecting the Laundryman. They would not protect Billy. They shot his cock off twenty years ago.'

'Go home Andrew. As soon as I've worked out what's going on here I'll stop by the house.'

When I pulled up outside my home I was in a daze. Part of my brain was saying, "How did you get here?" I had driven as if on automatic pilot. I had no recollection of the journey. It took me three attempts to get the key in the door. I was in a bad way. The house was too quiet. I needed noise; I wanted company. I called out for Tania but there was no reply. I went upstairs and knocked on her door. No answer. I turned the handle and went inside. The soft hum of the power shower drew me to the en suite bathroom. The door was open. 'Tania?'

'In here,' she said.

Tania's lean brown body was covered in suds. She was soaping herself up with her hands, hands on her breasts, then over her smooth, flat tummy, moving down between her legs then round to her bum. As the shower washed away the lather, it revealed her taut black nipples, and shaved vulva, glistening with droplets of water. I wanted her completely. I wanted to lick her perfect body from tip to toe. She stepped toward me and reached for the towel. 'Relax Stu, I think the time you've been waiting for has arrived. Loosen up. Say something sexy.'

'Billy's dead,' I said, and handed her the towel. I walked back through her room and down the stairs, past the drawing room and into the kitchen, where I poured whiskey into a tall glass. To the rim. I took three mouthfuls and tipped the rest down the sink.

Martyn didn't arrive till late. 'It's been accepted as a suicide subject to formalities,' he said.

'Will I need to attend an inquest,' I asked, 'given that I was the first person to find the body?'

'But you weren't the first person to find him; Debbie Cowans was.'

'Who?'

'Debbie Cowans. She works for Billy Carver - or used to - as an assistant solicitor. She has a garish appearance, orange hair -'

'And a pierced nose,' I said. Ms Punk. 'When did she find him?'

'Around 6:45.'

'Fifteen minutes before me?'

'Yes, she returned to work to collect some files, found Billy, left the office in distress and rang us on her mobile. The police that arrived at the office were responding to her call not yours.'

'Are you sure about the time she gave?'

'Positive. Do you have something to tell me?'

'No, but I may have something to tell you tomorrow afternoon. Do you have her address?'

'Sure.' He read it out to me. 'But I didn't give it to you.'

I planned to visit Debbie Cowans first thing in the morning. I needed to find out what really happened in the hours leading up to Billy death and in the immediate aftermath. 'What time did Billy die?'

'They reckon about 5:00 pm, give or take. Is that important?'

'I don't know,' I said with a sigh. 'What I really want to know is why he did it.'

'Don't beat yourself up on that one,' said Martyn. 'There is no answer to the question; at least, not one that will satisfy you. There never is.'

'What did you do with the note?'

'It has been included in the list of his effects. I have not specifically drawn attention to it. Let's face it, it's hardly a suicide note in the traditional sense of the word. That said, what you did was totally unacceptable.'

'I apologise, but you agree with me, don't you? Billy was not the Laundryman.'

'I agree, but not for the reason you gave. The Establishment will protect anybody who is prepared to do their bidding. Class, race, gender and socio-economic group simply do not come into it. I know Billy was not the Laundryman because he was too emotional. The Laundryman is ice cold. My fear, however, is that Billy knew who the Laundryman was.'

'Pity you didn't keep the £50 note. It could have been that he was leaving us a clue.'

Martyn removed a clear plastic envelope from his pocket. He slowly pealed apart the self-sealing lip and removed Billy's monetary suicide note. 'I said it was on the list. I didn't say I'd left it behind.' He placed the note on my low antique Chinese tea table. It was an ordinary £50 note on which was printed in black felt tip pen "The Laundryman." The "T" commenced on the Britannia's shield and the "n" ended on the portrait of Her Majesty the Queen. 'Does it mean anything to you?' asked Martyn.

'Nothing,' I said. 'You?'

'Nothing.' He turned the note over. The ink was clearly visible from the reverse side. The inverse "n" had been absorbed into the picture of an historic house in Threadneedle Street, and the inverse "T" had been absorbed into the left cheek of the portrait of Sir John Houblon, 1632 - 1712, former Lord Mayor of London and the first Governor of the Bank of England. We both saw it at the same time. I thought back to my meeting with Sir Kenneth Llewellin. *From this perspective the Laundryman is our friend. He ensures that the Treasury model of the economy actually works.*

'Is Billy saying - '

'I don't think so,' said Martyn.

'I hope you're right,' I replied.

'OK, I'm done,' said Martyn picking up the £50 note and returning it to the plastic envelope and resealing it. I showed him to the door.

That night I slept fitfully, waking often from troubled dreams: a football match with a human head as the ball, sharks tearing at the bodies of swimmers, people falling from tall buildings. The £50 note. By 4:00am I was just lying on my back awake, preoccupied and almost afraid to go back to sleep. The £50 suicide note. An icy chill ran through my body. The £50 Laundryman note. I didn't know what is was, but something was wrong.

Chapter 17

I made an early start. At 6:00 am I was standing under a cold shower, by 6:30 I was driving to the home of Debbie Cowans, aka Ms Punk, the erstwhile assistant solicitor to Billy Carver. The liar. She lived in a flat near Peckham Rye railway station. I knocked on her door at 7:15. She opened it in her dressing gown. She recognised me and invited me inside. There was sluggishness about her, whether from fatigue, grief or guilt. She offered me coffee. I declined.

'Well I need one,' she said, 'can't function without caffeine. Come, we can talk in the kitchen. It's about Billy right?' I followed her through to the small kitchen and leaned against the wall. She put the kettle on. 'Sure you don't want one?'

'Sure.'

'Poor Billy,' she said.

'Poor Billy,' I echoed. 'I thought I had found him first, but the police told me you found him at 6:45, fifteen minutes before me.'

'Yes,' she said with her back to me.

'Apparently you went back to the office to collect some files, found Billy hanging there, fled in a state of upset and rang the police on your mobile phone.'

'That's right.'

'But you lied, didn't you?'

'Did I?' She poured the boiling water into a large yellow mug and slowly stirred the instant coffee.

'Yes, you were not at the office when you said you were. I was parked outside. No one entered or left.'

Debbie opened the fridge, removed an open carton of milk and held it up to her nose. I waited. Satisfied, she added a little milk into her mug.

'You must have missed me.'

'Not a chance.' She turned to face me, toying with one of the studs in her ears. 'Tell me,' I said. 'I've said nothing to the police. I'm just trying to understand what happened.'

Debbie picked up the yellow mug and sipped the coffee cautiously. 'I was supposed to find him. I was supposed to go back to the office at 6:45, see him hanging there and call the police. You were supposed to arrive at seven, just as the police were responding to my call.'

'You knew I was coming.'

'Sure, Billy told me.'

'You knew he was going to kill himself?'

'He told me Monday evening.'

'And you didn't try to stop him.'

'No. He's a grown man – he was a grown man. And the cleverest man I've ever met. You didn't argue with Billy. Anyway, I'm a firm believer in euthanasia.'

'But Billy wasn't sick.'

'What do *you* call alcoholism?' I took her point, and left my silence to indicate that I had no answer. 'He asked me to help him,' she said. 'He was concerned that the light fitting would not hold his weight.'

'You were in the room when he hanged himself?'

'Yes.'

'You watched him kill himself?' I was incredulous.

'I never looked at him. I looked at the floor. My sole role was to help him should the light fitting not hold his weight. If he had fallen to the ground I would have helped him – removed the noose from round his neck. But he didn't fall.'

'You aided and abetted a suicide. That's a crime.'

'I beg to differ. I was present when a suicide took place. I neither aided nor abetted, as you put it. I would have helped him survive if it was necessary, but it was not. My conscience is clear, and so, I think you will find, is my legal position. *Thou shalt not kill; but needst not strive officiously to keep alive.* Arthur Hugh Clough.'

'He was being ironic.'

'It fits.'

'Why did he choose you?' I asked, adding improbably, 'Did you have more than a professional relationship?'

'I was not his type.' I looked at her bright dyed hair and pierced nose and lips and the contempt may have shown in my face. As retribution she told me the one thing I did not want to know. 'You were his type, Dr Stuart.'

On one level I must have known but the impact of her words hit me hard. "Tania's mine," I had said when Billy had spoken of a currently unrequited love. "More importantly, you are hers," he had replied. I suffered a crushing feeling of guilt. I realised that for all the words Billy and I had exchanged, I'd never really been listening. 'I'm sorry,' I said.

'Me too. Look, in reality the man drank himself to death. So we all watched him kill himself. I just happened to be there when he died.'

I took it upon myself to arrange his funeral. I ached for my lost friend and tried to understand his frame of mind at the end of his life. How, I tried to fathom, do you plan for your own suicide. What goes through your mind the morning of the day, the close of which you plan never to see? I understood the case of the terminally ill. I too had long supported euthanasia. When each day is filled with unbearable pain that will only ever end on death, then it seemed to me reasonable, even rational, to wish to hasten the end. But when you're in good health, when tomorrow could be better, why abruptly end the magic of life?

Was it a brave act or an act of cowardice? At first I couldn't decide. Some say suicide is "the easy way out." That was, I thought, a trite phrase that should only be found on the lips of the dull and the ignorant. Easy? Throwing yourself in front of a high speed train? Jumping from a high bridge into raging water? Standing on a chair with your head in a noose tied to the light fittings in the ceiling of your office, then kicking the chair away? Easy? I don't think so. Suicide, I decided, was the act of a brave person. And a short-sighted one.

For who knows the twists in the road ahead? Billy could have won key legal decisions that influenced an improvement in the law. He could have found requited love. He could have beaten his addictions and changed his life. He never tried, or if he tried, he didn't try hard enough. When, I wondered, did his light go out? Probably when the pain started. A long time ago.

'Stu,' said Tania from the stairs. 'We're waiting.'

'Five minutes,' I said.

Why? Why did he do it? When he looked ahead was the future he saw so dark? Was there nothing for him to look forward to? There must have been something. Moreover, wasn't he curious about events that would only unfold with the effluxion of time, those events that cause us to remark, "I never thought I would live to see the day?" The election of the first black US president, the complete legalisation of drugs, proof of life on Mars, finding the cure for cancer, peace in the Middle East. And on a more immediate level, wasn't he curious about the Laundryman: whether we were going to catch him, and how, and who he is? Or, as Martyn suggested, did he know?

The £50 note. And suddenly I understood. It was not a clue. It was a solution.

I joined the other mourners downstairs. BB, Tania, Martyn Clarke, Julianna and Anita, each dressed in black, were milling around in the drawing room, none of them quite knowing what to say or do. 'We're going to have a drink,' I said.

'So early?' said Anita.

'Yes,' I replied.

Julianna left the room, as we had previously arranged, and returned with a tray with six small glasses of whiskey and a large bottle of plain mineral water. She offered the tray around. Everyone took a glass. No one, not even Martyn, touched the water. 'To Billy,' I said.

'To Billy,' they replied, and we all downed our whiskey in one gulp. He would have been proud.

'Anita,' I said, 'I need to speak with you.'

'Go ahead.'

'In my study please.'

'Stu,' said Tania, 'we don't have time. We need to be at the church.'

'It will only take a minute,' I said.

Anita walked briskly to my study. I ambled behind. 'What is it?' she said. 'You made it sound conspiratorial in there.'

'Not at all. I need you to do something for me. Billy's death has raised all sort of issues.'

'Like what?'

'Mortality,' I said.

'Not for me,' she said, and I believed her. Anita would go on forever.

'The point is,' I said, 'I have no proper family. Notwithstanding our current estrangement, you have always looked after me in a professional sense. I now need you to do so in a personal sense.' I had intended this meeting to be businesslike, but I now felt myself overcome with emotion. I could not prevent my voice from breaking, when I asked her: 'Anita, should anything happen to me would you please arrange my funeral?' She was stunned. She said nothing, just looked at me with pity. I did not cry, but to my astonishment, tears formed in her own eyes. I ploughed on. 'I have put my affairs in order. Here's a key to my house. Everything you'll need will be here in my study, including who should be invited, the nature of the service and, of course, the money.'

There was a long awkward silence, eventually broken by a question that surprised me. 'Why don't you ask Tania?'

'Tania would not bury me.'

'No,' she said taking the key from my hand and making no attempt to brush away the tears now rolling sadly down her face. 'She's buried you already.'

I put my arms around her. 'Do you need some time?' I asked.

'No,' she said and pulled a handkerchief from her sleeve, patted her face and returned to the drawing room.

The funeral service was a disappointment. The vicar, it seemed, had reached into his service drawer and pulled out the standard funeral sermon. He described Billy Carver as a man who "loved life" – *he killed himself,* as a man who "loved his family" – *what family?* Billy Carver, he said, was "a levelheaded man" – *he was a manic-depressive* – a man who "knew only God's work" – *he was chasing demons all his adult life.*

I raised these points with George Fairlow as we walked behind the hearse following the coffin from the church to the burial plot. He didn't agree with me. 'He's a vicar, not counsel for the defence.'

'He should have tailored the service to Billy, addressed some of his pain.'

'He wouldn't have had time. Billy's pain was too complex.'

'I don't think so,' I said. 'I think it stemmed from racial exclusion.' I told him about Billy's hurt at being declined articled clerkships at top City firms despite his outstanding academic record.

'And you believe all that,' George replied. He turned and looked at me with disdain. 'Billy was a wreck long before he sought articles in blue-blooded City firms. At university he was fat, smelly and usually drunk. He was clever, sure, but he was at war with himself, as if he believed he had no right to mix with the upper crust.'

We walked on, George with his back ramrod straight and his chin in the air. George walked like a man who had a right to be. The confidence was inborn. 'He felt he had no right to mix with the likes of you is what you mean.'

'Yes, me and the others, his peers. We didn't look down on Billy. How can you look down on someone who thought like Lord Hailsham and wrote like Lord Denning? We admired him. He looked down on himself. That man's been hitting the self-destruct button for as long as I've known him.'

'Why?' I asked.

'I don't know. I never had the temerity to ask.'

Billy's coffin was lowered into the ground on manual pulleys. Slowly people took turns grabbing a handful of earth and throwing it down onto the coffin's lid, uttering as they did so, quiet words of remembrance. When my turn came I said, 'You'll always be in my life Billy,' without realising at the time how true that would prove to be.

As I walked from the graveside, Martyn Clarke sidled up to me. 'Can we talk?' he said.

'Sure,' I replied, 'about Billy?'

'Not directly. We have a lead. One of our undercover officers has reported that cash is starting to flow again. The Laundryman is active.'

'That's not necessarily good news.'

'I think it is. As far as our agent can tell the Laundryman is actively seeking funds. He seems to have substantially increased capacity, a new structure, a Five-Year-Plan.'

'Mycroft?'

'It would appear so.'

It had worked. I had lured the bear into the trap. BB had thought my plan too cerebral, preferring a course of direct action that had got us bound through the night to a rusting tractor in a disused barn. Anita, though she liked the plan, had thought it would not work. Martyn, himself, was sceptical. But it had succeeded. I punched air with excitement. The soft murmur of the surrounding muffled conversations fell to silence. I could feel a hundred eyes on me. Only then did I remember where I was. I felt my face redden with embarrassment. I grew hot with shame. What would they be thinking? What kind of imbecile punches the air with delight at a funeral? I hung my head and slowed my now uncertain pace, walking, as I did, on jellied legs.

'Don't be so hard on yourself,' said Martyn. 'Billy would have enjoyed that.'

We walked to my car and got in. 'That's my part done,' I said.

'Your part has just began,' Martyn replied. 'I can't arrest all of the purchasers of the Mycroft plan. There is not enough evidence. You'll have to narrow it down: from three to one.'

'Four to one,' I said.

'Four?'

'There are four purchasers of the Mycroft plan.'

'Joseph Feingold, Mansa Mussa and Kay Frisk. There's a fourth?'

'Yes.'

'You kept this from me?'

'Yes.'

'Why?'

'Because it's my solicitor Martyn, it's George Fairlow.'

It took the detective constable a little while to process this information. 'Let me see if I have this right: the solicitor who is defending you of money laundering charges has just become one of the four prime Laundryman candidates.'

'I know,' I said. 'It's implausible.'

'It's perfect,' he replied.

There was a tap on my side window. The hand was male and manicured. I turned my key to ignition, without starting the engine, and lowered the window. 'Andrew, I just wanted to say,' he stopped abruptly and his expression took on a faintly perplexed air as he realised the identity of my passenger. 'Detective Constable Clarke, isn't it?'

'Yes,' he replied. 'Good afternoon Mr Fairlow.'

'May I ask the purpose of this clandestine meeting?'

'Nothing clandestine at all,' said Martyn. 'We were reminiscing about Billy Carver. He was the solicitor to Dr Stuart's friend Tania Berkeley. We only met on a couple of occasions, and then in an adversarial context, but I liked him and wanted to pay my respects. Dr Stuart here was telling me he had an alcohol problem. I never knew. How did you know him?'

'We were at university together,' said George Fairlow, closing the conversation with Martyn Clarke. 'Andrew,' he said, giving his full attention to me, 'I'll call you later, but I will tell you this now. I do not think reminiscing with your arresting officer about the solicitor of your potential co-defendant is a particularly bright idea.' He did not wait for an explanation. In seconds he was erect, chin up and walking with the gods.

'BB was right about you guys,' I said to Martyn.

'Right about what?'

'He said you can lie, and you can.'

'I got us out of a hole,' he protested. 'Did you want me to tell him the truth?'

'No,' I said, 'you had to lie. I just didn't know you'd be so damn good at it.'

Martyn ignored me. 'Any more thoughts on the suicide note?'

'Yes,' I said, 'it wasn't a clue. It was a solution.'

'Explain.'

'There is a jurisprudential dilemma,' I said, 'known to every first year law student and it is this. The revered president is shot...' I set out the dilemma as I had to Tania, but unlike Tania he didn't offer an opinion. He just listened.

'So?' he said when I had finished.

'So Billy solved the conundrum. You don't simply kill an innocent man. You kill a man who is already dying. Or, as in Billy's case, he takes his own life.'

'Billy was dying?'

'He had a terminal disease.'

'I didn't know Billy was sick.'

With Debbie's words ringing in my ears, I repeated, 'What do you call alcoholism?' After a decent interval, I continued, 'Billy thought I was being set up as the innocent man and that I would never get out of it. So he put himself forward as the Laundryman.'

'I don't buy it,' said Martyn. 'That would be an extraordinary act of friendship.'

'No,' I said leaning back in the passenger seat and closing my eyes, 'it wasn't an act of friendship. It was an act of love. Unrequited love.'

I could sense that Martyn was uncomfortable. The silence grew heavy. Eventually he said, 'Then you should have left the note pinned to his cardigan.'

'I want to catch the Laundryman, Martyn, the real one.' I opened my eyes and released the car door. 'Let justice be done, though the world perish.'

Later that day, when BB and I were alone in my drawing room, I brought him up-to-date with everything, finishing with the information that the Laundryman had purchased the Mycroft plan and that Martyn needed us to narrow down the four suspects to one. 'So how do we do it?' asked BB.

'I don't know. We need a plan.'

'Let's get hold of Martyn and put our heads together.'

'No, Martyn said we're on our own.'

'And then there were two,' said BB.

'Agatha Christie's Ten Little Indians,' I said.

'That's not what she originally called it. When it was first published it was Ten Little Niggers.'

'She didn't mean anything by it,' I said.

'They never do,' said BB

I needed to move on. This day could become introspective to a painful degree. Funerals are a ritual to honour the dead, but their effect on the living is profound. It is a reminder of an uncomfortable truth, which we must fail to address so that we may live our day to day lives. It tells us starkly that we too shall die. BB and I should, and would, mourn Billy, but at this moment we had work to do, and sometimes work is the best medicine.

'Let's run through our four main suspects again,' I said. 'Just the two of us.'

'OK,' said BB, 'you start.'

'Joseph Feingold,' I said, 'the master manipulator. He has the front for it. And as Martyn said, he deals in cash all the time. What could be easier?'

'This is a London operation, Andrew. The man lives in Scotland.'

'Irrelevant.'

'OK then, why would he put all his energy, time and money into a song aimed at catching the Laundryman, if he's the Laundryman himself. He could have squashed that song in five seconds flat. Instead he promotes it. Come on, it doesn't make sense.'

'Yes it does. You've got to understand the way the man thinks. He is the best, the best in the world. Right now he is shafting the entire

Establishment and loving it. You're right, through the song he's giving the police a hand in catching him. But they won't catch him. No one will ever catch him because, in his mind, he's the best. You have to take a giant leap of the imagination to grasp the sheer magnitude of that man's ego.'

'Why would he do it? He has enough money.'

'Nobody in the world has enough money BB. You think he's got enough, because he's got more than you. Joseph Feingold probably thinks Bill Gates has enough because he's got more than him. Does Bill Gates think he's got enough? He hasn't taken early retirement. Everyone can use a little more money. Then there's the crack.'

'The crack?'

'The crack, the buzz, the sheer pleasure in doing it. You saw him at the castle. His appetite for everything is insatiable.'

'George Fairlow,' said BB.

'This one's too close for me,' I said. 'You have a go.'

'Right, he's a solicitor, a partner from one of London's top firms. He's snotty, from the upper crust. He's born to rule. He has friends in the very highest circles. He's untouchable. Now here's the twist. Billy was convinced he knew who the Laundryman was, right? Who introduced you to George Fairlow?'

'Billy,' I said.

'Right, look at it like this. Billy defends drug traffickers. He's got their confidence. Along the way they tell him or he finds out that his old university buddy is the Laundryman. You get arrested for money laundering. Now, in financial circles you're a big fish. So what does he do? He recommends you to George Fairlow so that George can keep a close eye on the case.'

'You're saying he knew from the beginning.'

'That's right.'

'Then he would have fed back to his buddy, as you put it, the outcome of the Brains Trust meetings and George Fairlow would have known all about the thinking behind the Mycroft plan and would not have purchased it.'

'Not necessarily, maybe as time wore on Billy got split loyalties, and chose not to tell him anything. Maybe he grew so tormented – '

'Don't,' I said.

'OK, let's approach it from another angle. George Fairlow is the Laundryman. He sees things getting hot so he introduces you to the man who protects him: a director of the Bank of England. The man tells you to lay off right?'

'Yes,' I said.

'He said the Laundryman is his friend?'

'You're taking it out of context BB. What he said was, seen from the perspective of the proper stewardship of the economy, which demands that this cash is deposited into the banking system, the Laundryman is a friend.'

'Same thing. And that's why Billy wrote "The Laundryman" on a fifty pound note. George Fairlow earns the big bucks. George Fairlow is the Laundryman.'

'Mansa Mussa,' I said.

'Your turn,' said BB.

'I'm Mansa Mussa. I'm not the friend of cabinet ministers and I don't run large public companies. I am never on the television. I am unknown to the criminal justice system. I work in the shadows. This is not about ego for me. It's about efficient money management. I launder like you have no idea. I transfer funds to the West from the national treasuries of African dictators. I funnel bribes from multinational companies to Third and Second World countries to secure large-scale engineering projects funded by the International Bank for Reconstruction and Development. I act as the intermediary between arms manufacturers and rogue states, circumventing sanctions and bypassing embargoes. And I do all this with a cool efficiency.'

'What about the laundering the money of the drug traffickers?' said BB. 'Sounds like you haven't got the time.'

'To the contrary, I need to wash the money of the drug traffickers. That is the oil that keeps my financial engines running smoothly. When the cocaine cartel clients get back their clean money it's probably been round

294

the world three times. My name is Mansa Mussa. I am the Laundryman.'

'Kay Frisk?' said BB.

'You liked her.' I said. 'She's all yours.'

With head and arms shaking BB started, 'My n'n'name is Kay F'f'ffrisk
— '

'Don't be cruel BB,' I said, restraining a giggle. 'And she didn't stutter.'

'OK, my name is Kay Frisk and I learnt a long time ago that all men are stupid. I learnt that neither education nor hard work gets you what you want in life, so I took a different path. I became a financial criminal. Seven years ago I embezzled a large sum of money from the company I was working for. Silly me, I got caught. My clever lawyer, you may know him, George Fairlow, got me off. Cost me a packet. I made a mistake. I was sloppy. Two years later I got busted for possession of cocaine. Georgie passes me to someone else, a grubby, horrible little coloured man. I get six months. But I learned a lot in prison. I've never been sloppy since. After a little rest, and financed by my ill-gotten gains, I became a launderer.'

'Too neat,' I said.

'As I said, all men are stupid. They would never suspect me, a well-educated, neat, prim, middle class lady, of money laundering on a huge scale. If I ever feel under pressure I put on the shakes, and the men can't do enough for me. I even told one rather foolish tax consultant that I was dying!'

'How does she do it BB? How does she launder? How does she make her contacts? It's not her world.'

'You don't know what world she's in. When you met her did you suspect that she had form?'

'You sound like Martyn, but you're right. No I didn't.'

'I don't know how she does it, but she does. My name is Kay Frisk and I am the Laundryman.'

'That's the lot. Who do you really think it is, BB?'

'George Fairlow. You?'

'Today, Joseph Feingold.'

'In the wheelchair?'

'That is not a problem in and of itself.'

'What does that mean?' BB asked me aggressively.

We had, perhaps, been working too long. 'It means his wheelchair's not a problem,' I said.

'No, not that' said BB, 'the "in and of itself" part. What does that mean?'

'It's just a phrase. Forget it.'

'I'm serious, what does the "in and of itself" add to "this is not a problem." I want to know.'

'It modifies it.'

'How? How the fuck does "in and of itself" modify anything?'

This had nothing to do with language. 'BB,' I said, 'why are you angry?'

'Because that's how you people keep me shut out. I ain't been to college. But I'm smart –'

'I know you are, BB.'

'Shut up! I'm smart right, and I'm kept out by that, by "in and of itself." It's the fancy phrase, the dinner party chatter, the "I'm a member of the fucking club" patter. It's the difference between being in and being out.'

'Rebecca dumped you, eh BB?'

'Yes,' he said.

And we both burst out laughing. We rolled up. We were literally on the floor kicking our legs in the air, releasing all the tension of the day. We laughed and we cried, as men do: when no one's watching. We cried for Billy and for ourselves. We cried through our laughter.

BB's face was shiny and his smile infectious. 'Serious, though,' he said, 'what does it mean? It means nothing, right, nothing at all?'

'It means,' I replied, 'that what you have identified as the problem is not the problem but something else may be. See, what you have identified is not the problem in itself or of itself, but –'

'Shut up,' he said, and we both burst out laughing again.

We were stretched out on the carpet when Tania marched into the room.

296

Face stern, arms folded, she said, 'This is supposed to be a solemn day.'

'We know Sis,' said BB.

'What is the matter with the two of you? It sounds like you're having a party.'

'This,' I said, 'is how we grieve.'

'With laughter?'

'Do you know a better way?'

'Maybe not,' she said unfolding her arms. 'I just don't know what to do. I've been in my room saying prayers.'

'You pray?' I asked with such incredulity that Tania could have been excused if she'd taken offence.

'Sure,' she replied. 'Don't you?'

'No,' I said, 'but I did know a pastor once, who claimed he'd prayed for my soul.'

'He told you that?'

'He told the police.'

'Stu – '

'It's a long story, another time.'

'OK, I'll go back up stairs and finish off the pastor's good work. What will you two be doing?'

'Setting a trap for the Laundryman.' When Tania had departed I said to BB, 'We might need to offer another superplan and see who takes it up.'

'What are you going to call that,' he asked, 'Son of Mycroft? It's a crazy idea. Full marks for getting us this far, Andrew. You've been fantastic, but no more tax plans or asset protection schemes. Now we go for direct action.'

'What's that then, four kidnappings?'

BB bridled at my sarcasm. 'Do you want my help on this, or not?'

'I do,' I said, 'I'm sorry.'

'Right,' he said. 'We know the Laundryman bought the Mycroft Plan. So it's either Joseph Feingold, George Fairlow, Mansa Mussa or Kay Frisk, right?'

'Right.'

'We have to contact each of them. We're going to approach the Laundryman direct. How much have you earned from Mycroft?'

'Gross? £4 million.'

'So you've got four million quid somewhere?'

'Of course not,' I said. 'I've had substantial funds to lay out for the structural matrix of Mycroft: offshore companies, trusts, limited partnerships and so forth, including of course the Anstalt. I've paid directors' fees, trustees' fees and nominee shareholder fees five years in advance. In addition, I have laid out for legal costs and bank charges.'

'So how much have you got left?'

'I don't know exactly.'

'Approximately?'

'Say, £3 million, but I need to make a provision for tax, so let's say £2 million.'

'Andrew, be serious. So you've got £3 million. Where is it?'

'In the Island Bank in Cayman.'

'Well, wire it back and draw it out in cash. It will be our bait.'

'You mean –'

'That's right,' said BB, 'we're going to trap the Laundryman with his own money.'

Chapter 18

'Tell me exactly how this is going to work,' I said.

'OK,' said BB, 'I'm feeling my way here. Give me some leeway. It goes something like this. Each of the four are contacted and told in a subtle way that there is a player with a substantial amount of money to launder. We make it clear that he will only deal principal to principal.'

'Three million isn't big in these circles,' I said.

'No,' he replied, 'but three million a week is. This is our player's takings for seven days, Monday to Sunday. He knows all about the Laundryman but has never used him. He wants to give him a try. He's ready to commit but he needs a trial run. We dangle this before Joseph Feingold, George Fairlow, Mansa Mussa and Kay Frisk, and see who bites.'

'And our player, he's fictitious?'

'No,' said BB. 'Our player is me.'

'Are you sure?'

'I'm positive. They must have a real person to deal with.'

'How do they contact you?'

'Mobile phone,' said BB thinking quickly. 'I go and buy a new mobile. Only six people will have the numbers. You, me and them. We just sit by the phone and see who rings. Then we set the trap, where we hand over the money and Martyn Clarke arrests him, or her.'

'Sounds too simple.'

'So was Mycroft, the idea, not the plan. The idea should be simple. It will become complex when we start to colour in the detail.'

'Why do we have to use real money? Why not a couple of suitcases full of newspaper.'

'The Laundryman will know what £3 million looks like, and the size of suitcase or suitcases it will fit into. Presumably we're going to grab him after he's taken the money. Surely he needs to be arrested with the cash. If he were arrested with two suitcases full of newspaper, his defence would be that he was on his way to the recycling pound. You're not thinking Andrew.'

'I'm thinking about my £3 million.'

'Then think about me instead. I'm the player. I will be coming face to face with the guy. If anything goes wrong I'm the one who's going to feel it.'

'You're right, BB. I lost my focus.'

'Don't worry about it. If I was putting £3 million on the line, I'd lose my focus too. Now, let's just keep thinking. How are we going to let them know and where will the exchange take place?'

'That's my field,' I said.

'Well?'

'I need to think. I'll tell you tomorrow afternoon. I'll be in Shepherd's Bush in the morning.'

'A client?'

'No, a past.'

BB looked at me quizzically, but he said nothing.

The next day BB had his new mobile and I had a plan. I suggested he called Kay Frisk first. 'Hello,' she said.

'Hi, I've been given your number by a player.'

'What are you talking about?'

'Just listen lady. The player said you can help me. I need you to sort out some financial documents for me, on a weekly basis. I will only deal principal to principal. This is a much bigger paperchase than you're used to. If you can help, call me back on this number anytime. But I want to move fast. They're burning a hole in my pocket.'

'Who is this?'

BB switched off the phone.

'Joseph Feingold,' I said, 'is different.'

'Yeah, he might recognise my voice.'

'No he won't. You never spoke to him, remember. I doubt he'd even recognise your face. He spent all his time looking at Tania. He's different for another reason. First, you're not going to get right through to him. He has an army of assistants to screen his calls. If you try the same approach as you did with Kay Frisk you'll get nowhere. You need to appeal to his ego.'

'How do I do that?'

'I'll give you his private number. He still won't answer it direct, but we'll be one level closer. He should be in the room when the phone rings. He'll want to know who it is. He's a control freak. Just ask to speak to the Laundryman. He'll come on the line. He won't be able to resist.'

'And then?'

'Wing it.'

Joseph Feingold was on the line almost immediately. 'Hey, who's this?' I could picture it, Joe in his wheelchair, phone to his ear, with Lucky Sucky kneeling before him. *Can't feel a thing, but I like to watch.* 'I hear someone wants to talk to the Laundryman.' I could hear the voice resounding through the phone five feet away. 'Go ahead. I'll pass on the message. How can the Laundryman help you?'

'I want to talk to the organ grinder,' said BB, 'not the monkey.' Dangerous, I thought, very dangerous.

'Now listen sonny. I've taken your call. For all I know you're some jumped up little shit of a reporter from the News Of The World, and if you are, fuck you, and you can print that OK? But if you're not, and you've got a problem, tell me about it and I'll see if I have a friend that can help you. You must know who you're talking to, so you know I got friends all over the world. You've got my private number so you must be connected, am I right? Of course I am. But if you think, even for a second, that I'm gonna show you my bare arse you're wrong sonny boy. Talk up, I can't hear you.'

'I've got some financial documents I need you to sort out on a weekly basis.'

'How much?'

BB looked at me. I nodded. 'Three mil.'

'Every week?'

'Every week.'

'He'll call you back on this number, if he's interested.' Joseh Feingold hung up. I had to admire the way he took total control of the exchange. Had he exposed himself? I didn't know. He was dangerously close to the edge but that, I thought, is where he lived.

'What do you think?' I asked BB.

'It's not him,' he said. 'OK, what's your approach for Mansa Mussa.'

'Similar, I think, to Kay Frisk, but play it with a little bit more respect. I have his own mobile number, which he asked me only to use in the case of an emergency. I assume this is the number on which he does his most private deals.'

BB dialled. Mansa Mussa was on the line after the first ring. 'The answer is no,' he said.

'I haven't asked you the question yet,' said BB.

'Who is this?'

'You should have asked that first. If the answer is no I'll take my business elsewhere.'

'Wait,' said Mansa Mussa. 'I was expecting a call at this exact hour. I didn't recognise the number, but that is not unusual in my line of business. People seem to change their mobile phones as often as their socks. Is this a new proposal?'

'Yes it is, but before we get to that, what was wrong with the one you just turned down?'

'Inadequate return on capital employed.'

'I thought you just collected commissions. Maybe I've got the wrong guy.'

'Maybe you have, but you will not know until you present your proposal, Mr?'

'No names, yet. Here's the deal. I need you to sort out some financial documents for me –'

'Financial documents, what financial documents?'

'On a weekly basis,' said BB.

'What financial documents?'

'I will only deal principal to principal.'

'You must explain the financial documents.'

'This is a much bigger paperchase than you're used to.'

'Slow down. Financial documents?'

'£3 million a week.'

'Oh,' said Mansa Mussa.

'If you can help, call me back on this number as soon as possible. I want to move fast.' BB switched off the phone.

'I asked you to be polite,' I said.

'I thought I was,' said BB.

'George Fairlow,' I said, 'is the biggest problem of all. How can I set up my own lawyer?'

'It's too late to turn back now,' said BB. 'Anyway, if he's not the Laundryman you have nothing to worry about. If he is, he's been setting you up from the time he took on your case. Come on, tell me, how do I handle him?'

'He's too grand for the phone,' I said.

'Rubbish, how do the others get to him.'

'I'm just not comfortable with you calling him. I think he will detect something.'

'That's different,' said BB. 'So what do we do?'

'We write. Remember Billy's suggestion at the first Brains Trust when asked how he would catch the Laundryman?'

'Yes, he said he would take out an advert.'

'That's right and he gave us the wording of that advert. I suggest we use it. We just put it in letter form and send it to the man you believe is the one we're looking for. It's a double whammy. You think Billy knew George Fairlow was the Laundryman? Billy believed that his advert would be instantly recognised by the Laundryman. If you're right, you'll get a call.'

'Can you remember Billy's words?'

'Pretty much,' I said. 'Let's go into the study.'

I sat at my computer and typed out the following text:

I have been referred to you by a colleague. I am an investor with a substantial portfolio previously in pharmaceutics, now mostly liquid, looking for an asset manager for the purposes of reinvestment in more diversified stocks and shares. I require total confidentiality. If you are able to help me personally, please ring the above number. If you are not, please completely disregard this letter.

BB was concerned. 'We're going into print. Let's say he's not the Laundryman, could he not pass this letter on to the police?'

'It's possible,' I said, 'but unlikely. There is nothing criminal in the letter. We will send it to his home address. George Fairlow is a very busy man. If the letter means nothing to him he'll probably put it in the bin.'

'He might call the number, just out of curiosity.'

'Fine,' I said. 'If he does treat him like the other three.'

'So we sit and wait for a call. That will be the signal to move into action. Have you thought about the drop?' said BB. 'OK, I recognise that smile, what is it?'

'I've got a name for the operation. It's a Holmesian classic.'

'Go on.'

'It shall be the Sign of the Four.'

Early the next morning as Julianna served coffee and toast to BB and me at the breakfast bar, Tania wandered into the kitchen dressed in her white silk dressing gown. 'Just a coffee for me,' she said to Julianna.

'Would you like to take it in the dining room Miss Berkeley?'

'No, I think I'll sit with my brother and my man for ten minutes. Hi BB.'

'Sis.'

'Stu.'

'Tania.'

'Have the two of you set up your trap yet?' she asked.

'We have,' I said. 'Tania there's something I need to talk to you about.'

'Go ahead. I have no secrets from BB and there's nobody else here.' Julianna placed a small cup of coffee in front of Tania. If she was hurt she didn't show it.

'It's about the money,' I said.

'What money?'

'Your money. The money found at your house, and at mine. Where did it come from? I need to know.'

'Why?'

'I'm appointing George Fairlow to represent you now. He can only do so if there is absolutely no conflict of interest between us both.'

'Then he needs to know, but you don't.'

'OK, I've had it.' For the first time ever I raised my voice to Tania. 'Forget about the need, I want to know. I demand to know!'

Julianna started to sing. Tania got up, leaving her coffee untouched, and defiantly strode out of the room.

Then the telephone rang. It was the mobile. BB grabbed it and I moved closer to him to hear what I could. BB hit the green button. 'Hello,' he said.

'This,' came the reply, 'is the Laundryman.'

When the Laundryman spoke, we were unable to determine whether the person was old or young, black or white, male or female. The voice was scrambled. It sounded like it was computer generated. This was a blow, but it made sense. We never thought it was going to be easy. The voice sounded artificial, each word being separately enunciated. For all BB knew he was talking to Professor Stephen Hawkings.

'You have something for me,' said the voice.

'Can you process £3 million a week?' said BB.

'Yes,' was the reply, 'Set up costs £250,000, then straight 15% commission off the top. Net funds transferred to any designated bank account in the world.'

'That's a bit high,' said BB. 'I'll take the set up costs but given my volume I was looking at 10% commission max.'

'Go somewhere else.'

'OK, revised to 10% after six months.'

'After twelve months.'

'Done.'

'Have you got the first £3 million?' asked the voice.

'Yes,' said BB.

'I'll call you in two hours to specify the arrangements.' And the phone cut off.

BB and I stood in silence for what seemed like an age. An observer could be forgiven for thinking that we had just received a call from the Pope. BB looked at me and I looked at him. We were star struck. Suddenly he was real. *We'd hunted down the fox that they called the Laundryman.* I felt both elation and fear, a heady mixture. BB was frozen in space and time. I took the phone from his stationary hand and placed it back on the bar. 'We have work to do,' I said, 'and only two hours in which to do it.'

'Why,' said BB, 'the ball's in his court.'

'Precisely, and I want it to be in ours. He wants to call back in two hours to specify the arrangements. I think we should have arrangements of our own. In short, where do we want to hand over the money?'

'Somewhere where Martyn Clarke and his team can be hiding.'

'Right, on our turf.'

'Well it can't be here. We give out this address and we'll never hear from the Laundryman again. We need somewhere neutral.'

'Preferably public,' I added.

'Somewhere safe.'

'Apparently safe for him; totally safe for us.'

'How about the university?' said BB.

'That's a good idea, but it's still tied to me. It would set off alarm bells.'

We sat deep in thought for several minutes. BB broke the silence. 'OK, I've got an idea, but it might sound wacky. Here goes: how about the Chessington World of Adventure.'

Wacky wasn't the word. It was completely off the wall. 'Why?' I asked.

'I took Rebecca there,' he said. 'It's neutral, it's public and it's safe. There are hills and valleys. It would be easy to hide. I'd meet the Laundryman at a ride, say, the Black Buccaneer. That's this large swinging boat. We sat right at the far end. When it swung up to the sky, I thought it was going to tip over. I had a feeling of temporary weightlessness, like an astronaut. Anyway, the ride lies in the low of a hillside. It would be perfect. Martyn Clarke and team would be in the hill watching with binoculars. I'd do the switch down below. You'd like Chessington. It's also wheelchair friendly, ramps everywhere, which would suit your candidate, Joseph Feingold.'

'Time out,' I said. 'Did the law studying, upper middle class Rebecca, who subsequently dumped you, enjoy the ride?'

'Yeah,' he said. 'She felt a little queasy afterwards, but that's part of the fun, isn't it?'

'Of course it is, BB,' I said. 'Of course it is.'

'You mean I blew the relationship on the Black Buccaneer?'

'Possibly,' I said, 'but let's move on. Chesssington is good. I like your thinking, but you've given me a better idea.'

'Let's hear it,' said BB.

I told him and he liked it.

As we waited for the Laundryman's call, Julianna made us a late Jamaican breakfast consisting of plantain, dumplings, spicy eggs, scrambled with pepper (and water), and thick hard dough bread. We ate at the breakfast bar in the kitchen, BB's mobile lying between the bottle of hot sauce and the pitcher of fruit juice.

'By the way,' I said, 'thanks for negotiating so freely with my money.'

'Had to get you the best deal,' he replied.

'Julianna,' said BB, 'how come you getting fat like plump cow.'

'Me jus' the same as before. Pure skinny white woman you look 'pon now, and you check me and find fault. G'way.'

'Don't worry,' I said to Julianna. 'She dumped him.'

And the phone rang.

'Hello,' said BB.

'Hello,' said the voice. 'Here are my instructions –'

'Hold on, I have some instructions of my own. I need to feel safe. I will not feel safe in your environment. Anyway, I want to see you. I want to look you in the face and know that my money is safe. This will be a one-time thing. After that my people can deal with your people. I need to do this, it's how I do business. When I look into your eyes I see your soul. Only then am I sure. And when I'm sure, I'm sure for life. I will tell you the collection point. You can choose the day and time.'

'I suggest some offices I use on occasion. You want to see me, you can see me there.'

'I will not feel safe in offices you occasionally use. I need a public place.'

'What do you suggest?'

'Baxter Hall.'

'Where's that?'

'It's England's finest Tudor residence. It's in Nottinghamshire.'

'Why?'

'It's big, public and safe. I want to see you coming.'

'Let me check it out I'll be back to you within the hour.' He got back in 20 minutes. 'I'll see you tomorrow 2:00pm. You will drive a brand new Previa peoples' carrier. Park it in block G. There will be a space. Leave a copy of Lightning's CD clearly visible on the dashboard. Walk to the Battle Room, with the car keys. See me, look me in the eyes, hand over the keys and the parking ticket and walk away.'

'When do I get the car back?'

'You don't.'

'Is this safe? What happens if someone steals the car?'

'No one will steal the car, I assure you. Now, describe yourself.'

'Single black male, tall, handsome and muscular, with a "don't give a shit" attitude. You?' The line went dead.

The deal was done. BB and I continued to kick around the details. 'If

I'm leaving the money in the car, when is the transaction complete?' he asked.

'When he drives away.'

'Even if he hasn't counted the money? Surely he can deny he knew that the money was in the car.'

'He's retaining a degree of deniability, I grant you, but it's not very strong, is it?'

'Wait,' said BB. 'He's not going to drive the car away. Think. What is he doing? What is his exposure? He's collecting keys. He's gone to Baxter Hall and collected some keys. These he passes on to another who drives the car out of the grounds of Baxter Hall to a discrete lay-by. He does a quick check on the money and rings the Laundryman, who sitting in the first class compartment on the 2:55 to Paddington. We will have achieved nothing.'

'We will have identified him.'

'It's not enough.'

'It just might be. Let me call Martyn Clarke.'

Martyn was bullish. 'I'll arrest him when BB hands over the keys.'

'Is that enough?'

'It's enough for an arrest. We trace the keys to the car. Inside the car is £3 million in cash. It's enough for us to hold him. Once we've got him under arrest we have a right to search his offices and his home. We can shake him down.'

'But, in taking the keys from BB he hasn't actually committed a crime has he?'

'No, but he'll think he has. This reminds me of a peculiar case that I was on about two years ago. In some respects it was rather sad. There was this really ordinary guy about thirty, with a beer gut, hair already receding, bad teeth, and everything. Went out to the nightclubs every weekend, couldn't get a girl. You or I might fix up our teeth, lose a bit of weight, do something stylish with the hair, not him. He started telling the girls he was a big time drug dealer. And he started to get laid. With one girl in partic-ular he started giving her sums of cash to pay into her account in return for cheques, said he need to wash his loose change. The sums were like £1,000 or £2,000. In fact each time he'd just withdrawn the same sums in cash from his own bank account. The girl felt important, started telling her friends, building up the story, you know, as girls do, and we got word of it. We arrest her. First she tries to protect him and then under some pretty robust threats she gives him up. He explains everything, proves it with bank records. We had to let her go. She thought she'd been money laundering, but in fact she had not.'

'What was his job?' I asked.

'He was an actuary.'

'And he couldn't get the girls with that?'

'Not the girls he wanted. As I said, it's a sad story. The point is, the Laundryman will be in the same position. When he takes the keys he will think he's laundering money. That's all I need to get started. I'll get the rest from the searches and shakedown.'

When I hung up Julianna burst into song. Tania was at the door. 'If you really want to know,' she said to me in a strong uncompromising voice, 'I'll tell you.'

Suddenly, I didn't want to know. 'OK,' I said.

'Upstairs,' said Tania. 'Oh, and Julianna, if I ever hear you singing in my presence again, you'll be looking for another job.'

Julianna stopped singing and started swaying to an imaginary beat. 'I didn't think I was here,' she said.

'Carry on like that and you soon won't be. Stu, I said upstairs. Now!'

I climbed the stairs as if I were carrying a heavy load, and tried to think of a reason why we did not have to do this today. I had a deep feeling of foreboding. Tania stretched out on the bed, lying on her side, supporting her head with the open palm of her hand. I sat on a straight-backed chair.

Tania smiled. 'We're very similar you and me,' she said. 'You create a picture for the taxman that is attractive and plausible. He collects some tax, by no means all, but enough. His files are in order and he's happy. Your client has saved tax. He's happy. The client pays you a fee. You're happy.' She paused. 'I do the same thing.'

'How?'

'I have clients just like you do.'

'Clients of the salon?'

Tania laughed. 'No,' she said, 'private clients.'

'Explain,' I said. 'And very slowly.'

'I cater for the fantasies of wealthy men. Every man has a fantasy. I fulfil it. At a price. I can be anyone they want me to be. No man is ever satisfied with what he's got. It's crazy. They'll pay whatever I ask.'

A scalding hot surge, akin to panic, ran through me. I was not hearing this. I clenched my fists to stop my hands from shaking. My neck and shoulders became tense.

'You look shocked Stu. You shouldn't. I've been a princess, a diva and a supermodel.'

I remained silent, confused, trying to take it all in.

'I've even been a hostage. One young white American entrepreneur wanted me to be his cleaner for an afternoon.'

And...? I thought. And what did he do? But I couldn't ask. I was incensed, but I wanted to protect myself. I didn't want to know. Instead I said, 'You know you were pandering to a racist don't you?'

'Really? He seemed nice enough. Maybe he had a black cleaner at home that he couldn't have, so he played out his fantasy with me. Not every cleaner is as accommodating as Julianna.'

I had nowhere left to hide. The truth was dancing through the room, taunting me. 'That's enough,' I said and got up to leave and in walking out of her bedroom I was walking out of her life. As I moved my whole body ached.

'Just before you go, Mr Brown,' said Tania. I froze. 'You are Mr Brown, aren't you Stu?'

'What?' I said.

'Mr Brown, the man with the precise instructions; that's you, isn't it?'

'I don't know what you're talking about.'

'Yes you do.' Her tone was accusatory, but it lacked any aggression. 'Sit down Stu,' she said quietly, 'I have something to tell you.'

311

I sat on the straight-backed chair and waited. I felt more like a prisoner than I did locked up in the police cell. I remembered Anita's stricture and, in an attempt to improve my mood, straightened my back and raised my chin. And I did feel better. Momentarily.

'Do you remember,' said Tania, 'some three years ago when Mr Brown requested a Somali woman in full traditional costume? She had to wear a full dress that covered her whole body from head to toe. It had a funny name. What was it? You must remember. Tell me. No? OK, and over her face she wore a veil. She went to your office in the evening, after work, of course, and followed the instructions you had specified to the agency. How did they go again? When she got to the office you would open the door. She was not to say a word.'

'You don't have to continue,' I said.

'But I do. You would lead her upstairs to your office and stand in front of your desk. She was to get on her knees, unzip your trousers and give you a blowjob, lifting her veil only high enough to get your cock in her mouth. After about five minutes she was to stand up and bend over the desk. You were to lift up her traditional dress but, unlike the traditional Somali woman, she was to be totally naked underneath. You would then enter her from behind. After you were done she was to rearrange her clothes and, without saying a word to you, go back down the stairs and leave by the front door.'

'How?...'

'And, of course she did all those things. Did you enjoy yourself Mr Brown? Did you enjoy me sucking your cock? Did you enjoy fucking me from the rear?'

'I didn't...'

'Of course you didn't know. But that was part of your fun wasn't it. The anonymity. Who was it last time? Oh yes, the businesswoman in glasses, with a slim briefcase. What was the briefcase for Stu?'

'Authenticity,' I said.

'And you talk to me about pandering to a racist. What was the Somali encounter all about? You know the veil you insisted she wore? Well, to get

312

the clothes I had to do some research. The veil is only worn by married Somali women, but you probably knew that didn't you? It added to your pleasure. Someone told me there's a term for your behaviour: sexual imperialism.'

'It was play acting,' I said. 'No one got hurt. Everyone got paid. Sexual imperialism is about exploitation.'

'You'd like to do it though Stu, wouldn't you, if you had the guts. You like to go to some third world country and just buy your sex from people who have nothing else left to sell.'

'No! You're not turning this back on me Tania. You're the whore.'

'And you're the John, Mr Brown.'

I paused and willed myself to calm down. 'So you still work for the agency?'

'No, I don't.'

'Then how do you know about my calls? Calls incidentally that I was assured were utterly confidential. I've paid a lot of money for that confidentiality. I am going after that agency, find out who's talking and close them down.'

'Haven't you got enough on your plate? Look, no one's talking. I know about Mr Brown because I own the agency. It's mine, Stu. That's where all the money came from. All the cash, the sterling, the dollars and the rest. You see when I told my solicitors that some of the money was yours, it wasn't a complete lie. I've been taking your money for years. Everybody paid in cash. That, as you know, was a stipulation. I couldn't just bank it. It would have raised too much suspicion. I started feeding some through the salon.'

'Where you work? So you colluded with the owners.'

'The owners have been straw men or, as you would call them, nominees, for the last two years. I now own the salon. I bought them out with my profits. Cash, of course.'

'You're a regular Joseph Feingold,' I said.

'So I was able to get rid of some of the money, through the salon and by other means. But there was always a surplus, particularly in foreign currency, and I kept the surplus at my house.'

'Where it was found and seized by the police.'

'Yeah, funny that. I think the police came here because my name appeared in an address book of one of the men they had under surveillance. The surveillance lasted some six months. So it was just by chance that the police chose that particular day to raid everyone's home. If they had come two days later the money wouldn't have been there.'

'Where would it have been?'

'Cayman.' Of course, I thought. 'When you left me with Paul Canolla of the Island Bank I first confirmed with him the laws regarding banking secrecy. Specifically, I asked that my affairs remained secret from you. He agreed. Then I told him about the money. He required an explanation, so I told him about the agency. He wanted proof that I earned the money in that way. He got the proof in his office.'

'You never —'

'No, I did not. In fact I didn't give him the proof at all. You did, in that little man to man chat that I had to leave the room for. You gave him the number, remember, of where he could receive personal attention on his next trip to London. Well, the number you gave him matched the number I had given him during our meeting.'

'Christ.'

'That's right. Paul opened an account for me and wanted to fly over personally to introduce me to what he called a co-respondent bank in London. They would take all my cash in the future and wire it across to my Cayman account on a weekly basis.'

'And Paul wasn't concerned about the source. No, why should he be? The money did not arise from an illegal activity and tax evasion is not recognised as a crime in the Cayman Islands.'

'Actually Paul didn't ask me about tax. I suppose he thought you'd take care of it.' She started to giggle. 'Think about it Stu, all that time in Cayman, and the time since in this house, you've been frightened to touch me in case you spoilt the love. You wanted it to be special. All the time you didn't know that you'd made love to me already.'

314

'I never made love to you Tania. I just fucked you, and it wasn't even you. It was a married woman from Somali.'

'You still haven't got it, have you? You're like all the rest. No man is satisfied with what he's got. The submissive husband wants to be dominant and the dominant husband wants to be submissive. The man who has love wants sex. The man who has sex wants love. Recognise yourself?'

When I stood up I was reeling. I felt as if I had been physically beaten. Tania remained reclined on the bed. So that was it. I understood. I now saw the whole picture, at least where Tania was concerned. I was just another John. 'You must hate me,' I said.

She flinched. 'No Stu, not at all. I think we can work. I really do. We just need to be honest with each other about what we want. I know things are bad today, and we're both in the middle of a criminal investigation, but I believe everything has happened for a positive reason, including the timing of the police raid.'

Rubbish, I thought. The entire mess of my life would have been avoided if the police had raided just two days later. Sure, they would have knocked on Tania's door, but they would have found no money. No money, no charge, and I would not have needed to stand bail. I would have remained out of DS Greenley's ambit. There would have been no Production Order, no arrest and no time sitting in a police cell. I would be working as normal, Anita would not have left me and I would still have my practice. Above all, I would not be hunting the Laundryman. I would not even know of his existence.

There was only one question that remained unanswered. One that Tania had put to me. 'It's called a hijab,' I said. She looked up, confused. 'The traditional dress worn by Somali women. It's called a hijab.'

I walked down the stairs and into the drawing room. I sat on the thick chenille stool, the incongruous piece of furniture for which I could find no purpose. This is what it's for, I thought, it's a low unsupported seat for the damned. BB entered sheepishly. 'I tried to warn you away,' he said. 'You wouldn't listen.'

'BB -.' I tried to get angry with him but I couldn't.

'Look on the bright side,' he said.

'There's a bright side?'

'Yes, she's not the Laundryman. Let's go catch him.'

Chapter 19

'I need to buy the Previa,' said BB, 'for tomorrow's meeting. Any ideas?'

'Go into my study, get onto the net, search for "Toyota Previa," print off a list of dealers, ring around and insist that the purchase is completed today. Remember it has to be brand new.'

'What's he going to do if I roll up in a second hand one, call off the deal?'

'Possibly, it would show that we were not taking the deal seriously. Remember also to insure it in your name. You can use my brokers.'

'Insure it? We're going to drive it once then give it away. What do we need to insure it for?'

'In case on the way to Baxter Hall we crash, or someone crashes into us, or someone steals the car.

'There's an idea,' said BB. 'When the Laundryman or his sidekick drives off in the Previa, we can report the car as stolen, get our money back.'

'No,' I said, 'but on the subject of money how are we going to pay for this? If you can agree the price over the phone, I can get Bertram Care, my personal banker, to wire the funds to them or issue a banker's draft.'

'Get me the cash,' said BB. 'Everybody loves cash.'

'I don't know who is worse, you or your sister.'

'My sister,' said BB.

'True,' I replied.

I telephoned DC Clarke. 'It's all set up Martyn. It will be handed to you on a plate. All you will need to do is arrest him.'

'I'm sorry Andrew, I can't help you.'

'What?'

'I've been taken off the case.'

'Why?'

'I don't know. They've allocated me to a big drugs case in Mitcham. I'm in charge. They tell me that if I bring this in, I'll make detective sergeant.'

'Martyn, we're close. You've got to stay with this.'

'No, I don't.'

'How do you know that the decision to pull you off isn't political? The Laundryman has enormous influence, you know that. Don't let him do this. One more day, that's all we need.'

'I've already gone further than I should have done. Sure I want to catch the Laundryman but being a police officer is my career. I will not jeopardise it by disobeying a direct order. It's over.'

'Martyn –'

'It has to be Detective Constable Clarke from now on, Dr Stuart. I'm sorry.' And he hung up.

'You heard that,' I said to BB.

'Yes I heard it and it's not good. We need to arrest the Laundryman in the Battle Room when a crime, in fact, has not taken place. That will be a problem now if we can't use Martyn. This guy is seriously wealthy. And ruthless. He has contacts in the highest places. The government don't want him caught. He could buy off anybody. Without Martyn he's going to walk in unchallenged and walk out with your money. We've got to call it off.'

'No, no, not now, we've come too far.'

'I don't see how you do it unless you go for a citizen's arrest, and if you did and it came out how you orchestrated this thing, you'd get prosecuted yourself. Not to mention that this would not play too well at your own money laundering trial. We've got to call it off.'

'No we don't,' I said, and reached for the phone. I had only dialled this number once before, yet my recall was instant. I doubt that I could forget the number if I tried. 'Hi Patsy,' I said, 'it's Andrew.'

'Hello Andrew.' She started to giggle. 'When are you coming round again? It was good seeing you. The pastor's back, but I'm sure we can sneak out.' She's going to sneak out, at 37 years of age.

'Soon,' I said trying to keep the sadness out of my voice. 'I was calling for Michael. Is he at home?'

'Yes, he's upstairs. I'll call him. See you soon!'

He was on the phone in an instant. I concluded that he must have been listening on the extension. I suppose he didn't need a private eye to watch over his mother. 'Hello,' he said.

'Michael, it's –' I hesitated, 'it's your father.'

'Hello Andrew.'

That felt like a smack in the mouth, but I continued. 'How would you like to arrest the Laundryman?'

His voice noticeably brightened. 'Is it you?'

'No, Michael, it's not me.'

'Oh. Then I don't see how I can. It's not my case.'

'It doesn't have to be your case. Let's say father and son were out for a day and you saw a crime being committed, couldn't you arrest the offender?'

'Technically, yes.'

'Well I'm taking you out on Friday. We're going to Baxter Hall. It's a stately home. Do you know it?'

'I know of it. I've never been there. Granddad never really approved of leisure activities.'

'I don't suppose he did.' I replied. 'So, you're in for a treat.'

'If this is for real I'll need to change my shifts. How will I get to Baxter Hall?'

'I'll come to the house and pick you up.'

There was a long pause 'What about granddad?' he asked.

'Fuck granddad,' I replied.

The next day we were on the road. BB was driving the brand new Previa with £3 million in cash in the back. I was following in my own car, with my son Michael, sitting by my side. When I had arrived at the house

319

he was standing outside. He got into the car without saying a word. As I turned the car around I thought I saw the net curtains twitch. I assumed it was Patsy, though it might have been the pastor.

Our conversation in the car was stilted. Michael wanted to give as little as possible of himself. I wanted to give everything. So I talked, which was fine, but when I asked a question, the silence that greeted it was long and awkward. Michael was virtually monosyllabic. Except when we were discussing the case. 'There is a small technical problem,' I said, 'relating to the arrest.'

'What's that?'

'At the time of the arrest the Laundryman will not, in fact, have committed a crime. He'll just think he has.' I explained the issues in detail.

'Was this a problem for DC Clarke?' he asked.

'No.'

'Then it won't be a problem for me.'

As BB drove into the car park of Baxter Hall and headed for block G, I hung back to observe. Block G looked virtually full. Three cars, however, parked in adjoining spaces, pulled out together, leaving BB spoilt for choice. It was either an act of serendipity or the Laundryman was making space for the Previa that would shortly be his own. I drove into the adjoining block F.

Aware that he was being watched, BB walked to the stately home on his own. Michael and I kept him in our vision as we walked some 50 yards behind. When he was very close to the house BB took out his mobile and rang a number I had dialled the day before. When the person answered he simply said 'Sign of the Four.' We saw BB being met by an uniformed attendant. Two minutes later another uniformed attendant met Michael and me. Two minutes after that the three of us were together in the administrative quarters of Baxter Hall.

'Dr Stuart, I was surprised to receive your call, surprised but pleased. You must be Mr Berkeley,' said Lord Baxter, extending a hand to BB. 'This way.' BB and I walked behind Lord Baxter, whose step was so dainty for such a large man. He had swapped his bright red waistcoat for a bright yellow one. If he had worn green trousers, I thought, he'd have been a walking traffic light. He led us up the stairs and into the control room, where five men maintained a watchful eye over 120 black and white monitors recording the live activity of every room in the house.

'Here you are, gentlemen. I believe you are interested in the Battle Room. This way.' He led us to three monitors in the corner, which showed the Battle Room from three different angles.

I looked at all three monitors. 'There are alcoves in the room that cast a shadow,' I said.

'Nothing I could do about those I'm afraid,' said Lord Baxter. 'It's the design of the room. They didn't have to consider the demands of CCTV in the 16th century.' The Battle Room was unusually crowded, as if it had been descended on by an official tour group or a school party. But there was no one holding aloft an identifying flag, and no children in uniform.

'There are too many people,' I said to BB. 'Look at those black youths. They don't seem that interested in the exhibits. Maybe the Laundryman brought some support with him.'

'No, they're waiting for me,' said BB. 'Boys from the Club.'

'You shouldn't have done that,' I said.

'They will cause no trouble, unless someone starts beating on me. Anyway, stop looking at my boys and start looking for the Laundryman.'

'Looking,' I said. Suddenly I saw everything I needed to see on one monitor. And, without my need to cover the clocks, time stood still. When BB spoke it sounded like he was yelling on the far side of nowhere.

'So put me out of my misery Andrew, can you see anyone there who bought the Mycroft plan?'

'Yes,' I said, but I was utterly transfixed. My throat was dry and anger seared through me. I couldn't take my eyes of the screen.

'Which one?' said BB. I couldn't answer.

'Is he in a wheelchair?'

'No,' I said.

'Strike Joseph Feingold,' said BB. 'Is it a woman?'

'No.'

'Strike Kay Frisk. Is it a black man?'

'No.'

'Strike Mansa Mussa. So it is George Fairlow, no wonder you can't talk. The conniving, stuck up son-of-a-bitch and to think you were paying him to protect you and all the time he's been -'

'It's not him,' I said, my eyes still focused on the black and white monitor.

'You said this person bought the Mycroft plan.'

'He did.'

'I've gone through the purchasers.'

'You missed one out,' I said.

'There's a fifth?'

'Yes.'

'Who?'

'The man who liked the Mycroft plan so much he bought the whole damn practice.'

'Hugo.'

'Hugo Maximillian.' I pointed him out on the screen. 'Go down there BB and give him the keys.'

I watched the monitor as BB entered the Battle Room, walked up to Hugo and exchanged a few words. BB looked deeply into Hugo's eyes. *When I look into your eyes I see your soul. Only then am I sure.* Hugo didn't flinch. He didn't need to. He was the Laundryman. BB handed over the keys. I left the control room and rushed down the stairs. I entered the Battle Room just as Michael placed a hand on Hugo's shoulder. My son. Pride swelled within me. 'My name is PC Michael Smith. I am placing you under arrest for conspiring to launder the proceeds of drug trafficking. You do not have to say anything. But it may harm -'

'Take your hands off of me.'

'- your defence if you do not mention when questioned -'

'Do you know who I am?'

'- something which you later rely on -'

322

'You'll regret this.'

'- in court. Anything you do say may be given in evidence.'

Hugo was enraged. 'PC Smith, you say? I am a director of one of Britain's premier banks. I don't expect you to understand the ways of high finance. They don't teach that to little rookies at Hendon. Remove your hand or your career in the police force will be very short lived indeed.' The black teenagers were visibly tense. They no longer feigned interest in Tudor armour. I feared violence. Hugo noticed me. 'Andrew?'

'Yes Hugo.'

'How strange to meet you here.' His voice, though strong, betrayed a degree of uncertainty. 'This is a terribly embarrassing situation. Talk to this boy. Tell him who I am. Clear this matter up for me, there's a good fellow.' Michael kept his hand firmly on Hugo's shoulder.

'The boy, as you call him, is a police constable. Address him as such. He's doing a job of work, an important one. Show some respect.'

'Whose side are you on Andrew?'

'The side of the good guys.'

'Does this nonsense have anything to do with you? For your sake I hope not.'

'Do what the officer tells you Hugo.'

Hugo tried to move toward me. Michael held his shoulder. BB looked around to identify possible accomplices. His boys kept their eyes on him. Hugo's eyes grew cold. 'If you don't resolve this now you will be lighting touch-paper that will eventually blow up all you hold dear. It's not too late to stop it.'

My son spoke next. 'It's far too late. He's no longer in charge of this situation, I am.'

'You have no idea what you're stepping into.'

'He may not,' said a voice I recognised, 'but I do.' I was heartened to see Detective Sergeant Greenley step out from an alcove in the shadows. 'Thank you PC Smith,' he said. 'We'll take it from here.' He led Hugo out of the Battle Room, accompanied by Michael and about eight men who I then realised were plain clothed police officers. BB followed them out to check on the car. He, in turn, was followed by his boys.

Lord Baxter entered Battle Room. He seemed pleased with himself, jolly even. He almost skipped up to me, his belly leading the way. 'I was a little worried you were on to me when you mentioned the shadows. We removed the light bulbs, you see, to give the detective cover. He called me yesterday, after you did. Always like to help the police. Never know when one might need a favour. Blind eye, and all that.'

'I understand,' I said. 'You did the right thing.'

'What a lot of excitement! I'm going to have to lie down.'

'That was the Laundryman they arrested,' I said.

'Who?'

'Just be careful with your management consultancy business. I would hate you to suffer a similar fate.'

'I don't think I need worry, not with my clientele, but thank you for the advice. Will you be sending me a bill?' He smiled the smile of the innocent.

'Don't put ideas into my head,' I said.

BB came back and reported that all was well. Greenley appeared shortly thereafter. He was as grim as Baxter was happy. 'I suppose I should thank the three of you,' he said. 'Nice trap, though you wouldn't have succeeded without me.'

'How did you know?' I asked.

'Michael called me. When we met I told him to stay very closely in touch with me, particularly if you came to him with any strange requests.'

'You thought I would turn to Michael.'

'Sure, once I had pulled DC Clarke off the case. Blood being thicker and all that. Martyn Clarke's a good man and a good officer, but I feared a leak. On the arrest he would have involved other officers and I feared the possibility of a tip off. He kept me fully informed. He'll get a lot of credit, but I couldn't take any more risks. I gambled on you turning to Michael, and I was right.'

I was uncomfortable. 'You felt confident my son would betray me.'

'No,' Greenley protested. 'It's just that Michael's adherence to the principles of law and order are very strong. A choice between the rule of law and the well-being of his long absent old man would pose no moral conflict in his mind.' Greenley scratched his unshaven chin. 'Where does he get that from I wonder.'

'His granddad,' I replied.

'You've got a good son, Dr Stuart. You must be able to take some of the credit. After all, he's got your genes. He's waiting for you outside.'

'He's not going back with you?'

'No, I offered. He said he'd wait for you. Go and talk to him.'

Greenley turned to BB and held out his hand. 'I never made out that report, about the assault on the officer in the execution of his duty. I figured, as Dr Stuart said, really we're both on the same side.'

'No we're not,' said BB and he walked away.

Outside the unpredictable British summer was confounding its critics. The sky was clear, the sun was warm and the breeze was gentle. Michael stood apart from the other officers. 'Ready to go Dad?' he said. My heart melted and I moved to embrace him. He moved back. 'One step at a time, OK?'

'OK,' I said.

Despite the success of the day, I returned to the house with a profound feeling of loss. Everything that mattered to me had changed. My business was gone, my reputation tarnished. The woman I loved owned the agency I used. Billy was dead. I also knew of corruption in the highest echelons of British society that I could never expose.

Julianna greeted me in the hallway. 'I've cooked,' she said.

'Not hungry,' I muttered.

'You must eat, and then we must talk. Things can't drift anymore Andrew. Tania's upstairs packing. You've got some decisions to make. Come on.'

She led me through to the kitchen where she had prepared a Jamaican feast: rice and peas, curried goat, yam, green bananas, dumpling, plantain and cabbage. The food was laid out on the table in stainless steel bowls, covered with glass lids, now all steamed up. My appetite returned. Julianna removed the plates from the oven with her hands.

'Use the oven gloves,' I said, but she didn't. She never did. Instead she carried the plates to the table resting them precariously on the ball of her hands and the tips of her fingers.

'There,' she said, having virtually dropped the plates on the dinner mats. 'Eat.'

I tucked into the food like a condemned man. I remembered how much these kitchen meals with Julianna were such a favourite of mine, before Tania. No ceremony, just wholesome good food and plenty of it. 'You said you wanted to talk.'

'I do,' she said. 'But it's difficult. Let's finish eating first.'

'No,' I said. 'It's good to talk and eat. It makes difficult subjects easier. Why do you think so much business is conducted over lunch?'

'Probably something to do with a tax write-off,' she replied and chuckled to herself. It was not a great joke, but I chuckled too. It just seemed the right thing to do.

'Andrew, I'm pregnant,' she said as she cut a dumpling and pressed some cabbage against it with her knife. 'Three months.' The dumpling and cabbage disappeared into her mouth. I could not look at her eyes. I watched as she chewed, very slowly, delaying the next words, or maybe inviting mine. I said nothing. She swallowed. 'I'm surprised you haven't noticed. BB did, said I looked like a plump cow.' Next up to her mouth was a fork full of rice and peas, with a small piece of red pepper on top. I looked down at my food, my appetite gone, and pushed my plate away. 'It's a girl,' she said reaching for her glass of pineapple juice. She drained the glass, reminding me of my dead friend. 'And I'm going to keep her.'

I sat very still, my arms stretched out together between my knees, my fingers intertwined and my elbows locked. Julianna continued, 'You said we should talk over dinner. I'm talking, but you're not.'

'I need to think,' I said. My head was spinning.

'Fine. While you're thinking think on this too. My deportation papers arrived yesterday. Detective Sergeant Greenley was good to his word.'

326

I got up and stood by the sink. Julianna joined me and put her arms around my neck. 'Listen Andrew, this is your chance to have what you want. Leave Tania, she's a bitch. I know you love her but she will only hurt you. Women like that only ride men for what they can get. I don't know the whole story, only pieces. But hasn't she hurt you enough? I spoke to BB. I told him about the baby. I needed to confide in someone Andrew. He told me you would never stay with me, that you were looking for love, not convenience. BB can be cruel y'know. But the way I see it is like this: you will find love here. Your daughter. That is the only person who will make you feel real love. Everything else is lust and sex.'

I eased her out of our embrace. 'Wait here,' I said.

Julianna stood directly in my path. 'You're going to her, aren't you.'

'I'm going to talk to her,' I said, 'there's a difference.' Julianna didn't budge. 'I'm going to talk to her and then I'm going to come back.' She reluctantly stepped aside.

Tania's door was open. She was leaning over a large suitcase which lay open on her bed, her perfect bottom facing the door. 'Don't get any ideas Stu,' she said, without looking up. 'I know your tastes.' She hovered in that position, enticing me to make a move. I yearned to, but I couldn't. She turned to face me, looking gorgeous in her white capri pants and short-sleeve, pale blue, cotton bodysuit. 'I'm moving back home,' she said. 'Unless, that is, you want me to stay.'

'No,' I said. 'Moving's good.'

'So this is it?'

'Yes, except that I will get the case against you dropped. We've caught the Laundryman.'

'Who was it?'

'A banker.'

I saw fear in her eyes. 'Don't worry, it's not Paul Canolla.' I turned to leave and, lingering briefly at the door, said, 'I love you.'

'No,' said Tania, 'you love the person you would like me to be. That is not the same. You don't know what you want. In a way, you're really quite sad.'

I walked down the stairs with her words ringing in my ears. Maybe I was sad. I used the agency to satisfy dark sexual needs, those needs I feared too closely to analyse. My instructions were always basically the same: the silence, the subservience, the blowjob and rear entry. Only the nature of the woman changed. I loved uniforms and costumes. I had ordered a traffic warden, a prison guard and a policewoman. The Somali woman was only one of my ventures into national dress. I covered the races of the world, including Eskimo. Nor did I stay in this century. I ranged from the cave-woman, through the Middle Ages and lingered for a while in the Tudor period (well, I had a special interest at the time). I took historical figures too. I no longer think of Elizabeth I as the Virgin Queen. Once I asked for a woman dressed as a man, complete with moustache. What frightened me was how much I enjoyed it. I only did it once. It was a little too close to the borders of Boys Town. But I was no sadder than Tania. I had needs and money. She satisfied my needs and charged me a fee. We were equal. We were, as the pastor would say, rooting around in the gutter together.

I returned to the kitchen and swooped Julianna up into my arms. I held her tight with her tummy, which was nurturing our baby, pressing against me. It did not take me long to make up my mind. 'How do you know it's a girl?'

'My hair has started to fall out.' She saw the puzzlement in my face. 'When your hair starts to fall out it's a girl baby. Everybody knows that.'

'There are more scientific tests,' I said, but she was having none of it. I eased my embrace and looked at the face of the woman who was carrying my child. 'I have a request.'

'What's that?'

'I want to choose her name.'

Events moved quite swiftly. The tabloids had fun for a week, calling for "Maximum Time For Maximillian," interchanging "Banker" with "Wanker," suggesting that the Coats Bank and been "stripped to its vest and pants" and other puerile wordplays. Lightning's record re-entered the charts. Joseph Feingold cranked back up the merchandising.

In due course I presented myself at the police station at the invitation of DS Greenley. BB drove me in our new Previa. 'In case,' he said, 'they pull any last minute stunts.' At my insistence, he waited in the car.

I was shown to an interview room, where a dishevelled DS Greenley was waiting to discharge me. 'I am pleased to inform you Dr Stuart that we will be taking no further action,' he said. 'You can collect your business files, personal files and other effects by arrangement early next week.'

I felt an enormous sense of relief. My life had fundamentally changed (not entirely for the worse), and I was glad it was over. Almost over. 'What about Tania?' I said.

'We never said we would let her go. Think about the money we found. She must be tied up in this somewhere.'

'She doesn't even know Hugo Maximillian.'

'No? Listen, how can I put this? We have her diaries; we have his.' The agency, I thought, and I remembered the fear in her eyes when I mentioned the Laundryman was a banker. I thought she was concerned about Paul Canolla. I was wrong.

She was a dark horse, a beautiful strong shiny black mare, and at some level I still loved her. She was wrong for me, of course. I could never trust her. Yet I continued to feel protective towards her. I continued to yearn for her. She was a Bitch with a capital "B" - but a Class Act - a Player. I just had to save her.

'Anything,' I said, 'just let her go. She's not guilty but she'll look guilty by the time the CPS have finished with her. Jail would destroy her. She's fragile. And I love her. And you owe me.'

'We can't let her go.' He paused for a long time. 'But if she left the country, I doubt we would expend a lot of energy looking for her.'

'You mean skip bail? This is her home. She would never be able to return to this country.'

'No?' he said and smirked.

'Anyway, she can't leave. You've got her passport.'

'Really, is that such a problem?'

'This is all outside my area of expertise.'

'Then you may wish to phone a friend.'

'DS Greenley,' I said, 'what about my bail money? If Tania absconds it costs me £250,000.'

'And your point is?'

'It's my money,' I said plaintively.

'That's the least of your troubles. We're holding on to the three million in cash that was in the back of the car.'

I had feared this, but I decided to play the innocent. 'Why?'

'It's evidence.'

'Can't you just get an affidavit from the officers who saw the money there? You're good at affidavits.'

'Funny,' said Greenley without a hint of humour. 'This case is going to be difficult enough. What have we got? The accused collecting keys to a car in the battle Room of a stately home. No, we need the money. We need to show it to the jury. We need them to see three million in cash. Your three million.'

'Martyn said this was just the set-up. He said you'd convict him on evidence you obtained from the shake-down.'

'"Set-up," "shake-down," what's the matter with you? I thought you were a tax consultant. You sound like Philip Marlowe.'

'It's the company I've been keeping,' I said, and got up and took my jacket from the back of the chair.

'I do have some good news, Dr Stuart, or should I say Andy Singley? Michael's grandfather gave me your real surname so I checked the files. Your statutory rape conviction, it must have been haunting you all you life. You changed your name and everything. I'm pleased to say we do things differently today. We're a little more understanding about teenage love.' Greenley ran his hand over his creased face and I wondered where this was going. 'Look, it was a long time ago. You were treated badly. You helped me. I'm helping you. The files are gone. Well, files never completely disappear but, as Mazzinni might say, when I hide a file God can't find it.'

My heart warmed to this crumpled disagreeable detective sergeant. 'Thank you,' I said.

'Forget it.'

I walked to the door and hesitated. 'Why was Mazzinni's name on the Production Order? You said he wasn't arrested as part of Operation Chalice.'

'We found his details at Tania's house when she was arrested. I can say no more.'

I'd asked her if she knew him. She'd lied to me. Again. But I was finding it increasingly difficult to get angry anymore. I pushed on. 'Why did Mazzinni name me as the Laundryman?'

'No idea.'

'I'm going to ask him.'

'No chance. He's on remand at Brixton prison.'

'Money laundering?'

'Perverting the course of justice. Arrested him myself. Won't have people lying on affidavits.'

'You might find one of your colleagues has already offered him immunity in return for naming me.'

'Apparently not. If he was under pressure to sign that affidavit it didn't come from us. Look, the case is over. Leave Mazzinni to me. We've got the Laundryman. Get on with your life.'

But I wasn't finished. 'You know, don't you, that another Laundryman will emerge in months.'

'Maybe sooner, the amount of publicity you've given the post,' he said.

'You're fighting a losing battle.'

'Dr Stuart, I am not a general in a war. I am a humble police officer. I find the criminals, arrest them and prosecute them, one at a time.'

'Never making a permanent impression on the big picture.'

'Who knows?' he said wearily. 'I do my job and if everybody else in law enforcement and the judicial process do theirs maybe the picture will change. But I can't account for everybody else, only myself. And I do my job as well as I can.'

'You do it very well,' I said.

'Thank you,' said Greenley and he allowed himself a rare smile. 'Now get out, and don't come back until Hugo's trial. We're going to need you. And BB. He'll testify, right?'

'Of course he will,' I said.

'No I won't,' said BB when I got in the car.

I was too weary to argue. Instead I said. 'Your sister is going to abscond. She needs a passport.'

'OK,' he said.

I was astonished. 'That's it?'

'That's it.'

I let it be. 'Greenley said something interesting today without, I think, realising it.'

'What's that?' asked BB.

'He described the Laundryman as a post, like an office of state. He seemed to be saying that the office would exist, even though its occupant had been arrested.'

'Maybe he's right, and maybe he knew exactly what he was saying. Let's not underestimate Greenley. Maybe he was saying it's not over.'

I looked hard at BB. 'It's over for you,' I said. 'But it's not quite over for me. I want to see Mazzinni. Greenley counselled against it.'

'But you're going anyway, right?'

'If I can. He's in Brixton prison. On remand.'

'No problem. You'll need to make an appointment, that's all, and bring some ID. Call now and you'll have a slot in a day or two.'

'He could refuse to see me.'

'He's banged up Andrew. Every prisoner likes a visitor. Even if it's only you. I'll call for you.' BB took out his mobile.

'You know the number?'

'The boys,' was all he said by way of explanation. 'Want me to come?'

'Thanks,' I said. We drove for a while in silence. 'Your Boys Club could use a large vehicle like this.'

'True,' said BB.

'Take it,' I said, 'but do me a favour first.'

'Say the word.'

'Drive me to Greenwich, to the Just In Case Veterans' Home. It's on Trafalgar Road.'

Chapter 20

Anita showed me into her small neat-as-a-pin office, which had a glass wall facing the lounge in which the veterans socialised. Again I had asked BB to wait in the car. I declined the tea and asked her, 'When did you find out?'

'During the boxing match. I watched and listened just like you told me. That was a good idea of yours.'

'BB's,' I said.

'Well, well.'

'Why didn't you tell me?'

'I was going to on the Sunday, but I changed my mind. It was a question of loyalty.'

'Loyalty to whom?'

'He paid my salary.'

'That's it? I didn't know loyalty could be bought.'

'Grow up, Andrew.'

'What about loyalty to the truth?'

'That's an odd concept for these modern times. If I were loyal to the truth I would have stopped working for you years ago. You turned truth on its head every day. A man comes to your office understanding that his income is taxable. You feed the income through an offshore trust here, a limited partnership there, maybe a foundation or two, you seek cover under a double taxation convention that would have been in no way drafted for the purpose to which you put it, and bingo, no tax! Same income, was it taxable or not? Where's the truth? You were a conjurer, Andrew, and I loved watching you do what you did, but there was little truth in it.'

'So you backed him over me.'

'Let me put it this way, Hugo was very concerned over the Baxter Hall meeting. He consulted me. He didn't know that I knew he was the Laundryman, he just put it to me, if you like, for risk assessment. I told him you got some of your best clients through such an arrangement.'

'You told him that.'

'Yes and as you know I can be very persuasive.'

'Did you know it was a trap?'

'Of course. It had you and BB written all over it.'

'Why did you tell him to go?'

'As I said, it was a question of loyalty. Couldn't see you going to prison now, could I? That would never do.'

'What about your job?'

'The bank should survive, otherwise I'll work here full time. I've got a little money saved.'

'I'd have thought you'd have a lot saved,' I said, 'from your own private laundering operation.'

'What are you talking about?' she demanded. Her face betrayed no fear.

'Hugo told me. He said I would blow up all that I held dear. He must have meant you.'

'Nonsense.'

'Weak perhaps, on its own, but try this on for size. The Just In Case Veterans' Homes are owned by the Inocace Trust. You showed me the Trust Deed, remember? You wanted me to interpret its provisions.'

'Yes,' she said, her voice steady as if she had no idea where this was going.

'You just couldn't resist it, could you?'

'What?' she snapped.

'Inocace,' I said. 'I. N. O. C. A. C. E. It's an anagram of "cocaine."'

Anita took a very deep breath and then, as she exhaled, she spoke her mind with characteristic vigour. 'You're wrong, of course, about having a lot saved. All the commissions I've earned have been spent on this and other Just In Case Veterans Homes across the country, all anonymously donated.'

'How did it get started?'

'Cyril, the son of one of daddy's old friends, suggested it. The homes, I mean. I gave him some of my own money to get started. In fact I helped him a lot in the beginning. But he was a man who liked committees and after a while I pulled away. The homes fulfilled a long neglected need but the demand for resources never stopped. The welfare of war veterans is not a popular fund raising cause. Funny, isn't it?' I nodded instinctively. 'Well, debts mounted. It was all going to crash. Cyril, of course comes running back to me. "What do I do? What do I do?" What is it with these men?' Anita did not expect a reply. 'I was working for you by this time. Do you have any idea how many clients I used to turn away without referring to you because it was utterly transparent that what they really wanted was a money laundering operation? And that's when I got the idea. I told Cyril I knew of an endowment that would bail him out, funded by a secret society of military men: The Inocace Trust.'

'Who drafted the Deed?'

'Me. Well, you really. It was based on a charitable trust document that you incorporated into the Corporate Cloning stage of a tax plan for a software millionaire not old enough to shave. Cyril was appointed a trustee, with the power to appoint others, which he did with a generous hand. I was largely forgotten about. I applied for the voluntary position here and got it. All the time I was privately funnelling the funds into the Trust that kept the Homes alive. Then they invited me to join their committee. Remember you told me that my duties as a trustee were to safeguard the Trust's assets? I am the Trust's assets!'

'How did you do it?'

'By controlling you, of course. *You,* the big, "I Am," who loved to say, "Only I see the whole picture." On two or three clients, Andrew, you only ever saw part of the picture.' She laughed triumphantly. 'It was all so easy. All the clients came to me first, and I allocated the work to you, piece by piece. I told you when to work and what to work on. Normally you only saw the clients for the grand theatre meeting. I was their day-to-day contact. On those few laundering operations I handled, I would tell them what to tell you so that the structure worked for them. It was really quite funny. I would tell them, they would tell you, you would reword it and I would type up the reworded meeting notes. Only I saw the whole picture Andrew, not you.

'Don't get me wrong, I genuinely admired your intellect. When this whole damn hunt for the Laundryman began, I did everything I could to divert you from it. I knew you would get to the bottom of it. I even played my trump card, the resignation. But not even that bought you to your senses. You sold the practice. I couldn't believe it. And like a gift from God you got me a job with all my old clients. I was worried a little about Francis Peartree, but Hugo was a dream. He believed the sole purpose of a bank was to make money. He'd been laundering for years. When I brought my little arrangement to him he was delighted. He couldn't contain himself.'

'I may have to tell the police.'

'Then I will follow the example of the best lawyer in London.'

'George Fairlow?'

'No, Billy Carver.' Her gaze was fixed and resolute. It exuded a steely calmness. I had to turn away. I looked out through the glass at the old men who were benefiting from Anita's largesse. Old men in old clothes, some playing checkers, some reading, some snoozing and some, I thought, wondering where they were. 'They are the heroes,' said Anita. 'They fought a world war. The police today think they are brave because they arrest inadequate men who want to sell drugs to other inadequate men who want to buy them. They arrest, at airports, stupid young girls who risk their lives by swallowing condoms stuffed with cocaine in return for less money than you make in an hour. And the police give themselves medals and titles. Those men out there faced down a tyranny. Look at them. Look! No post-traumatic stress disorder compensation for them. Oh no. They came home, leaving their friends dead on the battlefield, and tried to build a life, and when they grew old they were forgotten. They saved this country from the Nazis, and the government treat them as -' Her voice broke. 'My father was a hero. He deserved better.'

I couldn't deal with any more pain. I would let Anita be for the sake of our past professional relationship, her good works and her father's memory. It must be wonderful, I thought, to be proud of one's parents.

Later that evening BB and I sat in my garden and played a hard-fought game of chess. BB launched his usual brutal, combative attack. I weathered the storm and inched my way through a successful end-game. The air was warm and a soft breeze blew across the garden causing low whistling from the trees and shrubbery. The sky was clear and the moon three quarters full. It was so peaceful, sitting in the garden, with my best friend, the chess game won and the wine almost done. BB spoke into the stillness. 'There's something I still don't understand.'

'What's that?'

'Hugo is the Laundryman, right?'

'Right.'

'So he's the guy who called my mobile phone using the disguised voice, right?'

'Right.'

'How did Hugo get my mobile number? Only six people knew it: you, me and the four.'

We both looked at each other and, after a very short deliberation, we both smiled. We knew who had given him the number. It was obvious. 'I suggest you make a call,' I said.

BB retrieved the call register on his mobile, selected the private number, which the phone dialled from memory. 'May I speak to the Laundryman?' said BB.

'One moment,' said Lucky Sucky.

BB then placed the phone in the middle of the chessboard for us both to enjoy.

The voice boomed so loud the mobile vibrated causing the end-game chess pieces to dance over the board. 'I gave the Laundryman your number, and I know he called you, but listen, he's hit some problems, what can I say? I keep my ear to the ground. Have to. No legs. But you've got money, right? Ever thought of the entertainment industry? Sex, drugs and rock and roll. And why not? Good returns. We'd have to team up. And

338

you'd have to clean up. Do it right. You can't use the Laundryman, he's history. Hey, but there are others. Clean up and invest in some bands. They're all crap, but that's what the public like, see. Crap, am I right? Who am I talking to here?'

BB winked at me and we counted down together, three, two, one, 'You're right Joe!' .

The appointment HMP Brixton had given BB for our visit was for the following day. We arrived with passports and driving licences in hand. These were examined by a weary uniformed security officer who ticked our names off the approved visitors' list. We were searched on our way through to the visitors' area. It was little different to an airport search until they asked us to open our mouths and lift up our tongues. 'I'm not going to kiss him,' said BB. 'Couldn't hope to compete with all you handsome men in uniform.'

'That's it!' said the prison guard. 'You're not going in. I don't get paid enough for this sort of abuse. You can wait for your friend outside.'

I looked across at BB. The realisation grew warmly within me, like whiskey flowing into an empty stomach. 'Thank you,' I said. I had the final piece of the jigsaw.

When Mazzinni came into the large communal visitor room, wearing the yellow sash which identified him as a prisoner, he looked sallow and tired. He took his seat opposite mine. 'Hello Dr Stuart,' he said.

I got right down it. 'Who put pressure on you to name me as the Laundryman?'

'Does it matter?' he asked forlornly.

'It matters to me.'

Mazzinni did not answer my question directly. 'The £20 million,' he said, 'it wasn't mine. The money belonged to, how you say, a consortium.'

'A consortium of… ?'

Mazzinni just shrugged. 'Businessmen?' It was as good a euphemism as any. 'They paid me well. They wanted their money safe - asked me to hide it in a way that could not be traced to any of them. You came up with the perfect solution.'

'An offshore asset protection trust.'

'Right, and the beneficiaries, well, they would have been the business men who had contributed the piggy bank in the first place.'

'I see.'

'They asked me to use the Laundryman. And –'

'You thought it was me.'

'Yes,' he said.

'You were not alone. When did you find out you were wrong?'

'Wrong?'

'Yes, wrong.'

'They told me I was right.'

'They, who?!' I realised I was shouting. Other prisoners and their visitors had turned around. Two of the guards looked on intently. I breathed deeply, wrestling for control. In a calmer voice I said, 'Who were *they*?'

'Who you think? The businessmen. When the pressure was on, they couldn't move their money. They needed you out so that someone could take your place. I make a statement. They tell me what to say. I sign it. They send it to the police.'

'You'd already appointed me.'

'Yes, but I hadn't given you their names. You didn't want them remember. You said the names of the beneficiaries could wait. So they were safe. I'd paid you the deposit of course. But they say, hey, we write off £50,000 to move £20 million.'

'Why did you think I was the Laundryman?'

'You're not?'

'No,' I said. He seemed confused. 'You read the papers. You know they've caught the Laundryman.'

'He was a decoy, no? How you say, a patsy?'

I thought again of the jurisprudential dilemma. 'No,' I said. 'That was me.' I felt another chapter closing, another story coming to a sad end. I had one last question, prompted by BB's wisecrack. Leaning forward I said, 'The pilot who recommended me, I thought it was a man, but she was a woman right?'

'Yes.'

'I bet she looked great in her uniform.'

'Oh, yes.'

'Sexy.'

'Yes.'

'Only she wasn't really a pilot, was she?'

Mazzinni for the first time looked shocked. It was as if I had caught him out in a shameful secret. He paused, his head lowered to the ground. When he looked up his eyes were moist. 'I like to play, you know. I like women in uniforms. She wasn't always a pilot. Sometimes she was a princess. She seemed to know everything. So I told her I had some money to hide. Asked her where I should go. She recommended you. Well, you and someone else.'

'Who was the other person?'

'Him.'

'Who?'

'The guy who got arrested.' Hugo Maximillian, her client.

'Why did you come to me?'

'She said you were the best. Sorry I lied, but I'd paid her to be a pilot, so in a way she was a pilot, OK?'

'Not OK.'

'Would you have taken me on if I told you I'd been recommended to you by a beautiful, black, high-priced, London-based whore?'

'No,' I said softly.

'Do you want her name?'

It was my turn to lower my head. 'I know her name,' I said.

When I learned that Hugo had retained George Fairlow to act for him I was hardly surprised. George, as Billy had explained to me, was Establishment. Who better for the Laundryman? When I heard that Hugo had been granted bail I was astonished. And there was more. George telephoned to say that Hugo wanted to see me.

I was intrigued. I made my way to Bellows & Bellows on Chancery Lane. Mr Reception wasn't at his desk. In his place sat a very pretty blonde girl, who looked about nineteen years old. She smiled as I entered. I asked, 'Where is Mr…'

'Mr Cole?' she said. 'He's sick. In hospital. Doesn't look good, apparently.' His condition, however, had no effect on her own cheerful demeanour.

I felt sad for the man whose name I had never bothered to learn. 'Is there a collection for him?'

'No,' she said.

'I would like to start one.' I took out my wallet, withdrew a £50 note and handed it to her. 'Ask every client he met,' I said. 'He made us realise how fortunate we were.' Something, I thought, she would never do. I identified myself, asked for George Fairlow, she called him and directed me to his office. *Through the double doors, it's the third room on the right. His name is on the door.*

Hugo was in George's office sitting in the same visitors' chair that Sir Kenneth Llewellin had occupied the last time I was there. George, as was seemingly his habit, absented himself, this time on the pretext of some very pressing legal research, and Hugo and I were left alone. I sat in the other chair and waited.

Hugo looked drawn and tired. I guessed he hadn't been sleeping well. His tailored clothes had a shabby look about them. I thought, he hasn't changed, possibly for several days. As the sun from the window caught the side of his face it was clear that he hadn't shaved either. I doubt he'd brushed his teeth. I thought of my mother. Hugo's light had gone out.

'It was just business Andrew. I was providing a much needed service.' I remained silent. He fell into the void. 'You know what hurts?' he said. 'I was getting out. I was getting too old, wanted too many holidays. I needed to retire. I've been looking for a successor for the past two years.' He laughed with a pained regret. 'That's why I was recruiting YOU.'

The shock was glangorous, like the discordant pealing of a thousand rusty church bells. A wake up call for the blind. Just how much of the pic-

342

ture had I ever seen?

'You were perfect,' said Hugo in the monotone of the despondent. 'You had the skills, the hunger, the anonymity and the moral ambiguity. But I couldn't tell you, not up front. I needed you in the bank. To do that I needed to buy your practice. Did you really think I was interested in A J Stuart & Co? The original deal was way over the top in terms of price. I wanted you. *We* wanted you.'

He paused and looked at his watch. You have all the time in the world, I thought. Suddenly he was angry. 'But you blew it and for what? You could have been king. You just had to keep your head down. You stupid, stupid boy. Do you have any idea how much money you would have made? You could have bought ten thousand Tanias.'

'There's only one Tania,' I said. The dull ache in my stomach returned when I added, 'as you know.'

'Right,' said Hugo with a sneer. ' I fucked her but women were never my weakness. I prefer gourmet food and vintage wine, and absolute power. But I'll tell you this, Tanias cost about £100,000 a year max!' Hugo was a banker. He didn't toss out figures trivially. As much as I resisted, I could not help but do the calculation. Ten thousand Tanias at a hundred thousand a year represented £1,000,000,000. Hugo smiled at me. 'That's right,' he said, 'One billion pounds a year. And you had been approved by the powers that be.'

'What powers?'

'From Threadneedle Street to Whitehall to Parliament Square. They should have protected me, but they left me hanging out to dry. You'll know them soon. By name. I'm not going down alone.'

Yes you are, I thought. George Fairlow will protect the Establishment. He'll cut a deal. In spite of myself I felt sorry for Hugo. He was not the cold, methodical, precise and unemotional figure envisaged by Martyn Clarke. He was just a banker. And yet that made sense on many levels: money laundering is a business, an illicit one but still a business, and to launder money is to bank it. Martyn, however, was right on one point: the Laundryman would never have stood bail for Tania Berkeley.

I looked across at the pathetic figure of Hugo Maximillian and all I wanted to do was get away. He had the aura of decay. He was rotting in front of my eyes. I recalled the words of Mansa Mussa. *When my principal is himself subject to a coup, as he surely will be, everything he has done during his rule will be judged illegal. The incoming regime will brand him a traitor one second after he has been deposed.* He could have been talking about the Laundryman.

'Hugo,' I said, 'if you plan to bring anybody down with you, brace yourself, because you're going to get royally fucked. The Establishment did try to protect you. But you had become too sloppy, or too greedy, or too damn stupid.' He didn't even try to protest. 'As I see it the options you have are few. You can go to jail, do your time, come out and enjoy what's left of your wealth. You must have tucked a little away beyond the grasp of the Confiscation Unit.'

He giggled like a little boy. 'Mycroft,' he said.

'Then there is the Ernest Saunders Manoeuvre. You develop a "temporary" case of Alzheimer's Disease.'

He giggled again. He was not only rotting, he was regressing. 'Any more options?' he asked with a nervous titter.

'Yes,' I said, 'you can hang yourself in your office from a light fitting in the ceiling with a fifty pound note pinned to your cardigan.' He physically recoiled from the words and I took perverse pleasure in witnessing his distress. 'Personally,' I added, 'that is the option I would recommended.' I got up and walked to the door. 'No need to write on the fifty pound note. We all know who you are.'

In the corridor I brushed past George Fairlow without saying goodbye.

At the weekend Julianna and I planned our departure. 'Where will we go?' she asked.

'Well, we must start in Jamaica. That's where you're being deported to. After that I'll need to find some work, preferably highly paid. I'll have a look at Belize, perhaps, or one of the other less prominent offshore financial centres. Where would you like to go?'

344

'Somewhere hot.'

'I suppose I ought to do my own packing now that we're…'

'Yes,' she said.

I walked to my dressing area and looked at the rows of made-to-measure suits, the lines of crisply pressed double cuffed shirts and the racks of designer ties. I would take none of them. They were ill suited to the West Indies or South America. Moreover, I no longer needed to play the role. I had been through the crucible. I now knew who I was, and felt at ease, with or without the attire.

On the morning of our departure a letter arrived from Tania.

Dear Stu

BB told me about the understanding. He has arranged everything. Can't give you any more details.

Don't worry about the bail money. I'll make it up to you one day. I'll wear a hijab.

Tania x

I know I should have torn it up and thrown it in the bin. The letter was curt, ungrateful and cruel. But instead I replaced the letter in the envelope, which I folded and put in my pocket. It was from Tania. It was goodbye. Had I been alone, I would have cried.

BB drove Julianna and I to the airport.

'How much?' said BB when I told him in detail about my meeting with Hugo.

'One billion pounds a year.'

'Would you have taken it?'

I'd been asking myself that question ever since I'd done the calculation. As Hugo said, I would have been providing a much needed service. Or in the words of Sir Kenneth Llewellin, I'd have been ensuring that the Treasury model of the economy actually worked. There were moral issues, I suppose, but I was beginning to revert to my utilitarian stance: the greatest happiness to the greatest number. Then there was intellectual pride. I knew I would have been a brilliant Laundryman. 'I never got offered the job BB,' I replied. 'So I guess we'll just never know.'

'You'd have taken it,' he teased. 'You'd have been good.'

'The best,' I said.

Epilogue

I sit on a sandy beach in a small Caribbean island. Later this afternoon I will again meet with the island's Prime Minister to present the second phase of my program to turn this tropical agrarian economy into an offshore financial centre. For now I am content to watch little Billie splash about. Her favourite game is to stand still with her ankles in the water as the gentle waves come in and slap against her chubby legs. Occasionally a rogue wave hits her playfully in the chest causing her to tumble. Then she gets up screeching with delight and runs back to her daddy. My favourite game is watching her play her favourite game.

Julianna is not here this morning. She hops to Jamaica every two weeks for a couple of days to see her family and go shopping. I think she has a lover in Kingston. It doesn't bother me.

Life here is good. The weather is glorious. The pace is slow. I live well. I've even lost some weight. My hair is too long though, which is not a problem in and of itself. I got an e-mail from BB last night. Apparently Tania has opened a salon on the other side of the island.

THE END

ACKNOWLEDGEMENTS

With thanks for reading the novel in its various stages of completion:
Sonia Harris, Darren Foster, Nina Wöste, Veron Grant, Eileen Moxley,
Richard Murray and Nicole Manier.

With special thanks to:
Eddie Bell and Paul Moreton of Bell Lomax, my literary agents;
Rachel Hore, who edited my first draft;
Judy Hepburn, who did the final proofreading;
Stephen Beverley, who advised me on media law;
Bill Dew, of Black Limelight, who designed the book cover;
Martin Costello, Manager, Broadway Theatre;
Joe McHugh, Marketing Consultant; and
John Walsh, for telling my story.

Thank you for being there when it mattered:
Vivene Leslie, Anne Lamb, Mike Bonar, Mike Dickson, Ellie Kopiel,
Mairaide Stanley and Carole Roycroft.

With love and gratitude to:
Jadzia Kopiel for keeping the faith;
Beverley Tracey for all the encouragement; and
Lavern Archer for making it happen.